Dedication and Acknowledgments

For Marc Scott Zicree, who introduced me to Cal, Colleen, Doc, and Goldie, and who allowed me to shape their lives and tell their story. Living with them, feeling their pain, fear, and joy, writing it all down, has been an intensely satisfying experience of discovery. Thanks, Marc, for asking me to write this book, for your constant support and insight, for your patience and amazing flexibility.

SPECIAL THANKS:
To Elaine Zicree, for helping us to keep the characters honest, and for knowing Cal better than anyone.

To my husband, Jeff, for wondering how a musician's legal contract would be affected by the Change, for being a patient sounding board, and for naming my Bluesman. To Alex and Kristine, for putting up with a mom who walks around with her mind somewhere else, talking to people who live only in her head, and muttering Yiddish and Russian words under her breath.

To Cal, Colleen, Doc, and Goldie for taking me along on their journey.

And most especially, to Ray Bradbury, from whom I learned how to make reality behave.

Maya Kaathryn Bohnhoff
Grass Valley, California
June 2002

MAGIC TIME
ANGELFIRE

Maya Kaathryn Bohnhoff
created by
Marc Scott Zicree

An Imprint of HarperCollins Publishers

EOS

EOS
An *Imprint of* HarperCollins*Publishers*
10 East 53rd Street
New York, New York 10022-5299

Copyright © 2002 by Paper Route, Inc.

Interior design by Kellan Peck
ISBN: 0-06-105069-5

Library of Congress Cataloging-in-Publication Data

Bohnhoff, Maya Kaathryn.
Magic time : angelfire / Maya Kaathryn Bohnhoff ; created by Marc Scott Zicree.
p. cm.
ISBN 0-06-105069-5
I. Zicree, Marc Scott.. II. Title.

PS3552.0534 M34 2002
813'.6—dc21   2002024264

First Eos hardcover printing: December 2002

Eos Trademark Reg. U.S. Pat. Off. and in Other Countries,
Marca Registrada, Hecho en U.S.A.
HarperCollins® is a trademark of HarperCollins Publishers Inc.

Printed in the U.S.A.

FIRST EDITION

10 9 8 7 6 5 4 3 2 1

www.eosbooks.com

MAGIC TIME

ANGELFIRE

Introduction

Of Angelfire and Blindman's Blues

Welcome to the further adventures of Cal, Colleen, Doc and Goldie.

It's been said by many a megalomaniac before me, "I like to create worlds."

But I also like to share them.

It's one of the big reasons I work in TV. Whether it's taking my boyhood friendship with the late great Ted Sturgeon and transmuting it into *Deep Space Nine*'s "Far Beyond the Stars," or sitting around with a bunch of fellow writers and saying, "We've got twenty-two hours of *Sliders* to create—let's do something we've never seen before," it is pure, unadulterated joy to play in a shared yard with other creative souls.

If you've read *Magic Time*, you may suspect that it's a vision that has haunted me for years.

It was forged by several crucial moments in my life:

When the earth shook during the Northridge quake and the lights went out, and we all surged from our separate homes in search of the reassurance of companionship.

When riots seized L.A. and the night glowed red, palm trees burning like tiki torches flanking the Hollywood Freeway.

When El Nino howled, turning streets into rivers, driving people together, chilled and dispossessed, onto higher ground.

Those moments when all the clutter and noise of modernity were stripped away, and people crossed barriers of class and race and money to protect and hold on to each other, even in the riots.

Magic Time first emerged as the script for a two-hour television pilot, written by myself and my writing-partner wife, Elaine. But the land and characters continued speaking to me, demanding more elbow room.

Wherever I went, I found myself viewing a place through the lens of *Magic Time*, reshaping it into what Cal and his cronies might see and hear and smell.

I invited my friend Barbara Hambly along for the first trip, moving from Manhattan across a very altered world to Boone's Gap, Virginia. Then Maya Bohnhoff joined up, leading Cal and his friends in their search to Chicago and beyond.

Here's how we worked: we plotted out the journey beyond Manhattan more or less simultaneously. As Barbara and I wrote chapters of book one, we'd fire them off to Maya, and she in turn sent us the developing chapters of book two. It was an exciting time, as we would be inspired by each other, alter bits and pieces to match, polish it all together into a (hopefully) seamless whole. Along the way, new characters stepped up, insisting they be included, among them Barbara's Secret Service agent Larry Shango and Maya's fierce, heartbroken flare Magritte.

But let me be clear on one point—Maya wrote the book you now hold in your hands. I may have created the world and the lead characters, done minor course corrections . . . but this tale is all hers.

And what a tale it is.

As for the next installment, our intrepid band of chroniclers will be joined by Mr. Robert Charles Wilson, the brilliant author of *Darwinia*. Watch this space.

Now, however, switch off your pagers and cell phones, unplug the TV, turn your back on the computer and the internal combustion engine . . . and give yourself over to a time and place where all miracles—both dark and light—emanate from the burning core of our own true selves.

MARC SCOTT ZICREE
West Hollywood, California
June 2002

This, O my best-beloved, is a story quite different from the other stories—a story about the Most Wise Sovereign Suleiman-bin-Daoud—Solomon the Son of David.

There are three hundred and fifty-five stories about Suleiman-bin-Daoud; but this is not one of them. . . . It is not the story of the Glass Pavement, or the Ruby with the Crooked Hole, or the Gold Bars of Balkis. It is the story of the Butterfly that Stamped. Now attend all over again and listen!

"The Butterfly That Stamped,"
from *Just So Stories* by Rudyard Kipling

MAGIC TIME
ANGELFIRE

PROLOGUE

Manhattan, New York

"Your young men will dream dreams . . ."

Cal Griffin blinks up into my eyes and gives me a look that says he'd willingly crawl out of his skin if that would get him away from me. He glances at the building he is hoping to flee into and tries to pull his arm out of my grasp—not hard enough to succeed.

Around us, the chaos concert of city traffic is deafening. I put my lips close to his ear. "I'm telling you this because you talk to me, don't just look through. No such thing as coincidences. It's omens, Cal. Something's coming." A line of verse leaps into my head and off the tip of my tongue before I can stop it: " 'Metal wings will fail, leather ones prevail.' "

Cal stares at me, puzzled, wondering what I'm blathering about. That makes two of us.

I let go of him and step aside. "You keep your head low."

Cal nods mutely, turns to the doors. Just before he enters, he glances back, face going ashy when he sees me watching him.

"I'll see you later, Goldie," he murmurs.

"If there is a later," I say, and he falters, missing the revolving door. He has to wait for it to come around again.

I watch him vanish into the building, lost among all the other Suits. He doesn't believe me, of course. Can't blame him, but I had to try.

I wipe some powdered sugar from my chin. Time to go through the Dumpsters in search of another Gillette. This is a use-it-then-lose-it society. There are always throwaways.

The street empties as the Suits swarm into their termite towers. Anyone looking at me now would find it hard to believe I was once on my way to becoming one of them. I hadn't known myself then, hadn't known a strange truth about the world. Onion. The world is like an onion. One thing with many layers. Stinking or succulent, depending on how you look at it.

Good metaphor. I am still capable of good metaphors. Any other time, I'd be absurdly pleased with it, but not today. Today, my cleverness offers no satisfaction.

Because something's coming and it's going to be bad.

I spy Doc Lysenko manning his hot dog cart nearby. Someone else I should warn. I take a step in his direction, but with a suddenness that steals my breath, all the oxygen has been sucked out of the world. My legs threaten to fold up under me and I put a hand out to a nearby wall. Heat radiates from it—from the pavement—and the din of the city is like Thor's hammer.

What a world, what a world. Who would've thought a good little girl like you could destroy my beautiful wickedness?

Shit, Goldman, get a grip.

I send my mind into a ritual I started when I was nine: I take the sturdy brown tome down from the bookshelf. Needing inviolable privacy, I go into an upstairs bathroom and perch on the closed lid of the toilet. I open the book—*Encyclopedia Britannica*, Volume One—and begin reading: *This letter has stood at the head of the alphabet during the whole of the period through which it can be traced historically . . .*

Non compos mentis, my sister called me, and told me to look it up. I did, and then read from A to Z, passing through all the points between. A safe haven, a fortress where I couldn't hear Mom and Dad snarling psychobabble and legalese at each other. Order from chaos. I was transported. By words.

Words have power. Rituals have power.

My mind steadies. I have to get home, to hunker down and wait while there's still time. I slip into the narrow alley behind me, let it shield me from the noise. Dumpsters radiate hot garbage smell.

Funny how, even now, my nose is so easily offended. You'd think, given where I've been living lo, these many years, my sense of smell would've gone on permanent vacation.

I mentally run over the possible routes back to the underground, discarding Rockefeller Center for Grand Central. This time of day there'll be less scrutiny, easier to slip into the darkness. Just gotta be careful not to touch the third rail.

There is a rustling behind me, an odd, whispery sound.

Intriguing.

I turn. Wadded candy wrappers, stained sheets of the *Post*, and bits of excelsior that have tumbled out of the Dumpster are starting to swirl about in a minitornado, gathering speed. What's wrong with this picture is that there's no wind. None. In spite of this logistical oversight, the trash is still dancing in the air.

Abruptly the force swells, pushing the Dumpsters back and forth on their wheels, their heavy metal lids rising and then banging down again and again, like in a bad horror flick. My skin feels prickly; the smell of ozone charges the air.

Not yet, I think, *please, not yet*.

Doesn't matter that I've been expecting this; I'm terrified. Above me there's a crackling, snapping noise. And it ain't Rice Krispies. I look up to see blue electrical discharges whipping about in the sky. Dark clouds roil, casting a yellow-gray pall over Manhattan, over the alley, over me. I feel incredibly small and *watched*—by what, I don't know and don't want to know.

The blue lightning is ferocious, slashing in all directions with a sound like ice sheets splintering. And behind it another, greater sound, a low roar that vibrates through me, growing in power and rumbling the ground. I want to run, to hide, but I can't. I'm not even sure there's anyplace I *can* hide.

Sudden desire overwhelms me, a compulsion to leave the shelter of the alley, to *see* what is happening to the city. This is not *my* desire; this comes from outside, but it so invades me that I feel imprisoned, shackled from the inside out.

The pavement beneath my feet heaves and buckles, as if some massive serpent is struggling to burst forth from below. Obeying my captor's voice, I fight my way back to the alley mouth and peer out.

The sky is alive with blue lightning. It spits its hatred down at the city, frenzied fingers reaching out to every spire. The roar is deafening, a spike through my head. I clap my hands to my ears, but that does nothing. The sound is in my head, too, and now it rises to a scream.

The buildings are melting. Like ice cream cones on a hot day, dripping down—the entire city is liquefying. Proud towers turn to slag as the lightning dances its mad dance and the clouds enfold it like a shroud.

My mouth is open and I think I'm screaming, but I can't hear it against the shriek of the city. I fold in on myself, covering my eyes, rocking, defenseless. In what I know are my last moments, I surrender to it, realizing that no matter how much I prepare, how much I might *know*, in the end it will do with me whatever it wishes.

I open up to it, and the world falls away.

There's a jolt, as if the earth is taking one last token stand, and I realize I'm the only one screaming. I clamp my mouth shut, force myself to stop, and cautiously open my eyes.

The buildings are still upright; people still crowd the streets; but the cars, moments ago surging and huffing, are suddenly going nowhere. Sure, I might be looking at normal gridlock, but I know that's not what this is. The normal sounds of Manhattan have stopped, leaving something as close to silence as this city has known since Peter Stuyvesant stepped off the boat and wowed the locals.

And I, Herman Goldman, saw it coming.

I find my feet, supporting myself against the once again solid brick and mortar of the nearest building. "Your old men will see visions . . ." I murmur, and wonder if I can still score some antipsychotics at the Roosevelt's Free Clinic.

1

What the Trees Said

Suleiman-bin-Daoud was wise. He understood what the beasts said, what the birds said, what the fishes said, and what the insects said. He understood what the rocks said deep under the earth when they bowed in towards each other and groaned; and he understood what the trees said when they rustled in the middle of the morning. . . .

"The Butterfly that Stamped,"
from *Just So Stories* by Rudyard Kipling

ONE

I have that dream every night. The day the wheels came off the world. Bye-bye physics. Natural laws, who needs 'em?

And every morning I wake, realizing it's all real.

Okay, no buildings literally melted, nor did the sidewalks and streets actually roll like ocean waves. But the whole world experienced it, this moment of cosmic mayhem, this thing most of us refer to simply as "the Change." At least, we think it did. Nothing we've seen in the intervening weeks has suggested otherwise.

I have other dreams, too, also terrifying, also rooted in so-called reality. One of them is about a girl named Tina Griffin. Like our world, she changed—or began to change—in that moment of upheaval. So did a lot of other people. But Tina's in my nightmares because I know her. She is the reason we left New York, the reason we head inexorably west—because her brother Cal has the same nightmare, and because that's where the Megillah has taken her.

The Megillah is my pet name for what all the evidence points to as the cause of the Change. No one else calls it that. They have their own pet names for it: Armageddon, Doomsday, Kali Yuga, the Day of Judgment, the Real Thing.

Ek velt, Grandmother would've said: *the end of the world.*

Apparently, in elite government circles it was known simply as "the Source." A science project of sorts. Funny, the words "science project" usually bring to mind papier-mâché volcanoes and ant farms, not something that has the power to rip the world apart and put it back together all wrong.

But it appears that the Megillah has that power.

Tina Griffin, all of twelve years old, was one of the things it reassembled. And after it warped her body, clothed her in light, and granted her the power of levitation, it sorted her from among its other various types of "makeovers" and simply took her. And others like her. Where or why, we have no idea. Sort of a perverted take on the Evangelical Christian Rapture.

Before she was wrenched, screaming, out of her brother's arms in the tiny back bedroom of a run-down house in Boone's Gap, West Virginia, the changeling Tina spoke of *Something* in the West—a power, an entity, an Enigma. Something that came into the world with a roar and that now grows in it like a malevolent cancer.

And so, a Quest. Or a monumental game of hide and seek. We seek the Enigma and it . . . well, it doesn't so much hide as it evades. It's that thing you're certain is behind you in the dark. But a swift about-face only nets you empty air and a dark slither out the corner of one eye.

And whispers.

Since that moment in Manhattan when buildings did not melt and sidewalks did not ripple, I've heard its whispers. Which makes (lucky) me the only one with half a clue about what part of the West the Megillah inhabits. And that's about all I have—half a clue. I listen for it; I hear its Voice and we go. Tag, I'm it. Marco Polo. Games. Rough, deadly games.

Since leaving Boone's Gap our quest has taken us through varied terrain. Quiet pastoral countryside where cows and sheep still graze and watch our passing with little interest. Places where it seemed the earth had erupted in boils, or a giant hand had reached down, dug in, and tried to wrench the bedrock out through the grass and trees and soil. We avoid cities. Cities are places of unimaginable darkness and violence. I suppose they always were, but it's a different kind of violence now, at once more focused and more mindless, soul-deep and brutal.

There's violence of a sort in the country, too. And its effects have been devastating. We've seen ghost towns and ghost suburbs and ghost farms. But nothing like what we saw as Manhattan unraveled like a cheap sweater.

We see other folks ever so often. And ever so often we see not-folks. Ex-people who, like Tina, had their DNA radically rearranged. "Tweaks," Colleen calls them. I prefer "twists"—it's a gentler word. Although there's nothing gentle about what the Change has done to them. People tend to avoid them, and they tend to avoid people. Something I understand, completely.

Most often we don't see them, but merely *feel* them. Since some of them are rather unpleasant, it pays to be vigilant. You develop a sort of ESP about these things. The sense of being watched creeps over your skin and through your brain like a trickle of freezing water. When this happens, Cal's hand goes to his sword, Colleen's goes to her machete, Doc's makes the sign of the cross. Mine does nothing. At the moment, I carry neither weapons nor gods.

We're traveling on potholed tarmac today as we head for the border between West Virginia and Ohio. Cal and Doc are mounted on fine steeds (Sooner and Koshka, by name), Colleen drives our spiffy home-built wagon, while I ride shotgun. I mean that figuratively, of course. Since the Change, no one I know has yet figured out how to make a shotgun work. This is one of those good news/bad news things.

Our "wagon" is a pickup truck from which the transmission has been removed and the engine compartment gutted back to the fire-wall. It still has its vinyl-covered seats, but no roof, no windows, no windshield, and sawed-off doors. You can crawl from the front seat right over into the bed. It was, as they say, a find. Only cost us our bi-cycles and a couple of days work in the bed 'n' breakfast from hell.

Water barrels are ranked outboard down both sides of the truck bed, which has an awning that extends from the tailgate all the way out over the remains of the cab. We roll it down in the event of in-clement weather. The whole thing looks a lot like those old World War Two troop transports; only it's a brilliant shade of macintosh yel-low. For the first time in many days, the awning is rolled all the way up to the topmost strut of the support framework.

I glance at the sky and realize that's likely to change. It's a chill, cloudy afternoon—unseasonably cold. The sky presses down on the land like a heavy, gray sponge full of rain. Somewhere, there are calendars that say it's autumn, but it feels like half-past winter, and the trees are turning rapidly, as if hurrying to catch up.

Along the road ahead I see a strip of maples with prematurely nude branches. It's only when we get practically on top of them that I realize the leaves are merely transparent. They look like those blown glass things that once glittered in Manhattan shop windows. And as the moist breeze stirs them, I hear them, too—a fine shimmer of sound that's almost music.

Fascinating. The rocking of the wagon no longer seems so soporific. I swing out over the chopped-down door and hit the ground running.

A sharp snarl snatches at me from behind. "Goldman! What the hell do you think you're doing?"

Replying to Colleen's question while galloping into the forest would waste breath, so I don't bother. I make the trees and gingerly reach up to touch the crystalline leaves. They're beautiful, but hard and cold, with sharp, biting edges. A breeze moves through the branches and stirs them to song. I imagine an entire melody is cradled in those branches, but then I imagine a lot of things.

I'm enchanted. I take off my cowboy hat and carefully dislodge several of the leaves into the crown. They fall with a sweet tinkle of sound.

"What is it?" Cal Griffin peers down at me from his horse, hazel eyes darting from me into the deeper woods. His hand is on the hilt of his sword.

I hold up one of the leaves. Steely sunlight sparks cold fire in the tracery of veins. "We may have to rename a couple of seasons," I say. "How about spring, summer, shard, and bleak?"

Cal leans down from the horse and takes the leaf from my fingers. "Ouch. You're not kidding. I'd hate to be standing under a tree when these things fall. *If* they fall." He lays the leaf carefully on the palm of my hand. "Better get back in the wagon. Colleen might slow down or even stop for you if you apologize for scaring her like that."

I carefully tuck the leaves into the pocket of my buckskin jacket and set the cowboy hat back in its rightful place. As always, my hair—too thick, too curly, and too long—puts up an admirable fight, but I cram the hat down until it submits peacefully.

"Scare Colleen," I repeat. "Isn't that an oxymoron?"

He smiles fleetingly and jerks a thumb toward the wagon, which has come to a stop down the road with Doc hovering near the tail-gate. "Get."

"Maybe it's just a paradox," I say, moving away from the trees. "Or an anomaly, or a mere flight of fancy."

Cal clicks Sooner into a lope and leaves me to chug my way back to the wagon.

Colleen stays stopped to let me climb in. Then she gives me a chill glance, laces the reins through her fingers like she's done it every day of her life, and clucks the team into motion. In this nippy weather they are rarin' to go, as they say in the Wild West. They toss their heads, paw the ground, and pull at their bits. Colleen manages them effortlessly.

"You're sure good at that horsey stuff," I tell her, chipping at the brit-tle silence. "I guess it's because you're a native Cornhusker and all, huh?"

She gives me a cool green glance. "You think?"

I shrug. "Okay, I don't know why you're good at it. You just are. You've been around horses a lot, I'd guess."

She repeats the glance, then puts her eyes back on the crusty tar-mac ahead. One callused hand smoothes back her hair, which is al-most as spiky as her annoyance. Scissors still work, but Colleen is careless of such niceties. I think she does her hair with her pet ma-chete.

"Yeah. I got a horse when I was thirteen. Before Dad died. You never forget the feeling of the reins in your hands, the ripple of mus-cle between your knees, the smooth glide of a horse at a full gallop. To this day, whenever I get stressed out or pissed off . . ." A pointed glance. ". . . I walk myself through bridling and saddling a horse just to chill. Well . . . and to prove to myself I remember how to do it."

Her eyes go back to the road then, and she closes up tight as a clam. Conservation of intimacies, I guess. I play with my glass leaves, trying to shake music out of them.

After about five minutes of this Colleen speaks again. "You know what, Goldman? That's damned annoying."

I wrap the leaves in a handkerchief that's made its way into my breast pocket and put them away. "You know what, Ms. Brooks? No one's called me Goldman since my sophomore baseball coach. Well . . . and my probation officer."

"Your what?"

Loose lips, the curse of an unquiet mind. "Oh, look," I say. "A road sign."

There is, indeed, a road sign. It proclaims that there is a town not far ahead. Grave Creek. Nice, ominous little name for a town.

"Eight miles," says Cal, drawing his horse up close to the wagon. "If we hustle we might make it before the sun goes down."

On a clear day we'd have some wiggle room, but the oppressive cloud cover puts us uncomfortably close to twilight. Since the Change, out after dark is not something you want to be. If the world is peculiar when the sun is up (and it is plenty peculiar), it is insanely scary when the sun goes down. Colleen nods and clucks her team into a brisk trot.

Barely half an hour later we hear a shout from Cal, who's taken the vanguard. He lopes back to us through the gloamin', waving an arm. Doc draws up along our right flank to see what all the hoo-ha is about. Pulling up, Cal points southwest.

The clouds have lifted at the horizon and a baleful red sun glares at us from beneath the edge. Against the bleed of crimson, a water tower stands in sharp silhouette. Firelight flickers atop the squashed sphere.

"Civilization ho," I say.

"A lookout?" asks Doc, his eyes on the tower.

"Or a beacon," Cal says. "Maybe it's a friendly hello to wayward travelers."

Wishful thinking. "You know, there were these pirates up Newfoundland way that used to set signal fires on the cliffs to beckon to merchant ships. After the ships piled up on the rocks, the pirates would go out in little boats and collect the booty. Survivors were offered a choice: join the jolly pirate band or die."

"Judas Priest, Goldman!" says Colleen. "Do you have to be such a friggin' fountain of helpful information?"

Doc Lysenko hides a smile in the twilight over his shoulder. "Ah, a child's daydream. Didn't you ever want to be a pirate, Colleen?"

Colleen's face goes through the most amazing set of expressions: Doc has surprised a smile, but she aborts it and stretches it into a grimace, then inverts it into a scowl, then smoothes it into a look of prim disapproval. "What I want," she says finally, "is to be somewhere other than out in the middle of nowhere when night falls."

"Then we'd better get a move on." Cal turns his horse and leads on toward the looming silhouette of the tower.

Unaccountably, I shiver.

Our road descends into a shallow, triangular valley where the woods stand back from the edge of the grassland like spectators at the scene of an accident. The bottom of the triangle is a mile or two distant, and a second road runs north to south along it, merging with the one we're on. As we make the descent, my eyes are on the place where the town should be. I can just make out more flickers of light sprinkled about the base of the water tower. I do hope they're not pirates.

"We have company," murmurs Doc from our starboard bow. He's staring across the valley to the north-south road.

"Where?" asks Colleen, tensing.

"There." Doc's gesture is almost lost in the twilight.

A small group of people moves along the converging road toward Grave Creek, clearly visible against the dark woodland that hugs the road. They seem to be struggling with some sort of litter. Three of the people are very small. Children. Or munchkins, maybe. These days it could be either.

"I think they may have injured," Doc says. "They could likely use our help."

"Hold on, Doc," Colleen warns him. "Let Cal scope it out first, okay?"

Cal is already doing that, I realize, moving down into the valley at a leisurely, nonthreatening trot.

"I'll light the lanterns," I say, and do, suspending them from hooks—one on each side of the driver's box. Kerosene, no less. I just *love* modern conveniences.

Cal's nearing the floor of the vale when yet another group of folks comes out of the woods to our north. This new bunch heads down across the meadow on a course that roughly parallels the north-south road. There is a flicker of fire as someone in the road troupe lights a torch. There is no answering flicker of light from the folks in the meadow. They just keep pressing through the tall, dry grasses.

The newcomers, I realize, are moving very smartly. Maybe this is because they aren't hauling someone on a litter, or maybe because they're in a bigger hurry. The new folks overtake the first party and swing wide as if to pass them by. Then they veer sharply onto an intercept course, and suddenly it's as if I'm looking at them in a funhouse mirror. They become indistinct, fluid around the edges, a school of shadows flowing across the landscape as if pulled by currents.

By the pricking of my thumbs, something wicked this way comes. Hair rises up on the back of my neck and I wish I could borrow Colleen's machete—or Doc's faith.

There is a shout up ahead as Cal digs his heels into Sooner's flanks and tears off across the meadow.

"Oh, *shit!*" Colleen voices my sentiments exactly before she brings the reins down hard on gleaming horsehide.

The horses plunge into sudden and frantic motion—hot-blooded engines snorting steam into the twilight. The wagon jerks and my cowboy hat goes flying. Liberated hair tumbles into my eyes, blinding me. I hear nothing but the agonized squeaking of the truck's springs and the labored effort of the team. The truck is heavy, awkward, and probably a bitch to pull, but Colleen steers them off the road entirely and sends us bumping straight across the meadow. We're on a path that will take us directly into collision with the others . . . if our wheels don't fall off first.

Ahead of us, where the two roads meet, the first band of travelers has gathered to make a stand. There are seven of them. Three are children; two are women—one extremely pregnant. One of the two men is stretched out on the litter, brandishing a torch. The others have torches, too, and baseball bats, and a wildly barking dog. Slim defense against what they face. Advancing on them are strange, dark beings that are less men than shadows of men—vaporous, nebulous, writhing.

Cal rides Sooner into the breach between the two groups. His sword is still in its sheath, but he's swinging a loaded sling. Slowing Sooner only a little, he looses a scatter of golf-ball-size rocks into the shadow troupe.

Surprise! The rocks connect. The sound that results is not one I ever want to hear again. It is as if the air itself has cried out—a siren of rage that drowns out the baying of the dog and the thunder of our charging horses.

The shadows seem to melt back into the tall grass. But only for a moment. Then they're back. I try to count them and fail. The shadows uncoil and ooze forward, pressing Cal and his horse back toward the crossroads and the frightened refugees.

Colleen shoves the reins into my hands. "Take the team!" she yells, then rolls off the back of the seat into the truck bed, leaving me with a handful of fat leather noodles.

TWO

COLLEEN

My crossbow and a quiver of bolts were lying in the well behind the seat. I grabbed them as I went over. I'd barely touched down when the wagon veered sharply, slamming me hard against the left wheel well. If it hurt, I didn't feel it.

Just ahead a child screamed high and shrill. I barely heard it over the rumble of the wagon and I barely heard *that* over the bass drum in my chest.

I came upright and poked my head out through the support struts of the awning. We were still aimed more or less at the crossroads, but unless Goldman suddenly learned to steer a four-in-hand, we were going to trundle by to the north, behind the . . . whatever-the-hell they were.

Looking at them made me want to rub my eyes. They were shadows. Spooks. No kind of tweak I'd ever seen before. I couldn't tell how big they were, how fast, how nimble. From this distance I couldn't tell a damn thing about them, except that they were attacking.

Cal had gotten out of their way and was circling, maybe hoping to distract them, maybe looking for time to reload his sling. The tweaks followed his movement, reaching out like shadowy fingers. A chill streaked up my spine.

I was nocking an arrow when Doc flew past. Before I could do more than yelp, he pulled the lantern off my side of the wagon and galloped his mare full tilt at the tweaks, shouting and waving the lantern at them. I ground my teeth together and shot the bolt into the cradle.

The lantern did jack. If anything, light made these things harder to see.

Fine. I'll just have to guess what I'm shooting at.

I aimed into the pack of flickering shapes and fired.

The bolt hit something—I *heard* it—and one of the flickers stopped, suddenly solid. It flailed the air for a moment, then leapt. Straight at Doc. It was like a wave of quicksilver that covered eight or nine feet in a single bound.

By all rights Doc should've been dead. *Would* have been dead, if not for the blessed stupidity of animals. First, his horse shied, dodging the tweak but putting itself and Doc right between me and my target. Then this mutt torpedoed out of nowhere and started doggy-dancing all around, barking its fool head off. The horse bolted and Doc tumbled off over its rump. He and the lantern hit the ground with the sound of shattering glass. The dog disappeared, but I could still hear it barking.

My chance was gone; the wagon rumbled past the tweaks and onto the north-south road. The horses got tarmac under their feet and charged due north. I lost sight of Doc.

I jerked my head around toward the front seat and yelled at Goldman to bring us around. "Crank it!" I shouted, and mimed the motion at him.

He cranked, pulling us into a right-hand crash turn that I prayed wouldn't tip us over. Against the force of the turn I clawed my way to the right side of the truck bed and tried to see Doc.

He was about twenty yards behind us now, pushing himself up off the ground. The lantern had fallen four, maybe five yards beyond him, and flames were spreading swiftly through the dry grass between him and the tweaks, fanned by a chill westerly breeze.

The shadow-pack would be on him in a flash.

I hefted the crossbow and tried to steady it on the lip of the truck bed. I didn't have a clear shot, not arcing away like this. But if I had to wait until the wagon came around, it would be too late. I squinted through the fire and smoke and dying sunset for Cal, but he was riding away up the road with three children clinging to him for dear life. The other refugees were frantically dragging the litter along behind.

I was it.

Doc was on his knees, watching the tweaks from behind the spreading curtain of flame. Their bodies whipped as if caught in a fierce wind and they were making this freakish keening sound. Made my skin crawl.

They were afraid of fire.

I popped back into the truck bed, threw open a supply locker and scrabbled madly through the stuff inside. Ammunition. I needed ammunition. I found cotton wadding, cloth bandages, alcohol. I used a bandage to bind the wadding to the tip of the bolt in my bow, doused it in alcohol, and dug a cigarette lighter out of my back pocket. The small blue flame was a comfort. Scrambling, I made a handful of sloppy, drunken bolts, then slipped three of them into the magazine on the underside of the crossbow. The rest I slipped into my quiver.

We'd made a full 180 and were bearing down on the tweaks hard. Past the gleaming flanks of the team, I could see one of them circling to the left around Doc's protecting veil of fire. I swear to God I could see through the damn thing. I had to take a shot anyway.

I scrambled back into the driver's box, just about knocking Goldman off the seat, and used the frontmost support strut to drag myself upright. I lit the bolt, blinking at the sudden flare of light, aimed one-handed over the nose of the truck, and fired.

The bolt sailed into the shadow-thing and stopped dead. The tweak went solid. Its head twisted toward me, and eyes the color of magma speared me where I stood. In the split second I got a clear look at it, it went up like a bonfire. Bile rose in my throat.

We were almost on top of them now, and I didn't trust Goldman to steer. I nocked another bolt, then reached down to haul on the reins.

"Jesu-Christé!" yelped Goldman. Sounded like a legitimate prayer to me.

The team swerved sharply left, sweeping by the blaze and the beasts. Just as we completed our end-around, I clipped the bow to my belt, leapt Goldman and went overboard.

Mom always said I acted without thinking—used my gut instead of my brains. It was meant to be an insult. But since it usually followed the words, "You're just like your father," it was hard to take it that way. She was dead right, of course. I realized that as I hit the ground—hard.

I tucked and rolled to my feet. Doc was about fifteen feet away, crouched with a large shard of the shattered lantern clutched in both hands. I dashed the remaining distance, keeping my crossbow aimed at the fire.

"Hurt?" I asked.

He shook his head, eyes wild behind a veil of dark hair. But his voice came out, as always, rock steady. "Terrified."

Me, too. That fire was all that stood between us and a pack of demons that melted into the smoke and shadow like black cats on tar paper. Only the one I'd set on fire was solid. It rolled on the ground about twenty feet away, making a sound that will haunt me till the day I die. The stench of burning hair and flesh made my stomach heave.

Shadows don't have hair and flesh.

I sucked up close to Doc. Heat beat against my face. Somewhere, the dog bayed. "Let's get out of here."

"Which way?"

I grabbed his arm and pulled him toward the road to Grave Creek, praying the shadows wouldn't realize what their charbroiled buddy had—that fire can be outflanked if you half try.

We hadn't gotten far when they figured out the fire's limits. They did an end-around, steering clear of the burning husk, flowing to the rim of flame and around.

"*Bozhyeh moy,*" Doc murmured. The shard quivered in his hand, firelight dancing over the broken edges.

Cold wind nipped at us, and the air was getting soggier with the threat of rain. I didn't want rain. I *did* want the wind—it whipped the flames, churned dust and smoke, and made us harder for the tweaks to see (I hoped).

They oozed like oil, glowing eyes sinking toward the ground. I had no idea how many there were—four, maybe five. I had exactly three doctored bolts.

"They . . . are they *singing?*" Doc asked.

It was unmusical and weird, but singing was the only way to describe it. Down in my gut I knew what it meant. I brought out the lighter, flicked it open, and lit the bolt in my crossbow. It blazed bravely. The singing stopped. Not good. I steeled myself for the attack.

There was a dull rumbling, and a bizarre, yodeling wail cut through the smoky air and stopped all of us—people and nonpeople—in our tracks. Sounded like a damn cartoon Indian. Then the wagon swept into my field of vision with someone standing straight up in the driver's box like Ben Hur, wildly waving a torch.

Goldman. Bloody, frigging Goldman. The idiot was going to yodel his way right between me and a clean shot.

Horses are scared shitless of fire—not that I'd've expected Goldman to know that—and he was trying to drive the team straight into hell.

"Run!" I told Doc, and shoved him toward the crossroads.

He ran.

Goldman was fighting the horses for all he was worth, trying to get control of their heads. An experienced driver stands about a fifty-fifty chance of winning these little battles. Someone like Herman Goldman stands no chance at all. The horses revolted and he tumbled out of the driver's box, landing almost at my feet with the torch miraculously still in his hand. The wagon rumbled away toward the western woods.

I dodged the banner of torch flame and raised my bow. The arrowhead had gone out, alcohol exhausted. I cursed, flipped it out of the cradle and pulled another one from the clip. I'd just gotten it seated when they started singing again.

At my feet, Goldman howled and waved his torch practically in my face. I thrust the bow into the flame, burning my hand but lighting the barb. They were so close I imagined the heat I felt was from their eyes. Those horrible, flaming eyes were the only part of them that seemed not to move when you looked at them. Small comfort, but they made a good target. Knowing I wasn't going to get off more than one shot, I aimed at the closest tweak.

The singing stopped and there was a sudden, dense stillness.

Here it comes.

But the volcanic eyes turned westward, and then winked out—one, two, three, four pairs—as the tweaks turned tail and vanished behind the veil of flame and smoke. I caught a glimpse of solid forms, then there was nothing moving but real smoke and dry grass. Beyond the flames the dog's yapping faded.

I don't know how long I stood there like that, crossbow aimed at the dying blaze, Goldman quivering at my knees. Rain came softly, pattering on the top of my head and running down my face.

He moved first, getting slowly to his feet and taking about five steps toward the wall of fire, peering through its growing gaps.

I lowered the crossbow and set the safety. My hands shook. "Goldman, you nitwit! Where are you going?"

He turned to me, his face pale in the light of his torch. His lips moved, but if he said anything, I didn't hear it. Right about then, someone yanked me off my feet and dragged me up and across a saddle. Upside down, I caught a glimpse of blue-jeaned leg and a battered leather scabbard. Cal.

He rode away from the flames, and I was well-chilled by the time he set me on my feet several yards past the crossroads. He dismounted beside me while I grabbed stirrup leather and tried not to look as unsteady as I felt.

He gripped my shoulders, eyes scouring me for signs of injury. "Are you all right?"

I nodded, glad the early twilight hid my face. "How about Goldman?"

"He's okay. One of the refugees snagged Doc's mare and went out with me to get him. What spooked them? Was it the fire?"

I shook my head. "They were scared of the fire, but they were working out how to get around it when they . . . they just took off."

"Except for the one you shot."

He looked down the slope to where one of our new acquaintances led the exhausted wagon team back toward the crossroads. Beyond them the dying flames cast a strange glow over the meadow. You could still see the single corpse lying there, solid, unmoving . . . still smoking.

Cal turned, started to mount up again.

I grabbed his arm. "Where're you going?"

"I want to know what that was, don't you?"

"Not especially."

He looked down at me, rain dripping down his cheeks, matting his hair to his head. "I'm sorry, Colleen. You didn't really have a choice, though, did you? It would've killed Doc if you hadn't shot it."

I waved that aside. "Forget it. Let's get these people off the road before those sons of bitches come back."

There was just enough room in our covered wagon for our new friends. Cal had carried the kids a ways up the road and stashed them in an outcropping of rocks. That was where we loaded everyone up, lit every lantern and torch we had between us, and headed for Grave Creek. We hadn't gone far when the dog showed up, exhausted but grinning in canine bliss. He rode in the back, behind the driver's box, and panted happily in my ear.

The obvious leader of our refugees was a white-haired guy with a young face and glacier-blue eyes. His name was Jim — Jim Gossett. The pregnant woman was his wife, Emily. Two of the kids were theirs — a boy and a girl. The oldest girl belonged to the other couple — Stan and Felicia Beecher. Stan's leg was splinted, broken when they'd lost their wagon to what Jim's boy, Gil, called "pirates." That explained how they came to be wandering the outback so ill-equipped.

"It was a real wagon," the boy told me, "not a funky one like yours." He sat between me and his dad in the driver's box, seeming none the worse for wear.

Kids amaze me. They handle this shit a lot better than us so-called mature adults.

Jim said things were pretty bad up in Wheeling — a lot of looting was still going on in some parts of town. The hospitals were full to bursting; the shopping malls had turned into armed camps. "Then we get out here. First we lose the wagon, and then . . ." He shakes his head and shivers. "Weird shit. It was like the whole damn forest was watching us. Dog was going nuts for miles." He glanced into the one remaining rearview mirror. "Can we go any faster?"

I urged the team into a weary trot. Behind me, Goldman started humming a soulful little ditty under his breath.

"What's that?" asked Jim.

Goldman stopped humming. "What's what?"

"That song you're humming. I've heard that before."

"Huh. I thought I was making it up."

"No. No, I've heard that before," Jim repeated. He was silent for a long while, and we all listened to the hushed voices from the truck bed behind us and watched rain sparkle in the lamplight.

"Is this Armageddon?" Jim murmured. "I swear I never thought it would be like this. This isn't a war, it's a plague of madness."

Goldman started humming again. Guess he didn't have an answer, either.

Not far up the road we were swept up by the Grave Creek welcome wagon—a bunch of guys on horseback armed with hockey sticks and homemade spears. To each his own, I guess. They'd seen us tangle with the tweaks and had come out to help. They seemed legitimately sorry to have missed all the action.

They escorted us into town, depositing us in the E.R. of the Grave Creek Community Hospital, where Doc was an immediate hit. He slipped easily into the role of medic, applying patches and checking wounds in the harsh light of a brace of Coleman lanterns. Within ten minutes of our arrival the two nurses on duty were following his quiet direction as if they'd been doing it for years. For my part, I tried to be a good patient, sitting quietly while one of them slathered my burnt hand with something that looked and smelled like mint Jell-O.

The kids, being kids, only wanted to compare notes about the "monsters," and loudly interrupted every adult attempt at conversation. To them this was high adventure. They pretty much ignored Doc's swabbing and patching, and chattered to Cal, faces flushed and shining. The two girls, Lissa and Melanie, flirted with the good-looking guy—the only adult who seemed interested in their take on things—while Gil pretended he'd never been scared once.

Their parents were grim and silent and clingy. I met Emily Gossett's gaze over her son's head. She gave me a weak smile that was more a wince and clutched her little boy's shoulders so hard, he stopped talking, looked up and said, "What's wrong, Mom?"

Cal paced. He fielded a few questions about what we'd seen on our westward trek, but quickly turned the questions back around. I could just imagine him in a courtroom—suited and tied, curly, fair hair carefully trimmed and styled—summing up before a judge. But no judge'd ever heard questions like these: Had you, Jim Gossett, ever seen these particular tweaks before? Were they nine feet tall or ten? Did it seem to you they were a little transparent? Did they seem intelligent?

Objection, Your Honor: this calls for conjecture on the part of the witness. (Okay, I used to watch *Law & Order* now and again. Guilty pleasures.)

They had seen these tweaks. Or thought they had. They'd picked them up earlier in the day below someplace named Moundsville, but until sunset the tweaks had kept their distance. "Lurkers," Jim called them. The word put a chill into me.

Goldman, I noticed, had gone to ground in a corner, his back against the wall, his knees pulled up under his chin, his eyes open, staring at nothing. He'd been like that since we got here. Even while Doc patched him up he'd been silent. Not a gasp. Not an "ouch!" Not a peep.

This was unlike Goldman. He wasn't a quiet person in any sense of the word. Sometimes he seemed peaceful enough on the outside, but even then I suspected there was still noise in there, like the little wheels that run his brain never stopped turning. Cal once described him to me as having bees in his head. For a long time now the bees had been asleep; the wheels had stopped.

It was creeping me out a little, and I'd just about decided I was going to slip over and see what was up when I realized Cal was talking to me.

"You said they just wandered off," he said. "Any idea why?"

I blinked at him and shrugged. "Search me. They just split. They were afraid of the fire, but they'd figured that out. Maybe it was the rain. Maybe they don't like getting wet."

"Uh, no . . . no. It was as if they were, um . . . called off."

Cal and I turned in unison. Goldman had gotten up and wandered into the middle of the exam area. He stopped in front of Cal and tucked his hands under his arms as if to keep them still.

"Called off?" Cal repeated. "What do you mean, called off?"

"What do I mean, 'called off.' I mean, like . . . dogs. Like, uh, pets. Like a hunting pack that hears the horn or catches a new scent."

"*Whose* hunting pack?" asked Jim. He'd been watching Doc check his wife's blood pressure. "Those weren't any kind of animals I've ever seen."

"Hold on," I interrupted. "Anything might've drawn them off. It was cold, wet, windy. And, jeez, this is Goldman talking." I gave him a sidewise glance.

He was nodding, his eyes on Cal's feet. "Yes, that's right. This is Goldman talking, and he's a loon, so you can discount everything he says. But not this time. This time, *listen to me*." He looked up and hit Cal with a dark, laser beam gaze. "Someone or something called those guys off. I *heard* it."

"What did you hear, Goldie?"

Cal pays serious attention to everything Goldman says because, according to him, Goldman sensed the Change before it happened and tried to warn him. I had to admit I'd seen him do some pretty eerie things myself, so there were moments I could believe that. This was not one of them. Right now I was pretty sure Herman Goldman was not living on the same planet as the rest of us.

"Wait, wait," Jim interrupted. "*Guys?* What guys?"

There was a moment of awkward silence that was about as full of wretchedness as a moment can get. Cal glanced at me, then said, "In our experience the Change seems to affect only human beings."

I looked down, picking at the piece of gauze on my hand. Damn burn was already itching.

"Those were *people?*" Emily Gossett put a protective hand on her swollen belly.

I felt Cal's eyes on my face. He'd ridden down to the scorched field. Taken a close look at the body. Out of the corner of my eye I saw him nod.

"How . . . ?"

"How does it happen?" Doc Lysenko pulled the blood pressure cuff from Emily's arm and finished the sentence for her. His English is better than mine, but it's laced with the Motherland. "We don't precisely know. We know only that it is, em, selective. Few people are changed. But there is no way to predict who will be, or when."

The silence threatened to suck the air out of the room. Our two hovering nurses had stopped chattering, too, and turned grim attention to Stan Beecher's bad leg.

Cal turned back to Goldie. "What did you hear?" he repeated.

"Hear—what'd I hear?" He started humming.

"Oh, jeez!" I said. "He didn't *hear* anything because there was nothing to hear. Fire was roaring, those things were wailing like banshees, that damned dog—" I glanced over to where the dog in question snoozed peacefully under a gurney. "It was like you said, they caught another scent."

"*I* said that," said Goldman, jabbing a thumb into his chest.

Like that was real important. I said, "We know fire stops them."

Cal nodded. "That makes sense. Light sensitivity seems to be a by-product of the transformation. We've certainly seen that with the grunters. Tina . . . Tina was bothered by it too."

Every muscle in his face went tight, like someone had turned a ratchet somewhere in his head. Happened every time he spoke her name, and every time, it reminded me of losing Dad. Of course, where Dad went, there was no road back, and that was a long time ago, so it didn't really bear thinking about. We had at least a chance of finding Tina.

Cal glanced at Jim and Emily. "But you said you saw them in daylight."

"Only in the depths of the woods," she said. "They stayed in the shadows. They never once came out where we could really get a good look at them."

"Until the sun went down," Cal finished.

Emily nodded.

"I wonder how far they range," murmured Cal. "They could be local, regional—we have no way of knowing."

He was right. So far we'd only seen three sorts of tweaks that seemed to crop up repeatedly—*typy*, to use a term from my horsey past. We'd heard them called by various names—sprites or flares, trogs or grunters. Dragons. There was no other word for those. Grunters liked to skulk in shadows and holes, dragons favored skyscrapers or other aeries, and flares, we had been discovering, were becoming scarcer by the day. It seemed the Source, or whatever was at the bottom of this abyss the world had been slam-dunked into, was sucking them up like they were Gummy Bears.

And why? Of all the changes a power like that could make, why change *us*? People in general, I mean, because *I* sure hadn't changed. I couldn't fly, I didn't care to burrow into holes, and I didn't hear Voices with a capital V. None of it made sense to me. *None* of it. Cal had this deep conviction that everything we learned about our new world gave us a better chance of dealing with the Source, I wasn't nearly so sure. Hell, there were days I wasn't sure what we were doing on this road trip. I mean, sometimes a little voice in my head (small *v*) told me the best thing to do would be to just hunker down in some quiet backwater like Boone's Gap or Grave Creek and ride it out. Except that things were kind of looking like there was no "out."

"It's hard to believe they were once human," murmured Jim.

"Strictly speaking," said Doc quietly, "they are *still* human."

The memory of singed hair and charbroiled flesh rose up to choke me. I'd had about enough of this conversation.

Cal put a hand on my shoulder, as if he knew what was going on in my head. I like that about him. I hate that about him.

"Look," he said, "we're all going to need something to eat and a place to stay . . ."

One of the nurses, a young thing with Coke-bottle lenses and big, doe-brown eyes, pulled off her gloves with a snap. She turned her big eyes on Cal. "I can show you to the cafeteria."

"You have a cafeteria?" I asked.

She laughed and answered me without taking her eyes off Cal's face. "It's more like a hickory pit barbecue, but it's a source of food."

He smiled at her, no doubt making her day. "That'd be great." He looked to Doc. "Unless you need to keep them here?"

"Only Mr. Beecher," Doc answered. "The leg is most definitely broken."

Cal nodded, gave my shoulder a squeeze, and turned to gather his charges. That was when Goldman planted himself firmly in Jim Gossett's path and unloaded a gush of questions.

"On the way in, you said you felt as if the woods were watching you. What did you mean by that? Did you—I don't know—uh, feel dread, excitement, impending doom, indigestion, bad juju—what?"

We all stared bug-eyed at Goldman as if he were a space alien. (I've wondered.)

"We were *scared*," said Emily.

Goldman persisted. "But did you . . . did you *hear* anything? Did something *speak* to you?"

Jim cast Cal a fleeting and unreadable glance. *Is this guy for real?*
"I heard angels."

The voice was small and came from somewhere around Jim Gossett's kneecaps. Lissa had slipped unnoticed into the circle of adults.

Cal crouched so he could meet her eye-to-eye. "What do you mean by angels, honey?"

"Like angels singing. Oscar and I heard them. I think Gil heard them, too, but he pretended not to." She sent the little boy an arch glance.

"Who's Oscar?"

She pointed to the dog, who'd opened one eye at the mention of his name. The eye rolled shut.

"He heard them, I know he did, 'cause he barked at them and howled . . ." She paused to demonstrate, making Oscar's ears twitch. ". . . and he tried to run away to find them."

"Oscar barks at everything," Gil commented.

Cal glanced up at him. "Did you hear the angels, Gil?"

"It weren't angels. Prob'ly just deer or something."

"Deer don't sing," said Lissa.

"It weren't singing."

"But it was *like* singing—it *was*." Lissa looked up into the ring of grown-up faces. "Honest. Sure, Oscar barks at lots of stuff, but he hardly howls at all. He howls when he hears music. *That's* why I think it was angels. Because Oscar could hear them. Dogs can see *and* hear angels," she added.

"That was a movie," said Gil. "This is real life."

I swear to God, those were the most chilling words I'd heard all day.

"Real life," murmured Goldie, and wandered out into the corridor that led into the wards, his shadow stretching eerily ahead of him.

Cal's eyes followed him. He straightened and looked to the nurses. "Is there a hospital administrator here? Someone in charge?"

The nearsighted nurse—"Lucy" according to her name tag—nodded. "Dr. Nelson. He has an office right down that corridor to the right." She pointed in the direction opposite where Goldie had gone. "I could take you—"

"Thanks, but I think I can probably find it myself. I would appreciate it if you could show my friends to the cafeteria, though. Colleen, would you . . . ?"

"Play Bo Peep? No problem," I said. "I'm kind of hungry myself. I can keep an eye on Goldman for you while I'm at it."

He shot me the ghost of a grin. "Thanks."

Lucy took us to their makeshift mess hall. She pointed us at the chow line, which was hopping at this time of evening, and hurried back to the E.R. I didn't imagine for a moment that Stan Beecher's leg was the big draw.

I scanned the room. Even in the uneven lantern light Goldie wasn't hard to spot. He was a real fashion plate, if you thought a purple and red paisley vest and a green plaid shirt made the perfect ensemble. He was sitting alone at a table near the glass sliders that gave out onto a large patio.

Through the glass I could see ranks of grills and hibachis and other low-tech cooking devices—the kitchen, I guessed. There were five or six people scrambling to make sure all the cook stoves were completely beneath the awning and out of the rain, which was suddenly coming down in buckets.

I hesitated for a moment, then went over and plopped down across from Goldman, who was busy worrying a piece of bread to tiny bits. He didn't so much as glance up. I opened my mouth to ask how he was doing.

"Kids are very perceptive people," he told me. "They hear angels."

"Angels with hunting packs?"

"Maybe the two things are not connected. Just because two occurrences are synchronicitous doesn't mean there's a causal relationship."

I hate it when he talks over my head. "Yeah, and maybe there's not much oxygen on your world."

"I think somebody or something saved our bacon."

"You know what I think? I think our lurker friends had dinner plans, and that the only reason they backed off was to keep from becoming tweak flambé."

A spark of amusement crept into his dark eyes. "Oh, clever. And you continued the food metaphor. I'm impressed. But a minute ago you were suggesting the big sissies were afraid of a little rain."

Before I could offer a tart comeback, he added, "There's something in that woods, and I think it's important we know what it is."

"Goldman, I'll tell you what's in that woods—weird, creepy, bloodthirsty critters that were once-upon-a-time human beings, just like you and me. They didn't get called off. They just got scared because one of them bought the farm."

"And you were forced to kill him . . . or her. I'm sorry, Colleen." He gave me a liquid brown look of utter sorrow that bit through me like a north wind, then got up and headed across the room.

I was stunned. "What—sorry? Do I look like I need your sympathy?"

Part of me wanted to chase him down and make him take back his pity. Another part was just plain embarrassed, because people were staring at me. My dignity circuit kicked in. I grinned and shook my head, as if I hadn't just let him get to me. I was still sitting there about twenty minutes later when Cal came in and sat down across the table.

"Where's Goldie?" were the first words out of his mouth. They pissed me off.

"Just missed him."

Cal's eyes tried to catch mine and read them. "Did he say anything more to you about what he heard out there?"

"Nothing that made any sense." I changed the subject. "You talk to the admin guy—Nelson?"

He nodded, looking down at his hands clasped on the tabletop. Something about the expression on his face . . .

"What?"

He raised his eyes to the sheet of glass and looked out into the rain. Flames from the cook stoves were bright blossoms in the dark. Our reflections watched us watching them.

"They have some very real needs here, Colleen. They're short doctors, nurses . . . mechanics." He shot a glance at me. "You name it, they need it."

"He asked us to stay."

A nod.

"You're not seriously thinking about it?"

"I don't want to think about it, but . . ." He closed his eyes. "Just after you left, they brought in a kid with severe slash wounds. Deep slash wounds. I didn't think they'd be able to stop the bleeding. Dr. Nelson didn't think they'd be able to stop the bleeding. Doc did. And between the two of them, they pulled it off. The kid's unconscious, but Doc thinks he'll recover." His eyes opened and pinned me to the back of my chair. "When I first walked into his office a while ago, Darryl Nelson struck me as a man who was worn-out—almost used up. No light in his eyes, no hope. He said it was the end of a long day, but it was more than that. When he shook my hand just now . . ." He turned his right hand over on the table, palm up, and I realized the cuffs of his shirt were stained with blood. ". . .he was a different man."

I touched the stained sleeve. "That the kid's?"

He pulled a wry grimace. "I'm a paramedic now."

"And they need paramedics."

"They need everything." He sat back in his chair. After a moment of silence he looked at me, his eyes sharp and cool. "You know as well as I do that there's not a lot we can do in just a few days. This place has problems that would take an ongoing battle just to keep under control. But . . ." He gazed around the cafeteria at the little knots of people scattered around the room—families, children. "We can make a little bit of a difference here, and the rest could only help us."

I had to admit, the thought of setting up camp here, even for a couple of days, was awfully appealing. We were all exhausted. Even Cal, for all that he seemed to have an endless supply of high-voltage batteries. This wasn't an easy decision for him. Fear for Tina, fear that we'd be too late for her, for everyone, just hovered in the back of his head. You could see it in his eyes if you looked real close, as I often did.

"If you want to move on . . ."

He shook his head. "We're going to be here at least for the night. Let's just . . . be here now, or whatever Yoda said."

I snorted. The thought of Cal being here now was a bit of a stretch. "Yeah, right."

He almost smiled. "Look, why don't you go get some sleep? I'm going back down to the E.R. and make sure Doc doesn't pull an all-nighter."

He got up then, automatically reaching down to adjust the position of the sword that hung against his thigh. The sword he'd pulled, like Excalibur, from a pile of trash in the Manhattan underground. Sometimes I thought the thing was more than a weapon. A familiar, maybe—like a witch's black cat. Okay, that's creepy, but these days you found yourself thinking stuff like that all the time.

I gestured at it. "You're gonna forget to take that thing off one of these nights, and wake up with it fused to your leg."

This time he did smile, and the smile got all the way up into his eyes. It was a smile that made you feel, irrationally, that he saw the end of all this, and it was a *good* end. He laid a hand on the sword hilt. "Darryl said if you go to the admissions desk, they'd find a room for you. With a real bed."

"A real bed? I don't know if I remember how to use one of those."

He left, and I got a bite to eat—bread, jerky, dried fruit. Just about everything is dried or jerked these days. Then I fetched my pack out of the wagon and went up to Admissions and got myself a room on the ward. The guy there actually had me sign a guest register.

"Hey, when this is all over," he said, "these kinds of records might be the only way of tracking people down."

Either that made sense or I was groggier than I thought. I signed in and the guy handed me a towel and told me how to get to the showers. The *showers*, for godsake! I was so dazzled by the thought of showers that I didn't take offense at the suggestion that I needed one.

The admissions guy warned me that at this time of night the fires under the hot water reservoir had been banked down for hours and wouldn't be stoked until just before dawn. "Water might be a little cool," he said.

It was merely lukewarm. Felt great anyway. After, I dragged myself to my room, lay down on the bed and tried to sleep. I couldn't. I don't know how long I lay there trying, but I finally gave up, rolled out of bed, and wandered out into the hall.

From the ward I could look down toward the core of the building and the lobby, a two-story atrium with a lot of plate-glass windows and a skylight—almost like being in the open woods at night. I made my way down the hall past the gift shop (now a small supply store that took barter rather than money, according to Admissions Guy) and into the atrium. I curled up on a sofa in the lounge, my head resting on the arm so I could look up and see the sky.

The rain had stopped and the moon was still there, wearing a veil of clouds. She wasn't full; it looked like something had taken a bite out of her. No matter. As days passed, she'd wax and wane and wax again. And there were stars, twinkling like a promise.

Something in the darkness of the west wing caught my eye. A shadow shifted, oozed. Static electricity arced across every nerve junction in my body.

I rolled my head a little to one side so I could see the mouth of the corridor from the E.R., which opened right next to the door of the pharmacy. After a moment of watching, there was more movement. Someone or something had just slithered around the corner into the darkened store.

I put the thought of shadows or lurkers aside and rolled off the sofa to slink across the moonlit floor, keeping low and using the groupings of furniture as cover. I passed soundlessly through the glass doors and paused to let my eyes adjust to the deeper darkness in the cluttered room.

My ears found the movement first; a secret scuffling, as of really big mice, came from the storage area behind the pharmacist's counter. I crab-crawled across the front of the room, then slipped up and around the counter.

I could now see a tall figure standing at the head of a row of shelves filled with drugs of every description. A bluish flame glowed. By its light, he was reading something that hung from the shelf—a clip-board. Papers shuffled. He sighed.

He moved quickly then, down the row of shelving into even deeper darkness. I waited a beat, then scuttled forward to the head of the row of shelves.

The light flared again. He was kneeling at the far end of the row, exploring something on the back wall. The blue flicker revealed a cross-hatch pattern. Metal clattered on metal. He was trying to break into the lockup where I suspected they kept the really potent stuff.

I glanced around, looking for some source of real light. On the counter next to the deceased cash register was an oil lamp. I scurried, stretched and fetched, then fumbled the lighter out of my pocket.

The rattling was fainter and more purposeful suddenly. Whoever this was, he seemed to know how to handle locks.

I moved with all speed back to the shelves.

He'd doused the light, but even in the dark I could tell the thief was making progress. The rattling stopped and the door of the cage creaked open.

I crept up the aisle, holding the lantern and lighter at the ready. Inside the lockup, he was fumbling in the drawers.

"Damn it, damn it, *damn* it!" The voice was a croak.

I lit the lantern and thrust it through the door of the lockup. "Hey!" I said. (Original, huh?)

He froze, hands full of bottles and packets, something like pain in his dark eyes.

"Goldman? What the hell are you doing?"

THREE

GOLDIE

There are some moments in life you can only survive. Moments in which you find yourself desperate for oblivion, or a mantra—anything that will just get you through it.

I remember one night, coming up out of the subway tunnels near Central Park, running into a pack of young punks out hunting "moles," which, since I had a subterranean address at the time, included me. My life narrowed to a circle of dark figures with gleaming eyes, the ominous creak of leather, lips forming crude and entirely rhetorical questions, biting cold.

It was the last week of November, and Manhattan was lit up for the holidays—Chanukah, Christmas, Kwanzaa—take your pick. When the punks instructed me to take off my clothes, I suspected I'd get my fifteen minutes of fame by being the poor, naked, homeless schmuck found frozen to death on the first day of the holiday season. I'd make the headline news, and probably a handful of Sunday sermons as well.

I couldn't run; I couldn't fight; there was nothing I could do with the moment but just get through it. So, I thought of the Chrysler Building pointing up through the snow; a million frozen falling stars drifting down to blanket Fifth Avenue and catch in the bare branches of its hundreds of trees—and I spontaneously broke into "It's Beginning to Look a Lot Like Christmas."

The punks found a naked mole-guy singing holiday jingles amusing, which derailed some of their misdirected spite and got me through the moment until some friends from the underground came to bail me out.

My failed attempt on the pharmacy's goodies leads to one of these moments. There is no threat of physical violence here in Dr. Darryl Nelson's cozy first-floor office, but there is a circle of eyes—anguished, disappointed, disapproving. And there are questions, none of them rhetorical.

I discover again (as if I could have forgotten) that an enemy's hatred is less painful than a friend's disappointment. There is no mantra for this occasion; there is more at stake here than my dignity.

Cal's lips have stopped moving and though I haven't really heard him, I know the nature of the question. Doc, perched on the corner of a large antique desk, looks pensive. He is as reluctant to pass judgment as Colleen is to withhold it. I barely graze her face. It would be hard to read even if I cared to try. Where she sits, behind Doc in the window casement, she is half in shadow. Her condemnation, I can *feel*.

I pan back to Cal, whose eyes beg me to come up with a reasonable explanation for what I was doing in the pharmacy tonight. Moment of truth. Question is, what variety of truth? Half-truth? The whole truth and nothing but? Are they ready for that? Am I?

I open my mouth and a half-truth slips out. "I couldn't sleep."

I wait for somebody to feed me a straight line: *So, you were just looking for something to help you sleep?*

No one feeds me anything. I wonder if Cal the Earnest knows how hard it is to lie to him, or even withhold from him. I start again, flashing for just an instant on the cold sweat I woke up in about an hour ago. "I was having a hell of a time sleeping. I don't know, um, maybe all the—the stuff that happened today just, um . . ." That isn't it. Not really. I scratch my head. Time for a haircut. "I thought maybe some sleeping pills . . ."

Doc stirs. "You could have come to me, Goldie. I would have gotten you something, gladly. So would Dr. Nelson, I imagine."

No accusation. He exposes me with simple compassion.

"C'mon, Goldman," says Colleen. "You were after something a lot more potent than sleeping pills."

Cal raises a hand and she subsides, looking mutinous. He says, "If there's a problem, Goldie, let us help you."

He makes it so easy. Flashback to my parent's living room and three different pairs of eyes. If someone—anyone—had uttered those words back then . . . But they didn't, and the rest, as they say, is history.

You're just like Grampa Ziolinsky, Dad said. An impossible drama queen.

I take a deep breath. *Focus.* "Tegretol," I say, "I wanted Tegretol."

Cal's face is a total blank, then he glances at Doc, as if for a translation. In the miserable silence, I can hear flames fluttering in their lanterns. Doc raises himself slowly from the desk.

Cal shoots him a sideways look. "What's Tegretol?"

"A trade name for carbamazepine, a drug most often used to medicate epilepsy." Doc doesn't take his eyes from my face. "But this is not epilepsy, is it, Goldie?"

"No."

Now he nods, comprehension and understanding flickering in his eyes. "You are certain of the diagnosis?"

"I diagnosed myself when I was seventeen, but no one at home was buying. They went into denial and I went into college. I had to flunk out and hit the streets before a friend got someone in social services to listen to me."

You don't need medication, Dad said, you need self-discipline.

"How long?"

"I've been on carbamazepine for about eight years—on and off."

"Your last dose?"

"Months ago. I thought maybe the Change might . . . oh, I dunno . . . change that, too, but . . ." I shrug.

Cal says, "What is it? What's wrong with him?"

Perverse as it sounds, the metallic note of anxiety in his voice is music to my ears, because I hear neither anger nor judgment in it.

Doc turns his sad, gray gaze on my friend. "Goldie is bipolar, yes?" He glances back to me for confirmation. "Manic-depressive. This is a disease most commonly treated with lithium, but carbamazepine is sometimes prescribed for a particular type of manic depression—

rapid-cycling bipolar affective disorder is the clinical name. It can be kindled—triggered—by physiological or psychological trauma."

As always, the clinical terms, so cool and tidy, give me a chill. Even the warm, Slavic lilt of Doc's voice can't lend them heat. I realize I am shaking from stem to stern. Cal moves a few steps closer to me, entering my space, supporting me with his eyes, then with a hand on my shoulder.

Ah, a friend from the underground coming to bail me out.

I take a deep breath. This is okay. I'm just not used to sharing this crap with anyone. In my underground days, only Professor John had known something was seriously loose in Goldman's attic, and his only response had been to get me to the Roosevelt when I melted down.

"How bad is it?" Cal asks me.

I shake my head. "I don't know. Things have been so weird, I haven't had time to think about it." Except at night, of course, when I lie awake thinking about it, running down behavioral checklists and probing my memory. *Have I felt this before? What was that emotion?* "I keep . . . waiting for signals, you know? Wondering if I'm going to slide. For a long time—for as long as we've been out here—I've had weird shit happen to me. Some of it in my head. But it wasn't like either mania or depression. It was just weird. I wasn't sure whether I was just having a normal episode or whether the Change had—" I catch myself. What can I possibly have imagined the Change had done?

"A normal *episode?*" repeats Colleen. "What the hell is that?"

Cal stops her with a glance. "What's different now, Goldie? Why tonight?" he asks.

Well, now—that is the $64,000 question, isn't it? I suppose I could blame it on our brush with the Shadows, but that would be cheap and predictable. I feel something dark and viscous and suffocating moving around in the long, dark, convoluted corridors of my brain. I find I want it to stay there, where it's hidden itself.

"Insomnia," I say. "Lack of appetite. Jitters. A return to journal-keeping. Scary thoughts."

"What kind of scary thoughts?" asks Cal.

"Did I say 'thoughts'? I meant 'moments.' Scary moments. Vertigo. That sort of thing. Nothing earth-shaking." Just the usual sense of being dangled over the Grand Canyon by a hair. I tuck both hands under my arms.

"We all have vertigo in these times, Goldie," Doc tells me. "I would like to reserve judgment about giving you carbamazepine—if indeed we have any."

"Um, there's some lithium and some valproate," I say. "I don't respond well to lithium. I've never had valproate. I didn't find any carbamazepine."

"Under the circumstances, Goldie, I think you will understand if I do not leap to medicate you. We live in a time of unknowns and we have all been subject to unnatural stresses. Are you willing to wait? To see what happens?"

To see if I go flat freakin' crazy? Sure, why not? Panic flickers momentarily in my gut. But, no. He's right. Based on what I've told him, any other course of action would be premature. And I am altogether unsure I want to tell more, so I leave the other half of the truth where it lies.

Doc gives me some valerian root tea—surely the most foul-tasting swamp water in creation—and sends me back to bed. He promises it will relax me. I actually drink the tea. It helps. But it doesn't keep my masochistic mind from poking at itself.

I lie in the dark, wondering if I should have told whole truths and examining the experience—nightmare or hallucination or vision—that sent me to the pharmacy. I am in a dark tower—like a castle keep—full of dead-end corridors, subterranean passages, and moldering stone. This is blurry, indistinct. I know that outside is light and freshness and freedom, and inside is cold, dead murk.

Below, beneath the foundations of this ruin, is a cesspool of something black and oozing and malevolent. It boils there in relative silence, incongruously making a sound as benign as falling rain. But as I explore this dark place, looking for a way out, I feel it wake and begin to rise. With a dreamer's omniscience, I know it is coming up to meet me, climbing stairways, drowning corridors, filling rooms.

I climb, of course. In horror films, they *always* climb, while the viewer is thinking, *God, what a schlemazel!* because the *schlemazel* always climbs his way into a dead-end corridor.

I'm no different. I climb a stairway that I somehow know leads to a room with only one way out—straight down.

At intervals, I turn back and catch a glimpse of what has oozed up out of the bowels of the Tower. It's black and oily and gleams like liquid obsidian. And in the bulging tongue of stuff that licks up the stairwell after me, I see myriad almost-faces as if they were a swarm of insects in amber.

But it's what I hear that really makes my skin crawl. There is a voice for every face, a whisper, a growl, a cry, a shout. It's enough to make me rethink my certainty about multiple personality disorder. (Maybe Mother's diagnoses weren't sheer crap, after all, and I owe her an apology.) It also terrifies me, because in the same way that I can almost see the faces, I can almost hear the voices, almost understand what they're saying. And the closer I strain toward understanding, the more thoroughly, soul-chillingly scared I get, because I know that this thing *wants* me to understand, and that if I understand, it will engulf me, and if it does this, I will go ape shit, stark-raving mad.

Or I'll drown, which is pretty much the same thing.

The only out I see is off the top of the Tower into that cold blue sky, which—unless I should sprout wings and fly—would be fatal. Fall or drown—hell of a choice.

What's most disturbing about the dream is that it's progressive. Every time I have it, I'm a little farther up the stairs, and the voices are a little louder.

And this is why I wanted the Tegretol; I had a hope, however absurd, that it might deflate the nightmare/vision, because I suspect that I am not merely *in* the Tower, I *am* the Tower.

And the black ooze? I lie in the dark of my hospital room and hold my cupped hand before my face, concentrating on a spot in my palm. A flame sprouts there, cool, blue, and softly bright. It's pleasant, soothing to the eye, and quite outside the realm of *normal* human ability. I did this for the first time less than a day after the Change. Not as easily, but I did it. A very handy thing in a world in which batteries are never included.

Back then, I found it exhilarating. Now, my exhilaration is tempered with a little old-fashioned fear.

When I finally drag myself out of bed the next morning, I'm surprised I've been allowed to sleep in. I expected we'd mount up and be on our way, but such is apparently not the case. We are not moving on today, Cal tells me. And maybe not tomorrow.

I hope you're not doing this for me, I say, and teeter on the edge of guilt, an emotion I've worked hard to avoid. I don't need guilt, thank you, I have manias.

Cal tells me that, of course, it's not just for me, it's for all of us and for the people here who could really use Doc Lysenko's help setting up a real E.R. and an effective triage. Just a day or two, he says. No big deal.

Right.

Left to my own devices, I gather up a field kit—jerky, canteen, matches, a knife scavenged from the hospital kitchen—and follow inner promptings to the edge of town. It seems I have a Quest of my own.

From the city limits I can look down a long slope and see the swath of burned grass that marks last night's adventure. Beyond it, the woods stretch north and west, a giant's picnic blanket spread out along the Ohio River.

There is something peculiar in those woods, and I have, for some reason, fixated on it. It is a place where Shadows walk and Angels sing loudly enough for dogs to hear.

I look up at the sky, but it's hard to tell what time it is through the overcast. Mechanical watches still function, but it's been so long since I've worn one, it's hard to get back into the habit. I figure it's still fairly early, judging from the place where the clouds are brightest. Leaning against a convenient tree, I check my food stash, swish my canteen, and pat my knife.

"Going for a little stroll?"

Colleen is standing on the opposite side of the tree, looking nonchalant as hell. I suspect her presence is a function of Cal's concern, and the poor girl was unlucky enough to draw the short straw.

"Contemplating it."

"You still think there's something out there."

"Yup. Besides, I lost my hat."

"What a shame. You know, you might have been hallucinating."

"I've never once hallucinated while in the throes of mania."

"That was then; this is now," she says. "All bets are off, right?"

She has a point, however trite.

"You know, Colleen, I'd love to stand here all day discussing my mood disorder, but with this overcast, it's going to get dark early."

"Then I guess you'd better get going."

I start off; Colleen falls into stride with me. I realize she's also dressed and outfitted for the bush—belt packs, machete, the works.

"So," I say, "you got elected to keep an eye on the goofball, huh?"

"No. Actually, I figured you'd do something like this and I just thought I might tag along. Call it curiosity."

I think very hard about minding, then realize I don't. "You must be bored stiff if you'd rather baby-sit me than tinker with broken machinery."

"I don't do baby-sitting," she tells me. "But it's been a long time since I've been out for a lark in the woods."

I can't help but smile. "Not since last night, huh?"

"Goldie, if that's your idea of a lark, you really are crazy."

Sticks and stones . . . "You called me 'Goldie.' "

She shrugs. "You called me 'Colleen.' "

An unexpected turn of events: Colleen the Self-Possessed is venturing out on an adventure with Goldie the Strange and Unpredictable, notwithstanding she thinks I'm a raving loon.

We cross the meadow and enter the woods, with her silent as a post and me trying to sniff Purpose on the wind. We have wandered for some time without me sniffing a damn thing, when she says, "So, Goldman, what was all that about your probation officer? Were you just putting me on?"

"I'd never do that. You're not my size," I say, and add, "Ms. Brooks."

She mumbles something under her breath that rhymes with *duck doo* and then louder, "Don't be a dipshit. Do you really have a probation officer?"

"Not anymore. He converted. To something unpleasant and slimy, I suspect."

"Do you ever give anybody a straight answer?"

Why *am* I being so ornery about this? "I got into a little trouble a while back."

"Trouble," she repeats.

"Assaulting a peace officer."

Her head swivels around and big green eyes skewer me. "Whoa. You? Assaulted a cop?" Beat. "What happened? Were you drunk or something?"

"I don't drink. I don't do *something*, either. Not without a prescription, anyway. I was living in a tunnel community—"

She cuts me off. "Tunnel *community*?"

"Subway tunnels. Train tunnels. Under New York."

"Yeah, yeah, 'mole people'—I get it. But *community*? Isn't that a bit highfalutin' a word for a collection of losers and misfits?"

"Present company excepted, of course?"

"Sorry." She sends me a half-apologetic glance out of the corner of her eye, then turns her attention back to the ground, looking for signs of passage.

"No, you're right. Guilty on both counts. I put myself underground. But everybody's story is different. Some folks got put there. They . . . fell through the cracks, I guess."

"Into the sewer."

"Subway tunnels. Not a bad place really. There were about fourteen of us in this one compound—under Grand Central. Mostly guys, some couples . . . a family."

She's surprised. "A family? Mommy, Daddy, and kids?"

"Kid. Rachel. She was about four. Her dad worked in a body shop aboveground, saving money to afford first and last on an apartment. One night this cop showed up and started busting up the place."

The memory, I find, is still painfully sharp. It was late. Agnes and Gino had just put their little girl to bed; Gino was reading to her by Coleman lamp, and in came Officer Jordan on little cat feet. None of us heard him. He was just there, flashlight and nightstick and attitude.

Usually Officer Jordan was a pretty cool guy, a mensch, by any standard. We called him "Petey" and joked with him and talked baseball. Sometimes he'd bring sandwiches and cans of soup, and sometimes we'd invite him to join us for a meal. He even helped a few of our more chemically dependent fellows ease back into some sort of life.

But that night he got his first glimpse of Gino with his family and that big, friendly man turned into something Other.

He was going to take them in, but they couldn't let him, because they both knew that if he did, they'd lose their little girl to social services and their chances of getting her back would be slim and none. He knew that, too, of course, which made his actions even more inexplicable.

Some of us tried to get in his way, to give the family a chance to disappear. Things got ugly, and he pulled out his service revolver to subdue us, but by then Gino, Agnes, and Rachel were gone. Jordan came unglued. Fired his gun into the roof of the tunnel, over and over. Then he started breaking up the place, one piece at a time. He kicked their little orange-crate bookshelf to pieces, tore up their books, and used his nightstick on their scavenged dishes. Then he did something that just about broke me in two. And that's when I hit him. Square on the head with Agnes's toaster oven.

He ended up with ten stitches; I ended up in jail. I look back and think we both committed crimes that night. Weirdly enough, I think we committed them for the same reasons.

Colleen is watching all this storm debris flood back through my head. I wonder what she can read in my face. I look away through the trees, admiring the way the watery sunlight sparkles through their crystalline leaves, and she crouches to examine something in the dry grass and leaf-fall that I can't even see.

"So you busted up the cop?"

I can still see the shattered remnants of a family's pseudolife. The Winnie-the-Pooh they'd lifted from some library, torn and lying in a puddle of dirty water, the remains of a bowl of cereal soiling the cover; the clothing Agnes had so carefully washed that day in the warm leakage of steam pipes, shredded and filthy; Rachel's bed looking like it had exploded.

"He broke Rachel's doll," I say, as if that explains everything.

"You assaulted an officer for breaking a child's toy?"

"He ripped it apart with his bare hands."

She looks up at me—a long, measuring look. "I don't understand. Why would a cop do a thing like that, anyway?"

"Oh, I understand. He wanted them not to have anything to come back to. He wanted to get that family out of the tunnels, and I guess that was the only way he could think to do it. They didn't belong there. Crackheads and fuck-ups and psychos belonged there, not *real* people."

"Did he? Get them out?"

"They got themselves out after a while. But that time, they just moved somewhere else to rebuild. Somewhere deeper, safer."

"Kind of like most of the folks out here, I guess," she observes. "Moving, looking for a life, a home, a safe place."

I'm wondering if anyone can find those things anymore when

Colleen straightens and points with her machete. "This way," she says, and pushes off into the bush.

Just as I'm about to ask what she's tracking, we come upon a clear, well-used trail.

"Deer?" I suggest, but Colleen is already down on her haunches, checking out the spoor.

She shakes her head. "People."

"Anything else?" I ask warily.

"Not along here." She gives me a dark grin over one shoulder. "But then, I've got no idea what kind of tracks Shadows make."

We follow the trail until it forks. I argue for splitting up, but Commando Colleen is having none of it.

"There's no way I'm going back into Grave Creek and tell Cal I lost you out here," she says. "We stick together, you got that?"

"Why Colleen, I'm touched."

"Screw you," she mutters, and heads off on the western fork.

We've gone maybe fifty yards when I get a whiff of something, metaphorically speaking. It's as if a car has driven by with the windows open and the stereo blaring. A snatch of sound, a shiver of almost-recognition and *poof!*, it's zipped on by, leaving me standing on the curb playing Name That Tune.

Ahead of me on the trail, Colleen realizes I'm not right on her heels. She turns back and gives me this *look*.

"I think I heard something," I say.

"You *think* you heard something?"

"Yeah. Like a snatch of music. Only it wasn't music, exactly. It was, uh, something else."

She sighs. "Would it totally kill you to be coherent once in a while?"

I sigh back. "That way." I nod down the trail toward the West Virginia–Ohio border.

We continue scouting to the west. We find nothing, however, except a few stray folks picking wild grasses and herbs in the woods. They take a speedy hike when they get an eyeful of my bodyguard. I'd beat it, too, if I saw Colleen the Barbarian coming at me out of the bushes wielding her wonder-machete.

We shout after them about lurkers and loudly suggest they head south, into Grave Creek. They flee due north.

Colleen insists we track them down and warn them properly. This takes some time off our clock. It also sets Colleen to *kvetching* at me about the fact that we've been out here for hours with no more than the merest hint of anything peculiar. When she decides we've gone far enough west, she plops herself down to rest before we head back to town. We're sitting under a tall but twisted cedar (with comfortingly normal-looking needles) when this little tune pops into my head and starts running in circles up there. I start humming the little tune. Next thing I know, there are words, too. Words calling the poor, the wounded, the huddled masses to refuge.

" 'I lift my lamp beside the hidden door.' " Hauntingly familiar, and yet . . .

"Must you?" Colleen asks, and gives me a look that tells me her exact opinion of my vocal stylings.

I stop noodling on the song, which I have just grokked is a sort of lyrically mutated musical version of Emma Lazarus's inscription for the Statue of Liberty. Appropriate—everything else around here is mutated. And the song won't leave. It's circling in my head like it's got no place to land—words, music, chords and all.

I look at Colleen. She's just sitting there, back to bark, eyes closed. There are leaves in her sawed-off hair and a streak of dirt down the side of her nose. I decide not to inform her of any of this.

"You hear that?" I ask.

She opens one eye. "Hear what?"

"You tell me. What do *you* hear?" I watch her with all my senses.

She looks around. People always do that—you ask if they hear something and they *look* for stuff.

"Wind," she says. "Leaves rustling—uh, tinkling. Crows—I hear crows. And a stream. What'm I supposed to hear?"

"Huh. Nothing, I guess." I lean back against the tree trunk.

Colleen can't hear the music, which means one of two things. Either I am missing my meds worse than I thought or this is not natural music. It's something else.

I get up.

"Where're you going?" Her eyes are still closed, but her hands are snugly around the hilt of her machete.

"Gotta take a leak," I lie, and head off into the woods. I've got a bead on this thing and I am homing in.

I walk for about a half mile when I come to a ridge. Below me the twisted woodland drops away below into a streambed. I stop and wonder where to go next. That's when I *hear* the music. It's below me, down in that teeny, tiny river valley.

I slide down the scarp on my butt, ending up feet first in the creek, which is shockingly green and cold. I wade across, doing my laundry on the fly, you might say, climb up the bank on the other side, part a couple of little cedars, and there he is.

The first thing I notice about my music man is that he's playing a very cool guitar. It's a jumbo blond maple cutaway with a cedar top, mother-of-pearl perfling around the sound hole, and inlay all up and down its rosewood fret board.

Very cool.

He's fingerpicking this gentle blues thing to which he is singing the lyrics I've been hearing in my head. He has a harmonica in one of those wire neck braces, and every now and then he toodles a riff that reminds me of trains going through sleepy little towns late at night. It's a sound that tugs at the soul, that says there is a Place, a Safe Haven, a Refuge that I will find if only I go where the music takes me.

I disengage, tingling. The music is laced with a power that tickles my brain, stands my hair delicately on end, and makes my skin itch.

This is when I notice two other things about my Bluesman. One is that he has an audience. A handful of human people of various shapes and sizes are following him, smiling and looking *farmisht* and punchy, as if what's floating out of his guitar is an industrial strength euphoric. He's smiling, too, and his chocolate skin is gleaming with sweat.

The other thing I notice is that there is a flare hovering winglessly over his dreadlocks. A *flare*—like Tina. She—definitely she—is about the size of a twelve-year-old girl, and she is making a magic of her own that drapes a sequined mosquito net of aqua energy all around her musician friend.

This is no parlor trick. Not the sort of flashy crap I do to impress the natives. This music has a power I can feel deep down in my bones. Is that what's keeping his flare from being sucked out of real time back to the Megillah?

I join the Bluesman's audience, hoping to get a better look at the flare—hoping, against all odds, that it *is* Tina. I shuffle up beside the guitarist, copping the same beatific smile everyone else is wearing, and I look up at his floating friend.

The moment my gaze touches her, she feels it and looks back through eyes like topaz purie marbles; like suns. I swear to God, it's as if she's walked in through my eyeballs, taken the cook's tour of my psyche, and made herself right at home.

She's beautiful. Her hair, short and wavy, fans out in a pale titian halo within her nimbus of light, which cycles vivid, translucent hues—aqua, azure, violet. Her ears come to a graceful point amid the strands. She's a mermaid or a mist wraith or any one of a hundred beautiful, mysterious, and impossible creatures that are not supposed to exist in the here and now. She wears what looks like a white silk Chinese lounging outfit, trimmed in red and gold. Not standard mermaid issue, by any means.

And she's not Tina. This is not a child; this is a woman.

I wonder what she was like before. I wonder why she changed. I wonder why she's providing arcane sun block for her friend, and I wonder how far I will have to walk to find out.

I stay in lock step with the others, noticing that several more folks have come out of nowhere to do the same—a mother towing a scrawny little boy in tattered clothes, a girl of about twelve whose eyes are empty windows.

We've traveled maybe a half mile when a hand clamps down on my shoulder and I'm dragged unceremoniously into the bushes.

FOUR

COLLEEN

Damned idiot took more than a leak. He took a freakin' hike. It was a good five minutes before I realized what he'd done. Fortunately, he wasn't trying to cover his tracks.

When I caught up with him, he was shuffling along in the wake of some guitar-playing Pied Piper with a gaggle of other music lovers. I swear, except for the guitar, it looked like something right out of an old grade-B zombie movie.

Okay, there was another difference—these folks all looked blissed, as if whatever this guy was singing was laced with eighty proof Jamaican rum. Don't get me wrong, it was pretty music, and the guy was massively attractive in a Rastafarian sort of way, but I didn't get why everybody was so gaga over it.

I followed along, listening and inching my way over to Goldman, when the tune changed. I'm not much into music, but I recognized the song; it was the one Goldman had been singing earlier—the "huddled masses" thing.

My scalp tingled. I looked again at the faces of Goldie's fellow travelers. The tingle turned to a chill. These people were dazzled. Enchanted. Bewitched. This guy was hypnotizing them and leading them away to God-knows-where.

I was pissed. First, I tried to distract everybody by yelling and jumping up and down. They didn't even hear me. Then I concentrated on Goldman. I walked right up in front of him, but he just stepped around me, staring at the Pied Piper like he was having some sort of religious experience.

Only force made sense at that point. I grabbed Goldman by the collar of his flea-bit buckskin coat and threw him into the bushes. He landed hard, but when he came up I had his attention.

"What was *that*? Dammit, Colleen, I need to find out where they're going!" He clambered up and started after the parade.

I kicked his feet out from under him and brought him down again. "You're bewitched, you idiot! The music that guy is playing is magic or something. *Don't listen!*"

"Jeez, Colleen, of *course* it's magic. That's why I'm following him. That music has *power*." He tried to rise.

"No shit." I yanked him back. "Come on, Goldman, show some *cojones* here. Fight it. Don't let him get to you."

He was shaking his head. "No, no, no, no, *no*. You don't get it. I'm not bewitched, Colleen—at least not the way you think. I see what he's *doing*. What *she's* doing. Either they're working together, covering each other somehow, or he's drawn her in with the rest of them."

"What the hell are you babbling about? She, who? Who's working together?"

"Them—the two of them. The Bluesman and the flare."

I jerked my head up for a glance down the trail after the Pied Piper and his fans. *Shit*, I thought, *he's hallucinating*. Doc hadn't prepared me to deal with this. I had not clue one about how to deal with this.

I took a firm grip on his shoulders. "Look, Goldie. There is no flare. There's just a guy with a guitar, hypnotizing people. Hypnotizing *you*. You're seeing things."

He blinked at me, looking confused for a few seconds while his wheels spun and whirred. Then he said, "You're wrong, Colleen. I'm not seeing things. There *is* a flare. She's hovering over the guy's head. She's creating some kind of—of aura around him. Don't you get it? Somehow the Source hasn't found her—hasn't taken her."

He tried to move again and I tried to hold him. It wasn't easy. Goldman is tall, built like a big, lanky cat, and is about as hard to pin down. He struggled half to his feet and dragged me about a yard while I fought to make him hear me.

"There's no flare, Goldie! Listen to me—*there is no flare!*"

"I can see her. Why can't you?" He twisted and pulled himself half loose. "Come with me. I'll show you."

"That's part of his power," I panted, digging in my heels. "Maybe he . . . he makes people see whatever they want to see—whatever will make them follow him." Sounded good, anyway. I wondered if I dared risk concussing him with a swift kick to the head.

He stopped struggling, catching me off guard. I could hear the wheels again—*whir, click, whir.* "Now that almost makes sense," he admitted, "except for one thing. I didn't want to see a flare. I wanted to see *Tina.* This isn't Tina. This is someone very different. Someone I've never seen before."

"Then why can't I see her?"

He rolled his eyes and laughed. "Why can't penguins fly? They're birds. Birds fly; penguins can't fly. Does that mean penguins aren't birds?"

Brain freeze. Goldman used my paralysis to break free. I didn't react in time and ended up on my keester. While he ran for the trail, I was trying to drag myself out of the shrubbery.

Cursing, I lit out after him. He was faster than I expected and seemed to have a homing beacon on the blues dude. He cheated— cut corners, crashed boonies. This made him easy to track, but harder to keep up with.

By the time I caught up again, he was right back in the pack, as close to the guy as he could get, staring at the empty air over his head like there really was a flare up there. And all the while, Mr. Blues kept serenading his audience, wrapping his music and his voice and his words all around them, trussing them up like holiday turkeys.

I flashed on a dream I'd had last night—the one that had kept me from sleeping. I was a marionette. We were all marionettes. Off to the west, this faceless puppet master stood at the top of a dark, glittering tower with our strings in his hands and made us dance toward the sunset. In my dream I was *hungry* to go west. Awake, I knew that if we didn't go west, we'd never find Tina, or have a hope of understanding what was happening to our world, or have a chance to undo it or fight it.

Damned if you do, damned if you don't.

Suddenly, I was pissed again. Who was this guy and where was he taking these people? And why? What did he have to gain by hypnotizing Goldman, or that woman and her little boy, or that girl? The only answer I could think of made me even more pissed: he was a slaver. It was the only thing that made any sense.

I spent a moment swamped in a hateful, sticky confusion. I had to do something, but I didn't know what. There were half a dozen people here; I couldn't exactly run up and knock them all senseless. I had to cut the strings at the source. I pulled my machete, gave a wild-eyed whoop and launched myself at the Pied Piper.

It was like slamming into an electrically charged rubber wall. Something absorbed my attack, then kicked back like a mule. Fireworks went off behind my eyes. Lights flashed, chased, spun. I was spinning, too—through the air—head over heels over head.

I slammed upside down and backward into the trunk of an evergreen. Pain—bright, sharp, shattering pain—shot up and down my right side. I roared aloud and waited for a fall that never came. I was stuck to the trunk of that tree like a damned fly in sap; only it wasn't sap that held me. My legs and feet were tangled in a network of branches, and something held me tight against the trunk.

Looking up along my right side, I bit back a whimper. A broken limb had pierced that side of my jacket from the back and gone through the sweater and camisole underneath, knitting fabric to flesh. The shattered point stuck out through the jacket just above my waist, stained with blood.

Panic galloped from one end of my body to the other. It took me a long, crazy moment to rein it in. I was still breathing, I told myself. I hadn't punctured a lung. I wasn't dying; I was just stuck and hurt . . . and alone in a forest where feral shadows roamed.

And I *was* alone. The music was gone. Goldie's blues guy had blown me six ways from Sunday and strolled off, singing, into the sunset.

I took a calming breath and tried to figure out which was holding more of my weight—the network of twigs or the broken branch. My money was on the branch.

I pulled my chin almost to my chest, trying to see. Pain flared, making the sparks of light behind my eyes dance and twirl. I reached up and felt along the branch stub. Maybe I could somehow wriggle out of my jacket and get free. Tilting my head back, I peered at the ground. It was a lot farther than I'd hoped. Okay, maybe I could just fall a dozen feet onto my head and break my neck.

I looked back up at the limbs and branches at my feet, hoping to see something sturdy. There was nothing within reach that would hold my weight.

I jerked my left leg. It came free in a shower of pine needles. The world tilted dangerously and my side screamed.

Whatever I did, I had to do it fast, before I passed out. I closed my eyes, took as deep a breath as I could, and grabbed the stub with both hands. I'd count to three, then I'd try to get my other leg free.

"Don't move." Strong hands gripped my shoulders.

I felt weak enough to weep. "Damn it, Goldman. I thought you'd gone south."

"West, actually, but no. I heard you screaming."

"I didn't scream. Not out loud, at least."

"Really? Well, then you have very loud angst."

I opened my eyes and looked down toward the ground. He was looking up at me through those strange redwood eyes, his hands still on my shoulders.

"I'm going to climb up onto the branch behind you there." He pointed up toward my feet. "Then I'm going to grab your legs. I want you to try to ease yourself off that . . . snag. Don't worry about falling. I won't let you fall. I promise."

I hated that I felt reassured. "Shit, Goldman, don't be maudlin. Can you even climb a tree?"

"Never tried. But I figure if I can climb a steam pipe, I can climb a pine. Hold on," he added, and disappeared from my line of sight.

There was some scratching and scuffling behind me, then I was hit by a shower of pine needles and bark. I prayed there were no loose pinecones up there. A moment later he had a tight hold on my ankles.

I dared to look up at him. All I could tell was that he had somehow woven himself into the branches behind me and wrapped his arms around my legs.

"Okay," he grunted, "now, see if you can't get your clothes free of that snag."

"Problem. My clothes aren't all that's caught."

He was silent for a moment, then murmured something under his breath. "What can I do, Colleen?"

"A knife," I said. "Mine's in my boot. Little hard to reach just now. If I cut the jacket away from the branch, might help."

"Okay, hang on."

The branches creaked and groaned, I felt him fumble with my boot. A moment later something hit the ground.

"Shit," he said, then, "Sorry. I guess you'll have to make do with mine. Reach up toward me. I'm going to slip the knife into your hand, hilt first."

I reached. He got his knife into my palm without cutting either of us. It was smaller than mine—lighter. The handle was held together with duct tape. I prayed the tape would hold. I slipped the blade into the torn fabric at my waist and sliced.

The fabric slit so easily it caught me by surprise. I shot downward—only a few inches. There was a muffled snap and pain shot around my rib cage. I went cold all the way to the bone. It couldn't be a broken rib—it couldn't.

"Colleen?"

"It's okay," I panted, chasing the quivering, icy feeling out of my chest with hot determination. "I just slipped."

"I've got you," he said. "I won't let you fall. Try to get free."

I bit my lip and started hacking at the jacket. Finally, it slit all the way to the hem and fell away from the snag. I pushed gently on the broken branch; something tugged and my side shrieked.

"Oh, shit," Goldie said.

I didn't want to look. I had to look.

"I can't see," I said. Stars danced in front of my eyes; I fought blackness.

"Don't look. You've got a splinter in your side."

I almost laughed. A splinter. How mundane. I pulled my head up so I could see. I was a mess. The good news was that I hadn't impaled myself on the main branch, but on a shard about two fingers thick. I could see the bloodied tip angling out over my ribs. The bad news was that the other end was still attached to the branch.

"Give me the knife," Goldie said.

"Goldman, if I give you the knife, how are you going to hold onto me?"

"Good point." He shifted his grasp on my legs.

I shuddered as the splinter twisted in my side.

"Damn! Sorry. Okay, now give me the knife." I felt him take careful hold of the blade. "Let go."

I did, and gladly.

"This will no doubt hurt like hell," he informed me. "Are you ready?"

"Jeez, Goldman—what a question. No, I'm not ready. Cut the damn thing."

A kitchen knife is crappy for sawing wood. It took him several agonizing minutes to saw through the thing. I bit my lip, ground my teeth, growled, and panted like a dog. The splinter broke free of the tree in one final twist of agony.

Oh, God, I thought as the swirling specks of light gathered behind my eyes, *I'm going to pass out.* But I didn't pass out—not just then. I passed out when Goldman, having lowered me as far as he could without falling, let go of my feet. I came down on my back in a shower of needles and bark and an explosion of pain.

When I woke, there was icy water dribbling into my face.

"Drink," he said.

I obeyed, taking the squeeze bottle out of his hands. As I guzzled water, he said, "I thought about trying to extract that thing while you were out, but I couldn't tell how bad it was."

"You're not a doctor, so I'd just as soon you didn't try to play one."

"Yeah, well, I did manage to pull out some of the little bits and I cleaned around the wound and, um, put sort of a poultice on it. But Doc is going to have to perform the miracle today. I'm plumb out."

"Getting late," I observed.

He nodded, looking around at the striping of shadow and sunlight. "Help me up."

Getting vertical was hell. Walking was hell. Racing sunset was hell. I did not want to escape the clutches of some stupid pine tree only to become tweak chow.

At first I tried to be stoic and self-reliant, but by the time we reached the outskirts of Grave Creek, shadows were long, the sunlight was a tired red, and Goldman was practically carrying me.

When we reached the water tower, a cart came out to get us. I was so bloody glad to be off my feet, I nearly cried. Once we were settled in the cart, my side didn't seem to hurt so bad. In fact, it felt sort of tingly. I rolled my head along the rail of the cart to get a look at the wound, wondering what kind of poultice he'd put on it.

Goldman had his hand over it, as if to keep me from seeing how bad it was. The expression on his face was tight and dark. What did he think—that he could pull the damn thing out with his eyes? A snide and indignant order for him to get his hands off me popped into my head, then fizzled. Whatever he was doing, it wasn't hurting me any. Just felt sort of tingly.

I rolled my head back the other way, gazing out over the rear of the cart toward the blanket of trees. Among the slanting shadows floated several pairs of ruddy embers.

❦

I'd've refused a general anesthetic if they'd offered me one. But Doc gave me a local instead, then got to work cleaning and stitching. It was not a painless procedure. I meditated on packing my saddlebags, saddling and bridling my horse, and taking a trail into the Adirondacks. And I wondered what Goldman was telling Cal.

I could just imagine.

When we'd come in, naturally, the first question he asked was, "What happened?" I said, "Long story," and Goldman said, "Cal, we need to talk." When Cal seemed to want to follow my gurney into the E.R., Goldman added, "Now."

"Whatever he tells you," I warned Cal as the nurses wheeled me away, "don't listen!"

When the E.R. doors swung shut and cut me off, Goldman was already drawing Cal away toward Dr. Nelson's office.

A stupid thing to say, I reflected, as I watched Doc bandage my ribs. I really should know by now that any word spoken against his precious Goldie is a word Cal Griffin doesn't hear.

Doc put me in a wheelchair and started to roll me back to my room.

"I can handle it," I told him.

"No," he said, "you cannot. If you try to drive this chair on your own, you will pull out all of my careful work and you will begin to bleed. The wound was both deep and ragged, Colleen; you will not be able to bounce up and run away from this one. Besides, I imagine Dr. Nelson would disapprove of you bleeding on his so-clean floors."

"I gotta talk to Cal."

"Then I will take you to him."

I gritted my teeth all the way to Nelson's office. When I saw the look on Cal's face, my heart lurched. He looked like a crusade about to roll off to the Holy Land.

"What's he been telling you?" I asked, and cringed at how wimpy my voice sounded. "Did he tell you he saw a flare?"

"Of *course* he told me." His eyes were bright and the words bubbled out, mixed with laughter. "Why wouldn't he tell me?"

Behind me Doc repeated, "He saw a flare?"

"No," I said. "He did *not*. If Goldie saw a flare it's because he fantasized one."

The hope in Cal's eyes faltered. "What do you mean—he fantasized one?"

"I mean there wasn't a flare. He only *thought*—"

Goldman cut me off. "That doesn't make any sense. I told you before: if I'd been fantasizing, I would have fantasized Tina, not someone I'd never met. This flare was a woman—an adult. She was only generically like Tina."

In spite of Doc's magic herbs, I was bone weary and I hurt all over. I didn't have the energy to argue. But I had to. I couldn't let Cal break his heart on false hope. Again.

I grasped my wheel rims and pushed myself farther into the room, drawing a cry of protest from both Doc and my stitched ribs. "There was no flare, dammit, Goldie! There was a guy with a guitar and a bunch of sleepwalking zombies. He was a magician or a—a hypnotist, and he made you all see what you wanted to see and hear what you wanted to hear."

"Why?" Cal asked.

"So they'd *follow* him. You should've seen him, Cal." I nodded at Goldie. "He was . . . *smitten*. He was singing the guy's songs; he was following him like a little lost lamb; he was staring up at him like—"

"Like he had a flare hovering over his head," said Goldman dryly. Before I could crank out a comeback, he added, "How do you think you ended up in that tree?"

Brain tilt. "*He* did it—the blues guy."

"He didn't even see you coming."

Yeah, that's how it had seemed to me, too, at the time. But now it was hard to admit it. "He had a force field of some sort."

"Oh, you saw it, did you?"

"No, I didn't see it."

"Well, I *did*." Goldman thumped his chest. "*I* saw it. And I saw where it was coming from."

Cal's eyes were on his face, bright with hope. "The flare?"

Goldman nodded. "She was cloaking him in some way. Not to keep people away from him, I think—there was a little kid holding the hem of his jacket. But when Colleen came flying at him, the flare shot out this . . . blast of energy. Like a shock wave. Or a—a photon torpedo. That's what put Colleen in the tree."

It wasn't fair. It wasn't fair for me to be fuzzy and weak when I needed to be sharp and clear and strong. I bit the inside of my lip to keep from snapping and snarling.

Cal knelt by my wheelchair and met me eye-to-eye. "You didn't see any of this?"

I gave him the most straight-up, confident look I could muster and begged him silently to see in it how sure I was. "No, Cal. I didn't see anything but the guitar player."

"Did you feel any desire to follow him?"

"No. Not a bit. I just went along because I wanted Goldman *not* to follow him."

"Was it as Colleen said, Goldie?" Doc asked. "Did this man's music mesmerize you? Did these other people seem mesmerized?"

"I'd say they were."

I snorted. "Oh, yeah, but you weren't, right?"

"No, Colleen, I wasn't."

He sounded so calm and self-assured and—well, sane—while I knew he was nothing of the sort. Looking at Cal's face, it was clear the sanity card was one I didn't dare play right now.

"If I had been mesmerized," Goldie continued reasonably, "you'd still be hanging upside down in that tree."

Slam-dunk.

He turned to Cal, his eyes earnest, as if he was a wide-open book begging to be read. "There was a flare, Cal. Colleen couldn't see her—I could. It's that simple. Colleen didn't hear the music at first, either."

"I heard it," I protested.

"Sure, after you got within *hearing* range." He tapped his ear. "I heard it before that. That's why I went off on my own—to look for the source of it. And I heard it last night when we brought in the Gossetts and Beechers. The kids and the dog heard it, too. So did Jim. He caught me humming it and thought it was a song he knew. It was one of the Bluesman's tunes."

Cal gave him a long, searching look. "Are you saying this is what called off the Shadows?"

"I'm saying . . . it could be."

Cal turned back to me. "But you don't believe him."

Oh, God, but I wanted to sleep. "Oh, hell. Yeah, okay. I guess I believe him. Goldman was singing something about 'huddled masses' and driving me nuts. He wandered off, I followed, and— yeah—our Pied Piper friend turned out to have the song in his repertoire."

"If he heard what you couldn't hear, mightn't he have seen what you couldn't see?"

Put that way, it sounded reasonable, even to me. I should've known better than to argue with a damned lawyer.

"Yeah," I said. "Yeah, anything's possible, I guess." I was wilting. Melting away like the Wicked Witch of the West.

Doc's hand lit warmly on my shoulder. "Colleen needs rest. Perhaps we can explore the meaning of all this in the morning."

I could tell that neither Goldie nor Cal wanted to wait that long to explore anything.

"In just a moment," Cal said. "Let's assume that there is a musician drawing people into following him. And that there is a flare shielding him in some way—protecting him. Why? Why is he collecting people? Where's he taking them?"

"And for what purpose?" murmured Doc.

"Well, that's a no-brainer," I mumbled.

"And, um, how does he protect the flare?" Goldman was tugging at his lip, talking almost to himself. "How does he keep her from being sucked up by the Megillah? Or maybe the question is, how does he keep the Megillah from *finding* her?"

Cal looked up at him, his eyes intensely bright. "Where's she from? Maybe she's not the only one."

"The Source has Tina, Cal," I said, sounding surly. "There might be one flare or twenty or even a hundred where this guy is from, but not one of them is Tina."

"We don't know that, Colleen. We don't know *where* he's from. For all we know, he may have somehow gotten her *away* from the Source. She could be a direct link." Cal rose, looking over my head at Doc, ignoring me. "I want to know where she's from. And how he's protecting her."

"Or enslaving her?" asked Doc.

Cal's face was grim. "Or enslaving her. Enslaving *them*."

I lost track of the murmur of voices. When I came up out of my head-trip, blue and cream tiles were slipping by under the wheels of my chair. I turned my head so I could see who was driving. I recognized Doc's slender surgeon's hands and felt a flicker of disappointment.

"Guess I zoned out," I said. My words came out like mush. "No big deal, though, huh? I didn't have a whole lot t'offer the discussion anyway."

"You offered a great deal, Colleen. You do yourself a disservice."

I shook my head. "What is it about me, Doc? Why am I so damn dense? Why is this shit we're going through changing everybody but me? I'm like a—a rock. I just sit like a lump while the whole fucking world changes around me. *Evolves.* Why aren't I evolving?" Oh, dammit. I was going to cry. What the hell had he given me?

His hand came down on my shoulder, firm and consoling. "Colleen, you are beaten up and exhausted. So, I will ignore what you are now saying and advise you to do the same. Yes, you are, indeed, like a rock in many ways. You are stable, solid, dependable. Whatever happens, you can be relied upon to be where you are most needed. You are . . . an anchorage that the rest of us need."

I sniffled. God, I actually *sniffled*. "Cal doesn't need me. He just needs me to get out of his way. He makes a decision; I'm the one who's gotta argue it. He comes up with a plan; I'm the one who's gotta try to poke holes in it. You saw what happened just now. Shit, why couldn't I just shut up?"

Doc chuckled. "Because you care. You care that we don't get distracted—drawn off target, yes? As I said: you keep us focused. Calvin knows this as well as I do." Something soothing seemed to ooze out of Doc's voice—out of his fingertips—and fill my veins and arteries with warmth.

"You see, that's just what I mean," I complained. "You got this thing you do that just makes everything all right. The sky is falling and the world is crumbling and I hurt like hell and you say something and it's all okay."

Now he laughed. It was a free, natural laugh I'd hardly ever heard him use. "And you, Colleen, you have this thing you do, as well."

"What thing?" I wanted to know. "What thing do I do?"

He didn't answer me right away. Instead, he wheeled me to the door of my room, propped it open, pushed me inside and rolled the chair over to the bed.

I started to lever myself up out of the chair.

"*Nyet!*" he said sharply. Then he lifted me onto the bed, pulled a blanket over me, and perched on the edge of the mattress to look at me. His face, always neatly shaven, was all serious, solemn angles, hollowed out beneath the high cheekbones. He looked as weary as I felt, but there was an almost-twinkle in his eyes.

"The thing you do, Colleen, is to make things happen, not as our fears tell us they must, but as our hopes tell us they *should*. You defy all odds, you ignore all dangers, you acknowledge no defeat. If you did not do this thing you do so very well, neither I, nor Goldie, nor perhaps a single member of the Gossett or Beecher families would be alive tonight." He put his hand over mine where it lay on the blanket and squeezed it. "Be a rock, Colleen. Because it is a rock we need."

Tears leapt from my eyes, giving me no chance to call them back. Stupid. Weak.

He watched me for a moment, smiling this warm little smile he usually reserved for injured children. Then he leaned forward and kissed my forehead. "*Spatyeh, boi baba.*"

"What?" I murmured, already half asleep. "*What?*"

"I said, sleep, tough lady."

I seemed to have no choice but to close my eyes and let sleep carry away the tears.

FIVE

Am I sure, Cal asks me, that I can find the Bluesman again?

I just nod and don't mention that since I first heard it, I haven't been able to get his music out of my head. Admitting that might induce Doc to medicate me after all, and I suddenly find the prospect unsettling. I've connected with the music—or it's connected with me—and I don't want to risk jamming the connection. So I look Cal in the eye and give an emphatic, "Yes!"

We ship out as soon as Colleen is ready to travel, which, for the record, is two days later than she *says* she's ready. Doc has no patience with her macho sensibilities. Even at that, she heals up a lot faster than he expects.

We keep the horses, but leave the wagon with Dr. Nelson. Where we're going, a vehicle that size will be a liability. Besides, it'll make a dandy ambulance. Dr. Nelson and his staff display their gratitude in the form of food, clothing, and enough medical supplies to stock a small MASH unit.

Now we wander the wooded hills of West VA on horseback, trying to dial in the local blues station. We are not on the road long when I realize that my receiver has a bunged-up antenna. The music in my head is not much more than an echo—no, scratch that, a persistent memory. A memory that is almost as flaky as I am.

It's high noon and we've been zigzagging through the trees since daybreak when my radar finally kicks in. Oddly enough, Colleen notices I've connected before I do.

"Hey, Goldman," she says. "You're doing it again."

"I'm . . . what?"

"Singing," she says. "You were singing."

They all look at me.

I test the connection. "North," I say, and we go north.

Two miles later I've lost it again. It's like that all day—on again, off again—as we move north, then west, then north. I pretend confidence I don't feel and they follow.

On one late afternoon rest stop we consult a map of the world as we once knew it—another gift from the folks in Grave Creek.

Cal says, "If we continue this pattern, we're eventually going to meet the Ohio River." He grimaces. "That is, if the landscape hasn't shifted."

Once upon a time, you could look at a map created the previous year and assume the landmarks would have stayed right about where the cartographer put them. Not so, in this kinky new America. The Ohio River may or may not be anywhere near the wiggly blue line on our map. It might no longer be blue. It might no longer contain water.

Cal gives the cartoon landscape another long look, then gazes off into the distance, his fingertips tracing the map's blue line—up and down, up and down, like a blind man reading braille. The rest of us hunker in a circle, watching him. The wind sighs and hisses through the brush, and the leaves tinkle and moan—a sonata for theremin and wind chimes. I think I hear a dim fizz of static.

"Huh," Cal says. "This is going to sound weird, but . . . I can *feel* the river. It's still there. But . . . it's different."

"Different, how?" Colleen asks.

"I don't know. It . . ." He runs a fingertip over the river line again. "It's spiky . . . or something." He looks up at me. "Is that where we're headed, Goldie? The river?"

"We could go that way," I say.

His eyes hit me so hard I feel stung. "*Could?* How about *should?*"

Cal's monumental patience is wearing thin. I wish I could say something that would reassure him, but the truth is, someone's closed the door again and the music is just a memory.

"He seems to be angling toward the river, yeah."

Colleen pounces on the ambiguity. "*Seems?* God-bless-America, Goldman! We've been weaving around these woods for the better part of a day and the best you can do is *seems?* Have you forgotten how dangerous these picturesque woodlands can be after dark?"

"I haven't forgotten. Yeah, let's head for the river."

I sound less than convincing; a look passes between Cal and Colleen.

I stand, take up my horse's reins, and turn my attention up the trail. The cold, green smell of running water is heavy in the breeze. Waning sunlight pierces the fluttering crystals and shatters into a billion separate fragments of glory. I let them dance in my eyes and try to fan the song-memory into something more, but it resists. I find the whispered harmony of the leaf-chimes intruding. It surrounds the memory, winds through it, and alters it somehow.

"Goldie, where are you going?"

Cal's voice at my back stops me. I have started walking without realizing it—following something I didn't even know I'd heard. My horse, Jayhawk, nickers and nudges me with his head, as if to ask where I'm leading him. I'm not sure, but at least I realize that the song is not just a memory.

"He left a trail," I tell Cal. "I didn't hear it before, but I think I can track it."

Cal's face betrays his uncertainty for only a moment. "Then let's move."

We move. I sit atop Jayhawk with my eyes half out of focus, but my sonar is right on the money. The Bluesman's music shimmers in the glassy leaves. It's as if they've absorbed and refracted it, the same way they refract light. I guide the horse without really thinking about it, and we are heading due west, no longer angling.

We don't reach the Ohio River by sunset, but we do reach a stream. Mist has gathered and rain threatens and we are seriously nervous about who or what we might be sharing our camp with. Our options are dual and opposite: we can huddle in complete darkness and hope not to attract attention, or we can light our campsite up like a Christmas tree and hope the heffalumps and woozles will be scared away.

We choose darkness, with emergency recourse to light. We put the stream along one flank and a large rocky outcropping along the other. That takes care of two sides and gives us a sheltered corner in which to tether the horses. We lay three campfires across our exposed side, well packed with kindling and armed with extra wood. We set oil lanterns in the gaps between. We are armed to the teeth with weapons I have very little confidence in.

We decide to stand watch in shifts—two up, two down. Colleen and I draw first shift, and as fate would have it, it begins to rain. While Doc and Cal curl up in their little tent, Ms. Brooks and I try to cover the neatly laid fires with tarpaulins. Then we hunker down behind the central fire pit under a tarp—she with her crossbow, me with a machete that I suspect is more dangerous to me than it is to anyone or anything I might try to use it on.

We're silent for a long time, thinking private thoughts. I'm thinking about the flare—about her huge, bottomless, gold, cat-slit eyes—when Colleen says, softly, "You got people you wonder about, Goldman?"

"Wonder about?"

"Yeah. Like where they are, what they're doing. *How* they're doing."

"Yeah. Some friends in the tunnels. Some of the guys at a flophouse I lived in for a while."

"A flophouse?" she says incredulously.

I smile at the memory. "In the Bowery. Ten bucks a night, six-by-six room—but it was *my* room. I even had a guinea pig—Einstein. Anyway, I wonder about some of the guys there. I'd worry about them, but frankly, I think they're probably more suited to the life we have now than to the one we had. They're used to extremes in weirdness."

"What about your family?"

She had to ask. "Them, I try not to think about. And I seriously doubt they think about me. I doubt they even know I'm alive."

"Ouch. Don't go there?" When I'm silent, she says, "Okay, then, what about the folks underground? D'you ever think about that family you told me about—Gino and Agnes and . . . Rachel, was it?"

I'm surprised she remembers. "Yeah. I do think about them . . . a lot."

"Can I ask you something? How did people like that end up in the sewers? For that matter, how did you?"

"Subway tunnels, Colleen, not sewers. Some got into drugs or alcohol. Some just stopped believing in what they were doing. Some just couldn't manage what we laughingly call real life, and we stopped trying. Some . . . just weren't equipped to manage in the first place."

"And you?"

"Let's just say I had a disagreement with Mom and Dad about my college curriculum. So, I did what any red-blooded, Jewish-American boy would do — I ran away from home to find myself and . . . and got lost. That was a lifetime ago."

"What curriculum did you have in mind?"

"Art. Music. Religion. Mom protested that those were not practical pursuits. When I persisted, she got my father into the act. They'd put me through college if I wanted to study — you're going to love this — law."

She laughs. "Herman Goldman, Esquire, huh?"

"Over my dead body . . . almost."

I could just see her turn her face toward me in the uncertain moonlight. "Lawyers make good money."

"Uh-huh. And you've seen what it's done for Cal. Ely Stern had him whipped and he hated himself for it. Besides, I'm a musician at heart . . . or a monk."

"Lucky for us, I guess."

I like the thought. "Yeah, you're right. Huh. Imagine that. I'm in the right place at the right time. First time in thirty-five years."

"I wonder if that's what makes you more sensitive to the Source."

"What — being a musically inclined monk?"

"No, being . . . different. Thinking differently, I mean. Seeing things in the world — in people — that most of us don't."

Whoa. I am taken with the absurd idea that Colleen Brooks has just paid me a compliment, but before I can get all self-congratulatory, she says something that totally screws the mood.

"What's it feel like? When the Source . . . when it whispers at you, or whatever it does?"

Deep inside, something dark pushes up toward consciousness. I press it back down. "It feels like hell. That's, um, not a metaphor."

She won't give up. "You hear voices? Actual *voices?*"

I breathe out, watching the steam from my mouth dissolve into nothingness. *Be here now.* "I hear, I feel, I see. It's . . . complicated. You ever watch *Star Trek?*"

"Uh . . . yeah."

"Well, it's like the Borg. All those voices, coming out of nowhere, coming into your head, pulling at you from someplace dark and cold . . ." I see her shiver and add: "It's like I'm Unit Four of Unimatrix One, and the Source is the Borg Queen."

"You're putting me on, right?"

Actually, I'm putting her off. "You ever think about your ex?" I counter. "What was his name—Grumpy?"

"Rory. And that's a dodge," she accuses me. "If you don't want to tell me, just say so."

"So."

We talk for a while about the things we miss about so-called civilization. Oddly enough, we discover that we have the same number one item—truly hot showers.

The rain has let up and our conversation has degenerated into a laundry list of Most Missed when the horses suddenly get the yips. Words curl up and die on our tongues. We're on our feet then, and I quickly realize why Colleen kept shifting her position under the tarp.

"Should we wake them?" I whisper, nodding at Doc and Cal and trying to shake the cramps out of my legs.

"Not yet. Let's make sure it's worth waking them first."

Colleen moves to the horses—possibly to read their grapefruit-size equine minds—while I squint into the misty woods, hoping *not* to see fiery eyeballs peering back.

"Shit," I hear Colleen growl above the whinnying, then, "Wake up! Doc, Cal! C'mon, c'mon, come *on!*"

Behind me they stir, they stretch, they come to befuddled wakefulness, they realize where they are and bolt from their bedding. They are taking up weapons and stations when I see the first pairs of eyes. I glance behind me and wonder if the rocky outcropping before which our very nervous horses now quiver will be help or hindrance.

Lanterns flare at the periphery of my vision. I rip the lid off my fire pit and light up. The flames are sluggish, but they go. To my right and left I hear the rustle of tarps being whisked aside. Flames leap.

"Doc, stay with the horses." Cal's voice comes from my left. "Keep them calm. If the twists get past us, take them across the stream and get as far away as you can."

Doc argues, albeit unsteadily, "We should all leave. If we move now —"

"We could be separated," Cal finishes. He dumps wood on his fire; it spits bright cinders into the air.

On my right, Colleen hunkers down behind her own column of flame, crossbow locked and loaded. None too soon. Dark shapes materialize out of the shrubbery. As we watch, they go from solid to vapor—black on black, smoke on ink. They may not be able to surround us, but they can easily push us up against the rocks or into the creek if they attack.

They don't attack. They just melt into the trees and watch us. All we can see of them is those burning red eyes. After about an hour of this, they glide into a different formation. I can feel all four of us clench, expecting an attack. None comes.

Another hour ticks by. We speak in whispers, keeping each other alert. Cal wonders aloud what they're waiting for. I don't want to find out, I seriously don't.

"Just pray they don't start singing," Colleen says.

I take that as an order.

It occurs to me that we could be sitting here till dawn, and I wonder if our fires and lamps will last that long. We are destined to find out. My pile of wood is dwindling and Cal is dropping on his last log when Colleen swears.

"Dammit, the lamps."

They die as we watch. Then it begins to rain again. It's a gentle rain but it's killing our fires, and the dimmer the fires get, the closer the menace moves. I recall that Colleen theorized our shadowy friends were afraid of rain. I could say "I told you so," but decide it would be exceptionally bad timing.

The twists begin to make a sound that's less like singing than like wind through high-tension wires. Then they move, oozing toward us like sentient oil slicks. Like the thing in my nightmare.

Our pathetic horses are freaking. I can hear Doc desperately trying to calm them.

"Torches!" yells Cal, and lights one. Firelight gleams down the
wicked length of the sword he readies in the other hand.

The twists dance at the edges of the light, shapes shifting, now
solid, now ephemeral, always distorted, as if they're dressed in clothing that twists and deflects sight. They advance, they retreat, they
keen and wail, they eddy like candle soot. And I realize that they're
more than just *sensitive* to the light. They're terrified of it.

The fire I shelter behind leaps no higher than my thighs. I drop
the machete and hold out my arms—palms up, eyes closed—and
imagine four people and six horses inside a snow globe. My palms
tingle. My eyes open to a veil of blue-white light.

"Sonofabitch!" Colleen squeals like a five-year-old and leaps back
from the shimmering curtain.

Beyond the veil, our would-be gourmands shriek in fear and fury.
I want to laugh, not at Colleen (although I have to admit she looks
damn funny—kind of like a guerrilla goldfish), but at the sheer exhilaration of what I'm doing.

If they came like smoke, they leave like a buffalo stampede. When
the thrashing fades, the wood is as tranquil as a Robert Frost poem.
There is only the whisper of rain and the breathing of ten relieved
creatures in a bubble of light.

I hold the globe of light around us for another several minutes,
until I'm sure I hear nothing in the woods beyond. Then I let it go.
It does a Fourth of July fireworks fade. So does my energy. Hands on
knees, I pant like a dog.

"*Bozhyeh moy*," says Doc softly, and I think he crosses himself.

"What the hell was that?" Colleen demands, her eyes still raking
the woods.

Cal utters a single bark of laughter. "Cool." He grins at me sideways in the flicker of struggling firelight. "That," he says, "was a step
above your usual parlor tricks."

"I've expanded my repertoire. So, what do we do, boss? 'Do we go or
do we stay?' " I half gasp, half sing this last bit, then pull myself upright.

Cal sends me a quick glance before sinking to his haunches. "If we
could count on them staying away . . ." He shakes his head, flinging
water from his hair. "This weather is miserable for traveling."

"Look, here's an idea—why don't you and Doc stand watch while Colleen and I grab some sleep? If the horses act up again, wake me and I'll blow another bubble."

Cal surveys our soggy campsite. "I don't suppose there's any way you could set up a 'bubble' and have it stay put?"

"I . . . I don't think so. That took a lot of effort."

"Could I get you to try? Anything, Goldie. All it needs to be is flashy."

Flashy. "Okay. Lemme see what I got."

I fashion a ball of blue-white light, rolling it between my hands, feeling the texture of the power against my palms. They all slog over to watch me, looking like a gathering of drowned cats in the pale light. Rain drips from their hair, glitters on their eyelashes, and trickles down their cheeks.

I take my ball of light, set it about four feet off the ground, and let go. "Stay," I tell it, and step away.

It stays.

"You're still thinking about it," says Cal. "Walk away and make another one."

I do as asked. When I've finished and set the second globe, I glance back at where the first one was—and still is. *Cool.* A little Goldie goes a long way.

When I cozy down in dry clothes inside my pup tent, a perimeter fence of obedient light-balls stand guard over my sleep. I send them my last conscious thoughts.

When I wake at dawn, the rain has stopped and the sky is a bright blue, streaked with flame. The light-globes are gone.

"How long did they last?" I ask Doc over a hasty breakfast of dried fruit and flatbread.

"Almost two hours. It appears they extinguished when you entered deep sleep. But we had the fires up again by then."

I get my bearings, listening to leaves, and we mount up, striking out due west. Just after noon something changes. We are within sniffing distance of the Ohio River. Behind me the others discuss whether to ford the river or try to find a bridge. I'm idly wondering if there might be trolls under bridges these days when a window opens in my mind through which I catch the scent of a melody.

This is neither my memory nor the memories of leaves, this is the real deal. Without a moment's thought, I turn my horse and head due north.

"Goldie?" Cal comes up beside me. Sooner (a nervous Nellie if there ever was one) prances and rattles his bit. "Don't we need to find a place to cross the river?"

I only half hear the question. "River? No . . . he's on this side. Up ahead. North."

"Where?"

"Don't know. Somewhere. I hear him."

"What are we doing?" demands Colleen from behind. "We've been heading west all day. Why are we turning north all of a sudden?"

"Because, that's where *he* is."

She swings her horse—a big, red roan named Big T—right around in front of Jayhawk and cuts us off. "Look, Goldman, we are not out of danger here. Every night we spend in these woods is a night we risk attack. Crossing the river is our best chance of losing our Shadows."

"What makes you think they don't live on that side of the river, too?" I ask. "Besides, this isn't about avoiding Shadows. It's about finding the Bluesman and his flare friend. Crossing the river is also our best chance of losing *them*."

She gives me a hard glance and turns to Cal. "Look, Cal, I vote we cut our losses and get the hell out of these woods while we still can. We're heading west. Let's keep heading west until we find what we're after."

"I can handle the Shadows," I say.

"Oh, come on, Goldie. You did it *once*. Next time it might not work. Your juju doesn't exactly come through every time, does it? Besides, they might figure out that the fire isn't real."

"It wasn't the fire; it was the light."

Colleen snorts. "Says you."

She is about to say more, but Cal's patience has evaporated. "Cut it out—both of you. You sound like a couple of stubborn kids. I happen to think Goldie's right. I also think we don't have time for this argument. We have to keep moving."

"We sure do," Colleen says. "*West*."

"Yes, after we've tracked this guy down and answered some questions."

"It may turn out to be nothing," Colleen argues.

"Or it may turn out to be everything," Cal counters. "For now, we go north."

She meets him eye-to-eye for a moment, then shrugs and reins Big T out of my way. They follow me north along the Ohio River, down a corridor of crystal trees.

We ride until dark, then set up camp near the river. From our campsite we can hear one of the things that's different about the Ohio these days—it's not the gentle, meandering giant of lore and legend. This new, post-Change Ohio doesn't gurgle and murmur, it roars.

A short hike up the back of a low bluff in the waning sun, and we can see the difference, too. The Ohio is a froth of whitewater rapids, and our camp is downwind of a very impressive, if abbreviated, waterfall. It's loud enough to make sleep difficult.

Of course, I have the added impediment of guilt. For his faith in me and my abilities, I have repaid Cal by losing contact with our Pied Piper. I can no longer hear him. And because we are in an area of low brush, there are few glass leaves sending out good vibrations.

The river rapids are not loud enough to keep me from overhearing a muffled but heated disagreement after I've turned in. The participants are Colleen and Cal, and the first inkling of the subject comes when Our Ms. Brooks raises her voice to announce that Goldie is unstable and not to be trusted and, furthermore, Cal knows it.

This is not an unusual observation for someone to make about me, but since I realize it's leading up to something more portentous, I roll surreptitiously out of my sleeping bag and sidle up to the back of the rock behind which this fascinating debate is taking place.

"Look, Cal," Colleen is saying, "I know you don't want to say it, or even think it, but we both know damn well that Goldie is two tacos short of a combination plate."

I hear the delicate sound of Cal's eyes rolling. "He has a kindled mood disorder," he defends me. "It means he has . . . bad spells. It doesn't mean he's hallucinatory."

"He has a disorder, all right. One that causes him to have a very skewed take on reality. He *was* hallucinating, Cal. I was there. I saw reality. And in reality, *there was no flare.*"

"Then how did you end up in that tree?"

"In spite of what Goldie says, I think it had to have been the musician. He's able to pull people to him with his music. He could just as easily push people away."

I could picture Cal giving her that almost catlike look of puzzlement, hands on hips, skepticism in every word of body language—a lawyer's pose. "I have to take the chance that he's right, Colleen. I think you understand that."

"All right. Let's pretend for a moment that there is a flare. We have no way of knowing what her situation is. Maybe Mr. Blues Guy *isn't* protecting her. Maybe he's imprisoning her or maybe she's . . . I don't know . . . defective or weak or something and the Source didn't want her in the first place."

"If she's imprisoned, shouldn't we try to free her? If she's been passed over by the Source, wouldn't you like to know why? It might help us figure out why the Source is taking flares in the first place. It might even give us a tool to use against the Source."

Colleen utters a growl of pure frustration. "Yeah, and it might lead us on a wild goose chase that takes us in a completely wrong direction. We don't have time for wild goose chases, Cal. This world is unraveling a little more every day, and there's no way of knowing when it will stop—if it *ever* stops. You think following this guy might take us to the Source? I think it could just as easily take us away from the Source."

There is a long and pregnant pause, into which, at the most critical moment, Colleen murmurs, "God, Cal, I hate saying crap like this to you. I hate always being the—the prophet of doom. But this feels like a false trail to me. And a waste of time. *Tina's* time. *Everyone's* time."

No fair! The family card and the humanitarian card played in one deft move. And with a self-deprecatory spin, no less.

There is a crunch of leaves, and Cal says, "Do you think you need to remind me of that? Look, Colleen, you're asking me to make a choice based on a complete uncertainty. It's your word against Goldie's."

"Right, and you're taking his."

"Colleen, I believe you didn't see anything. I also believe Goldie *did*. Does that seem so strange?"

"Well, it—"

"Tell me, when was the last time *you* made fire leap out of the tips of your fingers or heard the Source whispering in your ear?"

Another pregnant pause. "That's not fair. He's a head case, Cal. Ask Doc. If you don't think he's worried about Goldie's mental state, you can think again."

"All right, Colleen. If it will make you feel better, I'll talk to Doc about Goldie's mental state. But I'm not going to make a snap decision. I think the best thing we can do is sleep on it and see where things stand in the morning. We're sure as hell not going anywhere tonight."

"Fine," says Colleen. Leaves crunch underfoot, then she says, "Cal, I'm really sorry. I know I'm a bitch. There are times I pride myself on being a bitch. This isn't one of them. I just don't want to see us . . . pulled off course."

"Don't worry. I won't let us be."

There's a moment of silence, then leaves crunch again, this time with an air of finality, and I sidle back to my bedroll.

Bitch. Witch. Snitch.

I run out of rhymes and concoct a plan: I will wait for Doc to commence snoring. *They* may not be going anywhere tonight, but *I* am. Of course, I'll leave a good trail so they can follow me—and they'll have to follow me. One way or another, we are going to find the Bluesman.

As luck would have it, Doc has trouble sleeping tonight, and I am half asleep myself, rapids or no rapids, when the window opens in my head and music comes cascading through—loud, clear, and achingly close.

I wait for nothing.

SIX

COLLEEN

Goldman was gone when I went to wake him and Doc for their watch. At first I hoped that he might've just hit the bushes to take a whiz (What *was* I thinking?), but I realized pretty quickly that some essential items were missing—his pack, canteen, and a machete— things a guy doesn't usually take along to the latrine.

We scrambled, packing up bedrolls and supplies and loading up the horses in record time. It was dark and misty and our lamps bounced light back at us from every billow. It was hardly ideal for tracking anyone, not even Goldman, who obviously *wanted* to be tailed. But at least we didn't seem to be drawing lurkers.

He had about a three-hour head start, but he was on foot and he didn't cover his tracks any better than he had the last time. In fact, to make damn sure we could track him, he'd left all sorts of crap helter-skelter in his wake. A game die, a little wooden top, a couple of bright-colored magnets, a red bandanna, the occasional comic button. (*Never meddle in the affairs of dragons, for you are crunchy and good with ketchup.*) When he ran out of his pack-ratty odds and ends, he switched to bits of buck-skin fringe.

Two hours into our little trek we entered an area of weirdness where the terrain was strangely lumpy. There were mysterious gullies and groves and eerie little hills that were just too neat and regular and flat on top. Now, I don't have a lot of imagination, but I couldn't shake the feeling that huge prehistoric beasts were crouched along the trail.

When the moon slid out of the clouds my mental image morphed big-time. I've been in houses where the owners have covered over everything with sheets for a long vacation. It's damn spooky. Suddenly, I felt like I was a mouse in one of those places, just waiting for something big and toothy to come flying out from under the sheets.

We came out onto a paved road, and I caught the scent of wood smoke. Less than a mile to the north we caught sight of a stand of trees that seemed to have a million tiny stars caught in their twigs. Campfire. We tethered the horses out of earshot of the camp and left Doc on guard. Cal and I crept up on the circle of light.

Bingo. Our boy Goldie was perched on a tree stump in front of a roaring fire, having a cozy fireside chat with the Bluesman himself.

I felt Cal's eyes on my face.

Oh, yeah, and a flare. She was resting on a fallen tree next to the Blues Guy, watching Goldie through huge, iridescent eyes.

"Yeah, I see her," I mumbled.

Cal pushed through the underbrush into the firelight, hand on his sword hilt. "Care to introduce your friends, Goldie?"

Goldie's new friends didn't want to be introduced. The Bluesman clutched his guitar and bolted into the bushes; his little flare friend shot skyward and vanished after him.

"Shit!" Goldman yelled, and followed without a backward glance.

Needless to say, Cal and I were hot on his heels. We were swallowed up in moments in a maze of hills and valleys. We turned right and left and right again, following Goldie's lead. Every turn was a right angle that took us deeper into a place I expected to have nightmares about for weeks to come.

I'd caught up with Goldie and Cal when our quarry turned one last corner into what I would've sworn was a dead end. The broad, shallow clearing was long, straight, and ran smack into the bottom of a huge, flat-topped hill.

We had them. I was sure of it. But when we reached the bottom of the hill, what had seemed like a dark smudge at the base turned out to be somewhat more than a smudge. It was the mouth of a cave. The

Blues Guy and his flare disappeared into it. And I do mean disappeared.

Cal, Goldman, and I came up short in a Three Stooges collision. The hole in the hill was filled with darkness so thick, I expected it to stick to my hands.

Goldman lifted a hand and blue-white light spilled out of it, rolling into the black and creaming it to a lumpy gray. We all pressed forward, straining to see into the pocket of fake twilight. All three of us expected, I'm sure, to see a passage—or worse, a bunch of passages—leading into the strange mound of earth, but there was no passage. The opening in the hillside was about the size of an elevator and went absolutely nowhere.

"Sonofabitch," I said, and didn't even feel the words fall out of my mouth.

We checked the little hole out thoroughly by Goldman's ball lightning, thumping and prodding and kicking at the rocks and dirt. We got nothing for our troubles but bruises.

"Maybe our eyes were playing tricks on us," Cal said. "Maybe they didn't even come in here. Maybe they turned and scooted into those trees." He nodded to the west where a grove of near-leafless trunks huddled in the gloom.

"They went in *here*," Goldman insisted, just as he'd insisted there was a flare.

He'd get no argument from me.

Cal studied the rocky wall for a moment, then said, "I'll go back for Doc and the horses. We may as well spend what's left of the night here."

He turned to Goldie, eyes glittering in the ghost-glow. "I hope you've got a really good story to tell."

Goldie snuffed the twisted little ball of light. "I'll be working on it."

"This is getting to be a bad habit with you, Goldman," I told him once Cal had sprinted away down the grassy path. "You get some wild burr up your butt and—*poof*—you pull a vanishing act."

"Yes, and you were trying to convince Cal I was hallucinating random flares. I had to prove you wrong. Sometimes, Ms. Brooks, my perceptions *can* be trusted. I took a calculated risk and it paid off." He squatted in the mouth of the cave, his back against the uneven wall. "So, you gonna say it?"

"Say what?"

"Oh, come *on*, Colleen."

"Oh hell, fine. You were right—I was wrong. There *is* a flare. Happy?"

"Her name is Magritte," he said.

We spent the rest of the wait in silence, peering warily into the mist and shadow, moving only when we heard the horses navigating the maze.

We made a hasty camp at the edge of the grove of seminaked trees, lit a fire, and hunkered down around it. Then Cal got in Goldie's face. He was angry, tired, and a little frustrated, and all of that bled into his voice.

"Why'd you run off, Goldie?"

"You want the long answer or the short answer?" asked Goldman in return.

"I want the truth, long or short."

"Okay. The truth is, I overheard you and Colleen discussing my mental state and I wanted a chance to prove I wasn't delusional . . . at this time."

Cal sat back against his log. "I didn't believe you were delusional."

"Yeah, but if you'd talked to Doc, you might. Look, I'm a classic case, I know that. And my former lifestyle didn't help any. Doc wouldn't have had any choice but to tell you that I show a number of symptoms of someone ramping up for hypomania."

Doc shook his head. "I would never have leapt to such a conclusion, Goldie. Nor would I have encouraged Cal to make a decision based on what might or might not be the symptoms of hypomania."

Goldie leaned into the campfire, his big, glittering, dark eyes on Cal's face. "It was like a door opened up in my head, Cal. Like the music was so close I was the one singing it. I had to go."

"Without us?" asked Cal.

"I'm an impulsive bastard. Forgive me. But . . . the music isn't always all that clear. It comes and goes. Tonight it came. I followed it. I knew you'd follow me."

Cal looked off into the dark. "Put that way, it almost sounds logical. Okay, I think I understand that part of it. What do you know about *them*?" His head jerked toward the Doorway to Nowhere.

Goldie's eyes lit up. "Okay. Um . . . his name is Enid. Enid Blindman. He's half Lakota . . . on his father's side. He's a musician—we knew that—and the flare's name is Magritte. Pretty, isn't it?"

Cal rested his forehead on his knees, hiding his face. I'd bet he'd like to borrow a cup of patience right about then. I was fresh out.

"Spill it, Goldman," I said. "Didn't you get anything but names?"

Goldie's eyes flashed briefly over the rest of us, then he said, "Before the Change—just before—Enid's manager signed him to a contract with an independent record label in Chicago."

"And what does this have to do with anything?" I asked.

"I'm getting to that. When the Change happened, his music got twisted. It affects people—attracts them. So, he uses it to gather refugees—lost sheep, he called them—and take them to someplace called the Preserve."

Cal's head came up. "Where's that?"

"I don't know. He didn't get that far. He just called it the Preserve. He says a friend of his—a woman named Mary—runs the place. That's where he takes all the people he collects."

"Why, Goldie?" asked Doc. "Why does he do this?"

"To save them. That's what he said. To save them from what's out here."

"And this flare," said Doc, "this Magritte—is she also called by him—held by his music?"

Goldie scratched around in his curly tumble of hair. "Well, no. Not exactly. They've got sort of a mutual protection racket going there."

"Protection?" repeated Cal. "From what?"

"Well, he's protecting her from the Source—they didn't call it that, but they understand that it's sentient and that it eats flares for breakfast. Enid said he saw a bunch of them taken in Chicago. He was there when it came for Magritte. That was when he discovered that his music could jam the Source. They've been together ever since. They fell in with this Mary and started working for her."

"And the flare's protecting him from . . . ?" Cal prompted.

"Oh, yeah. That's where the record deal comes in, sort of. It's his manager, if you can believe it. Some guy named Howard."

"Some guy named Howard," parroted Cal. "Why? What's this Howard doing to him?"

"Um, he didn't get to that part. We were interrupted." He had the absolute balls to give Cal a look of reproach.

Cal rubbed a hand over his face. To my utter disbelief, he was hiding a smile.

I glared at Goldman (the dipshit). "Look, can he protect any flare with this music of his?"

"I think so. It's a damping field of some sort—a jamming frequency. It creates a sonic veil that the Source, for some reason, can't penetrate."

"But when we came upon you," Doc observed, "he had stopped playing to speak with you."

"I had the presence of mind to ask him about that, actually," Goldman said, suddenly cheery. "It's sort of like my little balls-o'-fire thing, but a lot more powerful. A little touch of thought goes a long way. The real music's in his head." He tapped his skull. "And that just keeps going. There's something about this place, too. Enid said this place is lousy with power." He shook his head, looking up wistfully into the branches of our sheltering trees. "I can only feel its ghost."

We raised our eyes in unison to gaze around at the eerie, fog-draped shapes.

"What *is* this place?" I asked, and tried not to shiver.

In answer, Doc pulled something out of his jacket pocket and handed it to me. It was a brochure, damp but still colorful. It showed the front of a modern red brick building with a well-manicured lawn and box hedge. Below that was a big photograph of one of the unnaturally neat hills.

" 'Grave Creek Mound State Park,' " I read, " 'and Delf Norona Museum. Open year-round since 1978.' "

"Let me see." Cal snatched the brochure out of my hand, unfolded it on his lap, and read: " 'Grave Creek Mound is probably the most famous of the Adena burial mounds and certainly one of the most impressive.' " He stopped reading and looked up at us. "It says they hauled the dirt in baskets. Some of these mounds are over sixty feet high."

"And two thousand years old," added Doc. "It is comforting to meet with something of such longevity."

Comforting. Two-thousand-year-old burial mounds. *I will not twitch*, I promised myself.

"Where did you get this?" Cal asked Doc.

He shrugged. "While I awaited you, the mist cleared a bit. I saw a building just up the road—that building"—he gestured at the brochure—"and thought to investigate. It is not quite so tidy now."

"Did it look like anyone else had been in there recently?" Cal asked.

Doc shook his head. "Hard to say. Surely, there had been people there at one time or another. But as to recently, I couldn't say. Why do you ask?"

"I was wondering if this place might be part of the Bluesman's underground railroad. Maybe some of his lost sheep are hiding around here—"

Goldie was shaking his head. "He'd already delivered them."

"Delivered?" I repeated. Jeez, like they were pizzas or takeout or something.

Goldie just blinked his big brown eyes at me.

Cal folded the brochure back up and absently tucked it into his pocket. "That means the Preserve is nearby. Hidden, maybe, but nearby. Possibly even inside that mound. We should be able to find it by daylight." He stood. "You all get some sleep. I'll stand watch."

"Why you?" I asked. "You've already stood watch."

"Colleen is right," agreed Doc. "If anyone should stand watch, Calvin, it is me."

They argued about it while I slid into my bedroll. I'd stood watch, too, and what I needed now was sleep, not a pitched battle.

Doc won. Cal was asleep in a matter of seconds. Goldie palmed one of his little "balls-o'-fire" and wandered over into the mouth of the cave. As if it could make the dead end any less dead. I slept.

When I woke, there was almost-sunlight creeping about the glen through the mist. The mounds were a lot clearer now, but they hadn't lost any of their weirdness. Hard to believe they were like this before the Change, too.

After a freezing sponge bath in a nearby stream, I came back to camp to find Cal up and about. Doc was heating water and cobbling together a breakfast. Goldie was nowhere in sight.

Exchanging glances, Cal and I wandered over to the foot of the mound. It rose, green and velvety and sculpted, a good forty or fifty feet above ground level. Mist curled out of the little cave like steamy breath. My imagination woke up, and I was staring at a big green animal with a gaping mouth. A shiver rippled up my back.

Goldie was in the cave, sitting cross-legged on the floor like a Buddha, staring at the blank wall as if it was going to do something fascinating.

"Hey, Goldie," Cal said. "Doc's throwing some breakfast together."

Goldman didn't answer. He just got up, raised a hand as if to wave us away, then stepped into the rocks and earth as if they were billows of fog. He disappeared.

"Damn," I said, and meant it.

SEVEN

GOLDIE

Normally, I wouldn't even think of stepping through a wall of rocky earth, but as milky sunlight oozes into the cave I come to the obvious, if insane, conclusion that that is the only place Enid Blind-man and Magritte could have gone. I can still feel the pull of his music. It comes from a place so right under my nose I could put my hand out and touch it.

At dawn, at that moment when the local patch of reality gets its first dusting of enlightenment, I have a moment of mind-altering clarity. The rock and earth seem no more substantial than last night's mists, and I just step through.

I hear someone shout my name, then there's silence and darkness. I take another step and the silence is replaced with the slow drip of water and the whisper of air and something else that I don't hear so much as feel. My eyes adjust to the new reality—a pocket of misty light. Firelight, I think, because of the way it waxes and wanes.

I stumble and fall forward a few steps. Dirt and sand crunch comfortingly under my feet. I put a hand out to steady myself and touch water-slick rock. I'm still in the cave. I smell cave, hear cave, feel cave, and, as my eyes focus, I see cave.

Impressive. Someone's mimicked rock and earth so well that it took me half the night to see through it. I wonder how far into the mound this goes.

Any second, I suspect, Cal and company will realize what's happened and come blundering through after me. Question is, do I wait around for them, thus triggering another round of recriminations and explanations and apologies, or do I plow right on in?

I plow, heading for the source of the dancing light. The narrow passage widens out and jogs right. It meets a broader corridor with a ceiling so high it seems to connect with outer space. There are torches here, stuck in crude sconces along the rough walls. To the left, the corridor descends farther into the earth; to the right, it rises. The sound of rushing water comes from the lower branch; above, I hear something that's almost music.

I swing upward to the right, passing so close to a torch that it should've singed my hair. It doesn't, because it's putting out no heat. It's also completely silent. Someone here has gotten the faux-glow thing down to a fine art. I touch a finger to the flame.

"You're one stubborn son'vabitch, aren't you?"

I wheel to find the flare, Magritte, floating about five feet up the passage from me in a wash of pale violet light. She throws me off balance, like misjudging a step.

"So I'm told," I answer. "The Preserve, I presume?"

She tilts her head, looking me up and down with those amazing golden eyes and making me acutely aware of my sartorial shortcomings. Reflexively, I try to shove hair out of my face.

"The doorway to it. A doorway," she amends. Her voice is soft and carries the lilt of the bayou. "You shouldn't've come here. Mary don't want people to come here without they been invited."

"Sorry. I don't mean to gate-crash, but it's very important for me to understand how Enid protects you from the Source."

"I know." She seems sincerely empathetic. "But I don't think you *can* understand it. It's just something he does. What you do gotta understand is that Mary's built this whole world here, and she'll protect it." She floats closer. So close I can see the subtle wrinkle of concern between her pale brows. "You should go."

"I can't. I need to talk to Enid. I need to at least try to understand what he does—how he does it. Maybe it's something I can learn."

She shakes her head. "No one's been able to learn it. Not even Kevin Elk Sings, and he's a medicine man *and* a musician. You gotta turn back around and get outta here, before you get caught. She'll do whatever it takes to protect this place from the wrong sort of people."

"We're the *right* sort of people, Magritte. I promise you."

"Nice words," says a new voice, "but cheap. How do I know I can afford to believe them?"

If Magritte's voice is cloud, this one is rock, iron, steel. The woman it belongs to doesn't even come up to my shoulder, but even at first glance I can see she suits her voice completely. She's what they used to call a handsome woman—strong-featured, with a square jaw and pale eyes that could cause chilblains with prolonged exposure.

Before I can answer her question, which I suspect is rhetorical, two large and very substantial gentlemen appear on either side of her, making trust irrelevant.

"Mary McCrae?" I bow slightly. "Goldie, a.k.a. Herman Goldman. I see I have some convincing to do."

"You're welcome to try, Mr. Goldman, but I can only promise to listen." She gestures for me to move up the slope past her. I'd be crazy to decline the invitation.

The cave broadens out into a large rounded room with a natural stone pillar at one end. There's a sooty niche in the center of the formation—someone's been using it for a candleholder—and faded graffiti on the walls.

There are grunters here, squatting on their haunches and doing grunter things: chowing down on something unrecognizable, guzzling from steamy clay mugs, and leering at us out of their milky, slug-trail eyes. I can't contain a shiver.

Mary is amused at my squeamishness. "We are not what you'd call an elite society, Mr. Goldman."

"Really? I somehow got the idea you were only interested in 'the right kind of people.' Um, what kind are those, exactly?"

She stops and drills me with those pale, miss-nothing eyes. "The kind who need refuge, a community, a place to belong. The kind who want a chance to maintain a grasp on their humanity. Can you understand that, Mr. Goldman?"

Do I understand? My years of being looked past, stepped over, and

even spit on are not so long gone. I remember someone we encoun-
tered in our first days out of New York. A boy named Freddy. At least,
before the Change he'd been a boy. After, he was alone, scared, and
no longer completely human. In an alternate universe, Freddy might
have come west with us to find this place, but he'd run off because
he was no longer like us.

"I do understand," I tell her, and change the subject. "Do all the
mounds connect to the caverns?"

She gives me a sidewise glance out of the corner of her eyes. "At
times."

So I've seen. I start to ask who designed her "drawbridge" when
we reach a concrete stair that spirals upward. I'm reminded of my
dream-stairway to oblivion and experience a moment of sharp, clear
panic. But this stair goes up into sunlight. Not that wishy-washy post-
rainstorm stuff, but golden, unambiguous sunlight. I hold my breath
and climb.

At the top of the stairs I stop dead. Before me is arranged a campground of sorts about a large irregular sward of grass laced with neat
graveled paths. Among the encircling trees are cabins, summer cottages with canvas walls, travel trailers, campers, RVs, and tents. Directly upslope there is something I have trouble wrapping my mind
around. It looks like a little Wild West town complete with saloon,
assay office, church, train station, and jail. All is bathed in a golden
glow, as if I'm looking through a cinematic filter.

Reality check, please.

The world pauses to watch me. My hostess also watches, an unreadable expression on her face. There is a pleasant ringing in my
ears—the music-not-music I've been hearing since I got here. It seems
to come from all around me. Everywhere there are people, both natural and processed. I see a few more grunters plying the sunny clearing, wearing shades or carrying umbrellas and bundled up as if to keep
any exposed skin from being touched by ambient light.

Sounds cute, huh? They are *not* cute. They are creepy. There are
also some tweaks here I've never seen before.

My breath catches in my throat. I see another flare—a white-
haired boy, who stares at me through azure eyes as if *I'm* the oddest
thing in this picture. An instant later he darts behind a tree.

Mary is watching me closely; she doesn't miss my reaction.

"How many . . . ?"

"The fireflies? Seven now." A shadow crosses her face and is gone. She gestures toward the one-horse town, urging me forward.

The town ambles up the hill, at the top of which is a large lodge with smoke curling cozily from its several chimneys. Picturesque in the extreme, but nowhere—*nowhere*—is there a single burial mound of any kind.

"Where am I?"

My hostess sweeps a strand of graying hair out of her face and smiles. "Not where you expected to be, apparently."

"Where are the mounds?"

"About two hundred miles southeast of here."

My brain tilts and I do a full 360, taking in everything around me. She's not joking. The landscape is similar—karst topography, in geologese—but the trees are of different varieties and—behold!— they are not made of crystal. In fact, they're still green.

But the dead giveaway is the sign. It is posted not more than fifty feet from where I stand and it doesn't say one word about the Adena mounds or the Delf Norona Museum. It says: OLENTANGY INDIAN CAVERNS, DELAWARE, OHIO: ORIGINAL CAVE ENTRANCE. There is a chunk of exposition beneath this in charmingly rough-hewn letters that have been chiseled out of the wooden plank and painted yellow. I don't have time to read it, except to note that it speaks of the religious ceremonies of Wyandotte Indians, and of oxen falling down holes. I'm being ushered to the Lodge.

As we pass through the campgrounds, I see where the musical aura of this place comes from. There are wind chimes everywhere—in the trees, on the buildings, and on clotheslines strung between. The chimes are made of glass, metal shrapnel, bits of fired pottery, hollowed-out wooden tubes.

Clearly, this is more than a fashion statement. My musician's ear notices something else about them, too: they seem to be playing the same scale of notes so that, in the whole gentle cacophony, there is never a note out of tune. There is only harmony. And if that isn't rare enough, they're singing away without a breeze to stir them.

Okay, so why hang wind chimes everywhere, then go to the trouble to tune them and keep them moving even when there's no wind? And *how*? I hope Mary McCrae likes to play Twenty Questions.

We pass a cleared area marked by concentric circles of logs laid out on the ground. At the center of the area is the smoking remains of a large fire. Clearly a gathering area of some sort. We bypass the Wild West town, cutting straight up the hill. I see only the backs of buildings. Faces in windows.

The Lodge is an archetypal construct of wood and stone and slate shingle. It looks quite perfect sitting there among the trees—serene, rustic. I'm ushered into an office on the first floor—a pleasant room with knotty pine walls and red and green plaid furnishings that trigger a ghost-memory of summers long ago when I was almost happy. A cabin in the Catskills, a white-haired old gent who laughed a lot and who had my mother's smile.

I shake myself. Mary is asking if I won't please be seated. I do please, taking the middle of the plaid sofa. She perches across from me on the edge of a large desk. The substantial gentlemen both leave; Magritte stays. A moment later Enid comes into the room looking almost sheepish. He sidles to a chair on my right where Magritte is in restless hover, but he doesn't sit, he hovers, too, in a manner of speaking, half leaning against the chair.

"Enid tells me you tracked him here," says Mary.

"I did. We did—my friends and I."

"Why?"

"He didn't tell you?"

"I'd like to hear it in your words, if you please."

"We have a rather special interest in Enid's music."

"You wouldn't be the first. Enid's ability is quite exceptional and rare. What's your particular interest?"

"One of the men I'm traveling with—Cal Griffin—has a twelve-year-old sister who is now a flare."

"A what?"

"Like Magritte," says Enid quietly. "A firefly. The Storm got her, too, he said. Like in Chicago." He lowers himself to the arm of the chair.

Mary's sharp eyes soften just a bit. "I'm truly sorry, Mr. Goldman. But if the Storm got your friend's sister, how can Enid possibly help her?"

"We're headed west to where the Source—what you call the Storm—is gathered. If Enid really can shield flares from the Source, maybe he could help break them free of it." *Maybe,* I think, *he could do more.*

Now Mary's eyebrows shoot straight up into her fringe of salt and pepper hair. "You're tracking the Storm? How?"

"It's a little talent I have, I guess. I'm like a compass. It—um— pulls me." And the sign on *that* door says: Do not enter.

Mary nods and glances at Enid. "And your ability to see through our defenses—to *walk* through our defenses—is that also a 'little talent' you have?"

"Ah . . . apparently." I don't like the way this conversation is going. Especially since I now suspect that the others aren't right behind me after all.

"You'll understand, perhaps, if I tell you this concerns me."

She slides off the desk and meets me eye-to-eye though I'm sitting. She is shorter, I realize, than Tina, but her stature is not a matter of physical size. This is One Big Woman.

"Usually, people don't come here without an invitation," she tells me. "In fact, since Enid and Maggie and I came here, no one has come through that portal that we haven't *led* through. This is a place of refuge, Mr. Goldman. A preserve of human life. And your 'little talent' could put its very existence in jeopardy."

I look over at Magritte. Her eyes are wide with what I think is concern (though flare eyes can be hard to read, and that little puckering between her brows could be annoyance). Enid is examining a knot in the floorboards. No help there.

"I'm no danger to you, Mary." I try to reassure her. "My friends are no danger to you. All we want is to talk to Enid in the hope that maybe he can help us."

"This compound"—she makes a sweeping gesture with one arm— "is locked in a vault that is somehow folded up in space. We don't understand how. All we understand is that to keep it hidden, we have to bar the doors and windows and mind the locks. You picked my locks, Mr. Goldman. How many more like you are there at home?"

Several things flash through my mind at once. One is Mary's choice of words; these are *her* people, *her* place, *her* locks, *her* gates I have crashed. Second is a quandary: Do I tell her there is one of me or many?

I opt for the truth. "There aren't any more like me. At least, not among the people I'm with. None of them saw Magritte until Enid let them. None of them can see through your defenses or pick your locks."

"No?" She turns on her heel, starts to pace. "But you could let them in."

"I was kind of hoping you'd do that."

"So they can talk Enid into leaving us to find this Source?"

"Not necessarily. He may be able to share his talent with us in another way. He might know something we don't, something we can learn. Pardon me, but I kind of got the idea from Enid that helping people in need is your shtick."

"My shtick." A smile lifts one corner of her mouth. "Well, it's a nice story, Mr. Goldman. It touches the heart."

Her pacing brings her back into my face. "I have over 120 souls here. And more coming, by invitation, every day. What if you're not what you advertise yourself to be? What if you have other motives that I can't begin to divine? Or even if you're sincere, what happens if the only way Enid can help you is to go with you?"

I hold up my hands in surrender. "Fine. I'll leave."

She grimaces. "So you can gate-crash again with reinforcements? Try to put yourself in my place. Would you trust you?"

Well, now. Given what the world is coming to, she has a point. Lesson number one in post-Change reality is that if it was ever true that nothing is what it seems, it now goes double.

"If there's anything I can do to prove we're harmless . . ."

Her mouth curls up at one corner. "And how would you go about doing that, Mr. Goldman? How can you be sure you *are* harmless?"

I can't.

She's silent for a moment, her eyes on my face, poking, prying, scanning. Then she steps back a pace. "Enid, find our would-be friend something to eat. He is not to go near the caverns. I'm going to call Council."

"Yes, ma'am," says Enid, docile as all get-out. He beckons with his dreadlocks.

I am dismissed into the care of the Bluesman and the flare. They lead me to a large, bright kitchen where the wood stove puts out too much heat and where a pot of tea is boiling—eternally, I suspect. I pull off my ratty coat and get a bowl of some sort of grain porridge and a cup of the industrial strength tea. While Enid and Magritte huddle at the kitchen table and speak in muffled tones about some-thing—most likely what they should do with me—I stare moodily out the window, down the hill to the center of the camp, where the rhythm of early morning activity has established itself.

It's like watching a dance of insects. They beetle around the fire pit, stop and chat, exchange containers of some sort. Near the residences, people are also busy, beating rugs, hanging laundry, tending animals, scratching at the ground. Very normal in a bucolic, medieval sort of way.

While I watch, the rhythm of the dance changes. From several of the cabins, people emerge as if propelled—two here, one there, an-other over there, a fourth and a fifth. They converge on the camp center, homing. On their way, they tag and draw along a woman hanging laundry, a man weeding neat rows of something green, an-other man deep in conversation with a group near the fire pit. From there, they start up the hill toward the Lodge. The people around them, the people they pass by, take note, following their progress, pausing to comment on it.

Call me squeamish, but this display of synchronicity makes my hair stand on end. I swallow a suddenly tasteless mouthful of porridge and set down my bowl. Okay, it's not *Children of the Corn*—the peo-ple coming up the hill are chatting and smiling as they approach—but I am seriously weirded out, nonetheless.

"She called Council," Magritte says from beside me. Her voice re-minds me of the wind chimes. She seems slightly ill at ease.

"Is that a bad thing?" I ask.

"Not a bad thing," says Enid. "The Council protects us, is all. They'll do what's good for the Preserve."

"Ah. Which may not be what's good for me and my friends." Or the rest of the planet. I turn to look at him as straight up as I can. "Look, I meant what I said. Let me go and I'll take my friends and get out of here."

Enid drops his eyes. "That's not my decision."

"What about the little girl?" asks Magritte. "You ain't just gonna abandon her?" Her eyes, for a moment, show me as deep and dark a maze as the one I traveled to get here. It doesn't take special powers to see that Tina's plight has some special significance for her. After all, she was close to becoming Megillah-fodder herself.

I shrug. "I could tell Cal there was no way Enid could help. But I'd be lying, and I'm not real good at that."

Her aura seems to fade toward transparence for a moment. Then she looks to Enid, *through* Enid and right down into his soul.

He puts up his hands to ward her off. "Hey, no, baby. Don't ask me that."

She says, "What if he could convince the Council—convince Mary—that it was a good thing?"

"How's he gonna do that, Mags?"

The look they exchange is loaded with subtext. There's something here I'm not in on.

"With your ability," I say, "you might be able to free more flares—more fireflies. You might be able to free them all."

Shaking his head, Enid slumps farther into his chair. "No, man. No way I can do that."

"Then maybe I can. I've managed to harness a few twisted talents. I can see and walk through your portals. Maybe I can learn to do what you do, or maybe I can help you do it."

Enid grins at me unexpectedly, the furrows alongside his mouth becoming deep smile lines. "Sort of a sideman, huh?"

"Or a side*kick*."

He reaches up to rub his eyes, which are bloodshot, I assume from lack of sleep. "It's not the same thing. The portals is one thing; the music is something else."

"I'm willing to try if you are. Look, if Mary is as dedicated to freeing and protecting people as you say, then isn't this a golden opportunity? A talent like yours could save a lot of enslaved flares. We can find the Source—the Storm."

"You seem awful sure of that."

"I am." Sometimes I wish I weren't. "But let's say we *can* free some of the flares. The missing piece in the scenario is where do we take them where they'll be safe?" I smile. "Nice place you got here."

Enid and Magritte exchange another verbose look, then Enid says, "Lemme go talk to the Council," and leaves me alone with Magritte.

I feel her beside me, a cool, blue furnace. I have a swift and unworthy fantasy about what it might be like to make love to her. It shocks me. She is looking at me with those giant cat's eyes while this slithers through my mind, and the sudden one-two punch of lust and shame drive me over to the hearth, where the heat from my face is lost in the fire. She follows me, so my relief is short-lived.

I try to keep my mind on the problem at hand. "So you were in Chicago when this happened to you?" I ask without looking at her.

"Yeah."

"Was it sudden? I know with Tina—my friend's sister—it happened gradually, over several days. We thought she'd gotten some sort of radiation poisoning."

Magritte's hands make a series of vague little gestures before she says, "Poisoning, huh? Yeah, it took a while for me to get poisoned, too." She giggles, but there isn't any mirth in it. It ends in a strange little hiccup.

I glance at her face and surprise something both bitter and desperate in her expression. "Was it painful?" I ask. "Tina was in physical pain up until . . . well, until it was over. After, she seemed . . . relieved . . . released. I think there was a different kind of pain, then."

She grimaces, her sharp little flare teeth making her seem feral. "Sounds like sex."

Well, that catches me napping. I'm speechless, and what's left of my lust flares (you will pardon the pun) then shrivels right up.

"I don't know what I'd've done without Enid," she says in a voice like the rustle of dry leaves. "Out of the frying pan, into the fire . . . Uncle Nathan always said that about me."

She turns her face away; the flames paint it gold and red, even through her aura of rippling light.

"How close did you get to the Storm before Enid—"

"Struck by lightning," she murmurs. "You ever been in a tornado?"

"Ah, no . . . an experience I've managed to avoid, living in Manhattan."

"Stay in this part of the country long and you won't be able to avoid it. Tornado just sucks up anything that gets close. Even at a distance, you can feel the power of it. Like a magnet, pulling at you. You see it; it dances in your eyes. You know it's a quick trip to hell, but it's so powerful, so *beautiful*, that part of you wants to walk right up and touch it. You *want* it to take you."

She pins me with her eyes, suddenly dark as the underbelly of a thunderhead. "Storm was like that. One minute I was dancing for *him*, the next minute I was dancing for the Storm."

I recall someone a lifetime ago talking this way about cocaine. She got struck by lightning, too, in a manner of speaking. One night, in a cranked haze, she walked right onto the third rail in our tunnel.

"Dancing," I repeat. "For Enid?" I'm trying, I realize, to wrap my mind around their relationship, as if it matters.

"No, not Enid. Enid is my friend." She lays subtle stress on the last word. "He was there to save me from one thing, and ended up saving me from something worse."

"You knew him before the Change?"

"He played at the club I worked before his manager got him a break. After, he'd come back to check up on me, make sure I was okay, talk about getting me out of there. He *tried* to get me out of there." She shrugged, spilling radiance into the air. "When all the weird shit came down, he was there for me. In the wrong place at the right time, I guess."

Darkness flitters across her face again like the shadow of wings. It's the same look I glimpsed earlier when she asked if we'd abandon Tina. I have the sudden conviction that Magritte knows a lot about abandonment. I fight the urge to stroke her cheek. Did I mention I'm a lousy fighter?

She doesn't flinch away from my touch as I expect. Instead, she turns into it, fixing me with her whiteless topaz eyes, wrapping me in a tingling veil.

From my fingertips, gold-white light fans out across her cheek and bleeds into her own vivid aura. A luminous mist glides over my hand, my arm, my head. It envelops her, too, and in a moment we're engulfed in a veil of something kinetic that is both hers and mine. The world is shut out. I hear no shimmer of wind chimes, no snap of flame, no life-noise from the camp outside, not my own breathing, not even my own heartbeat. I am aware only of our mutual amazement.

The opening of the kitchen door pulls us apart. The combined aura explodes soundlessly and the outside world rushes back in. I am dispossessed.

"Council wants to see you," says Enid, and if he is aware of having interrupted something, he hides it.

The Council meets in a large parlor I suspect was once the staff lounge. There is a huge braided rug around which sit nine people on chairs, bench seats, and pillows. They are an interesting mix, five women (including Mary), four men. They are racially mixed, too—three blacks, one Hispanic, one Asian, two Native American. Mary is the sole Caucasian. They are old and young. Fresh and worn.

Their clothing suggests diversity of social strata, as well. The Asian gentleman wears a sweater that is obviously cashmere, but his L.L. Bean boots are muddy and scuffed. The Hispanic woman next to him is dressed in ill-fitting overalls and a man's flannel jacket—Kmart wardrobe. They both have very clean but very chapped and callused hands.

In the once real world, clothes said something about who you were. Now I think they might only say something about where you've been. The Change has been a great equalizer, I suppose, whatever its faults. Perhaps it's true that no evil happens that does not bring good in its wake. If there was ever a time you couldn't judge a man by his clothes, it's now.

I smooth the loose tails of my own gaudy purple and green plaid flannel and await their verdict.

"Enid has explained what you're proposing," Mary says. "On the surface, it sounds ideal. Like Kismet. You have a way of tracking the Storm; we have, just possibly, the means of freeing its slaves and an underground railroad ready to receive them."

"But?" I prompt.

"Mr. Goldman," says the Asian gentleman, "we have had a number of people approach Enid during his sojourns with an interest in using his talent. Ultimately, they wish to seek advantage from it over their unfortunate fellows. Machines such as we once relied on for services no longer work. There is only one means of replacing them that does not require arcane talent."

"Human machines," I murmur. The ambient temperature in the room drops a few degrees and I shiver.

He is nodding at my reaction. "In a word, slaves. So you see, there are people in our new world who have a need, and others who will attempt to fill it. Commercialism, Mr. Goldman, at its most despicable. Out there, human beings are once again becoming a commodity. I think you will understand how some would find Enid's talent attractive in that context."

"I do understand. And I understand that your mission is to protect all of this. I don't know what I can do to convince you that my friends and I are no threat. Look, um, maybe if I tell you what we know about the Change and the Storm, you'll understand *our* mission."

They exchange glances, then all eyes go to Mary. She nods.

"There was a government project code-named 'the Source.' I don't pretend to understand the physics behind it, but I do know that it went pretty horribly wrong. We . . . met one of the scientists who'd worked on that project. He'd been changed by the disaster—not like anyone we'd ever seen. Not like anyone we've seen since. We suspect that when the project went south, something terrible was born. You call it the Storm; I call it the Megillah; I've heard it called other things. It's powerful. It's sentient. It sees. It senses. It hungers."

Even at a distance, you can feel the power of it.

"And for some reason it's most hungry for flares, people who were twisted like Magritte was. Like my friend's little sister, Tina. She was twelve when the Storm took her. Look, I don't want to sound like, um, like Mr. Sob-story, but since you seem to be in a position to decide my fate, I think you should know the kind of person Cal Griffin is. He's been taking care of Tina since their mom died and their dad ran out on them. Well, not quite in that order, but it's a complicated story. The point is, he's spent most of his adult life protecting her. But he couldn't protect her from the Change or from the Storm." I glance at my musician friend, where he leans against the door frame. "Cal wasn't as lucky as Enid, or maybe the legal profession just doesn't lend itself to sorcery, but there wasn't a damn thing he could do to stop what happened to her. It was like Magritte said, a—a tornado just sucked her away from him. Since then, we've been on a sort of quest—Cal, Colleen, Doc, and me. Cal is determined to find Tina and free her and the other flares the Source has taken. More than that, he intends to find some way of defeating the Source."

A ripple of surprise circles the room.

Mary watches the reaction of her fellows closely then turns to me. "And you and your friends accompany him. Why?"

I pause to consider this. "Before the Change, I lived on the street. People stepped on me, over me, and around me on a daily basis. Most of them took me as just another crazy. While insanity is a great defense against all sorts of abuse, I . . . I admit I slip in and out of reality more easily than the average guy. Cal always treated me like a man, even on my bad days. Sometimes he even treated me like a friend. So when he says we can find the Source and do something about it, I believe him."

"Why?" Mary asks.

How to describe Cal's possession by this mad *vision* that we four merely human beings can confront and conquer the unknown? That we *must* do it. "Because *he* believes," I say at last.

The Native American fellow, who appears to be in his early fifties, leans forward, eyes intense. "This Doc you mentioned, he's a real doctor? A medical doctor?"

Duh. I should have my head examined.

I nod eagerly. "Yes. Yes, he is. He was a surgeon in Russia, but he knows a great deal about general medicine, and he's absorbed book-loads about herbal remedies. He's had to."

I neglect to tell them that before the Change, Doc was peddling hot dogs on Manhattan street corners.

Mary says, "I know what you're thinking, Delmar, but I'm not sure we can afford to let ourselves be seduced by need."

I'm not much of a seducer, but it doesn't hurt to try. "If you need a doctor, Doc Lysenko will be only too happy to assist. He can train nurses, medics. He might even be able to recruit some doctors from Grave Creek."

Mary draws a deep breath as if I am taxing her patience mightily. "Mr. Goldman . . ."

"Goldie." I give her my most winsome and lopsided smile. It even worked on my mom . . . when I was ten.

She grimaces. "Goldie. We are charged with protecting these peo-ple and with adding to their number. Right now, I can't send anyone out through that portal because your friends are camped right in front of it. From what you've told me about Cal Griffin, I suspect he's not likely to leave without you."

She's right. Stunning thought. Being left and leaving, I realize, had become rather a lifestyle for me.

"We could bring them in," says Delmar.

"And then what?" asks the Asian gentleman. "It doesn't sound as if they intend to stay."

"We could stay long enough to help with your medical needs."

"We *need* a doctor, Mary," says a black woman with tight, graying cornrows. "Even a temporary doc would help."

"We need more than that, Letty." Mary looks at me. "Well, Mr. Goldman, you've given us a lot to think about. Enid, why don't you and Magritte show Goldie around while we try to come to consensus here?"

We stroll outside—or at least Enid and I stroll; Magritte swims the air between us like a sea wraith. I congratulate myself that I'm no longer a prisoner. Now I'm a tourist.

I peer into the forest as we make our way down the hill in front of the Lodge. It seems to go on forever, blurring to a misty green in the deepest reaches. A thin haze rises up from the far treetops and forms a shining bowl overhead. In a trick of the eye, the sky looks more golden than blue. The temperature is almost balmy.

They give me the cook's tour. I see vegetable gardens, windmills, a water tower that catches rain and flows it out to the cabins and vegetable patches. The Lodge and some of the larger outbuildings are on wells. There's a waterwheel, too, snuggled up against a deep channel cut from a fast-running stream. It's nearly complete. It will be a working mill, Enid tells me, used to grind wheat, corn, and various seeds and nuts into flour.

"That's something else we gotta go outside for," says Magritte. "We haven't been here long enough to harvest much."

"Mary said she wasn't sure why it was cut off from the outside. Any theories?"

"I sure as hell don't get it," says Enid. "That's more up Maggie's alley. She's got a kind of sense about these things. It's got something to do with the old tribal magic, I think. That it, Mags?"

"Mags" nods. In the sunlight she looks like an archangel, sans plumage. Her hair is pale flame and her skin gleams like opal. She makes me hurt inside.

"There was Wyandotte Indians around here," she says. "They used the caverns to protect them from the Delawares. Sort of a hideout. There's an old Indian Council Chamber and some other places they used to have ceremonies. Power's real strong down there. *Real* strong. Some folks even say they seen 'em. Or their ghosts, I guess. Especially in the old Council Chamber."

Some folks. "Have you seen them?"

She hesitates, then nods. "So's Kevin Elk Sings. His daddy, Delmar, was a chief, and his mama was a medicine woman, so he sorta comes by it natural. I don't know why I see 'em. Maybe because I'm like this."

"Is that what protects the flares while they're inside? This power? Or maybe the ghosts?"

They exchange glances, then Magritte says, "Sort of. When everything changed, the Preserve got cut off, somehow. You can't walk in or out, except through the portals. You try to walk out, you just end up somewhere back inside."

Sounds familiar—Boone's Gap had a similar if more sinister means of dissuading escape. "And the Storm can't get in?"

"Not with Enid here."

Enid again. I'm in awe. Enid's a regular one-man show. "How do you do it?"

He gives me a weary smile. "Wish I knew."

"So, how did Mary find this place? Does she have some sort of talent herself?"

Magritte glances at Enid and says, "We found the Preserve—me and Enid. We both saw it, but he made it open up. With his music."

I'd be more surprised at that if I hadn't felt the power of Enid's music for myself. "The music opens the fold *and* draws in the sheep," I murmur.

"If they hear it," says Enid. "Some people got too much anger to hear it. It kind of picks who it wants to come in."

"It picked me," I say.

Maggie treads air, turning to Enid. "He's right. It *did*. It did pick him."

He stops, sagging back against the trunk of a pine tree to look up at her, a crooked grimace on his dark face. "What—so now you're thinkin' he belongs here, or some cosmic shit like that?"

"I can't stay—" I begin.

But Magritte cuts across me with, "Enid's the only one who can open this place up." Her eyes meet mine, making me dizzy. "Except now . . . there's you."

Enid looks up into the branches of the pine and says, "Dammit, Maggie."

Well, *this* puts a new spin on things. "How do other people—"

"Enid has to open the portal for them. When we're out on the road, no one else goes in or out. Scares poor Mary just about to death that something's gonna happen to him out there."

"There's literally no one else that can do it?"

"We can," says Magritte. "Fireflies, I mean. But without Enid we don't dare go outside. We don't dare."

Enid shakes his head and the little bells woven into his dreadlocks sigh musically. "Dammit, girl, you got the biggest mouth on you. She's right, though. Kevin Elk Sings can see the portals, but he can't open 'em. It's taken a month of Sundays to bring in the folks we got here."

Catch-22. "So there'd be some benefit to me staying here."

Both of them are looking at me with wary gazes, Magritte's eyes going from azure to silver. She says, "I'd be lyin' if I said no, but even if you did, there's no way the Council'd let Enid go. Gettin' in and out is one thing. Keepin' the lid on this place is something else."

"Are you sure you couldn't train this Kevin Elk Sings to—"

"Tried it," says Enid. "The kid's got a ton of talent or power or whatever you want to call it, but it's real raw. And me, I *do* this stuff; I don't know *how* I do it. Makes it damn hard to teach someone else." He shakes his head and gazes out over the parkland. "Hell, I wouldn't even know where to start."

He looks like hell, I realize—gray beneath his chocolate skin, eyes weary.

"This must take a lot of energy." I gesture at the bright golden haze on the meadow.

"More every day, seems," Enid says, and adds, "So, your friend Cal's a lawyer?"

Okay, we change direction. "Uh . . . yeah. Or he was, anyway—before things got interesting."

"He know how to find loopholes in a contract?"

"I'm sure Cal can find loopholes with the best of 'em."

"Think maybe he'd be willing to help find one in mine?"

"Why? Any contract you had before would have to be void now."

"You'd think so, huh? But you'd be wrong. Mine just sort of changed shape."

I'm fascinated. I've seen many strange and terrifying twists and tweaks in our topsy-turvy world, but a twist of law is unique. "I thought this Howard what's-his-name was the problem."

Enid doesn't answer. He doesn't even seem to have heard the question. His eyes are closed, and his skin glistens with sudden dew.

Magritte touches his hand. "You go on back to the Lodge, Enid. Get some sleep. I'll stay with Goldie."

He starts to open his mouth, then just nods and levers himself away from the tree trunk. We watch him make his way back up the hill, walking like a man three times his age.

"Is he sick?" I ask.

Magritte is silent. When I look at her, her violet-blue aura is dancing with darker hues. "He . . . It takes a lot out of him, all he does."

She seems about to say more when someone pops out of a nearby cabin and waves us down.

"You're wanted up to the Lodge, Maggie," she says. "Pronto."

We go up, pronto, and I'm introduced to Kevin Elk Sings. This might have been a pleasant event, except that he brings chilling news from the West Virginia portal: Cal, Colleen, and Doc are under attack.

EIGHT

COLLEEN

I've seen Goldman do some pretty surprising shit, but this took the biscuit. I had time to shout "Sonofabitch! *Goldman!*" (as if it helped) and make a grab at his coat. I grazed my knuckles on solid rock. The raw pain was enough to push me over the edge of a line I hadn't even known I was hugging. I let out a roar and threw myself at the wall, beating my fists against it.

Cal broke into my raging, grabbing my shoulder and shaking me, hard. "Colleen! Come *on*. This isn't accomplishing anything."

"What d'you propose I do, Cal?" I asked sarcastically. "Say 'Open sesame'?" I gave the wall a vicious kick. "Sure. Why not? *Open-fucking-sesame!* Oh, look—nothing happened. Now what? *Now what*, Cal? You're the college grad. Got any bright ideas?"

Running off at the mouth, Mom called it. I did it whenever I got thrown for a loop. Whatever I was feeling went straight to my mouth without passing through my brain. Right now I was furious and scared and, dammit, I wanted Cal to be as furious and scared as I was. Now I bit my tongue—way too late.

Cal had closed his eyes. Counting to ten, no doubt. Now he opened them and asked, "Did the kick help?"

"No, damn it! It didn't do shit! Stupid question."

"Here is another: What has happened that you two are shouting at each other?" Doc had come over to hover outside the cave.

I straightened. "Oh, nothing much. Our friend Goldman just pulled the ultimate disappearing act, is all. He walked through that wall." I pointed.

Doc shot me a sharp glance, then edged into the little space. Cal stepped outside and I followed him.

"Look," I said. "I'm . . . I'm sorry I lost it. It's just . . . I feel so help-less when stuff like this happens. I hate feeling helpless."

He turned to look at me, his eyes already forgiving me for the ridiculous outburst. "No shit."

I took a deep breath of the moist, chill air. Cleared my head a lit-tle. "So, what do we do now?"

Cal glanced back into the dark little doorway. "What goes in must come out. And when it does, we get in."

"So we just sit out here and *wait*? What if he never comes out? What if there are a thousand ways into the Preserve, each as . . . picky about who gets in as this one?"

"And what if the sky falls, Chicken Little?" He was laughing at me, but gently—giving me the space to pull on a wry grin and turn my anger inside out.

"News flash, smartass—it already has."

"That doorway could open again at any moment, Colleen. I think the best thing we can do is make sure we're ready to go through when it does. Let's saddle the horses and pack up." He was digging around in his pockets.

"What're you looking for?

"Map."

"A map? What the hell good is a map?"

He cast me a glance out of the corner of his eye. "You forget, I don't read maps like the average guy."

Something hopelike stirred in my chest.

"*Intiryesneh*," said Doc.

"Huh?" I swiveled my head to peer back into the dark recess where Doc was on his knees, checking out the wall.

He gestured at it. "Interesting. It seems . . . blurry to the eye and . . ." He pressed the palm of his hand against the rock. ". . . it feels very strange, too. Almost, em . . . fuzzy."

He glanced up at Cal, who left off looking for the map and got down next to him on all fours. "I'll be damned. You're right. This does seem less than solid, doesn't it?"

Looked perfectly solid to me.

Doc nodded. "Yes, exactly. It seems like real earth and stone, but . . ." He pushed at the rock. "Less than solid, as you say. Goldie went through here?"

Cal nodded. "If I hadn't seen it, I wouldn't have believed it."

"Then I suppose we must wait until he comes out again. There is breakfast to be eaten." His eyes grazed mine as he rose. "Patience, like most virtues, is easier on a full stomach."

We saddled the horses and packed first, then ate quickly, our eyes on the little cave. I suspect each of us was rehearsing what we were going to say to Herman Goldman when he came back up from the underworld. (Jeez, who names their kid Herman, anyway?) Of course, the longer we waited, the louder and nastier the rehearsals got. Damn Goldman. By the time he got here we'd have all run out of mad.

As it happened, we didn't so much run out of mad as had it scared out of us.

Cal had gone back to the cave. I could hear him tapping at the wall with something heavy and metallic. (That's no way to treat a good sword.) Doc and I were sandwiched between a couple of horses, packing up the last of the kitchen items, when Doc yelped and leapt back, bumping me and knocking me face first into a bag of drying mushrooms that was dangling from a pack saddle.

"*Bozhyeh moy!*" he said, and I sneezed and came back with "Sonofabitch!"

I turned to see what he was *bozhyeh moy*ing about. Over the rear end of the packhorse I saw a guy peering at us from the trees at the edge of the camp, about twenty-five feet away. At least, it looked like a guy at first glance. Young.

I stepped out from between the horses, hand on my knife. "Hey! Either get lost or come out here where I can see you."

He smiled. That's when I realized this was not a normal guy. If you were to mix everything you'd ever seen that was dangerous, dizzying, vile, putrid, and charming into a smile, this would be it.

Smiling Jack chose option number one, leaving nothing but a bobbing tree branch to mark where he'd been. He didn't reappear. Imagine my relief.

We moved the horses up to the cave and gave the camp and clearing a thorough last look. Then Doc and I went to hover outside the cave, where we watched Cal in silence for a while.

"Anything?" I asked finally.

He made a negative noise and shook his head.

I gave the area around the mouth of the cave a nervous once-over. Tree limbs shivered in a chill breeze and a mist was caught like cotton wadding in the branches.

Great. Another soggy day.

I beckoned to Doc and we moved to secure the horses on their grazing line, strung out along the perimeter of the mound.

"So what does that mean," I asked as we worked our way back toward the cave from the end of the line of horses. "Boshuh . . . bozeh . . ."

"*Bozhyeh moy?* It means 'my God.' "

At the end of the line I squatted down, my back against the steep berm of the mound. "You a religious man, Doc?"

He seemed surprised by the question and answered slowly as if he had to look at each word as it came out. "Yes. Yes, I am a religious man. An anomaly, yes?"

"An anomaly," I repeated. "I'm not quite sure how to answer that." In fact, I didn't have a clue what the word meant, but I wasn't about to admit it.

He shrugged, glancing down at me. "I merely mean that, with all that has happened, it may seem . . . foolish to believe in a God."

"Hey, no, really," I protested. "I wasn't thinking that at all. Although, I gotta say, the whole idea of evil is sort of weird. I mean, why would God invent a devil? What—He didn't think life had enough challenges?"

He smiled, his eyes straying out over the clearing to the billows of fog that pressed into it. "Perhaps God did not invent evil. Perhaps all He did was invent man."

"Yeah, but He gave us the tools for evil. Look at the Source. All that power. Look what they did with it. What it's become."

"Tools, Colleen, are neutral. They are neither good nor evil. Good and evil are in the using."

He reached down, picked up a rock, and held it out to me in the palm of his hand. It was river-worn, a flattened oval of reddish brown. The sort of stone that would skip well.

"Is this a weapon or a tool? Hmm? Does not the answer depend *only* upon whether I choose to hit you in the head with it, grind corn with it, or skip it across a quiet pond?"

I laughed because he had seemed to read my thoughts. "Okay. Good point. I heard somebody say that about fire once: in the hands of a wise man, it warms the house—"

"In the hands of a fool, it burns it to the ground." He turned the rock in his fingers. "In the hands of a fool . . ." he repeated softly.

"Catholic?"

"Russian Orthodox."

"Ah." Like I knew the difference.

He was still smiling at me, still balancing the rock in his hand, when my alarms went off. So did the horses'. They whickered nervously and yanked on their tether. The fog was practically lapping at their butts, and something dark swam through it.

I tried to stand, but my feet slipped out from under me, landing me on my ass. Doc immediately knelt to help me up, and it was while we were in that awkward position that I saw Smiling Jack again over Doc's shoulder. He was much, much closer, seeming to ride the crest of the fog.

"Shit!" I flung myself up, using Doc's shoulder for leverage, and just managed to get my knife free of its sheath.

Jack wasn't alone. There were four more guys just about like him, only less guylike. They were all young and recognizably human, but there was something *wrong* about them. Their features seemed distorted—like I was looking at them through a warped window *and* a thick mist.

Doc turned, saw them, and moved to shield me. This was absolutely the wrong time for that chivalry crap. I shoved him roughly toward the mouth of the cave, which was about eight feet farther to our left along the mound. Our mounts were tethered on the far side. My crossbow hung from the pommel of my saddle, for all the good it did me.

I brought my attention firmly back to our friends. "What d'you want?" I demanded.

"Want?" repeated Jack.

Well, at least he could talk. "Yeah, want. If you've got your eyes on our food, fine. We'll share, but that's about all we're good for."

He smiled, his weird, amber eyes sweeping me up and down. "Not *all* you're good for. Huh-huh-huh."

I realized that was supposed to be a laugh. The rest of them picked it up: "Huh-huh-huh." My skin tried to crawl off and hide.

"You with him, huh?" Smiling Jack was facing me, but his eyes were on the mouth of the cave.

"Him? Cal?" I glanced at Doc, whose face was so rigid it might've been cut from stone. "Yeah, we're with him. Why?"

"He did this," Jack informed me.

I shook my head. "Did? What—did what?"

"*This!*" He snarled the word, pounding himself on the chest with a clenched fist, his lips drawn back over sharp, uneven teeth. There was pain in his eyes.

"I don't get it, Jack. How could Cal have done . . . whatever you think he's done? He doesn't know you. He's never even seen you."

His face twisted into something not even half human. "*Jerry!*" he shrieked. "My name's JERRY! He don't know us, 'cause we can't touch him." The smile came back (oh, how I wish it hadn't) and the other guy-things echoed it. "Can touch *you.*"

They all took a floating step toward us, in perfect unison.

Doc clamped a hand on my upper arm so hard it hurt.

"Whoa! *Whoa!* What? How did he do *anything* to you? How?" I flashed my knife and was embarrassed at the way my hand shook.

Jerry-Jack's head swiveled strangely on his shoulders like he was trying to shrug off a yoke. He opened his mouth—and the other Jacks opened theirs—and they all let out this *sound*. It made my stomach heave and my eyes water because I knew I'd heard it before and—oh, God—I never wanted to hear it again.

Doc murmured something in Russian and took a step toward the cave, pulling me with him.

Jerry's head made another roll. "Mu-u-usic! Damned mu-usic. *Burns.*" He brought his face forward, eyes wide and feral and almost glowing with hateful and familiar red light. "He play. You pay."

Enid. He had to be talking about *Enid*. Before I could even take that in, they flickered and half faded into the mist. Then they moved—

smooth as smoke. I was only half ready, but Doc was fully primed. He let loose with his rock, catching Jerry-Jack in his nearly invisible head.

The tweak went solid again and dropped, distracting the others and giving me time to cut the horses' tether. They bolted in all directions, covering our dash for the cave. Fog and tweaks roiled and danced, and a crossbow bolt shot from the cave to bring another one down.

Cal yanked both of us into the cave with him.

"Thanks," I panted. "How'd you get the bow?" Damn, but I was glad I'd taught him how to use that thing.

Cal slipped a second bolt home. "They were focused on you. I was able to get to your horse before it spooked."

"Great. Give me the bow and some bolts."

He grimaced. "Last one. I couldn't get the quiver free before they attacked."

He handed me the bow anyway and drew his sword. Awkward, with us all crammed into this rocky closet, but it came free of the scabbard with a deadly whisper.

The tweaks had stopped circling their floundering buddy and were moving on us again, like smart ground mist. Cal raised his sword; I held up the crossbow, threatening. They stopped, eyes gleaming, and faded into the mist.

The clearing was silent except for the wounded one's muffled keening. We listened to our own breathing. We counted seconds. They weren't done with us.

"Are these the same tweaks we saw before?" Cal murmured.

Saw? "Hell, how could we tell? But there's four of them. That's how many there were left."

When they reappeared, they'd armed themselves with rocks. They didn't hesitate to use them. I took the first one in the thigh. I heard another strike with a soft thud and Doc cried out. I fired the crossbow, but another stone smacked my shoulder and the bolt flew away into the fog. I pressed myself into the rubble, gritting my teeth against the pain and disappointment. Except for my knife and know-how, I was defenseless . . . unless I could bludgeon one of them to death with my crossbow. Cal's body quivered against mine, dread and adrenaline racing between us like an electrical current.

Rock rang on steel, thudded on bone. Doc moaned and slumped, falling across Cal, who only just pulled his sword out of the way before it did damage.

I jerked forward to stop Doc's fall, but a stone grazed my temple and then I was falling, too. A haze of sparks rose up to swallow me and the sound of a vast crowd roared in my ears.

Something had me. It jerked me off my feet and sucked me backward into the roaring darkness.

Hate to admit it, but I think I screamed.

II

Above, Below, and Here

Suleiman-bin-Daoud was strong. Upon the third finger of his right hand he wore a ring. When he turned it once, Afrits and Djinns came out of the earth to do whatever he told them. When he turned it twice, Fairies came down from the sky to do whatever he told them; and when he turned it three times, the very great angel Azrael of the Sword came dressed as a water-carrier, and told him the news of the three worlds: Above, Below, and Here.

"The Butterfly that Stamped,"
from *Just So Stories* by Rudyard Kipling

NINE

I look down upon a valley from a high place. Where I stand, exactly, I cannot see. Below me the land is beautiful and serene; towns are scattered across it like gems on velvet, bright against the moist, lush green.

The biggest of the gems is a city that stands afar off, at a river's edge — a cluster of crystals thrust into the sky, aloof. I do not recognize it, but feel I should. It is not a real city, but an archetype, I know these things even in dreams. The analytical mind. I decide the city is Kiev, my home.

I dismiss analysis and attempt to absorb the serenity — to breathe it in with the perfume of wet earth. I give myself a moment of this — a gift to myself — but a moment is all I am allowed. For the moment is drowned in the wail of sirens.

As I look down from my eagle's nest, the gleaming, crystal city belches smoke.

A war?

When my eyes penetrate the smoke, I find that the city is a city no longer; it is an ugly, sprawling industrial complex. Gone are the buildings of my imagined Kiev, in their place, the ungraceful pilings of a nuclear reactor. The single fluted tower that has always reminded me, with much irony, of a minaret, tells me all I need to know.

I have been here, and know that the smoke is not smoke, but something far more sinister. I am instantly afraid. I don't want to be here. I *cannot* be here.

In the villages and farms there is an awakening. A froth of humanity boils from the buildings. Somehow, they are at once antlike and individual; I see the masses and I see faces among them, and I am plunged with them into terror.

I must find a way down from this cliff, but my frenzy accomplishes not a thing. There is no way down. I can only run back and forth along the edge of my aerie, a flightless, dithering bird, trapped by its incapacity.

Fevered, I look again to the pylons of Chernobyl, but again they have changed. Where they squatted like broken gargoyles, there is now a tower. It is black like the candles I have seen in the windows of dark, cluttered shops—a votive to a demon. It glistens as if in a sheath of oil or water or glass. It terrifies me for reasons I cannot name. It terrifies me more than the leaking reactor.

The cloud now reaching to embrace the countryside is neither smoke nor radiation. It is a swarm of insects small as gnats. I tell myself this is a good thing, that these mites cannot possibly be as fearful as the horrors brought by the cloud of radiation.

But the comfort is false; the swarm overtakes the fleeing people and swallows them. They produce their own horrors, for their bite not only draws blood, it destroys and distorts so that what emerges from the swarm is less than human.

Yes, yes, a fine conceit. The Change—I understand. I protest this heavy-handed dictator of a dream. *You may stop now,* I tell it.

But it doesn't stop. And though I dream knowingly, I cannot stop myself from wishing I could fly from this cliff.

Damn dreaming. Let me *help!*

As swift as thought, I am in the valley. The insects have flown, leaving a countryside that is twisted and torn, and people who are also twisted, dead or dying.

"Dr. Lysenko! Here!" I recognize the voice of a colleague—a Dr. Kutshinski. But his is not the only voice.

"Dr. Lysenko! I have no more dressings. What do I do?"

"Doctor—my daughter—please, won't you look at my daughter?"

"I can't find my wife. Help me find my wife!"

"Viktor, what's happening?"

This is Yelena's voice, and it stops me in my fevered tracks, for she cannot be here. She is at home in Kiev. Safe. Still, I jerk my head up from the man whose wounds I cannot heal, a man whose flesh boils as if liquid and falls away from his muscle and bone.

"*Gdyeh?* Where?" I ask. "*Where?*" I rise.

Someone thrusts a syringe at me. Yes, at least I can stem the flood of pain. But when I reach for the syringe, my hands are manacled.

I cannot suppress a cry of futile rage. Impotent. Shackled. Yes, that's how it was—*is*.

In the face of futility, I struggle against Shiva (*for behold, I have become the destroyer of worlds*), struggle to become a preserver of lives.

The dream becomes confused, muddy, horrific. I am awash in death and blood, while creatures that are mere parodies of humanity press around me. Always, I am conscious of the Tower, looming over the valley, casting its shadow, drawing my eyes. Though my hands are locked together, I toil.

"Viktor, will you come home? Your time there is done."

"No, Yelena," I tell her, patching flesh that will soon explode with malignancy of one kind or another. "Can't you see how much there is to be done? Can you not see the need?"

"Papa, when will you come home?"

That is Nurya, whose voice is like the sweet song of a flute.

"Papa? *Papa!*"

I weep. Can they not understand? These people *need me*.

"Wait," I tell my wife and daughter. "I'll be home when I can."

They fall silent. Too silent. I turn to see where they have gone and the field hospital dissolves away.

Around me, rain falls. The lights of police cars slither across the slick road and rainbows squirm in shallow, oily pools. The tow truck comes back onto the road now, our little car dangling at the end of a thick chain not unlike the ones I wear. Water streams from it. In all other ways, it seems as normal as the last time I saw it parked in the narrow lane behind our flat.

I look up and the Black Tower is there, like a funeral candle, upthrust from the trees. Its sides, slick and greasy as this patch of road, reflect no light. Somehow it is to blame for this. Or perhaps I am to blame and it merely witnesses my guilt.

Fury, blind and useless, builds up beneath my heart and pushes upward. I raise my hands to rage or supplicate, I am unsure which, and find they are no longer chained.

I wake, or at least I am moved to a different reality. Here, there is light. Sunlight, golden and warm, shrouds all. Then out of the haze comes a being of such beauty, I am stunned to the soul.

It is a girl. She floats a little above me in a halo of blue-white light. My heart leaps. And I dare to hope . . .

"Oh, he's awake," the girl said, and flitted away.

So, I wasn't dead after all, and this was not heaven and that was neither Nurya nor an angel. I was alive. Absurdly, I was disappointed.

My vision cleared enough for me to see that I was in a mere room. A sunny and pleasant room, to be sure, but a place built by human hands. I gingerly moved arms and legs. My left knee throbbed, convincing me to lie still.

Reflection overtook me. Heaven was not a place to which I hoped to go, but a place I had once lived and from which I had been expelled. I gazed down at my unchained hands and wondered at the language of dreams.

"Welcome back."

Colleen stood to one side of the door, which was now open, and through which came Cal, Goldie, and a flare—a woman, not a little girl. This must be Enid's flare, Magritte, whom I had taken for an angel named Nurya. Last into the room was a tiny woman with dark, graying hair and piercing eyes.

Cal came to sit at the edge of the bed and gripped my shoulder. "You gave us quite a scare," he said. He looked weary and perhaps a little anxious.

I had nothing to say, so I tested my voice by asking the first question that came into my head. "How long . . . ?"

"Almost six hours." The tiny woman moved to the foot of the bed. "We have no doctor here, only one nurse and a medicine man. Do you think you might be concussed?"

"Possible."

"Head hurt?" asked Cal.

"Among other things."

"Well, at least we can offer something for that," said the woman. "But I'd advise you to eat something."

My stomach growled on cue and I managed a weak smile. "Advice I shall take, thank you."

"I'll see to it." The flare bobbed and was gone in an aura the color of sky.

I did not miss the way Cal's eyes followed her; she was like Tina— yet unlike her.

"Is there anything else we should do for you, Dr. Lysenko?" my hostess inquired.

Doctor Lysenko. How odd it sounded, still. For years no one had called me that, and now it was my name again, my reality. "Observe me," I said, "in case I should do something peculiar."

She smiled, her pale eyes kindling. "Now, I like that in a person— humor under duress." She looked to Cal. "I expect you'll want to compare notes and catch him up on things. I'll get Cherise to have a look at him . . . in case he should do something peculiar."

She left, and Goldie moved to take her place at the foot of the bed. "That was Mary, of course."

"I had suspected as much." I looked at Colleen, who leaned against the doorjamb, aloof. She seemed more than usually subdued. "You are all okay?"

Cal nodded. "Thanks to Goldie's new friends. Colleen took a knock to the head, too, but fortunately it was just a glancing blow. She never lost consciousness."

"Ah. You are a better man than I am, *boi baba*," I told her.

She smiled, and the others threw me a puzzled look. Is muttering Russian a sign of concussion? Well, if not that, perhaps rhyming is.

"We are in the Preserve?" I asked.

Cal's face became instantly animated. Whatever gray ghost had haunted it passed without rattling its bonds. "This is incredible, Doc. We are *hundreds* of miles from Grave Creek."

"I don't understand. The Preserve is not in the Adena mounds?"

"The mounds are only a portal to the Preserve, they link to it across miles of Ohio landscape."

"But how? By what mechanism?" I found what he was saying

strange but not impossible, and it struck me how much like a dream reality had become.

"Unknown," said Goldie. "The only thing the two sides of the portal seem to have in common is that they were both Native American cultural and religious centers. It makes a strange sort of sense."

What a perfect turn of phrase. What other sort of sense could it make? "They came through the portal and brought us here?"

Cal nodded, "Just in time, too."

"And we have found Enid?"

The smile reached his eyes. "It's just like Goldie said—Enid's music has the power to render a flare invisible to the Source. Magritte isn't the only flare here, and he's protecting them all."

I tried to sit up but thought better of it. "Then this place would be safe for Tina as well?"

Cal's expression was suddenly guarded. "If we need a safe house for Tina, this could be it."

"Except for one small fly in the ointment." Colleen spoke at last. "Enid can't leave. Seems he's the one and only Key Master for the portals that lead into this place. If they lose Enid, these people are trapped."

"There must be a way," I said, believing it. "We cannot have come here without reason."

"Divine Providence, Doc?" Colleen crossed her arms over her heart.

"I doubt a theological debate is the best medicine for a possible concussion," Cal interrupted. He touched my shoulder again. "Neither is anxiety. Rest. Let us worry about Enid." He nodded to Goldie, and the two of them slipped from the room.

Colleen moved as if to follow, but did not. She let the door fall shut behind them, then swung back to look at me, her eyes subtly invading my thoughts.

"Are you sure you're all right?"

We spoke the words together; our voices harmonized. Self-conscious laughter followed. I'm not certain why two human beings should be embarrassed at having spoken in unison, but it seems we were.

"I'm fine," she said. "Sore, but whole. You, on the other hand, have a nasty gash on your forehead and a knee the size of a cantaloupe."

I put a hand to my head, gingerly. A gauze bandage blocked inspection. "I, too, am fine."

"Yeah? How many fingers am I holding up?" She showed me her fist.

"None," I said, smiling. "Or all. It depends on how you look at it."

She retreated again behind folded arms. "Doc, who's Nurya?"

Breath left my body in a rush, leaving me winded. "What?"

"When you were coming around, you seemed to be having one hellacious nightmare. You shouted for Nurya. When you saw Magritte, you said the name again." Color swept her face. "Shit, I'm sorry. I'm just too damn nosy. Forget I asked."

So, she had not come into the room with the others. She had been there all along. It was she the flare had spoken to before leaving to find Cal.

"Nurya was my daughter. My little girl." Even now, after so many years, the tears emerged easily.

Colleen sat on the edge of the bed—coiled, tense. "What happened?"

I could not look at her face, so I read answers from the pine knots in the ceiling. "You remember Chernobyl, yes?"

"Well, sure. It was all over the news. Even teenagers pay attention to the news sometimes. Christ, don't tell me she got caught in *that*."

"No. *I* got caught in that. Because of my expertise in triage. The disaster was . . . worse than even the American media made it. Doctors were brought in from everywhere. I was to set up a triage unit, then go home. But I couldn't go home. There was too much to be done. What I failed to realize was that there was something to be done at home, too. My wife, Yelena, had contracted meningitis. She wouldn't tell me this, but Nurya said her mother wasn't feeling well. I simply didn't hear her over the cries of the dying."

I hesitated, testing the words as if they were an unknown trail. "Yelena was driving herself to hospital when she lost control of the car. It plunged into a stream. They drowned."

Colleen had been watching my face. Now, she turned away. We sat in silence for a time, not looking at each other.

She was the first to speak. "My dad died when I was fifteen. He was two thousand miles away on some damned military training junket. He served in Vietnam for two tours of duty and then went to Texas to die of a heart attack giving a friggin' seminar. He'd had a two-pack-a-day habit for years, and I'd just managed to nag him into giving up cigarettes. For a long time I thought maybe I just hadn't nagged enough." I could feel her eyes shift to my face; it was a gentle pressure. "It's not your fault, you know."

"Is it not?"

"You were needed—"

"At home. I was needed at home. There was nothing I could do for those poor souls that any other qualified physician could not have done. But only *I* could have made a difference to my family."

Colleen made no reply. I had silenced her, and her silence was damning. Physician, heal thyself.

"So you came to America to start over," she said after a moment, "as a hot dog vendor." The expression on her face was so dubious it made me laugh.

"It was a life."

"This is better." She said the words with stark certainty and meant them for both of us.

Our eyes met and locked. Détente.

"Yes, better," I agreed.

"Doesn't make us freaks, does it?"

"What if it does?"

She looked away. "Yeah, what if it does? Thanks, Doc." Her eyes met mine again at a slant. "You must have a real name."

"Doc will suffice."

She pursed her lips and gave me a look of grave disapproval.

"Viktor," I said. "My name is Viktor. With a *k*."

"Well, Viktor with a *k*, thanks."

"For what?"

She didn't answer, but stood and looked down at me and smiled. "Huh. Turnabout. Last time it was me flat on my back."

The door opened. Colleen tensed; an instinctive movement. It was Magritte with a nurse and food.

"Well, I guess I'll just go check on our progress," Colleen told me. "Later."

"Yes, later," I agreed, but she had gone.

TEN

"So, you're a lawyer, Mr. Griffin. A most maligned profession."

Mary seated herself across from me in front of the fireplace in her office. Between us, a low coffee table of burnished pine held an odd collection of artifacts: arrowheads, a grinding rock, a rattle made of wood and leather.

" 'And He said, Woe to you, lawgivers also,' " I quoted, " 'for you load men with burdens hard to bear and you yourselves do not touch the burdens with one of your fingers.' Gospel of Luke, Chapter Eleven, verse forty-six. Even God doesn't think much of us as a tribe."

"But I'll bet you were one of the *virtuous* lawyers, weren't you?"

I shook my head.

Her eyebrows rose. "A cynic?"

I laid a hand over my heart. "A fallen idealist."

"But repentant?"

I shrugged, smiling in the face of accusing memories.

"Were you any good at it?"

I had to think about that. "I . . . yes. Yes, I was good at it. But not cutthroat enough to be truly great."

"Are you cutthroat enough to take Enid away from us?" Mary Mc-Crae didn't pull punches.

"I don't want to take him away. I just want to borrow him."

"For how long?"

"I don't know. As long as it takes."

"Days? Weeks? Months?"

"In months it could be too late."

"For what?"

I had to search my head and heart for the right words. "I think the Source is gaining strength. I think that's why things are continuing to change. At some point it may be too late for anyone to do anything."

"So, if Enid were to go with you, you might be able to 'pull the plug on the Source,' as Goldie put it . . . or you might not."

I nodded.

"And if not?"

"Then we do what we can and come back here to regroup." *If we're still alive.*

"Either way it could be weeks before Enid returns. *If* he returns. And while he's gone—"

"I know. You're stranded."

"Worse. We have no consistent way to protect the flares, as you call them."

"You protect them now while he's away. How?"

She studied me, as if trying to decide how much to tell me. "A battery of sorts. Look, Mr. Griffin, let's assume for a moment our . . . flares could be shielded inside the Preserve long enough for you to get where you're going and back. Enid's talent is essential to us in other ways. We wouldn't survive long without it. Refugees aren't the only thing that comes in from outside. *Everything* does: food, clothing, equipment. Even if I could ensure everyone's safety, I must be able to open the door."

I read her eyes. "Goldie," I said.

"Goldie. You think that's an unreasonable request?"

"No, but I can't ask him to stay. I can't *afford* to have him stay. He's our bloodhound. He's how we track the Source."

She gazed at me for a moment. "So he said. No one else can do that?"

"The Change is selective, Mary. You know that better than anyone. It chose Goldie and Enid, but not me or Doc or Colleen."

She was nodding. "Or me, for that matter. In my past life . . ." She paused, smiled. "Listen to me, sounding as if I'd died and been rein-carnated. In my past life I was conversant, Mr. Griffin. I spoke the language. I knew the drill. I could perform because I knew the rules of engagement. There is a new language; I don't speak it. There are new rules; I don't know them. I don't know the drill anymore—I'm winging it. It's as if I've gone suddenly blind and Enid is my seeing-eye dog."

"And Goldie is mine."

"Your what?" Goldie was standing in the doorway of Mary's office, looking from one of us to the other.

"Lucky rabbit's foot," said Mary wryly.

I decided to cut to the chase. "Goldie, Mary would need you to stay here and take Enid's place if he comes with us."

He was unsurprised. "Sure. Makes perfect sense, except that you'd be in dry dock without me."

"You're that sure?" Mary asked.

Goldie nodded. He wandered farther into the room, coming to squat by the coffee table.

"You couldn't show them on a map?" she pressed him.

He chuckled, his eyes picking over the odds and ends on the table-top. "Mary, I don't know if you've tried using maps lately, but they can be awfully unreliable. Things aren't where they belong. The Ohio is a whitewater theme park ride, and there are invisible corridors between Ohio and West Virginia. And it's still changing. Isn't it, Cal?" He glanced up at me, his eyes ice-pick sharp, reminding me that the Change hadn't left me completely untouched.

If I were to twist suddenly, I wondered, *what form would I take?* I turned the thought aside.

"So you can't just divine where it is on a current map and let them extrapolate?" Mary asked.

He picked up the rattle and fiddled with it, turning it over in his hands. It responded with a soft scrape of dried beans. He seemed fascinated by it. "I could point to . . . oh, South Dakota and say it's there. I could even point to the Badlands and say it's there. But the Bad-lands covers a hell of a lot of territory. The reality is: I feel a pull; I take a step. If it's the right step, I feel the pull get stronger. If I take the wrong step . . ." He shrugged. "Right now, all I know is that the pull is coming from somewhere west of here."

Mary sat back in her chair and looked at me. "So, that's it, then. I can't let Enid go. And you can't let Goldie go. An impasse."

I looked down at my hands. They were clenched, knuckles white. I relaxed them with effort. "Mary, I know you care about the people here. I understand that you want to protect them. But they're a handful of people out of the millions—maybe billions—who are homeless, helpless, confused. When we left New York, it was coming apart at the seams. People were dying—worse, they were *killing*. Even people who didn't change behaved like animals."

"And your point?"

I looked up at her. "If Enid stays here, he can save a handful. If he goes with us, he could save billions."

Mary flushed to the roots of her hair. "You overstate your case, Mr. Griffin. We have no way of knowing how widespread—"

"Did you hear what I said? We came here from *Manhattan*. We can vouch for the fact that the Change has affected New York, West Virginia, Ohio. Planes have fallen out of the sky, there's no electricity, and the landscape in some places is as twisted as the people. You came here from farther west. Is it any different on this side of the Ohio?"

"Don't push me, Mr. Griffin. And don't try to manipulate me. Perhaps you think because I'm a woman you can do that. You'd be wrong. I can tell when I'm being jerked around."

"Cal doesn't jerk people around, Mary," Goldie said quietly. "Right now he's just trying to get you to look at the big picture. If we get to the Source and unplug it, which Cal believes we can, then it doesn't just help your folks, it helps everybody."

Her eyes struck me with the force of an arctic storm. "*Why?* Why do you believe you stand a snowball's chance in hell of doing *anything* against the Storm? You saw it—what it did, what it's still doing. What makes you think you can do *anything*?"

I had to smile. How many times a day did I ask myself that question? "Would you believe me if I told you I had a vision?"

Into the silence that followed, intruded a soft, rhythmic thudding. A peculiar vibration tingled under my feet. Goldie obviously felt it, too, because he put down the rattle and stood, looking puzzled. Mary raised a hand, as if to command silence, and sat listening to the eerie drumming. It seemed to come from everywhere, to be in the room with us.

When the vibration ceased, Mary rose. "Excuse me. I have to go. I'm assuming you won't be leaving right away." She was gone in a wash of tension I swear pricked my skin.

Goldie and I stared at each other for a moment, then I asked, "*Is it in the Badlands?*"

He gave me a look he could probably patent. "Now I'm a travel agent? How the hell should I know?"

We moved by unspoken consent to stand on the Lodge's broad veranda. Down the hill, mellow afternoon sunlight tumbled through trees that were still green into an odd, gleaming mist that seemed to fit the forest like a woolly, translucent bonnet. It reminded me of Boone's Gap, but this mist seemed benign, like a child's favorite blanket. There were no angry ghosts in it. It was pleasant here, from the clutter of cottages and tents to the song of wind chimes. If it were not for Tina—no, if it were not for the Source—I'd consider staying. God knows, we all had talents we could put to use in a place like this.

"Bagel dog with kraut," Goldie murmured.

"Excuse me?"

"Things I Miss Most. Your turn."

"You have to ask?"

"Now now. This is supposed to be a lighthearted exercise in distraction. The category is Things We Miss Most About Life as It Once Was."

"Okay. Um . . . Starbuck's . . . double latte, tall, vanilla."

"Figures. Low fat milk, too, I'll bet," he said, and when I nodded, he added, "Yeah, I figured you for a low fat kinda guy."

"But if I had to do all over again? Whole milk and hazelnut."

"You devil."

"*Could* you learn to do what Enid does?"

He sobered and his eyes dropped to his feet. "Tried it. That's what I was at this morning before Doc came around. I don't get it."

"Maybe it just takes practice."

"*Practice? Practice what?*"

"Okay, trial and error, then."

"Look, you remember the light-globe I used to scare away our Shadow friends?"

"How could I forget?"

"It's a form of visualization. I imagine the globe; that somehow gathers the photons together and it's there. That's roughly the way Enid makes his shield around Magritte."

"All right, so you understand the mechanism. So far, so good."

"No. No good," he said, shaking his head. "I work with light. Enid works with sound. They're two different types of energy—at least so far as the Change is concerned. Enid creates a sonic shield around Magritte, so the Source can't *hear* her. I could create a light-globe, but all that would do was keep her from being eaten by the local wildlife. It wouldn't block her from the Source." He paused to chew on his lip and pick at a knothole in the porch railing. "It's not just Enid. It's Magritte. They do it together." He made a spasmodic gesture with his head. "The shield, the jamming thing."

"Wait. You're telling me . . . What are you telling me?"

He shrugged. "They're a duo. A team. Batman and Robin, Scully and Mulder, lox and bagels. You can't have one without the other. Symbiosis. And no room for cream cheese."

"You and Magritte don't have symbiosis?"

He glanced away from me so quickly, if we were standing in a courtroom, I'd have smelled guilt.

"What?" I prompted.

"Nothing."

"Something."

He wagged his head back and forth and sighed. "Magritte and I . . . we have some sort of . . . rapport. We connect. Or maybe she just makes me hot. I don't know. But we don't have what she and Enid do. Besides which, he needs *her* protection as much as she needs his. Protection from this Howard guy."

"Howard? Refresh my memory."

"His manager. The guy he's hiding out from here. Irrelevant at the moment. The point is, I just don't seem to have *it*—whatever *it* is."

"Full circle. We're back to Enid."

He shook his head. "You heard Mary. He's their lifeline."

"She said something about a battery—the thing that protects the flares while Enid is gone. What did she mean?"

He gave me an odd look and held up a finger. "Listen."

"To what?"

"Shh! *Listen.*"

I heard a dog barking down the hill, water gurgling and splashing, a chorus of wind chimes. Goldie started humming. It took me a moment to realize that the tune was in perfect harmony with the wind chimes.

Enid used *sound*. "The wind chimes?"

He grinned. "Cool, huh? I haven't verified it yet, but that's my theory. It would explain a lot. Such as why they're all over the place, why they all play the same set of perfectly tuned notes, and why something keeps them moving even when there's no breeze."

I looked up at the row of chimes along the eaves of the Lodge. There was no breeze, but they were rocking and sending out a sheer veil of song. "What keeps them moving?" I asked.

"Don't know. Haven't had a chance to ask anybody who'd say anything more than, 'Well, uh, they're *wind* chimes.' "

I grimaced. "I hope the answer isn't 'Enid.' "

"What if it is?"

"Then our job gets a little harder." I put a hand on his shoulder. "There's a way to do this, Goldie. If we can't account for all of Enid's talents, then we have to make Mary see that if we don't shut down the Source, and shut it down soon, *nobody* will be safe *anywhere*. Not even here."

Goldie's eyes met mine, grim, troubled. "Cal, there's something you should know. Enid's sick."

A cold fist wrapped around my stomach. "How sick?"

"I don't know. Magritte says it's just that he's doing too much. Maybe she's right, but intuition tells me it's something more. He's pretty used up."

"Does Mary know?"

"Would she admit it if she did?"

🌣

Goldie was right about Enid—he was used up. It was hard to miss. He was right about Mary, too; she didn't admit it, even when Doc offered to take a look at him.

"Why? He's just very tired, Dr. Lysenko," she insisted. "He does an awful lot for us here, and with winter coming on outside, we've been keeping him especially busy. He just needs rest."

I tried to read her face, but she would've made a fabulous poker player; I couldn't tell if she was lying, in denial, or telling the Gospel truth.

I figured Goldie was in a better position to read that situation than I was. If Enid wouldn't tell him, chances were good that Magritte would. She seemed to trust him—something he found bemusing, but which didn't surprise me. In a matter of days they formed a peculiar triad: Goldie, Magritte, and Enid. Nothing sexual, except perhaps in my friend's fulsome fantasy world, but something musical and—I don't know—spiritual, I guess.

I wondered if I still believed in spiritual things. I vaguely recalled that I once had. That Tina had. Or perhaps Tina was the believing part of me, and apart, I believed in nothing but Tina herself.

Doc was up and around on the second day of our stay, limping but mobile. By the end of that day he'd become a fixture. Surprise, surprise. He fit in here, the same way he fit in at Grave Creek; the same way he fit in on the corner of Lexington and Forty-second, the same way I have no doubt he'd fit in in the operating theater of any major urban hospital.

Doc Lysenko, chameleon.

I didn't fit. So I put myself to work, mostly in the infirmary Doc was helping them piece together. A good place to gather information. There were moments I'd look up from a task and watch everybody fitting in, and I'd try to imagine what life would be like if we found Tina and brought her here. Would I fit then? If Tina was the part of me that believed, was she also the part of me that *belonged*?

Colleen understood this. She didn't fit in any better than I did. We were misfits together, Colleen and I. Where Doc could get absorbed in the Preserve's medical needs, and Goldie could just get absorbed— period, Colleen stayed focused. That helped *me* stay focused.

"It'd be really easy to get sucked into this place, wouldn't it?" Colleen said at the end of our first day in the Preserve. "Just too good to be true."

I gazed down the long hill at the evening view from the veranda of the Lodge and realized that she'd put my feelings to words pretty much exactly. "Who wouldn't want a haven like this?"

She laughed, and I could feel the warmth of her gaze on the side of my face. "You. You're already planning our next move, and that sure as hell doesn't involve hanging here."

"No. Because you're right, as it happens. This place *is* too good to be true. Mary says it's locked in space and time. But it's not locked. And it's not safe. The world outside is going to keep changing."

"Until someone or something stops the Source."

I turned my head to look at her. Her eyes met mine—open, frankly questioning. Did she take that for granted—that if the Source was somehow conquered or dispersed, the Change would simply stop? I didn't.

"I don't know," I said. "I hope so. I hope it's that easy."

She laughed again. "Listen to the man—'easy'! . . . Well, I guess there's only one way to find out, huh? We just have to keep going until we get . . . wherever it is Goldman is leading us."

"Looks that way."

The moment stretched out between us, silent, as we stood eye-to-eye on the veranda in the soft light of fey torches. I wanted to lean into her, to touch her, to establish something constant between us.

But then she pulled her eyes away, looked back down the hill and said, "So what's next?"

"Next," I repeated, pulling my thoughts back from the edge. "Next, I get to know the flares."

There were seven of them, all but one pulled from the Source's radar at the point of Change. The one exception to that serendipity was Javier, who had changed while in the Adena mounds. There, he had apparently been protected from the Source by whatever power the place held. The same power, I suspected, that linked it to Olentangy.

Javier and his family had been vacationing in West Virginia when the Change came. He was thirteen. His mother and father were also here. They no longer spoke of making their way home; they now understood that to do so would mean leaving their son behind. They stayed. They fit in.

The flares liked the Preserve's little chapel. It was the light, Magritte said—the way it slanted through the stained-glass windows, making rainbows in the shadows and tinting their auras with the vivid hues of flame, ice, and Saint Elmo's fire.

They didn't seem to mind when I crashed their little gathering the morning after our arrival. I perched on the edge of a pew while they arrayed themselves about the altar like kinetic votive candles. If the gathering was odd, so was the chapel. The altar sported the usual cross, along with a menorah, a Lakota ceremonial pipe, a doll-size Buddha, and some relics I didn't recognize.

A Bible verse stirred my memory: *And My house shall be called a house of prayer for all nations.* Maybe we were seeing the fulfillment of prophecy.

We talked about the Preserve, about Mary, about Enid. I mentioned the wind chimes casually, commenting on how many of them there were. The other flares turned to Magritte in eerie unison, and Magritte gave me a long, searching look and said nothing. And when I asked them about the Storm, there was a silence so deep I could hear the candles burning.

Then a girl with the unlikely name of Faun asked, "What's to know about the Storm? It's why we're all here. That's enough, isn't it?"

"How did it affect you? How did it call to you? My sister talked about hearing a Voice or Voices. 'The one and the many.' Is that what you heard?"

They exchanged glances, and for a moment no one spoke. Then Javier said, "It wanted me to belong to it. The way I belonged to my family. It *told* me I belonged to it. It made me think . . ."

"Think what?"

"That it was where I was meant to be," he finished. "That I wasn't like my mom and dad anymore. I was . . . different. And I needed to be with my own kind."

"Maybe you shouldn't talk about it, Javy," said Faun. "You know how it gets when you think on it too much."

Javier looked from me to Faun and back again. "Your sister's like us?"

"Yes. She wasn't as lucky as you are, though. It found her."

Auras rippled and shifted hues. Eyes, deep and mysterious as twilight, traded glances.

"When I was in the mounds," Javier said, "I could feel it calling me. Somehow, I knew it couldn't reach me as long as I stayed where I was. But after a while I *wanted* to leave the mounds. It made me want to leave. To go find it. Mom and Dad kept me there . . . and then Enid came. They were so scared. I've never seen them so scared." He shook his head. "Then, I didn't understand why."

My blood chilled. "Do you now?"

He didn't answer, but glanced over at Magritte, who hovered lightly above the pew on which I sat like a lump of coarse clay. "Should we tell him about Alice?" he asked.

Magritte's expression went through a series of changes as she decided again how far she could trust me. "Enid found Alice up on Put-in-Bay Island. She was in the last of the Change and the Storm'd come for her." She said the words as if they were dangerous. "Enid got to her just before the Storm did, and we barely made it back into the cave. But Alice . . . wasn't very strong. When she'd hear the Storm, she'd listen. One night, she just left. She went back through the northern portal to the island and it got her. Enid followed, to try and bring her back, but it was too late."

"What do you mean, when she'd hear the Storm? I thought you couldn't hear it inside the Preserve."

"Sometimes you can," said Javier quietly. Terror and longing merged uneasily in his eyes, and I remembered Tina telling me that she wondered if she ought to just embrace the power tugging at her, heed the voices telling her how perfect a union it would be.

I remembered, too, as clearly as if I lived it again, our last moments together in the Wishart house in Boone's Gap. The simple white board structure had held something too complicated and paradoxical for me to comprehend: two men, one less than a man, one more than a man. Bob Wishart, crippled, disintegrating. His brother Fred— *Doctor* Fred Wishart—a cocreator of the Source. Coauthor of the real Doomsday Book.

A piece of the One.

In the moments of quiet I tried to avoid, I could still hear Fred's voice, gentle, trying to explain to me and to Tina why he held a tiny mountain mining town in deadly thrall.

If I let go, I'm destroyed, too. Something bad needs me to be whole. Something bad.

I'd been warned. And when Fred Wishart had been sucked into the void between Boone's Gap and whatever place the Source inhabited, Tina was gone with him, torn away by an unnatural wind. Gone, while I lay in an impotent heap, stunned, broken, knowing her terror as starkly as if it had been me in the Storm's embrace.

I wanted never to feel that combination of emotions again.

"I don't want to talk about this anymore," said Faun. "And I don't think the rest of you should talk about it, either. It's bad luck."

The others seemed to agree. They drifted away in silent consensus, Javier giving me a long backward glance. Only Magritte stayed.

"They're scared," she said when they'd gone. "The Source is evil, but it has a pretty voice. I think that makes it more evil, don't you?"

"Yes," I said. "I also think that makes it more dangerous. You say you can hear it in here. How is that possible?"

She just looked at me and shook her head.

"The wind chimes—Goldie thinks they're what protects you when Enid's gone. Is that what they do? Is that when you can hear the Storm—when Enid's gone?"

Her lips curled. "That Goldie's pretty sharp."

Yeah, and I wished he were here. Maybe he could get her to open up. "What makes the wind chimes work, Magritte? Does Enid do something to keep them moving? Is he the only one that can do that, too?"

I watched her glide along the altar, touching the sacred things there one after another as if they might protect her. Her movements had the feel of ritual—as if this were something she performed regularly as a ward.

"Look, Magritte, I know Enid is sick. Is that why the Source gets through sometimes, because he's getting too weak to stop it?"

She swung around to look at me, her eyes wide and stricken. When she spoke, her voice was nearly a whisper. "When it came for me, I felt its touch. It was the same touch I felt every time I . . ." She hesitated, her hand cupping the little Buddha. "My johns really liked it when I started to change. They said it was like doin' an angel. I was with a john when I changed final. The Storm came quick and sudden and it touched me. It was like somebody'd took that john and multiplied him times a million."

Her hand had clenched around the Buddha. Now she let go, stroked it gently, and moved on to the next relic. "I don't ever want to feel that touch again. I'll die first."

I didn't have to ask if she meant it. I tried to put Tina out of my head, to stop thinking like a brother and start thinking like a strategist. "I don't want you to feel it, either. I want to stop the Storm.

Completely. And it's possible that you and Enid might be instru-
mental in that. Maggie, I need your help. Tell me about the wind
chimes. Is Goldie right—are they what protects you inside the Preserve?"

She was silent long enough that I thought she wasn't going to answer me. Then she said simply, "Partly."

"Partly. What else is there?"

"Enid's music. Us fireflies. And this place. It's a powerful place. It
all kind of works together. But when Enid's . . . when he's gone, we
have to work harder to tune out the Storm."

"How do the chimes work? Do you know?"

She shook her head. "Enid says they scramble the signals. So we
don't hear the Storm clear and it don't hear us."

"Does Enid have to move the chimes?"

"No. Anything can move 'em, but you can't count on the wind
around here, so he keeps them going. It's in the music—in his head."

"Maggie, do you have any idea why the Source wants you?"

She looked up from the altar, her face caught in a fall of bloodred
light from the window behind the altar, the white silk of her tunic
stained with it. "It's hungry," she said.

The strategist sat silent while the brother faced the horrible possibility that his sister might be dead—that the Source, for whatever reason, literally devoured flares. I forced my throat to make sound. "Do
you . . . do you think it kills the flares it takes?"

"Not the way you mean. A pimp doesn't kill his girls. At least not
all at once. He just uses them up, bit by bit."

Nausea swept me. I fought it down. "Maggie, can you hear the
Storm now?"

Her eyes locked on mine, she shook her head. "Not right now. But
I think some of the others do. I know Faun does. She's not very strong."

"And Enid? How strong is he?"

She stared at me from those bottomless eyes for an eternity. "I
think he's dying."

I caught up with Mary in the caverns, walking into the middle of a
scene that involved a trio of snarling grunters and a red blanket. The

problem: one of them had it; the other two wanted it. They were in the process of ripping it apart when Mary stepped in and snatched it away from them. They turned on her in unison, showing fangs, reaching for the lost prize.

Adrenaline kicked in; I drew my sword and got in the way.

If the grunters were surprised, Mary was outraged. "What the hell do you think you're doing? Put that damned thing away!"

I stood my ground between her and the grunters. "They were about to jump you."

"They were not. And I'd appreciate it if you wouldn't talk over them as if they weren't there. They're *people*, dammit. Regardless of what they look like."

I lowered my sword slightly and gave ground—a little. I glanced at the grunters. They dropped into defensive postures, eyes shuttling warily back and forth between the two of us.

Mary, meanwhile, swung a backpack down from her shoulder and pulled out more blankets. "This is a different sort of place than you've been before," she told them. "There's no treasure to be hoarded here. And there's enough for everyone to have what he needs."

They shuffled forward in unison, still snarling, eyes darting suspiciously. One reached his hand out for the red blanket. Mary smiled and gave it to him. He clutched it to his chest, grunted out something that sounded like "Thanks," and headed off into the gloom. The other two dove for the backpack.

"Blue!" said one. "Want blue!"

"Mine!" said the other. "Blue *mine!*"

In another second they'd be fighting again.

I took a step forward. "Hey, fellas! Why are you here, huh?"

They both turned their milky eyes up to me and blinked.

"Didn't you come here to find a more human life? Didn't you come here because you didn't want to end up alone, or wandering around with a pack of animals?"

Mary picked up the cue and grabbed a couple of blankets, which she held out, one to each grunter. "He's right, boys. Try to remember what brought you here. You want to be better than what your friends outside have become? Well, being better starts here."

"You're a natural," she commented as we made our way back to the surface after the incident.

Tweaked torchlight fluttered and ran across the rough walls, making and unmaking shadows. It was hard not to suspect them of harboring danger.

"A natural what?"

"Leader."

"I was going to say the same of you."

"Bullshit. If you're so impressed with my leadership, why the hell did you run me over back there?"

"Run you over? Mary, I thought they were going to tear you to pieces. They can do that. I've seen them."

"So have I. But you forget—the very fact of their having followed Enid in here shows that they're different. You saw it yourself. They're better than that."

"I only hoped they were."

She stopped in the middle of the room the tour signs called "Indian Council Chamber" and smiled up at me, her hands clasped in front of her like a schoolteacher . . . or a Buddha. Torchlight turned her graying hair to deep gold, burnished her face, and softened the lines there.

Breath caught in my lungs; she reminded me, sharply, of someone from a past I'd lost. I hadn't thought of my mother for what seemed an eternity, and suddenly her ghost was standing an arm's length away.

"Well," she said, "it seems your hope was rewarded. Your cynicism didn't get you anything but hollered at." She turned and began walking, now raising a hand to greet one of her subterranean citizens— human and twist—now reaching out to touch the moistly glistening walls.

Neither of us spoke again until we came out at the top of the spiral stair. The sound of wind chimes was heavy in the air. Mary struck out across the campground.

"Magritte says Enid is dying," I said.

Mary turned around so fast, I thought I heard static electricity. "Magritte isn't a doctor. But she is young and emotionally needy. A desperate combination."

"We brought you a doctor. You won't let Enid see him."

She shook her head and began moving in the direction of the Lodge. "Enid is just very tired. I told you—"

I matched her stride. "What you've told me doesn't tally with what I've seen. He can't stay awake. Sometimes he can barely walk straight. From what Goldie says, sometimes he can barely *stand*. The flares can hear the Source whispering to them through Enid's Veil. I know you've already lost one, and I know it was while Enid was here."

She paled, stopped. "Who told you that?"

"The flares."

She started walking again, anger in every line of her compact body.

I stuck to her. "Come on, Mary. You're in denial. And there's nothing to be gained by it. You're going to lose Enid one way or another."

"So better your way?" she asked bitterly. "The flares will be destroyed—"

"If you don't move now to shore up the Veil," I finished.

"How?"

"As Magritte described it, the wind chimes are a focus for power—the flares' and Enid's. They provide a sort of sonic veil, but only if they're kept in motion. Good so far?"

She nodded, slowing her pace slightly.

"Then what we need is a way to keep them moving."

She snorted. "Are you God now, Mr. Griffin? Can you make wind?"

"We don't need to make wind, we just need—" I broke off and stopped walking, distracted by the sight of several sets of wind chimes sharing a clothesline with some laundry. As I watched, a woman with a baby on her hip and a basket at her feet pulled the laundry to her by rotating a pulley wheel mounted on a tree trunk. The chimes shrilled.

Goldie would have called it an epiphany. Whatever it was, it shot adrenaline into my veins.

"Need what?" Mary asked, her eyes on my face.

"That." I pointed at the rig of pulleys, wheels, and line. "A system."

She glanced at it and shrugged. "Yes, but driven by what?"

"Something that never stops moving."

Her eyes came back to my face, the anger gone. "Water."

For a moment, at least, Mary McCrae and I were on the same page.

We gathered rope, string, twine—anything that could be strung on the odd assortment of wheels we collected. Since there was a limited amount of rope, Colleen and I sweated over a homemade map of the Preserve's inhabited area, plotting the most strategic places to set up lines, calculating how they would be connected with the locus of the system, the waterwheel.

It was nearly complete, lacking only the integration of its internal gears and the mounting of its big wheel. Colleen cheerfully volunteered to aid in that effort, declaring that waterwheels were right up her alley. Maybe, but her mechanical know-how was unfortunately offset by her lack of people skills. The engineer heading the project, Greg Gustavson, was not keen on the idea of having a "little girl" tinkering with his machinery. I don't know if that slowed the wheel's completion. I only know it wasn't ready when we needed it.

I was in the company of flares that day, or at least, of three of them—Magritte, Faun, and Javier. Of all the flares, it was Javier who reminded me most of Tina. Like Tina, he was intelligent and, like Tina, he had a way of seeming older than his years and a direct gaze that was sometimes disconcerting.

We were in the chapel again, a place I found as calming as the flares did. Maybe it was the warmth and light. Or maybe it was the smell of beeswax, wood, and incense. It felt as if time had stopped there, and the world seemed a normal and safe place.

The first inkling I had that there was anything wrong was when Faun, in the midst of a colorful story about her marvelously dysfunctional family in Nashville, stopped speaking and began silently to cry. Her azure eyes were wide and fixed on the large window above and behind the altar, and I thought she was just feeling the pain of remembrance. But then her lips opened and she uttered a high, inhuman wail, so piercingly sad that it brought tears to my eyes.

Javier and Magritte stiffened, their eyes going to the same window. I rose, following their gazes.

The window was pictorial: Noah's ark sat upon a grassy landscape while dark storm clouds, filled with lightning, billowed overhead. Animals looked up, two by two, and Noah, in the prow of the great boat, also had his face upturned, his beard wind-flung, his hands raised as if casting a spell or warding off the storm.

The light that had been falling through the window a moment before was gone, dulling the bright glass. The chapel darkened.

Faun wailed again and jerked upward. Javier echoed her, putting both hands over his upswept ears, crushing them against his skull.

Magritte turned frantic eyes to me. "Oh, God, I *hear* it! *Enid!*"

I understood in a chill jolt. Something was wrong with Enid. The Veil was unraveling. It had been a close, still morning; I already knew there was no breeze to move the chimes.

Without warning, Javier was pulled toward the rafters like a puppet on strings. Maggie grabbed him with both hands and began to sing Enid's "Refugee Song," wordlessly, her voice high and trembling. Javier's upward movement stopped, leaving both flares suspended above the altar.

I turned and bolted from the chapel. There were two sets of chimes hanging under the eaves of the porch. I could make a shield of them.

The courtyard had been awash with morning light earlier. Now shadows swam across it, sucking away the sun, devouring the Preserve's protective aura. Delmar Crow stood on the porch of the leather shop across the way, staring at the sky.

I shouted at him as I reached for the chimes, kept shouting as I yanked them from their hooks and shook a wild cascade of notes out of them. "Flares! In the chapel! The Storm's getting at them!"

Delmar's eyes swung to the chapel, realization dawning. He made a gesture of comprehension at me, then turned and disappeared into the leather shop.

Swinging the chimes, I turned back into the sanctuary, driven by the sudden, insistent sound of drumming, which seemed to come from everywhere at once. I was terrified that in the moments I'd been gone, Magritte and the others had been taken. But I heard her voice as I crossed the foyer, still reeling out song, trying to scramble the signal. I elbowed my way through the inner doors, chimes singing with every movement.

All three flares hung in midair before the altar, linked only by Magritte's hands. She burned bright, white-hot, her delicate features twisted with effort. Faun and Javier were guttering flames. Their auras were no longer radiant and lucent, but pulsed with muddy reds and purples. Above them in the rafters a malignant shadow spread its arms, pulling them upward into its embrace. Its voice was like the hiss of whitewater, swiftly building to a roar.

I moved without thinking, chimes tangled in my fingers, rushing up the aisle, leaping, grabbing, managing somehow to get my arms around the struggling flares. I felt the warm chill of their changed flesh, the homely fabric of their clothing. I was surprised when my human weight had an effect; they dropped suddenly and my feet met the chapel's firm floorboards.

Magritte sobbed in my ear. Her voice faltered. We were buoyed upward.

"Keep singing!" I shouted.

"Scared," she keened, and turned the cry into a note and the note into a trill of song.

"Me, too," I murmured, and wondered how long we could keep this up. My arms around the flares, the chimes I held were useless. And Magritte was weakening.

There was a crack like thunder and the ceiling above us ripped apart in a hail of debris. The Storm surged into the breach; I could feel and hear the alien wind, sucking at us from above. It stirred the chimes tangled in my hands, but the chaos voices drowned out their song.

Faun let out a cry of despair and fury and twisted in my grasp, her fists striking glancing blows across my shoulders. Javier screamed. We were being lifted again, tugged from the solid earth toward the looming shadows. I looked up. The Storm's maw was gaping, black, eternal and ablaze with unnatural, translucent flame in a thousand hues. And behind it Something smiled, unseen, and hungered.

I don't ever want to feel that touch again.

I tightened my grip. In response, Faun lashed out with a charge of pure, freezing energy that blinded all my senses. My arms went numb, my legs spasmed, my head exploded with hot-white pain. Faun twisted away and flew upward. Javier shot up after her, slipping from the circle of my arms.

I grabbed desperately, clumsily, losing the wind chimes. But I caught one thin ankle with a hand that seemed part of someone else's body. With the other hand I captured Magritte, crushing her against my side. I would not let go. I swore it to myself, to Tina, to God, to the Source. I would die before I'd let go of either of them.

Enid's voice cut through the storm fury like a velvet knife, accompanied by a sheet of chime-song. Melody reached up into the blazing darkness and joined battle with it.

Above us, in the Storm-mouth, Faun twisted this way and that, a stray ember thrown from a fire to die. Javier reached after her. The unearthly wind crescendoed, roaring, wailing like a maddened animal, like a lost soul. Then it was gone so suddenly that all sound, all sensation, seemed to have been sucked out of the room.

And with it, Faun.

I quivered in the aftermath, dimly aware of Enid's voice flowing around me. Javier was a dead weight in my arms, his fey light extinguished. He weighed no more than a young child. My legs felt as if they were made of rubber, not flesh and bone. I sank to my knees on the hardwood floor.

Magritte, halo dimmed, sagged against me, panting. She touched Javier's face with a trembling hand. "He'll be all right," she whispered. It may have been a promise or a prayer.

We both looked to Enid. He still sang, desperation in his eyes, sweat gleaming on this face. His voice was raw and his fingers faltered on the strings of his guitar.

I got to my feet, passing the limp Javier to Delmar, who had come into the chapel with Enid. "We've got to get the waterwheel online," I said. "I'll need Colleen, Goldie—hell, I'll need everybody you can get."

Delmar nodded. "I'll take care of these two. And pray the others got to safety."

"Where will you take them?"

"Down. Into the caves."

I headed for the unfinished millhouse, trying to keep my eyes from being drawn to the sky. I knew what I'd see. The weak shimmer of chimes, powered by human hands, held the Storm at bay, but it hadn't been repulsed. Its unnatural clouds roiled overhead, licking the treetops; I felt them as a hot weight on my soul.

Mary met me near the center of camp, Goldie and Kevin Elk Sings at her side.

"Magritte." The name tumbled out of Goldie's mouth the moment he saw me. His hand clutched my sleeve.

"She's okay. How did you—"

"Delmar," said Mary. She seemed dazed, wounded. "The drums."

"Faun," I said.

She nodded. "I know."

"There was nothing I—"

"I know. If there were a way you could have saved her, she'd be here now. But the others . . . you . . . they're still with us." Her eyes came in to sudden focus, locked with mine. "We've got to protect them."

At the millhouse the great wheel was still, poised above the water. A cascade of curses rolled from the open door. We dove inside.

The obscene litany came from a stocky gentleman with an impressive shock of white hair and five o'clock snow on his jaw. Within the halo of white, his face was the color of a boiled lobster and glistening with sweat; a sledgehammer was clenched in his fist. Like Thor or Vulcan, Greg Gustavson must surely be capable of tossing thunderbolts.

Colleen was here, too, crouched above him in the confusion of large wooden gears that formed the mill's mechanism.

Greg ceased cursing long enough to look at Mary and say, "Before you ask, it can't be done. She's not ready. The clutch isn't finished, and if it were, the wood'd be too green yet."

"Great Scotty's Ghost," murmured Goldie.

I looked up into the recesses of the building. About a dozen feet above our heads a beam as big around as a century oak stretched the width of the millhouse. It was suspended from the ridgepole above its cradle by a web of ropes. Along with the framework of gears that would drive the grinding plates below, there were several pulley-wheels, their lines threaded through the millhouse walls through small, high windows. They connected the mill to our system of chime lines. They were useless without the wheel.

I swung up next to Colleen amidst the machinery and knelt to inspect the clutch "Scotty's Ghost" had mentioned. I could feel the Storm above us, circling like a vast bird of prey, muttering to itself, looking for another opening.

"What's the good news?" I asked.

"The good news is the gearbox is finished. The bad news is—"

"I didn't ask for the bad news."

Colleen shot me a sideways glance. "Well, you're gonna get it anyway. Bad news is, these brakes need work."

She ran her hands over the curved wooden brake pads that were intended to slow or stop the wheel. "These are smooth," she told me. "Too smooth. It'd be a miracle if they could brake this thing under normal circumstances; there's no way they'll survive if the shaft hits the cradle moving."

"Which it will do," said Greg Gustavson from below, "if the wheel catches running water."

"We have to get it in the water," I said. "*Now.*"

Colleen met my eyes, then looked down at the engineer. "What if we bypass the clutch and—"

"If you drop this thing in the water without a clutch, it'll tear the whole mill apart," he snapped. "We've got to be able to disengage the gears."

"Or stop the water," said Kevin quietly. The boy hovered behind Mary, working his hands around and around the barrel of a wooden flute. Somehow I got the feeling he never put the thing down.

Greg shook his head. "The lock's not finished yet, Kev. We got caught with our pants down. We're not ready."

"How fast can you get the wheel into the cradle?" I asked.

Greg shot me a glance that asked who the hell I thought I was to come onto his turf and start issuing orders. "In a matter of minutes, but what's the point? I told you, if that wheel hits the water in motion—"

"Then Kevin's right," I said. "Our only chance is to stop the stream. Then we can lower the shaft into the cradle and use the brakes to control the momentum."

"*If* we rough up these braking surfaces," said Colleen.

Greg snorted. "Hell, that's the easy part. How're you gonna stop the stream?"

❀

Kevin and Goldie followed me from the mill while Greg, Colleen, and a couple of volunteers worked on the brakes. Mary hurriedly gathered a crew of brawn to manhandle the wheel.

Just above the millhouse the waterway narrowed before cascading into the broader, deeper channel along which the mill was being constructed. I tried not to hear the roaring of the frustrated Storm above the treetops, tried not to imagine its hot breath as we checked the lay of the land, the orientation of trees, the availability of large rocks, logs, branches, anything.

Near the mill, uphill from the stream, a large hunk of granite caught my eye. Apply the right leverage and we could roll this thing downhill into the current right about where the stream fed into the millpond. That would block it only partially and would leave us with the additional problem of getting the boulder out of the water again, but right now I didn't see an alternative.

The sweet, clear tones of a flute floated up to me, mingled with the purl of the stream. I turned. Kevin Elk Sings sat cross-legged beside the flow, flute to his lips. He seemed to be playing to the water. Goldie squatted beside him, eyes raptly on the flute player.

I heard steps behind me. Shadows fell across the face of the boulder. I tried not to notice how dim they were in the growing darkness, what strange colors they cast.

"What are they doing, Calvin?" Doc asked.

"Not sure," I said.

I turned. Doc wasn't alone. Delmar Crow and several other men were with him. "Look," I said, "here's the situation. We need a dam. Gustavson and Colleen are getting the wheel ready to go in the water, but first we have to *stop* the water from flowing into the millpond."

Delmar nodded, slapping his hand against the granite flank of the boulder. "You want to start with this?"

I nodded. "We'll need leverage."

Leverage came from a pile of scrap lumber stacked in the lee of the mill. We dragged out three long pieces and hurriedly worked them under the boulder's flank.

I looked down the hill, mouth open to warn Goldie and Kevin out of the way. The sound stopped in my throat.

The two of them were just about as I'd last seen them, except that Goldie had moved closer to Kevin, the fingers of one hand resting on the barrel of the flute as if in a caress or a benediction. Just beyond where they crouched, the water eddied, curled, and slowed as if an arctic wind breathed over it. Then it folded back on itself and ran, with all the speed of syrup, back the way it had come.

If Kevin could keep this up, the millpond would be empty in a matter of minutes. I held my breath, feeling as if I were on the verge of an epiphany. But as I watched, the water fell back into its normal state, and my epiphany drained away with it toward the mill.

Kevin slumped on the bank with a wail of frustration.

I nodded to Delmar. "We're on. Let's get this thing in the water." I wrapped my hands around a rough two-by-four. "Doc, can you go down there and get them out of the way?"

He threw me a sideways glance. "I am prepared to help here," he said.

"Doc, we need them out of the way."

He moved off down the hill, gait stiff, but no longer limping. At the water's edge, Goldie gave him an argument and Kevin was slow to move, but he managed to get both of them out of the path we hoped our boulder would take.

It took more than the three tries requisite in most fiction, and Goldie, Doc, and Kevin had to add their strength to the effort, but in the end we heaved the boulder out of its bed and watched it roll ponderously into the stream. It splashed down about where we'd intended, but then rolled back toward the mill, leaving generous floodgates on both sides.

"Now what?" Goldie had to shout, making me realize that the roar of the Storm had grown.

I could no longer hear the wind chimes, and had to glance at those nearest us to even see that they were moving. Around us the woods flickered with strange, uncertain light and our shadows squirmed and writhed on the ground as if sinister life grew within them.

"Now we build a dam," I answered.

Delmar was already headed for the pile of scrap lumber. The rest of us followed. We hauled everything we could lay our hands on down to the stream, then Delmar and I plunged in to start the water wall. We were joined by two men who could have easily passed for defensive linemen. Their names were Tomas and Hagen.

Our backs against the boulder, we worked desperately to seat the odd-size planks across the stream's mouth. The water was glacially cold; in a matter of seconds hands and feet were numb. Wood slipped easily from frozen fingers, forcing us to grapple with it again and again.

When we had built an unsteady, shifting, four-foot wall, the others plunged into the stream with us, forming a human brace against the water. Only Doc was left on shore, ferrying materials from the mill.

It was working, but so damned slowly. And the stream was stubborn. It breached the wall in a dozen places and foamed over the top, blinding us. The roar of the water bled into the Storm chaos until I couldn't tell one from the other. We needed more wood.

I glanced up to where Doc hovered on the bank, a short piece of board in his hands. "Too small!" I shouted. "Longer!"

He hesitated, then dropped the board and scrambled up the bank. It seemed an eternity before he was back, struggling with several longer pieces. He was trying to pass one of them out to us when he missed his footing and toppled into the stream just above our would-be dam. The force of the water slammed him into the leaking wall and sent Kevin Elk Sings tumbling backward into the dwindling millpond. Water shot through the unmanned gap.

Delmar shouted and lunged to cover the hole. Kevin scrambled as well, out of the water and around the end of the dam to help Doc clamber out of the water. The cavalry arrived, after a fashion; several more people hurried down the slope to tackle the pile of wood, pass us lumber, and lend brawn to the dam.

While Doc sat watching them, gasping for breath, Kevin turned to the millpond. "It's falling!" he cried after a moment. "Water's falling!"

He was right. The water was at my waist, then at my hips, then at mid-thigh. I had no way of knowing if it was enough, but we couldn't wait any longer. I could distinguish between the sounds of stream and Storm now, and the Storm was the louder of the two.

I pressed a shoulder into the wall and waved at Kevin, shouting to get his attention. "The wheel! The wheel!"

He got it, turned and ran, slipping and sliding in the water that now lapped up the bank. Doc was nowhere in sight.

I worked myself around so the dam was at my back and I could just see the mill past the curve of the boulder. Beside me, Delmar did the same. Along the ridgepole stood eight men and women intent on an array of tethers that ran down to and around the wheel's massive hub. At some signal I could neither see nor hear, the phalanx of brawn leaned into the cant of the roof; ropes went taut.

From inside the mill there was a crack like the breaking of a tree limb. The top of the wheel tilted back toward the mill as the nether end of its shaft dropped into the inland cradle. A moment later there was a second crack and the wheel sagged toward the creek bed. Its weight hit the lines hard, pulling the team on the roof forward.

Breath stopped in my throat and I mentally pulled with them. Who knew? In this mangled reality, maybe willpower had a real effect.

The wheel stopped moving, suspended by the ropes. Then ponderously, a few inches at a time, it slid downward, groaning like an aged dinosaur, and slipped into its cradle. The water lapped at it but lacked the power to move it.

On the millhouse roof the rope team stood down, except for a lone figure that straddled the ridgepole, apparently waiting to signal us when the gears were engaged.

"Problem!" Delmar yelled in my ear. Water cascaded over his head in a foamy veil. "We just let go this stuff—it hits the wheel—could damage it!"

Damn. He was right. We'd have to dismantle our dam piece by piece, and try to lose as few of those pieces as possible.

I opened my mouth to shout back when I heard music. Flute music. Kevin stood above us on the stream bank, trilling out a melody that cut through the shriek of the Storm in gentle defiance. Around us the roar of water diminished. Less of it poured over the top of the dam. What did come over cascaded in slow motion—lazy banners of foam.

With the Storm winds pressing low enough to whip the treetops, I trained my eyes on that ridgepole silhouette. Praying it would move, would tell us we were ready to put the Storm to flight.

A second later my prayers were answered. The man pulled himself to his knees and waved both arms at us, shouting as he did: "Away! AWAY! NOW!"

We hauled scrap lumber out of the water as fast as humanly possible. I still had one foot in the stream when Kevin stopped playing and water exploded back into the pond, carrying away the few small pieces we'd missed.

I crab-crawled up the stream bank, panting, and watched as the flood rushed around the boulder, catching the wheel and turning it.

There was a great creaking and the clatter of meshing gears, then lines moved on their wheels and the wind chimes stirred. All around the camp's perimeter, they sang—loudly enough to be heard above the Storm's fury.

Another sound carried down to us there on the bank of the mill-stream—a roar of celebration from the millhouse. The men around me echoed it.

Delmar pounded my back and laughed in my ear. "Look!" He pointed to the sky. "Look! It goes!"

I looked. My own laughter bubbled up from someplace hidden, catching me by surprise. I pumped my fist at the sky. Already the Storm was retreating, being replaced by the burnished gold of the Preserve's strange mist. We had, with a perfect synthesis of the physical and the metaphysical, averted disaster.

"Nice work." Goldie squatted beside me, grinning like the Cheshire cat. Kevin Elk Sings hunkered next to him, flute still clutched in his hands.

Yeah, it was good work. "Kevin, you really came through there. Thanks."

He gave me a self-conscious smile. "I didn't want to let you down. You were all putting yourselves on the line. I don't have lots of muscle; this is the only thing I do well." He turned the flute in his hands, then smiled again, rose, and moved away toward the mill.

"That was quite a piece of work," I said.

Goldie nodded, eyes speculative. "Wasn't it, though?" He got up and followed Kevin, leaving only his grin behind.

I pulled myself to my feet amid celebratory and congratulatory chatter and looked around for Doc, afraid he might have hurt himself again. I didn't see him, and before I could go looking, Mary caught up with me.

"I suppose I should thank you," she said. "You pulled off one hell of a save, Mr. Griffin. Something I doubt I could have done, under the circumstances. This thing blindsided me."

"I didn't save a damn thing, Mary. We did it, all of us. And we're not safe—not yet. This is a temporary fix, a salve. It's not the cure."

She nodded, looking away toward the mill, her arms folded defensively over her heart. "The cure is defeating the Source."

Neither of us spoke for a moment. Then she said, "You were

right, Cal. Enid is dying. I don't pretend to understand why, but I doubt it's any natural disease. Whether I can afford for him to leave us or not, the simple fact remains that he's going to leave us." She turned to look up at me, her frosty eyes bright with tears. "If there were some way you could save his life, Cal Griffin, I would gladly let him go with you."

I was stunned. "I'm not a miracle worker, Mary."

"No? What do you call what you just did?"

"We did. And I don't know. But it wasn't a miracle."

"It might as well have been. I can't do what you do. I can't . . ." She groped for words, her hands making futile gestures in the air. "I can't *drive* people the way you do."

"Maybe not, but you've already done something I know I couldn't do: you've molded an incredibly diverse group of people into a thriving community. To me, *that's* a miracle. One I doubt I could reproduce."

"But they needed you to—to focus them just now. I . . . After Faun . . . God, Cal, I felt so *lost*."

Impulsively, I put my hands out to take her shoulders. "For a moment, Mary. For only a moment. None of us are one-man or one-woman shows. How far do you think I'd have gotten if I didn't have Doc and Goldie and Colleen with me? Where would any of us have been if you hadn't rescued us from that dead-end mound cave? I needed you then, you needed me in this emergency. I'm good at emergencies, I guess. But after I'm gone, this community you've built will need someone who can hold it together. That's what you're good at."

She took a deep breath and met my eyes, the light in them suddenly wry. "You know, I think you'd make a good lawyer."

I laughed, dropping my hands from her shoulders. "Yeah, so I'm told. You know I've wondered: what were you before all this?"

She shook her head. "Unsatisfied. Tried being an executive secretary—oh, pardon, an executive assistant—tried teaching. I liked teaching, but frankly, it was a depressing occupation. Then I started a day-care center outside of Dayton."

She'd surprised more laughter out of me.

"What?"

"I had you pegged as an administrator, a judge, or a politician." *Or the Dalai Lama.*

She pointed a stern finger at my forehead. "Young man, I ought to wash your mouth out with soap for that last crack."

A smile tugged at the corner of her mouth, and I suffered another sharp pang of déjà vu. She turned and headed toward the Lodge, then paused and glanced back over one shoulder. "I was an administrator's *secretary*. Now, don't you think you'd better get yourself into a change of dry clothes?"

There was, I thought, following her, something to that old truism about who really runs an office.

ELEVEN

DOC

"Got a minute?"

I looked up from the table where I was grinding herbs to paste and found Colleen in the doorway of the Preserve's little apothecary shop. It seemed to me that I often saw Colleen in doorways, as if caught between coming and going. I gestured for her to come in.

She hesitated but entered, nodding to my two assistants, who variously filled containers with homemade remedies or folded bandages, some of which would accompany us on our westward journey, some of which would go to their own infirmary.

She came to stand close beside me, leaning as if to peer into my mortar, and said, "Can we talk someplace private?"

"Certainly."

I picked up the tray on which I worked and carried it to the back room, calling back over my shoulder for her to come help me. There was less light here, but it was private, as she had requested.

"Light me that lamp, please?" I nodded at an antique copper oil lamp that sat on a shelf across the room.

She fetched it without hesitation, lit it, and brought it to the counter where I had set my tray of herbs. She dipped her head toward the preparations, then wrinkled her nose. "What *is* that?"

"Wintergreen," I said. "Good for rashes and abrasions. Is that what you came to ask of me so privately?"

"No. How's the leg?"

"It will serve. Colleen, what is it?"

The room darkened, the oil lamp spat, and we breathed in harmony while she watched me play at being an herbalist. I did not prompt her again. She would speak in her own time.

Finally, she said, "I fell asleep, if you can believe it. Right after supper. Just now woke up."

"It has been a draining day for everyone," I said. It certainly had been that for me—and sobering. I glanced at her sharply. "You are not ill?"

"Huh? Oh . . . no. Nothing like that. It was just . . . I had a dream."

"Yes?" I hoped it was nothing like my dreams.

"I dreamed of being cornered in that little cave in the mounds. It reminded me of something I'd forgotten."

I stopped crushing leaves and gave her my full attention.

"I remembered what the tweak said just before the attack."

"What he said? As I recall, he was barely coherent."

"He was coherent enough to know what changed him."

I shrugged. "The Source changed him, of course."

"No, not the Source. The tweak said, 'He did this.' "

"Did . . . ?"

She put a hand on my arm and shook it. "*Tweaked* him. I thought he meant Cal at first, because he was looking into the cave when he said it, then I realized he was talking about Enid. I'd forgotten it until the dream put it back in my head."

"Perhaps you dreamed that as well?"

"No, Doc. I didn't dream that. I *remembered* it. Don't you remember? 'The music burns,' he said."

I struggled for memory. "Vaguely, I recall . . . You are saying . . . ?"

The look in her eyes chilled me. "That Enid's music does more than attract refugees."

※

I watched Colleen pace the lounge. In the silence that always follows disclosure, six pairs of eyes followed her, only to drift away when the meaning had fully penetrated. All but mine.

Enid seemed to sink beneath the weight of the revelation. He was a deflated man, cornered, his eyes wary.

It was Mary who first looked his way. "Were you aware of this, Enid? That your music . . . had this effect?"

Colleen stopped pacing and made a gesture that brought to mind a scarecrow in a high wind. "Don't pretend you didn't know!"

"Colleen," I said softly, and she moved away to a hearthside chair, where she sat, folded up.

Mary seemed not to have noticed her. She moved to Enid and laid a hand on his shoulder. "Enid?"

He nodded, eyes still on the rug between his shoes. "I knew . . . I knew my music could do . . . stuff like that. I just didn't know how bad the leak was."

"The leak?" Cal repeated.

"Sometimes," Magritte said softly, "neither of us is real strong. When he gets shaky, I hear the Storm. When I get shaky, there's leaks."

"We've seen no evidence of it here."

"It don't happen here. It happens out there." Enid canted his head to the wall. "Everywhere I go, I leave a trail of tweaked shit. Mostly rocks and trees. Sometimes animals."

"And people," muttered Colleen under her breath. I think I may have been the only one to hear her.

"Tweaked trees," repeated Goldie.

Enid glanced at him. "You seen 'em."

Goldie nodded. "Uh, yeah, and followed them here. *Wow.*"

Enid looked as if he might cry or rage. "I swear to you all, *I did not know about those people.*"

Beside him, Magritte hovered solicitously, hands fluttering toward him like frightened birds. She was the only flare not sequestered in the caverns tonight. The others were weakened, and it was feared they might be able to hear the Source whisper to them even through the veil of music. Mary McCrae was taking no chances.

"How long?" asked Mary. "How long has it done this?"

"Always," Enid said. "Ever since the Storm. In here, I'm safe. And things are safe from me. That's why I've stayed."

"But you went out time after time," Mary said. "Why?"

He looked up, finally meeting her gaze. "Because you needed me to. I figured the good I did outweighed the bad. If I didn't have Magritte, it'd be worse."

Mary shook her head. "Why, Enid? Why didn't you tell me?"

"You might not have let me go out. And you needed me to go out. *They* needed me to go out, the folks I've brought in. You gotta understand, Mary, I didn't know about these guys Colleen's talking about. I mean, I seen 'em. And I knew my music . . . *did* stuff. But I didn't connect it all." He closed his eyes, his face gray. "Shit, no, that's not right. I just didn't want to. Didn't want to know."

Beside the fire, Colleen made a soft sound that was either a moan or a growl.

"How did this happen?" Mary asked.

"Howard," Goldie guessed.

"Howard," Enid agreed. "I s'pose you could say I got some contractual difficulties." He glanced over at Cal, eyes pleading. "I was hoping maybe you could help out, being a lawyer and all."

Calvin stirred, a look of incredulity on his face. "You're serious? A *contract* you signed with your manager is making your music . . . backfire? When Goldie said Magritte was protecting you from your manager, I had something a little more . . . physical in mind."

Enid sighed. It was a sound that seemed to come up from the pit of his soul. "When I was hungry, barely scraping by on gig money, Howard and I made a gentleman's agreement. Handshake deal. He did real well by me—got me choice gigs. *Great* gigs. I played at *Legends*, man—Buddy Guy's club. This was no small shit. He got me seen by people—the *right* people. So, I signed an exclusive with him. He got me a recording deal with an outfit called Primal Records. Also exclusive. I gig when Howard says 'gig,' and if Howard doesn't say 'gig,' I don't. You follow? According to the contract, if I play without his say-so, there's repercussions."

He laid a subtle stress on that last word, and I could not help but think what a strange word it was, at once bland and full of threat. And, in this case, most descriptive. I could almost see the twisted consequences of Enid's art ricocheting through an equally twisted reality, finding circuitous paths to unexpected victims.

Repercussions.

"But how can you be sure it's the contract?" asked Mary. "Maybe it's coincidence or something completely unrelated."

Smiling what was not at all a smile, Enid reached into the inside pocket of his jacket and fetched out a thin sheaf of papers. Without ceremony, he crossed to the fireplace and tossed them into the flames. Then he put his hands in his pockets, leaned his shoulder against the mantel and watched them burn. We watched with him.

When the pages had completely blackened, Enid picked up a fireplace poker and stirred them to ash. Then he turned, reached into his jacket pocket a second time, and pulled out an identical sheaf of papers.

"When I left Chicago, I left this behind. I mean, with all that shit going down, who's gonna think to take along a damned contract? But while we were on the road, I opened up my guitar case and there it was, lying on the bottom, all neat and tidy. I've tried tearing it up. I've tried throwing it in the river. I tried burning it three times, sayin' prayers and singin' hymns all the while. I've even had Mags try to get rid of it. It comes back. Every time."

Cal was nodding, and I could see the lawyer mask slip into place and his eyes become winter landscapes. He held out his hand. "Let me take a look at it."

While the others hovered over the document, speaking in hushed voices, I slipped over to Colleen's chair and perched upon the arm. "May I ask," I said, "why you are so much about the discovery of secret treachery?"

She turned her head enough to see me, but her eyes met mine only for an instant. "I wouldn't expect you to understand. You're not cynical enough."

"Oh, yes. I'm such an idealist, such a Pollyanna. Always, the rose-colored glasses."

"You *are* an idealist. You see people the way they want you to see them. You buy their hype."

"Ah. Do I?"

She sat up straighter and met my eyes. "You do. It's an endearing quality, Viktor, but stupid, and will probably someday get you killed. And it's not just you. Goldie is hot for that cute little flare, and Cal's hot for the Source, and he looks at Mary McCrae as if she were . . . I don't know, Joan of Arc and Mother Teresa rolled into one. Somebody has to keep a straight head."

"And that would be you, yes?"

"Somebody has to."

"And how do *you* see them, *boi baba?*"

"As they are. I see them as they are."

"*Vitsishye glaz choozhoi da nyeh vidishyeh svoy,*" I said.

"What?"

"A proverb of old Russian grandmothers: 'The eye that sees all things sees not itself.' "

"Yeah, well, I know a few proverbs myself, like: 'Trust no one.' And: 'If something seems too good to be true, it probably is.' "

"Ah. And I suppose it's because you are such an untrusting person that you are marching off into the heart of darkness with the rest of us?"

"I'm marching into the heart of darkness, as you put it, because it improves the odds. I'm not good with people, Doc, but I've got damn good survival skills, which have really come in handy lately, wouldn't you say?"

She was right, of course. She had skills that very much increased the odds of Cal getting where he needed to go and doing what he needed to do. I could not help but contrast them with my own, which were conspicuously lacking.

Even Colleen's dream had reminded her of something that now might be of use. It had reminded me only of a lesson I had learned most recently from my failure at the mill—that while I might be an asset in a medical emergency, I could be a liability when the goal was simple survival. An unpleasant truth. And despite Colleen's belief to the contrary, my glasses were not rose-colored enough to disguise it.

TWELVE

I'm no entertainment lawyer, but legalese is legalese, and the intent of the contract was crystal clear. It relieved Enid Blindman of a great deal of personal control over his career and the music it rode in on.

The parties named in the contract were Enid himself (hereafter referred to as "the Artist"), Howard Russo (hereafter referred to as "Management"), and Primal Records (hereafter referred to as "Primal Records").

Stripped of that squishy outer skin that legal jargon provides, the stipulations were draconian: the Artist was not to perform his music except with the express written consent of Management. Outside of Primal Studios, he could only record it by "special arrangement" with Management and Primal Records. And heaven help the poor fan who bought a bootleg tape or CD.

All in all, it was a fabric I was more than familiar with. I had constructed contracts like it with my own two hands and glibly defended their provisions, trying to be worthy of Ely Stern's regard. The thought turned my stomach and made my skin itch. I recalled that Tina's skin had itched while she was changing.

If there were a God, I'd pray that He let me redeem myself in some way *before* I mutated into something in keeping with my occupation. *Alas, alas for you, lawyers and Pharisees.* If I changed right now, I might end up as a viper with good intentions.

I gave the contract a second thorough reading, underlined a few clauses, jotted a few notes, then sat back and stretched, aimlessly clicking the point of my pen in and out. It was late . . . or early, depending on how you looked at it. The Lodge's roomy lounge was quiet except for the snap and crackle of the fire in the grate. Beyond the aura of the lamp, it was swathed in moody but comforting shadow.

Mary had gone up to bed, Colleen and Doc were curled up in opposing chairs on either side of the fire. They seemed in emotional opposition just now, too. It bothered me—the strange static between the two of them. But I couldn't afford the head space at the moment to worry it or puzzle it out. Later, I told myself. Later, I'd talk to Colleen.

Enid was drowsing, too, his breathing labored, his lanky frame draped over one end of the rustic plaid sofa. Magritte had fallen asleep and come to rest on the sofa's lumpy padding, her head in Enid's lap. Goldie was hunkered down at the fireplace, trying to make coffee.

I had contemplated putting this off until I'd had some sleep, but it was hard to look at Enid and imagine sleeping. In all probability I wouldn't be able to sleep anyway until I'd at least gotten a handle on the legal issues. There was a mystical part of me that hoped I might ingest the contents of Enid's contract while my very literal consciousness was half asleep, then digest it while I was *fully* asleep.

Maybe, I told myself, half seriously, I would dream the answer. My dreams had not been terribly productive lately, although they were predictable. Inevitably, I would find myself in a maze that seemed to be made of wet or oily glass. The maze was dark and full of cryptic, disturbing sounds that shredded the senses. Its thick walls seemed to ripple and pulse as if alive.

I always started out leading Goldie, Doc, and Colleen through the maze, while I whispered or shouted, "Follow me!" at intervals. But at some point I'd turn around and realize they were no longer behind me. I could only hear their voices, nearly buried in all the other voices and sounds. They'd call my name and plead with me to find them, but the walls of the maze closed in and the glistening corridors went on and on, and though I turned this way and that, I never came any closer to finding anyone.

In the past few nights a new element had entered the nightmare: through the translucent walls of this stygian fortress, I could see a vague, glowing form. It seemed to shadow me as I searched, becoming clearer and closer. At length I would see that it was a flare, and that the flare was Tina. I would throw myself at the glass, trying to break it, while she pressed herself against it as if, like light, she might pass through.

The dream would end with us face-to-face, separated by viscous, cold translucence. Her face was a wraith-blur behind the glass, pale and distorted. Her eyes were no more than deep smudges of shadow, and though her mouth moved, it was the others I heard, still crying out to me to find them.

" 'Earth control to Major Tom,' " Goldie sang, practically in my ear.

My weary nerves failed to leap. "Hey," I said.

"You've been suspiciously sphinxlike for a very long time. Anything?"

"Goldie, I'm not even sure what I'm looking for."

"I believe 'legal loophole' is the operative term."

"What good would a legal loophole do? This thing's not operating in the same continuum it was written in."

"Ah, yes, and . . ." He perched on the corner of the little table, rocking it. ". . . if the contract is tweaked, then any loopholes in it would be tweaked, too, right?"

I laughed. "You're trying to apply *logic* to the situation?"

"Meaning Goldie doesn't do logic or logic doesn't apply?"

"Meaning, logic doesn't *necessarily* apply."

"Yeah, but I'll bet *twisted* logic does."

He had a point. I gave my faltering attention back to the contract, smoothing the paper. My fingertips left a smear of pale violet light across the page.

"Whoa," said Goldie, and leaned in closer. "Do that again."

I brushed the paper a second time, tracing a line with my fingertips. Where I touched violet, the type glowed and gave up an answering charge of green static.

My skin crawled, my scalp tingled, and hair rose up on the backs of my arms. While I watched, the letters and words began to wriggle as if trying to free themselves of the paper. In a matter of moments the sentence had rearranged itself on the page.

"God," I whispered, "are you seeing this?"

"God's not answering," said Goldie. "But Goldman saw it. Nice light show. What does it mean?"

I read: " 'The Creator hereby agrees that he will know no other Master, nor will he enter into any covenant by which his creation will be employed for the benefit of any entity but his Master, without his Master's express permission.' "

"Pardon me? Where are you reading *that*?" He put his head next to mine and squinted at the page.

I pointed. "Here. Right here. Where the text rewrote itself just now."

"Whoa. Back up. What do you mean, rewrote itself?"

I raked a hand through my hair in frustration. "Just now—the light, the living word. You said you saw—"

"I saw the light; I didn't see . . . Read that again."

I did.

"Okay," he said. "When I look at it, it says: 'The Artist hereby agrees that he will sign no other contracts for his services, nor will he enter into any agreement to perform, record, or write original lyric or music without the express written permission of Management.' "

"Damn. It would sure make me feel a lot better if you could see it, too."

"Why? I'm a nut case, remember?"

"See what?" Enid had padded over to us, quiet as a cat.

I pushed the contract across the table and indicated the passage that was still giving off soft green radiance.

His brows rose. "What language is that?"

"What do you mean?"

He ran his own finger over the passage. "This part, here, is in some weird language I never seen before. What is it?"

In answer, I translated the next passage, whereupon I saw English words that were entirely arcane; Enid saw words that were not even English; Goldie saw the glow of light, but no change in the text.

At least we all saw *something*.

Goldie wasn't content with that. He seemed to go inside himself for a moment, silently chewing his lip. Then he said, "Give me your pen."

"My—"

"Your pen—your *pen!* The one you've been making notes with."

I fished it out of my breast pocket and handed it to him. He took it and laid a hand on the contract, clicking the pen top in a snappy staccato.

Just when I found myself fighting the urge to hum "Black Magic Woman," he chuckled. "Bingo," he said, and read the arcane version of the first clause.

"I don't—"

"Transference. An inanimate object with which power is channeled transfers power. In layman's terms, it rubbed off on me."

"Where did you pick that up?"

"Irrelevant at the moment." He nudged my shoulder. "Come on, Dr. Jones! Decipher the rest of that hieroglyph."

There was a strange creeping sensation in the pit of my stomach, not unlike the day I first stood, solo, in front of a judge. My skin was tingling with something I couldn't name; first the map, now this. I had begun to think I was impervious to the Change. Now, I felt as if it had trailed a cold, slimy finger across my soul, leaving a slug trail.

I took a deep breath and passed my fingertips over the remaining text. The words wove themselves into an arcane tapestry describing an unnatural covenant. A covenant that resulted in nothing more or less than the spiritual bondage of Enid Blindman.

" 'If the Creator should strain or break the bonds of this covenant of blood and spirit without the Master's leave, the consequences shall be upon him, and upon those creatures to whom he binds himself in spells of mist.' "

" 'Like acid and oil on a madman's face,' " Goldie murmured. "So *that's* the backlash—the consequences visited on Enid and the people who hear his music."

"But not all of them," I noticed. "It's random. Or at least inconsistent."

"Spells," repeated Enid, sounding dazed. "It says that? Spells?"

"It says that," I assured him. Which in itself made me wonder how this contract was still binding. I read on, looking for a possible mechanism for Enid's liberation. Near the end of the contract I found one.

" 'If the Creator wishes his release from the bonds of this covenant, he must seek such release from the Master alone. Face-to-face and spirit-to-spirit must the suppliant Creator seek his deliverance in the place where the covenant dwells. The Master, alone, may grant it.' "

I sat back in my chair.

Goldie echoed the movement, making the table groan. He let out a low whistle.

"The Master," repeated Enid. "That'd be Howard?"

"Presumably. I wonder if he's even aware of what's happened to this contract."

"I dunno. Howard's kind of a shithead capitalist sometimes, but he's not *mean*."

"You mean he wasn't mean *before*," Goldie observed. "He might've turned into something that'd make a Ferengi look like a Keebler elf."

Enid was nodding rhythmically, as if affirming something whispered by an invisible companion. He looked down at me finally, face set. "I gotta go to Howard. That's what all this means, isn't it?"

Goldie and I exchanged glances. Had I just uncovered something that was going to send us on yet another detour?

I glanced at Magritte, still sleeping peacefully in the arms of gravity, her aura dimmed almost to invisibility. Her flesh no longer glowed; it was merely pale. Her hair was no longer flame; it was merely strawberry blond silk. She looked almost like a normal woman, with little about her of the dryad. She looked completely vulnerable . . . and reminded me forcibly of Tina.

I brought my eyes back to Enid's face. It was more gray than brown and gleamed with a sudden cold sweat.

"That's it, isn't it?" he asked me. "I gotta find Howard and get him to let me use my music the way I want to use it. But how do I do that? What do I say? What's the loophole?"

"There is no loophole," I said. "You don't need one."

"The hell I don't. This thing's sucking the life out of me!"

"When did you sign this contract, Enid?"

"Last February. Why?"

"And did it say any of this stuff about 'spells of mist,' and 'spirits,' and 'covenants' at that time?"

"Hell, no. Think I would've signed it if it did?"

"Well, when you track Howard down—"

"Shit, I don't have to track him down. I *know* where he is."

"How?" Goldie asked.

"You know that little something you got goin' with the Storm? Well, I got something like that goin' with Howard."

I kept my lawyer face on. "Where is he?"

"Chicago. Didn't imagine he'd ever leave. He hasn't."

"Oh, shit." Goldie murmured the words just loud enough for me to hear, then got up and went to the window, arms wrapped around himself as if he'd caught a sudden chill.

I half watched him as I spoke to Enid, wondering if I'd ever be completely at ease with his sudden mood shifts. "Well, what you say to Howard is that this contract is not the same one you signed in February of this year. It's changed. Basic law, Enid: no party may change a contract after it's been signed. This is no longer legally binding."

"Then why's it still eating at me?"

I tapped the release clause.

"So, I gotta meet the little shit on his turf? Well, so be it."

We woke Mary and the others then, in the deep, dark heart of the night, and told them what we'd found. When the telling was over, we sat in silence for a moment, listening to the newly set fire roar in the grate while Doc fed it wood and Colleen poked it into submission.

It was Mary who ended the hush, her eyes on me. "My God, it's like something out of somebody's Book of the Dead. So you think if Enid goes to Howard and confronts him with the changes in the contract, he could get out of it?"

"If this legal twist parodies real law, yes."

"And that will cure him?" She glanced at Enid, worry darkening her eyes. "That will keep these . . . side effects from happening?"

"I can't be sure, but it seems to me it's the only chance he's got. Unless he stops playing music altogether."

Enid stared at me. "I can't do that. Music's in my blood. In my soul. If I stop playing, I lose myself and . . ." His eyes moved to Magritte. "I lose everything, everybody I care about. There's no way in hell I can do that. No, I gotta follow this thing through. I'm going back to Chicago, and I'm gonna settle this—" He hesitated, looking to me again. "Chicago wasn't where you were headed."

"Enid, I'm not exactly sure *where* we're headed. We follow Goldie's lead in that. Chicago may not even be out of our way."

"It's not," said Goldie quietly.

I glanced over at where he sat, perched on the arm of a chair, Magritte hovering beside him. "What? Something about Chicago we should know?"

He shook his head, his eyes on the frayed knee of his jeans. "Don't know."

This was really the wrong time for Twenty Questions. "Did you . . . see something? Hear something? What?"

"Nothing I saw. Or heard. Just . . . a feeling."

"Convenient," murmured Colleen.

Goldie glanced at her, then met my eyes. "Look, if we expect Enid to help us free anybody from the Source, we need to free him first. That puts the Windy City on our itinerary, wouldn't you say?"

He was right; Enid wouldn't survive the trip otherwise.

"And of course, Magritte is going with us." Colleen stirred the fire absently, not looking at us.

"Sure she's going with us," said Enid. "Why wouldn't she go with us?"

Colleen gave the logs a sharp jab. Sparks shot up into the flue. "Because if she does, you'll have to shield her. And if you shield her—"

Magritte's aura flashed azure and violet. "I gotta go with you," she said. "I gotta protect Enid."

"If he doesn't play, there's no reason to protect him," Colleen argued.

"No, you don't understand," Enid said. "If Mags doesn't cover for me, Howard gets control."

I shook my head. "Gets control?"

"Of me. Of my music. He pulls me to him. He . . . Look, you know that old story about the red shoes?"

Know it? I lived with it. I used to tease Tina that she practiced as if she wore those damned slippers and that if she didn't take them off once in a while she was going to dance herself into a coma. "One of my sister's favorite stories," I said. "You put the shoes on, you can't stop dancing."

Enid nodded. "Howard gets a hold of me, I can't stop playing. I can't control what I play. And I can't control what the music does."

"Well, considering what it does when you *do* control it," said Colleen, "that's a damn ugly thought."

Damn ugly. I wondered how many more dire revelations Enid had tucked away in his guitar case.

He sank to the sofa, eyes on his hands. When he spoke, his voice was barely above a whisper. "I've turned trees to glass and rocks to powder. I've turned water to blood and I've made rain burn. And worst of all, I've twisted *people,* and those people *know* what I done to 'em. My songs are supposed to soothe souls. To lift them up. D'you know what it feels like to have them . . ." He lost his voice and struggled to recover it. "I gotta get free of this thing, dammit! I'll do anything to get free of it."

"Well, I always say," said Goldie, "when God opens a door, He closes a window."

Enid ignored him. "Every time I use the music outside the Preserve, I have this dream. There's a chain around my neck and there's a chain on my guitar. And the chain leads to this tower. I try to pull myself off the chain, but the Tower says, 'You can't go, boy. You belong to me. Your songs belong to me and your soul belongs to me. Read it.' And then this wind comes up and the pages of that contract dance all around me while I try to gather them up. But I can't lay a hand on 'em."

A chill from the heart of a Manhattan January had risen up out of my breast. "A tower?" I repeated. "What was it like?"

Other voices echoed mine. "Was it shiny and black?" demanded Colleen, and Doc asked, "Did it glisten, as if wet?"

"Sweet Cherry Garcia." Goldie, half standing, sank back to the arm of his chair, his face ashen.

I could see it in their eyes. "We've *all* dreamed . . ."

Everyone spoke at once, fear and discovery tumbling out into the room. I raised my hands. "One at a time! Doc?"

He nodded, flashing a haunted look, before he turned his face back to the fire. "In my dreams of Chernobyl, the Black Tower is there. It watches everything I do. I, too, wear chains."

"Marionette strings," murmured Colleen. "We're all connected to it by marionette strings and it's making us dance."

Goldie picked at a frayed patch of denim on the leg of his jeans. "I'm inside it. Or maybe it's inside me." He kept his eyes averted. "I try to get out, but there *is* no way out. Except to die."

"I'm inside it, too," I admit. "I'm trying to find Tina, but instead of finding Tina . . . I lose all of you."

"I . . ."

The whisper of sound drew every eye to where Magritte hung, still, in the air next to Goldie. Her usually bright aura seemed smudged and muted, and she had wrapped her arms about herself like a cocoon. She quailed a little under our collective gaze, gliding backward. Goldie reached out a hand to her, stopped just short of touching her. Soft light seemed to pulse between them, or perhaps I imagined it.

"It calls to me in my dreams," she said. "It has my uncle Nathan's voice, and the voice makes pools of black, like oil on a road. I try not to, but I fall into a pool and it gets all over me. It gets inside me." She looked at Goldie then, and I realized that her aura had completely taken him in. "And I drown," she finished.

The fire made sounds that should have been comforting. Then Doc spoke the words we'd all been thinking: "What does it mean? That we're being called? *All* of us? By what? Is this the Source? Or is it something else?"

"It can't be the Source," said Colleen. "The Source is in the West."

"Chicago *is* west," murmured Goldie.

"Yeah, *North*west. You never said it was in the *North*west."

"I never said it wasn't."

I cut across the argument. "*Is* it, Goldie? Is the Source in Chicago? The last time you talked about it, you said something about the Badlands."

"I said, 'what if.' *What if* it's in the Badlands."

"We've all dreamed about the same place. Are we going to find it in Chicago?"

He shook his head. "I wish I knew. But I don't know. I won't know until we're moving again. Maybe it's the Preserve. Maybe it distorts my Source sense just like it distorts the space around it. I don't know. All I know is, I've dreamed of that tower for weeks. In all that time, I never thought of it as an actual place. I thought . . ."

"That it was the Source?" I finished.

"No, that it was *connected* to the Source in some way. That it was . . . um . . . something the Source had put . . . in me."

"Looks to me like it's put something in all of us," said Enid.

"Well," said Colleen, "it really doesn't matter, does it? Either way, we're going to Chicago. Question still remains, if Magritte goes along to protect Enid, how do we protect her?"

"I'm strong," protested Magritte. "I've got real good at jamming the Storm all by myself. Enid's so weak sometimes, I've had to. Besides, you don't have a choice. One way or another, I'm coming with you."

Doc murmured something in Russian and sketched a gesture over his heart. He turned from the hearth. "And I am not," he said.

Colleen stood, poker in hand, staring at him. "What? What are you talking about? Of course you're coming with us."

He kept his eyes on my face. "I am a liability to you, Calvin. Events have conspired to teach me this. This leg . . ." He patted his left thigh. "This leg will not let me go where you need to go. It has refused to heal as I might have wished. I am slow to move and I doubt I could sit a horse all day—"

"Then we'll wait until you're better healed," I said. "We'll rest more often on the road."

He smiled without humor. "You see, already you are planning around my disability. On the road, I would only slow you down, Calvin. At best. And if you face the Source sooner rather than later . . ."

"That's ridiculous. I'm sure we can deal with your—"

"*Perhaps I don't want you to deal with it.*" His voice was harsh, ragged. He took a deep breath and went on in gentler tones. "Soft tissue damage is difficult to recover from. Aggravate it and you take a chance of causing a chronic injury. Something from which there is no recovery." He lowered his eyes. "I have no desire to be a cripple."

"Shit," said Colleen under her breath.

Doc glanced at her, then said, "I shall stay here. Here, I can do something for the good." He turned to Mary. "This place needs an infirmary. While the others go upon this quest, I shall help you build one."

Mary said, "Doc, are you sure?"

"You need a doctor. Enid does not need a doctor. He needs a good lawyer." He gestured at me. "Now he has one."

Mary's eyes moved from Doc to Enid to me. She nodded silently.

Now was the time to say that we had started this journey together and must finish it together. To give words to the sudden realization that Doc had somehow taken over the care and feeding of that tiny, cowering believer in my soul, the one I thought had disappeared with Tina. But I couldn't say any of those things, because to do so would have been the height of selfishness.

I was silent.

Colleen gave the logs a vicious stab, then dropped the poker, scattering ash across the hearth. We locked eyes for a moment, her face frozen in an expression I couldn't begin to read. I expected a sarcastic remark, an outburst of some sort. But she merely brushed past Doc without a glance and left the room.

After a momentary hesitation, he followed.

Goldie pulled the contract out from under my numb hands and handed it to Enid. He made his own exit then, giving my shoulder a light squeeze as he passed me by.

Irrelevantly, I realized he had kept my pen.

THIRTEEN

DOC

She was standing out under the trees behind the Lodge, looking to where, in an ordinary place in a normal world, the sun would eventually rise. I hobbled to her side, but she did not so much as look at me.

A soft wind, carrying the perfume of darkness, curled among the trees and stirred the chimes to song. Night birds chanted somewhere above our heads in branches I could see only as short strokes of midnight against the violet-brushed pewter of the Preserve's perpetual cowl of mist. I listened with her for a time to the muted night music, watched as the moon marked its path in a pale blur across the watercolor sky.

"You are angry with me," I observed finally.

She made an impatient noise. "I'm not . . ."

In the silence, the birds and I waited to hear what she was not.

"I'm not angry with you. That would be childish and stupid."

"Then what?"

"I'm mad at life, at everything. I'm mad at Goldie for seeing that damn portal, and for prying into this place. I'm mad at Cal for following him in here, and I'm mad at me for following Cal. I'm mad at the Source and the government and Fred Wishart for doing all this shit—" She gave the universe a broad gesture of inclusion. "And I'm mad at God for letting them do it."

"I thought you did not believe in God."

"I don't. I'm too mad at Him. It's my way of getting even, I guess." A smile tempted her lips; she spurned it.

"Ah. So I am the only person here you are *not* mad at. And you are pleased I will not be going west with you."

She turned to look at me. "I didn't say that."

"Then what *did* you say?"

Her breath sailed out on a banner of steam and she dropped to the grass, arms wrapped about her knees. "All right, dammit. I'm mad at you. There, are you happy?"

I lowered myself down next to her, taking great care to keep my left leg straight. "No. And you are mad at me because . . . ?"

"Does it matter?"

"To me, yes. It disturbs me to have friends angry with me. Even if their anger is justified . . . or perhaps most especially so."

"So, you think I'm *right* to be mad at you."

"No, not right. I merely meant your anger is understandable. But you were going to tell me why I have earned it. Surely, you understand why I am staying." I rubbed my knee.

"And that's supposed to make it easier? Okay, Viktor, look: I'm a hick from the sticks. Horses, I get. Nature, I get. People, relationships, that sort of thing—I *don't* get. Not since Dad died." She picked up a long twig from the ground and began to strip it of its bark. "I . . . depended on Dad. He was . . . the foundation of my safe little world. When he died, the world crumbled and I was alone. I've been alone ever since. Until now."

"Your mother was still alive, I thought."

She laughed—a sharp, unpleasant sound. "If you could call it that. I was never as close to Mom as I was to Dad, but our relationship was okay. Better than okay. I loved her and I thought she loved me. But after he died, everything I did was wrong. Everything I said. I was too tomboyish. Too much like a guy—"

"Too much like your father, perhaps?"

She looked as if I had punched her and left her breathless. "Whoa. Wow . . . Now that you mention it, yeah. She said that a lot: 'You're just like your father.' I started to wonder why she'd ever loved him at all if he had so many flaws. You're saying I was . . ."

"Your father's ghost."

She pondered that for a moment. "Now, that would explain a lot."

"Sometimes," I said, "we fool ourselves into thinking that a cold, hard shell around the heart will protect it from the fire of grief. Perhaps it can, though I have doubts. I do know that such a shell can also protect the heart from the warmth of other things: love, joy, closeness."

She turned to look at me again. "Who's that aimed at, Doc? Me, Mom . . . or you?"

I smiled. "Just a hick from the sticks, eh?"

"Yeah, okay. I'm not *that* dense. It's too little, too late, but I guess I understand that Mom was just dealing with her grief the same way I was. Badly."

"Too little, too late?"

"She died about eleven years ago. Cancer." She poked the now naked twig into the mat of leaves, grass, and cedar needles on which we sat. "I guess what I'm most mad about is that I've let myself get attached to other people for the first time in years."

Odd. What sparked anger in Colleen touched me only with a warm, bittersweet sorrow. "I, too, am attached, Colleen. But I am not parting company with you forever. And you will still have Cal and Goldie. You are, I think, especially attached to Cal."

Now, she looked away from me down the hill. Shadows flirted in the underbrush and danced counterpoint to nodding boughs and singing chimes. "Yenta," she said.

Surprised into mirth, I laughed. "Yenta?"

"I learned it from Goldie."

"But, I am right, of course."

She didn't answer directly, but shrugged and said, "I don't know what to think of Cal. I'm . . . attracted to him. I admire him . . . a lot. He's a great guy . . . a good man. But sometimes I feel like I have more in common with you or Goldman, if you can believe it. Cal and I are so . . . so terminally different."

"They say that opposites attract."

"Uh-huh. But he's such a . . . such a square peg, you know? He's the kind of guy I try to *avoid*. All that white knight crap, true-blue, honor-driven, stand-up . . ." She shook her head. "That's for clingy bimbos. I can take care of myself."

"I would not argue that point. Except to say that in every human being's life there will be times they need other people. As Cal needs you and Goldie and Enid to help him find Tina."

"He needs Goldie and Enid. He needs *you*. Why does he need me?"

"You are the rock, remember?"

Her twig speared a leaf. "Oh, yeah. How could I forget?" She pulled the unfortunate leaf from the sharpened twig and crumbled it in her hand. "This is gonna sound weird, and I'm not sure it makes any sense, but here it is: I do have feelings for Cal. But at the same time, it seems like—when it comes to this team of ours—I'm the odd man out."

"Perhaps this is because you are a woman?"

"Don't be funny."

"I would never."

"I feel . . . isolated. Okay, okay—" She raised her hands in a gesture of surrender. "I isolate myself. I get that. But what I don't get is that somehow, in spite of that, you make me fit."

Now it was my turn to be startled. I understood what she had said about attachment. I understood her fear of it. And I had begun to suspect that I had stepped into the void of her father's absence. But that I somehow reacted with her as if we were two chemicals, that I had not considered.

"It isn't me, Colleen," I said. "You make yourself fit."

She shook her head, brandishing the twig as if it were a pointer. "Uh-uh. No, no, Doc. This time I got you. Goldie thinks I'm a freak of nature, and he's probably right. Hell, I even scare myself sometimes. Cal . . . I don't know what Cal thinks. But you—*you* accept me, as is. Which sometimes feels really good and sometimes makes me damned uncomfortable. And you know why? Because you make me *think* about myself. About who I am and what I'm doing. And why I'm doing it. Like right now. You keep me honest." She turned her face toward me and her eyes filled with the moon's ghost-light. Even so, I could not see all the way to the bottom of them. "When you're gone, Viktor, who'll keep me honest?"

"You will keep yourself honest, Colleen," I told her. "Because Cal will need your honesty."

She nodded and flipped the twig end over end into the night. "Yeah? Well, I think he *deserves* yours." She turned on me, her eyes glittering in the moonlight. "Why are you *really* doing this? Staying behind. You're not afraid of being crippled. That's the biggest load of crap I've ever heard."

Stunned, I shoved words from my mouth. "What I told Cal—"

"You told Cal shit. Don't think I didn't notice how careful you were to not say anything that was an outright lie. And you're not afraid of dying, either. You've faced death over and over with us. *With* us," she repeated fiercely. "What is it, Doc? What *are* you afraid of?"

I couldn't answer her immediately. The words simply would not come. When they did, it was with great difficulty. "I am very afraid of death, Colleen."

"Oh, bull—"

I grasped her shoulder. "Listen to me. Perhaps I am not afraid of dying, but I live in constant fear of causing death. Even before this injury I was a liability. At Grave Creek you and Goldie threw yourselves into danger to rescue *me*. At the mounds, at the mill . . . I was an albatross, over and over putting the rest of you in harm's way. How many times can I do that before the worst happens?"

"I suppose as many times as the rest of us are around to bail you out."

"You should not have to 'bail me out,' as you put it."

"Why not? You do the same thing for us." She patted her ribs. "I have a neat little row of stitches to prove it."

"It is different with me."

"How? How different? What—the rest of us are allowed mistakes, but you're not? The rest of us can limp along, but you can't?"

"Colleen, if I were to be responsible for harm coming to any of you . . ." I shook my head. "I can face death. I could not face that."

"I see." She sat in silence for a moment, arms wrapped around her knees, staring into the darkness. "Are you going to tell Cal the truth?"

"Cal would not accept the truth any more than you have."

She turned to look at me again. "He *shouldn't* accept it. Don't do this, Doc. *Please* don't do this. We're weaker without you than with you. You could bung up both legs and that'd still be true."

I had no reply. I could only wallow in keen awareness that this hurt more than I had expected.

She studied me a moment longer, then put one arm around me in a swift, fierce embrace. It was a gesture I did not expect and it stunned me anew.

She stood, brushed off her jeans and jacket and looked down at me. "You look like hell, Viktor. Get some sleep."

I sat and listened to the rhythmic tread of her feet, solid and sure on the earth. Then I rose to do as she commanded.

"It's amazing how fast those soft tissue injuries can heal up, isn't it?"

Cal's voice caught me in mid-stride, freezing me. He stepped from the shadows beneath the boughs of a tall cedar, blocking my path up the hill, his eyes pointedly on my left knee.

"Well, Doc, aren't you happy? You just got up out of a crouch without using your hands. And you didn't even wince. That's got to be a miracle, right?" He took a step toward me. "Or not."

"And how long were you standing there?" I asked.

"Let's assume I was standing there a long time. You have something you want to tell me about your leg?"

I couldn't see his expression, but I knew I had no further room for evasion. "My leg is fine. It barely even aches. My leg . . . is not the issue."

"I didn't think so. You know, I never would've taken you for a superstitious man."

"I am not—" I protested.

"An albatross? What is that, if not rank superstition? Colleen's right, we've all needed help. We've all done things that put others in danger. That's not likely to change. She's also right that we're weaker without you, no matter what condition you're in." He held his hand out to me, his eyes holding mine. "Come with us, Doc. *Please.*"

When I hesitated, he said it again: "*Please.*"

I gave in, clasping the hand he offered, feeling a strange mixture of dread, gratitude, and relief. "I do this against my better judgment."

"So noted."

He turned and started up the hill. I fell into step with him. We had gone only a few strides when he said, "She called you 'Viktor.' "

"That is my name."

"You never told me."

"You never asked."

He was silent for a few strides, then said, "Sorry. I should have."

FOURTEEN

CAL

"Hey," I said.

Colleen looked up from her fletcher's task, a half-finished cross-bow bolt in one hand, a roll of thin leather binding in the other.

Terminally different. That was where I'd come in last night. Were we really? I hoped not.

Between her and her able assistant, Matt, the resident weapon-maker, a pile of bolts and longer arrows grew on the table in the leather shop's large, tourist-friendly workroom. We would not lack for armaments on the next leg of our journey.

"Hey, yourself," she said. "Give us a hand?"

I hesitated. A request from Colleen for help was extraordinary in itself; the idea that she'd let me handle the ordnance was doubly so. I was a good swordsman (with high school and college fencing tro-phies to prove it), but she openly despaired of the way I handled the complexities of archery.

"You're sure?"

She glanced at Matt (usually called Young Matt, to distinguish him from his father, Old Matt), and pointed at the bundles of stripped and smoothed wooden shafts that needed to be turned into deadly projectiles. "You wanna get out of here any time soon?"

I sat down at the table. "What do I do?"

She pulled a longish shaft out of a bundle and held it out to me. "You take that very, very sharp knife and you cut a notch yay deep in one end of the shaft." She ticked a mark across the shaft with her thumbnail. "Then you cut three slits yay long . . ." She scored the other end of the shaft vertically. ". . . around this end. Equally spaced. Use the razor blade gadget there for that. And if you cut yourself, please don't bleed on the binding. Liquid makes it stretchy, and we don't want it to get stretchy just yet."

Young Matt stifled a chuckle and squinted at the arrowhead he was attaching.

"I won't cut myself," I promised.

I don't know what Cal thinks, she'd said. What I thought was that even with shorn hair, she was beautiful, the way a wild mountainside is beautiful. More than that, she was vital. Strong. Capable.

Colleen smiled and went back to slipping sharp, nasty-looking bits of metal into the notches she'd cut in her crossbow bolts. "Talk to Doc since last night?" she asked, eyes on her work.

"You mean since he dropped his little bombshell?"

She peered intently at her wrapping job. Apparently satisfied, she set the barb aside. "Yeah, that. Did you . . . ?"

"We talked."

She gave me a sudden, sharp glance. "Well, is he coming with us or not? Because I can't believe you'd let him get away with faking that bum knee and that crappy attitude. And I told him that . . . more or less." She fell silent for a beat. "Well? What did you say to him?"

I blinked at her, wanting to laugh, forcing my face to remain solemn. "I told him . . . he wasn't an albatross."

She stared at me for a moment, then lowered her eyes. "Oh, you heard all that. So you understood what he was doing."

"Yeah, faking a limp."

Colleen swatted at me with a length of leather thong. "That wasn't what I meant. I meant the *reason* he was faking the limp." She leaned across the table toward me and lowered her voice as if it might keep Matt from overhearing. "God, Cal, I swear he actually thinks he's going to get us killed. Like he's a—a jinx, or something. Like what happened with—" She broke off, flushed, and shook her head.

"Like what happened with what?"

She shook her head again. "Nothing. Um . . . just, you know what happened at the mill with the dam. All that. He has a clumsy moment and turns it into a disaster."

Colleen is a terrible liar. I reached over and stopped the movement of her hands. "That's not what you meant. What were you about to say?"

She looked down at our entwined fingers. "Nothing I should've." After a moment she glanced at Matt, then back to me. "Has Doc ever talked to you about Chernobyl? Or his family?"

"I know he lost his family. And yes, he told me he was at Chernobyl. It must have been horrific. Are the two things connected?"

She gazed at me unfocused for a moment, then said, "He felt like he didn't make a difference then. Like he was in the wrong place at the wrong time. Here, in the Preserve, he *can* make a difference." She shrugged. "I guess that's really what he's all about. Making a difference. Making . . . choices." Her voice seemed to die in her throat.

"What?"

She shook herself visibly, looked down at her work and said, "Just a little lightbulb going on in Colleen's head. So, what did you say to him?"

I tapped the fist she'd knotted around one of the pencil-thin dowels. "Aren't you afraid you're going to break that?"

"Don't be a shit, Griffin. What did you *say* to him?"

"Sorry. I told him you were right."

She sat back and looked at me wryly. "Really. Oh, well, I'm sure *that* changed his mind." She wet a binding and began wrapping it around the notched joint between barb and shaft.

"Actually, it did." I glanced at the contents of the table. "What are you planning on using for feathers?" I asked Matt, aware that Colleen's eyes were making holes in the side of my head.

"Whatever's lying around." He pulled a basket of junk out from under the table. It contained a motley collection of actual feathers, plastic playing cards, business cards, and other junk. "Feathers," he said.

"Very eclectic."

He shrugged, smiling. "Works."

Colleen's hand clamped firmly over mine. "Back up! Doc isn't staying? You talked him out of it?"

I looked up and met her eyes, and the breath stopped in my throat.

I was suddenly aware of every sensation in my body—the quickening pulse, the tingle of subtle electricity on my skin, heat warming my face, other, more intimate responses.

What do you mean, I'm a square peg?

I had a vague impression of Matt glancing back and forth between us before bending back to his work. Colleen's smile went from bright to bashful, as if we were two kids at a high school dance and I'd just asked her for the next waltz. Then her eyes shifted away from mine toward the door to the outer room.

"Oh," she said.

I followed her gaze. Doc stood in the open doorway, a fat backpack in his hands. Something passed between them, swift as thought—a secret conversation that made my ears burn. I felt myself flushing.

The moment passed and Doc raised the pack. "I have finished the med-kits. We will have two."

Colleen got up to take the bag and pretended to stagger under its weight. "Jeez, Doc! I hope you didn't rob Peter to pay Paul."

"Pardon? Oh, no. Cherise said they could well afford this. They have already a good collection of basic supplies. They lack organization."

"Not for long," she said. "I'm sure you'll have that infirmary up and running in no time. Then you'll be bored stiff."

Doc looked past her to me. "You didn't tell her?"

"He told me. I was faking. But you're the expert at that, aren't you?" There was another silent exchange, at the end of which Colleen punched Doc lightly on the shoulder. "Albatross."

⚜

We spent the next several days prepping for the journey. While Colleen marshaled supplies and decided how to distribute them among pack and saddle horses, I plotted our route, compulsively checked and rechecked the mechanics of the chime system, and worried about what would happen to Magritte when we stepped out of the safe confines of the Preserve. That was a question we still had no real answer to, other than Maggie's repeated assurances that she was stronger than the other flares and better able to protect herself from the Source. Having seen how she'd been the day we lost Faun, I was hopeful, but not certain.

Doc spent his time doing what he could in the Preserve's small infirmary, giving Cherise and her two volunteer nurses pointers on everything from dosages to the fine art of surgical stitchery.

Enid rested for the most part, though he did open the portals to allow foraging parties in and out. If they were going to be cut off from the outside for any length of time, Mary's little community was going to need all the food, seed, and other supplies that could be brought in.

It was Goldie who concerned me most. In the days leading up to our planned departure, I saw him so rarely, I began to think he was a figment of my imagination. The one opportunity I had to talk to him, he artfully dodged me.

He was cheerfully stuffing his face in the dining hall one morning when I wandered in, feeling like reheated animal protein. Despite the early hour, the place was buzzing with activity as Olentangians lined up at the fruit and grain bar for breakfast, chattering like a bunch of tourists on holiday. Only the snatches of conversation I caught informed me that their concerns were more pressing than any tourist's.

Goldie had parked himself at one end of a laden trestle from which he was snatching random food items.

"Well, if it isn't Goldini the Magnificent, Master Escape Artist," I said.

He bowed deeply from the waist and performed a flourish with a tortilla-filled hand. "My fame precedes me," he mumbled around a mouthful.

"So, what have you been up to?"

"Busy."

"Busy. Doing what?"

"Stuff."

"Stuff."

"Is there an echo in here? Stuff—you know, things to do. Don't nudje, I'm keeping myself busy." He moved away from the food toward a less occupied corner of the room.

I picked up a muffin of some sort from a large ceramic bowl and followed him. The muffin was an unappetizing shade of green, but tasted of berries and honey.

"That's not the point," I said. "I was hoping we could all be highly productive during our last days here."

"Who says I haven't been productive?"

"Goldie—"

"I told you, I've been busy. Productively so, in fact. Now stop sounding like my father, okay? You're scaring me."

A hint of annoyance had slipped into his voice, and I realized he looked about as tired as I felt. Dark circles and lines of strain stood out around his eyes.

"Fine. Just tell me what you're doing."

He took a last bite of tortilla and washed it down with a swig of the local tea before setting his cup on a bus cart. "Say, did Colleen mention that there's a portal north of here on Lake Erie?"

I stumbled over the change of direction. "Uh, Magritte mentioned it, actually. Someplace called Put-in-Bay?"

"Yeah. I guess Mary considered moving the whole Preserve up there because it's so isolated, but the weather is too inclement; the Veil can only do so much."

"And you mention this at this juncture because . . . ?"

He grinned. "Well, um, partly to sidestep the issue of what I've been doing, and partly because I noticed when I was up there with Colleen that the weather is really, really bad outside the Preserve and I think we'll need to be better prepared for that." He caught his breath and added, "We've got a lot of ground to cover—a couple of states worth."

He'd succeeded in distracting me, at least momentarily. "This northern portal, is there any way we could use it to get closer to Chicago?"

"Yeah, but there's this little problem."

"Which is?"

"A lot of very deep, very cold water. Put-in-Bay is an island, re-member? Accessible only by airplane or ferry."

"Or rowboat?"

He flashed another grin. "Two words. Winter. Great Lakes."

"That's three words."

He shrugged. "Gotta go." He started for the door.

"Whoa! Whoa! Where are you going?"

"I'm late for my flute lesson," he said, not even slowing, and was gone.

Under other circumstances the whole scene might have been

funny, but under *these* circumstances it made me uneasy. Was Goldie slipping out of touch with reality into some sort of manic episode? If he was . . .

I stopped the train of thought. There was no time for it now and too much to do.

During that last week, the weather turned decidedly colder even within the protected precincts of the Preserve. Mary made certain we were well-provisioned with warm clothing, blankets, dry kindling, and other necessities of winter travel, but I was still uneasy. We had hundreds of miles of open terrain to cover in a midwestern winter, which I had every reason to believe would be even harsher with the Change. And through it all, we would be taking the chance that at any moment Enid would have to start "jamming" to keep Magritte safe.

I shook off a tremor of real fear and put my mind to the business of preparation.

Mary had maps. I got one and did the math. Assuming that Chicago was where we'd left it, we were looking at about a 250-mile trek, as the crow flies. None of us being crows, and given that we'd no doubt have to take evasive action to skirt Indianapolis, the journey could easily exceed three hundred miles. At an average of twenty to thirty miles per day, that gave us road time of ten days or more. At last report from the northern portal, it had begun to snow.

Almost against my will, I also checked the map for "anomalies." They abounded. There was some sort of ragged edge around Indianapolis. What it was, I couldn't tell, but I had a sharp if fanciful vision of the city perched on a towering scarp, below which wild rivers raged. Or at least I assumed they raged; under my fingertips, they felt just as the Ohio had, rough and spiky.

I decided the best route would be to take Highway 317 northwest, swinging far to the north of Indianapolis and passing close to towns with such charming names as Arcanum and Nineveh. I found myself wondering if the Biblical story of Jonah was neither myth nor metaphor, but rather the way the world operated then. Maybe a man could live inside a giant fish. Maybe there was a God—one with a peculiar sense of poetic justice. And maybe the Source was something that had always been with us. Something that had just been trapped in another dimension for uncounted centuries, or locked up in a celestial prison house until human intervention had caused an inopportune jailbreak. Maybe Jonah had known the Source and simply called it by a different name.

I straightened from my map reading. "Doc, you're pretty familiar with the Bible, right?"

He glanced over at me from where he sat, cutting various sized bandages from freshly washed but irregular hunks of fabric. "I am familiar with it, yes."

"Isn't there something in the Revelation of Saint John about God locking Satan up someplace and then letting him loose at the end of the age to torment the world?"

His gray gaze was contemplative and level. "That is metaphor, my friend. The seemingly simple words speak a complex truth, which they can either illuminate or obscure, depending upon who reads them."

"And how do you read them?"

"I understand them to mean that what torments the world is man's insatiable thirst for control."

I nodded. "I guess the prophecy applies either way, doesn't it? It sure seems as if someone let Satan out of jail."

"I thought you were plotting our course." This came from Colleen, who was bundling barbs and arrows on the floor near where Doc sat. "What's that got to do with the devil?"

I rubbed my eyes, feeling suddenly light-headed. "Must be getting punchy. Maybe I'll take a break."

"Good timing!"

Goldie entered the cabin on a wave of kinetic energy, rubbing his hands together fast enough to make static.

"I was just going to suggest that you *all* take a break and come for a little walk underground."

His face was flushed; his eyes were overbright, and for a moment I had the sickening thought that he was on something, or worse. He stopped in front of me and I realized that his jeans were soaked from the knees down.

"Well, don't everybody move at once. Just line up in alphabetical order and file politely out the door." He made a shooing gesture with both hands.

"Where would we be going on this little walk?" Colleen asked, not even preparing to move.

"I told you: underground. There's something I want you to see." He imitated a praying mantis again and giggled. "You're gonna love this."

I exchanged glances with Doc and Colleen. Both looked uneasy. Doc rose slowly and put his bandages aside. Colleen, taking the cue from him, followed suit.

"Please, show us," Doc said, and smiled.

Goldie rolled his eyes, shook his head and laughed. "Jeez, you guys are a piece of work. Fine, if thinking that poor old Goldman is about to leap out of his head will get you into the caves any faster, so be it. Walk this way."

He did a creditable Igor, hunching his back and dragging one foot behind.

I wasn't sure whether I was supposed to laugh or cry, so I did neither. I just followed, Colleen and Doc close on my heels.

Ten yards from the door of the cabin, Goldie straightened and shook himself all over. "Man, that gets old fast. How'd Feldman do that through an entire movie?"

He cocked a glance back over his shoulder. "Oh, there you are." He crooked a finger and took off again.

Down in the cavern, he led us through the Indian Council Chamber, then took a left-hand passage rather than the more or less straight-ahead one that led to the Adena portal. After a silent walk of about twenty yards or so we came to another branching of the ways. Again Goldie took the left-hand trail.

Colleen, just behind me, tapped my shoulder and whispered, "This is the one that goes to Put-in-Bay cave."

Goldie turned back with a finger to his lips. "Ssshhh."

"Now he thinks he's a librarian," muttered Colleen.

"Quiet, Miss Brooks," said Goldie. "We don't want to do detention, do we?"

Colleen fell back, muttering obscenities under her breath.

Yards of faerie-lit tunnel slid by around us and I found myself internally oohing and ahing at the sheer beauty of the glittering rock formations. God's jewel box. Another passage opened up in the left arm of a Y junction. The lights continued to the right; Goldie ducked under a diamond-studded curtain of limestone and forged into the darkness of the leftmost branch.

I hesitated.

Behind me Colleen protested, "Goldman, you lose your compass or something? It's that way."

A shower of gold light cascaded down the left-hand passage from Goldie's hand and rolled into the junction where the rest of us stood in confusion.

"Nope. It's this way." He beckoned, releasing the ball of light into the moist air, then turned and led on, a second tweaked lantern floating above his head.

The passage twisted and turned a bit, then opened up into a huge, sandy-bottomed chamber from which I could hear the gurgle of running water. The golden light did not touch the walls on the far side of the room, giving some indication of its size, but it sparkled like stars in the waters of a tiny lake.

It was into this body of water that Goldie plunged up to his knees. He splashed across to the other side, where Kevin Elk Sings sat cross-legged on the floor, flute in hand, wearing the same gray look of exhaustion that Goldie did beneath his flush of excitement. Mary McCrae stood behind him, looking bemused. Magritte hovered at her shoulder. Goldie's light globes and smaller, starlike motes of gold floated about them, casting luminescence over the glistening floor.

"Good, you're here," said Mary. "Cal, do you have any idea what this is about? They're all being annoyingly mysterious."

I shook my head. "I haven't got a clue."

"I am not wading through that," announced Colleen from behind me.

"It's the only way across without going all the way to the end of the chamber," said Goldie. His voice echoed strangely off the walls.

I sighed and plowed through the flood, gritting my teeth against the bone-jarring cold. On the other side I found myself facing a curving wall of pale flowstone that glittered as if set with jewels. It blended upward into a vaulted ceiling that was lost in the void.

"Okay," said Goldie, "everybody stand just so." He arranged us all in a semicircle behind Kevin. "Maestro?" Goldie nodded to Kevin, who rose in a single, fluid movement and began to play.

The melody was familiar, but twisted. Appropriate, I suppose. It took a moment for me to recognize it as a piece from the Who's rock opera, *Tommy*. Rolling out of Kevin's flute, it had an ageless quality, as if generations of Lakota Sioux might have played it.

At almost the precise moment I placed the song, Goldie's face lit up in a brilliant smile and Kevin began to move toward the wall, still playing. He strode up to the wall and stepped through it as if through a curtain of stars. The music echoed momentarily, then faded.

"Pretty slick, huh?" Goldie asked.

It was, indeed, pretty slick. "Uh, yeah," was the best I could manage.

Mary put a hand over her mouth, her eyes wide. "Kevin did that? Himself?"

The music faded back in and Kevin reappeared. He stopped playing the moment he was clear of the wall. Behind him the stars winked out.

Goldie, Mary, and Magritte broke into spontaneous applause, and Kevin bowed, grinning and flourishing his flute.

"Now," said Goldie, "the really slick part. Kev is going to take you all through the portal."

He did, too. Instead of passing entirely through the sparkling wall, he stood, half in and half out, and literally changed his tune. The wall no longer seemed quite solid. It looked like a slightly cheesy special effect I'd seen in countless old science fiction films—a filmy veil of sequins through which our heroes would step into . . . ?

We passed through gingerly—like a bunch of cats on snow—and emerged into another cave. Silvery light poured down onto us from somewhere up a gently sloping passage.

I hesitated a moment, then climbed up and into the light with Mary beside me. A cold wind slashed through my wet jeans and sucked the air out of my lungs. Tiny ice crystals brushed my face and swirled in little eddies over the ground. Visibility was poor, but in the murky distance I could see that we were surrounded by a group of hillocks.

The others emerged behind us and stood gazing about.

"I'm confused," I admitted. "These can't be the Adena mounds."

"Blue Mounds," said Kevin. "About twenty miles southwest of Madison, Wisconsin."

"Madison? Damn." Colleen was obviously impressed.

"So, have I been productive enough?" Goldie asked me.

I opened my mouth to answer, then realized Magritte had come through the portal with us and was treading air near Goldie. The chill wind moved into my heart. "Should she be out here?" I asked him.

Goldie's smile didn't reach his eyes. "She has to come out here, Cal. She doesn't have a choice."

I watched the expression on Magritte's face as she glided a little farther from the mouth of the cave, was aware that Goldie's eyes were on her, too. "Do you feel . . . anything?" I asked. "Hear anything?"

She nodded. "I hear it—the Storm. Like far-off wind."

"Does it hear you?"

"Maybe not yet, but it will."

Goldie took a step closer to her and for a moment they seemed to be enveloped in a veil of light. I'd seen the effect before, and thought Magritte's aura had simply expanded to take in Goldie. Now my imagination tried to tell me that Goldie had a faint aura of his own.

"Right now we're in a sacred place," said Kevin. "There's power here. Outside . . ." He shrugged and fingered the flute.

"Let's go back into the cave," said Goldie. "I'm freezing my ass off out here." He turned back, Magritte moving in unison with him. The aqua-gold halo remained intact.

Back in the comparative warmth of the cavern, Goldie stepped us through his trail of discovery. "It hit me the day the Storm got in—at the waterwheel. Kev's music allowed me to see the . . . the patterns of power around the water. When I touched the flute, I could see the same patterns around other objects. Even after he stopped playing, I could see them just by touching the flute. I realized the same thing happened, to one degree or another, whenever I picked up one of Kevin's or Delmar's ceremonial artifacts."

"Transference," I said. "You talked about that when we were trying to figure out Enid's contract."

He pulled my Parker out of his jacket pocket and clicked it. "This," he said, "is how we figured out where that portal ends up. Transference. You have this little thing going with maps. Kevin can see portals. In fact, he found this portal himself. I sat him down in front of it with a map and this pen. It was kind of like dowsing. The transference allowed him to sense where on the map this puppy opened up."

"We transferred the ability to open portals the same way," Kevin said. "Goldie learned to play my flute well enough to—how to de-scribe it—endow a tune and then the flute itself with—well, 'Gold-ieness,' I guess you'd call it."

Colleen snorted.

"Hey, don't laugh," said Goldie. "It works. Like I've always said, a little Goldie goes a long way. It took a lot of woodshedding, but I got to where I could play the portal open with Kev's flute. Then he took over and worked until *he* could play it open."

"I thought you couldn't do sound," I said.

"Ah!" he raised a finger. "True. I *can't* do sound. But I *could* visu-alize the notes. I converted them into light." He laughed. "I can con-vert music to photons! They couldn't even do that on *Star Trek*. All they could do was make Tachyon fields."

"Yeah," said Colleen, "but at least their Tachyon fields always work."

I shot Colleen a glance. *Don't step on him. Not now.* "You said you used a map," I said to Goldie. "You still have it?"

Goldie pulled it out of his jacket pocket and handed to me. I un-folded it, found the Blue Mounds, and traced the path southeast toward Chicago. I looked up at the others.

"Thanks, Kevin. This little discovery is going to cut our trip just about in half."

It should have been the best sleep I'd had for weeks. We were moving on, after all. Together. With a real chance of finding the Source, and a means of protecting Tina from it and bringing her to a place she could be safe. There was even a chance we could do more than that with Enid's ability.

During daylight hours I did a pretty decent impersonation of a man who'd come to accept all the weirdness. But at night, when no one was looking, I could easily imagine that a team of gerbils went into full throttle in my head, their little wheels spinning madly until they exhausted themselves.

This was the stuff of which dreams were made.

Pause, rewind, replay. The gerbils reeled out half-waking dreams of sequined portals with musical keys, sonic shields run by wind chime batteries, and legal jargon that resulted in toxic songs. Goldie saw "patterns of power" when Kevin played his flute. Richard Dreyfus looked at a pile of mashed potatoes and said, "This is important."

I thought about flares.

I wasn't sure—I couldn't be sure—but I suspected that what the Source wanted flares for was power. What was it Magritte had said: it used them up, bit by bit.

The way a flashlight uses up batteries.

The gerbils chugged along, trying to carry me toward an epiphany while I strained toward sleep and mumbled, "I don't get it."

The Quran, so Goldie tells me, records how Muhammad received his revelation from God through the archangel Gabriel. The angel visited the Prophet-to-be in his cave on Mount Hira, held out a book and said, "Read." Muhammad, being illiterate, could not read, and told Gabriel as much. Three times Gabriel commanded Muhammad to read, and three times, the Prophet said, "I cannot." Then, miraculously, he read. He got it.

There was no commanding angel in my dream; there was only Kevin Elk Sings, failing to play a dam and succeeding in playing a key. There was no gleaming holy book; only a contract that slithered with tweaked legalese. There was no nation-building Prophet; only a Manhattan Pharisee, doggedly trying to read—to "get it."

It took me more than three tries, to be honest, but as I dipped into an exhausted sleep, I had read a word. And the word was "analogues."

All of the warped abilities with their strange new connections were *analogues* for the things the Change had voided. They were machineries. They didn't work exactly as the old machineries had, but they worked in a parallel fashion. While material physics no longer applied, we now had a new physics—a physics of imagination.

In the old physics, there were laws. If you knew how to apply them, you could make things happen—internal combustion, electricity, nuclear fission. I was willing to bet the new physics had laws, too. The trick was in application.

Albert Einstein had been a prodigy of the old physics. Somewhere between here and our final destination, we had to become prodigies of the new.

FIFTEEN

DOC

W ind. An arctic wind, full of rain that could quickly turn to ice. That was the substance of our world. It blew horizontal to the ground, stinging as if made of microscopic shards of glass. I was transported to the Russian hinterland and knew not even an atom of homesickness.

The low tent in which we spent our nights shuddered like a drunkard forced to sobriety, fabric popping loudly enough to wake a deaf man. But not Goldie. And, as if to challenge the wind, Goldie snored.

Somewhere near dawn on this, our third day on the road to Chicago, I decided to take my chances in the open, got up and dragged my sleeping bag out to where our night watch huddled in the lee of an outcrop of rock.

"What are you doing up?" Cal asked, his voice only just audible above the railing of the wind.

"I find myself unable to sleep with the noise."

"The wind?"

I nodded. "Yes, that too."

Cal chuckled and glanced at his watch, a venerable mechanical device—the only kind that works in our new world. "Well, it's pretty close to morning anyway. Not that you can tell from that penlight on the horizon. Everything all right in the tent?"

He meant Magritte, of course. Since we had left the relative safety of the Blue Mounds, she had lived in a state of unease, expecting that at any moment the Source would pounce on her. But it had not. She could hear it, she told us, had to distract herself, steel herself against it, but the call was muted. "Like I'm hearing it from inside a bubble," she'd said.

Still, we resorted to physical restraint at night—she was literally tethered to Enid in the event the Source should break through her "bubble," forcing him to sing. He had gone only days without blocking the Source, and already I could see improvement in his health. The grayish cast was gone from his skin and he slept soundly, which was more than I could say for myself.

"Things are quiet," I said to Cal, "after a fashion. At least, everyone else is asleep."

I peered into the unrelieved charcoal gray of the Wisconsin landscape. Sunrise, we already knew, would bring little real relief from the gloom. Wisconsin seemed to be perpetually in twilight. "You were raised in Minnesota, yes?" I asked.

"Uh-huh."

"And Minnesota is near Wisconsin, yes?"

"You could say that."

"Are autumns usually this harsh?"

Cal tilted his head within the hood of his anorak. A banner of steam marked the movement before being stretched and flayed by the wind, and I wondered, irrelevantly, if we would ever again see a jet's vapor trail. This led to the unwelcome memory that hundreds, even thousands, of people must have been aloft at the moment the Source exchanged our universal constants for its own inconstants.

"Winters up here," Cal said, "have always been hard, but I've never seen it like this so early. When I was a kid, we'd get snow by Thanksgiving most years. Nice, fluffy snow, like a blanket over everything." He paused, and I suspected that he had gone back in time to a place that seemed kinder through the filter of recent events. "I always knew when it'd snowed the minute I woke up. There's no silence in the world like the silence the morning after a first snow. And the light. The light is different. It seems to come from everywhere, like . . . like in the Preserve."

Ah, now that was the sound of homesickness. I had heard it in my own voice when once I spoke of Kiev. Then I had not yet understood that home is not a place, but the people in it. I had no people in Kiev now. Everything I had was here. This was not true of my friend, Cal.

"We will find Tina," I said, "and take her there so she, too, can see the light that comes from everywhere."

He glanced away from me. "I don't want to take her there, Doc. If we have to take her there, that would mean there's still something to protect her from." He turned back to face me, his eyes burning. "It's not enough to just get Tina away from the Source. We have to shut the Source down."

"Then we will."

He laughed without humor, and breathed out a long jet of steam. "You know what I was sitting here wondering just now? I was wondering if I'd be sitting here wondering if I'd accepted that job in the D.A.'s office in St. Cloud instead of buying the New York hype."

"The New York hype?"

"You know—if you can make it there, you'll make it anywhere. I wanted to make it."

"And what has New York hype to do with your being here?"

He did not answer me directly. "You know what I wanted more than anything, growing up? Not to be like my father. Not to do to the people who loved me what he did to us." He shook his head. "Maybe it's genetic."

"Meaning? You are nothing like the man you described to me, Calvin. That man was selfish, shortsighted—"

"I worked evenings and weekends. Tina took buses to ballet practice, cabs to recitals. A prima donna with no one in the audience to cheer just for her. She was lonely, Doc. And I was trying so hard to fit into Stern's zoo, I didn't notice until she was beyond my reach."

"Calvin," I objected gently to his self-reproach, "you have always done for Tina what you felt she needed."

He shook his head. "We've all seen it, Doc. The Source twists people physically who have already been twisted by life. And Tina . . . There was a hole in Tina that I put there. The Change had plenty to work with."

The snow changed to a wafting mist. The wind eased to a mere moan, which seemed, at this moment, to come from within Cal Griffin himself.

"Now we argue nature and nurture," I observed. "You and Tina have had much the same experience, yes? An absent father, a mother struggling to make a home for her children. The painful loss when she died. Yet, only Tina changed. Have you not considered that this perhaps was due to her nature?"

He made no answer.

I leaned close to him and put a hand on his arm. "There is an old Russian proverb: 'Shit happens.' "

He let out a bark of laughter. "Old Russian proverb, huh? Is that a literal translation?"

"No. The literal translation is 'You go uphill and the devil grabs your foot,' but the point is the same."

He nodded, smiling at me from the depths of his hood. "I'm going to go scramble up some breakfast. Believe it or not, it's morning." He stood, stretched, and made his way to where the supplies lay beneath their protective shroud of nylon. In a few paces he was no more than a vague shape in the lightening gloom.

"Nice try, Doc." Colleen stepped into the place Cal had vacated.

I shook my head. "I am not sure he listens."

"Why should he? You don't. I'm beginning to think it's one of those 'guy' things. Only affects people with that broken X chromosome."

She had surprised me yet again. "What do you mean? When do I not listen?"

She crouched next to me. "Viktor, for a wise man, you have some surprising gaps in your smarts. They say a person can't talk and listen at the same time. You're living proof of that."

"I don't—"

"What did you just tell Cal: Shit happens? Why can't you take that to heart? I bet somewhere, deep down inside, you still blame yourself for Chernobyl."

My face grew warm, damning me, and I had to deliberately misunderstand her. "Nonsense. I have never blamed myself for Chernobyl."

"No? But you made yourself responsible for the victims. Every one you lost, you punished yourself for. Just like you punish yourself for Yelena and Nurya."

The anger that forced its way up into my heart was raw and searing. I meant to direct it at her for daring to trespass on this, my sacred ground, but this sudden rage did not bear her name. "You cannot pretend I was not responsible for them. I *was*. *That* was the gap in my smarts, as you call it. I made a choice between the good of many strangers and the good of those few I loved. The choice was a lie. There *was* no choice. I told you, I had so little effect at Chernobyl. At home—"

"And what about the choice you made back there at the Preserve? Wasn't that a lie, too?"

For a moment I felt like a tiny ceramic man in a child's snow globe, frozen and senseless. I turned to look at her without volition. In the wan morning light her face was more solemn than I had ever seen it. Not even a spark of humor reached her eyes.

I thought of all the possible responses I could make, but only one was honest enough to be uttered. "History repeats itself," I murmured, and felt the chill of this Wisconsin dawn drive itself into the marrow of my bones.

I had not even let myself consider what it meant for me to be back there, within the relatively safe confines of the Preserve, while she and the others were out here, facing what only God knew. There, I was one of many, while they would have been only five against the unknown. Cal had been absolutely right, of course, for any one of us to be absent increased the chances of failure.

"And how is it," I asked at last, "that you realized this, when I did not?"

Her gaze did not waver. "I *listen*. I listen to the people I trust. Especially when they can tell me things about myself even I don't know." She raised her hands in that so typical gesture of surrender. "Okay, so it doesn't happen often. In fact, I haven't really listened to anybody since . . . well, probably since Dad died. People worth listening to are a rare find."

I tried to imagine her as a teenager with a teenager's faith that the people in her life today would be there tomorrow and the next day, and the next. I imagined a girl who smiled much and worried little, whose mouth turned up at the corners, and between whose brows no lines of worry had yet settled. I thought I had seen her in brief flashes over the past weeks, so I knew she had not been completely conquered by the *boi baba*.

We woke the others to a hurried breakfast before hastily packing our goods back onto our well-chilled horses, who had sheltered the night behind a pair of extra tents. As we worked I wandered through the door Colleen had opened in my mind and visited the room that lay behind it.

"What was a thing your father told you about yourself?" I asked her as we distributed the last of her gear across her horse's pack.

"That I shouldn't follow his footsteps into the military."

"And why was that?"

She cleared her throat, then said, in a voice of gravel, " 'You wouldn't take orders well, Chief. They'd bust you the first time you were insubordinate.' "

"Chief?"

Her lips curved. "A nickname."

"I take it, then, that your father was never insubordinate. This surprises me, considering what you've told me of him."

She grinned, letting the teenager peek out. "Oh, Dad was *never* insubordinate. Not in any way they could prove. He had a talent for saying things with a smile that . . . well, that might've started a fight or a court-martial if someone else'd said it. I sometimes thought Dad was too laid back, too easy. Now I realize that was a survival tactic. It was his way of staying true to himself in a world that wanted him to conform. Maybe it was his way of daring the world to change him. The immovable object resisting an irresistible force."

"You are also good at resisting the irresistible," I noted.

She shook her head. "Too good. There are some changes I *want* to make. I'm just not sure I can." Her eyes strayed to where Cal moved among the pack animals, checking cinches and tarps.

In a moment he glided between us, granting each a tired smile. "Ready to go?"

"Ready," said Colleen and returned the smile.

He gave her a quick, one-armed hug and patted my shoulder before moving to mount his horse. Watching him, Colleen shrugged and shook her head, then swung up into her own saddle, making herself busy with the packhorse's lead.

The wind was in our faces as we set out. The day was much like the days before, a freezing, gray blur, during which I considered that riding bareback would be warmer for both myself and my poor horse. Her name, I was told, was June, but I called her Koshka—meaning "cat"—for that was what she reminded me of, not in the least because she so disliked being wet.

Theoretically, one could stay dry beneath one's down or leather jacket and waterproof poncho, but in reality the wind drove icy shrapnel into every slit. Koshka, I had no doubt, was even more miserable than I.

There was no possibility of conversation, no landmarks to entertain the eyes. The world quickly narrowed to the view between my mare's ears. I could barely make out the glow Magritte spread about herself at the head of the column, so I kept my eyes on Colleen's back and wondered how it is that flares do not seem to feel the cold.

The weather did us the favor of clearing toward afternoon. There was even a sun in the sky. I had become so used to the Preserve's golden bonnet and Wisconsin's gray snood that for a brief moment I did not recognize it. The temperature rose enough that I put back my hood and gazed about.

We traveled off the beaten track but in sight of it as long as the sun shone. But as soon as dusk began to settle, we came down onto the road—County Highway 14, according to the signs. We were now in Illinois, I realized, and probably had been for some time.

Snow had blown across the road, cushioning our horses' hooves. Above the soft lowing of the wind, we could not hear the sounds of our own passage. We saw no one—no people, no domestic animals. Nor did we see signs of them. The farmhouses that we saw from afar were dark, their access roads covered with pleated coats of snow and ice except for the occasional track of fox or field mouse. Whether there were no people or no people fool enough to brave the storm, we could not tell.

Now we were able to speak, but didn't care to. The cold, the constant wind, the stinging snow, had drained us. Even Magritte was subdued, having come to rest on the rump of Goldie's gelding. Her bright aura had dimmed, but not died. Still, she was obliged to wrap herself in one of our sleeping bags for warmth.

At that point when the day teetered between twilight and darkness, we arrived at the crest of a hill. The sun, like a baleful red eye, glared at our backs from the western horizon, while below, the land disappeared into a gloom so deep no feature could be discerned. It was a peculiar, thick, unnatural darkness that made the hair rise up on the back of my neck.

Cal halted atop the hill, perplexed. "We should be able to see *something*. There are towns down there. We should be able to see fires, smoke . . ."

"It's weird. It almost looks like a—a canyon," said Goldie, making a north to south sweep with one arm. "Or a black hole."

"It's *supposed* to be fringe towns and bedroom communities—incipient suburbia. They wouldn't have electricity, but . . ." Cal shook his head.

"Well, whatever it is, we're sure as hell not going to find out tonight," said Colleen. She gestured with her head. "Judging by that cloud mass up north, we're in for some weather."

Cal forced a long, steaming breath between tight lips and nodded. "You're right. We should make camp." He glanced back over his shoulder at the ribbon of snowy road behind. "There was a farm back about half a mile. I'd like to go check it out."

The house had been gutted by fire, but the barn was intact, a fine, sturdy building with thick double doors and shuttered windows. It was empty of life, except perhaps for some mice. There was also hay, grain, and a number of other things that would be a welcome supplement to our supplies. I couldn't help but wonder what happened to the animals and the people that had lived here; of them there was no sign.

We scavenged unburnt wood from the house and built a fire in a trash barrel, while Goldie set light-globes blazing. Then we bedded down the horses and ate our supper, none of us, I suspect, tasting much of the dried meat, fruit, and flatbread we consumed.

After our meal, Cal spread his map out on a bale of hay and pored over it, while Colleen hovered at his shoulder. Enid sat next to me on a bale just opposite them, watching silently. On an adjacent bale, Magritte slept at the end of her tether, her aura drained away.

Enid had taken his harmonica from his pack, but not to play. Instead, he turned it ceaselessly in his hands, end over end over end. "This is a weird time for me," he murmured, slanting a gaze at Magritte. "Here I been jamming twenty-four/seven, trying to keep music happening—now I gotta keep music *from* happening. It's unnatural. And I gotta wonder how long it can last."

"Have you any idea how it is the Source has not heard her?"

A sort of music came to us from Goldie, out of sight among the box stalls. He was humming and singing in turns, tapping out rhythms on whatever surfaces presented themselves.

Enid turned his gaze from Magritte to follow the sound, a faint smile touching his lips. "I got my theories."

"I don't get it." Cal's voice pulled my attention to where he and Colleen studied the map. He ran his fingertips over it in a gesture that reminded me of a circus Gypsy reading tarot cards. When he was done, he shook his head. "We should be approaching the outskirts of Woodstock by now. But there's nothing there."

Enid straightened. "Where'd it go?"

Cal searched the map again, a smear of violet brilliance following the movement of his hands. Tangled networks of light leapt into being, culminating in a knot. To the east and west of this gleaming web was darkness.

"That's Lake Michigan," said Cal, pointing to the easternmost point where the light cut off abruptly. "I'd expect it to be dark. In fact, I'd be worried if it wasn't. But I have no idea what this is." He tapped a finger in the middle of the lightless area on the map.

It lay between our present position and the knot of light I knew must be post-Change Chicago. An enigma.

"Are you sure you're reading that right?" asked Colleen.

Cal glanced up over his shoulder at her. "I . . . Yes, I'm sure it's right. I mean, it's *wrong*. There should be something there."

"You mean there *used to be* something there," said Enid.

Goldie moved from the stalls at the back of the barn to pace along its front wall, still humming, providing accompaniment with a little wood and skin rattle he had pulled seemingly out of nowhere—a gift from Kevin Elk Sings. Enid tracked him for a moment, then turned to watch Magritte sleep.

Colleen sighed and dropped to a crouch next to Cal, leaning wearily against his leg. "Maybe we're just plain lost."

The drumming suddenly quit and Goldie said, quietly, "We're not lost. Chicago's on the other side of that hole in the map, we just need to find a way to get across it."

Cal turned to look at him, standing before the barn's double front doors. "You're sure?"

"I'm never sure of anything. You know that."

Cal glanced over at Enid, who shrugged and said, "I don't know about Chicago, but Howard's still there."

"On the other side of the void?"

"Yeah."

Cal stood and turned to Goldie, the map in his hands. "And is the Source on the other side of the void, too?"

Goldie smiled uncertainly. "You're asking me?"

"Who else would I ask? Goldie, we've been on the road for days, moving straight toward Chicago. I haven't asked you if the Source is there because I figured if it was, you'd tell me. And if it *wasn't*, you'd tell me. You haven't said a word, one way or the other. Now, I'm asking. What's your sixth sense telling you about the Source?"

Goldie looked down at the rattle. "My *sick* sense, you mean."

Cal's hands clenched on the map, crushing it. Pale violet light seeped from between his fingers. "Goldie, we're practically on top of Chicago—or at least we ought to be. And we're coming in from the West. Is the Source east of us now, or west?"

There was no sound in the barn but the hollow chuckle of fire in the barrel and wind tormenting the riven walls.

"Wow, what do I say? Never could tell my east from my west."

"Goldie, dammit! You—" Cal stopped the words with visible effort. "You've been hedging this since before we left the Preserve. What is it you're trying so damned hard not to tell me?"

Goldie's eyes darted around as if seeking a place to hide. "That I don't know what to tell you. I'm getting mixed signals. Static. Too many voices."

"Voices from Chicago?"

"Sometimes."

"And was it just coincidence that Chicago was where Enid and Magritte needed to go?"

Goldie's eyes met Cal's in a collision I felt as a sudden tightness at the back of my neck. "I'm not making this up, Cal. Yes, I thought it was farther west before, but things change. That's the nature of life nowadays, isn't it?"

"Jesus Christ, Goldie—if I asked you if something was black or white you'd tell me it was gray!"

"Things *are* gray. Things have always been gray."

Cal threw the crumpled map to the floor. "Goldie, for God's sake, can you *please* stop sounding like a fucking sphinx? I've had enough riddles and conundrums and—and puzzles to last me a lifetime. Right now I need answers, and you're the only one who has them."

But Goldie was shaking his head. "I don't have answers, Cal. I never have had."

"No, of course not. You don't have answers; you just have manias. How convenient."

"Cal!" Colleen scrambled to her feet and stood poised, as if ready to put herself between the two men.

Goldie's laughter was harsh. " 'Convenient' isn't exactly the word I'd use."

"No? What word, then, Goldie? What word would you use to describe the way your sense of direction comes and goes? Huh? You tell me in one breath that the Source could be in Chicago. In the next, you tell me you're not sure. One moment you're setting course with abandon, and the next you're dithering around like a—a—"

I finished the sentence for him. "Like someone with an extreme mood disorder? For the love of God, Cal, where are you going with this?"

Goldie drew back, shadows falling across his face. "No, Doc, it's . . . it's okay. He's right. I'm . . . two bricks short of a load. Common knowledge." He dropped his eyes to the rattle again before going on, his voice a raw whisper. "Look, Cal, I'm sorry I can't be more clear-headed. More . . . like you or Doc or Colleen. But I've tried everything I can think of to keep up my end of this. Up to and including opening genie bottles I'd just as soon leave corked. You can't imagine some of the scary shit I've had to let into my head to be able to hear those Voices."

"Goldie . . ." Cal said.

"Yeah, I know what you're thinking: 'Jeez, Goldman, you eat scary shit for breakfast.' Granted. But it costs me to stay connected to the Source. To hear those Voices night after night. When I'm on the edge, Cal, they make stepping over sound . . . easy." He raised his eyes to Cal's face, and Cal went white at the look in them. "Sometimes it's all I can do to hold on to the little piece of sanity I've got left in here. I know you want yeses instead of maybes and answers instead of riddles. But I don't have them. Not right now."

There was a vacuum in the room. No one spoke or moved. The wind rattled the doors and pried at the windows.

Finally, Cal spoke, his voice careful, gentle. "Then we'll make do with maybes and riddles. I . . . I know you're not making this up, Goldie. But I'm blind right now. I'm not sure what we're facing."

A ghost smile touched Goldie's lips. "Welcome to my world."

Cal's expression changed subtly in the exchange their eyes made. "Yeah. I . . . I get it," he said finally. "If you . . . sense anything, hear anything—"

"You'll be the first to know. Trust me." He turned back into the rippling shadows and disappeared into the stalls.

Cal picked up the crumpled map and smoothed it against his stomach. "I'm sorry, you guys. I . . . I don't have any excuses. It's just . . . another day in a long nightmare."

Colleen laid a hand on his arm. "Don't beat yourself up over it. Everybody's worn-out and a little tired of surprises."

Cal shot a glance back into the shadows where Goldie had gone. "I'm worried about him. He's our compass. Always pointing almost due west. Now it's as if . . . the pole has moved. Maybe it's these dreams we've been having . . . maybe they're confusing things."

"Well, one thing I'm not confused about," said Enid. He pointed toward the southeast corner of the barn. "Howard is that way."

Cal took a deep breath. "Then we go that way."

Enid nodded, as if content with that, and lay down on his hay bale, pulling his sleeping bag over him. I realized how hungry for sleep my own body was. I had laid out my bedroll in what was left of a haystack along the inner wall of a stall. Now I went to it and crawled in, facing the common area, almost numb with cold and weariness. I could see Cal and Colleen standing where I had left them, both looking at the hard-pack floor rather than each other.

After a moment Cal dropped the map onto a hay bale and moved to stand by the fire barrel, where he made business of warming his hands. Colleen hesitated, then followed him.

"Could the Source really be in Chicago?" she asked, her voice low. "Is that what we'll be facing on the other side of the void?"

"That's one of the things that doesn't feel right. All this time, I've assumed that when we get to the Source, I'll know it. I'll hear it, or I'll *sense* it in some way. And I thought . . ."

"What?" prompted Colleen, her eyes tight on his face.

"That when the time came, there'd be something for us to use—some tool or weapon or . . . knowledge that we don't have now. Some way to defeat it. We've got Enid, but I don't know how he fits. His music is like a shield, but is it a weapon? And . . . I've always assumed that *I'd* find it—this weapon—whatever it is. The way I found the sword. I feel as if there's a piece missing. Something I'm not understanding."

Colleen shrugged. "Maybe we have the missing piece but we just don't know it. Or maybe it's out there, somewhere." She tilted her head toward the same wall Enid had pointed at moments before. "Or maybe it's here, inside us. Not just one or another of us, but all of us together. You found the sword, but Goldie led you to it, didn't he?"

Cal tilted his head and smiled down at her in the fire's glow. "You say the most amazing things."

She took a half step back from him. "What? What'd I say that's so funny?"

"Not funny, profound. You said something . . . Doc might've said, or Mary maybe. That it isn't just one of us—it's *all* of us." He took back the half step she'd given up. "I wasn't laughing at you, Colleen. I wouldn't laugh at you."

She opened her mouth to respond, sarcasm battling something else in her expression. But before a word could come out, he bent his head and kissed her.

I rolled over onto my back, casting my eyes deep into the darkness of the hayloft. Good. This was the way it was supposed to be, was it not? It was what Colleen had hoped for. Clearly, it was what Cal wanted. It was what I had expected, encouraged.

Then why did I feel no contentment?

Fierce, sudden wind slammed against the barn's broad flank. The entire structure shuddered as if the earth had bucked beneath it, and the front doors blew in, admitting wind and sleet mixed with rain.

Colleen and Cal were startled into action, while I sat up as if on a spring. They had pushed the doors shut and lifted the oaken latch bar into its iron cradles before I could struggle from my bedroll. Dirt and hay scooted across the floor, pursued by the chill wind that stole beneath the doors and through every seam and crack.

Cal pulled a hand through his wet hair and grimaced. "Looks like it's going to be a rough night."

It was.

SIXTEEN

CAL

When I was thirteen, I broke through the ice on a neighborhood pond and plunged over my head into glacial water. When I got out and Mom sat me down in front of the fire, I felt as if she'd thrown me right into the flames. I was feverish and freezing, my skin burning even as the chill of the pond burrowed deep in my bones.

I felt like that now.

Colleen stood not two feet from me, brushing dust from her hands and jeans. She looked up, caught me watching, and colored.

"Well, I guess we . . . I'd better turn in," she said. "I'm sure tomorrow's gonna be a long, weird day."

She was right, of course. But sleep wasn't what I wanted just now; I wanted to talk. To her. I wanted to explore what had just happened. I wanted to kiss her again. But she was headed away from me toward her bedroll.

"Colleen . . ."

She glanced back at me warily. "Yeah?"

"Do I need to apologize?" I asked, lacking anything better to say.

She colored. "No. You don't need to apologize, I just . . . I'm real tired right now. Don't know whether I'm coming or going. I'm not sure that's the best time to . . . you know."

No, I don't, was what I wanted to say. *Maybe it's the best time in the world. Our defenses are down. We're not so careful, so-damned-in-control.* But I didn't say that. I let her go off to her bedroll and moved like an automaton to unroll mine.

That was when I saw something in our peculiar domestic picture that wasn't right. Colleen and Doc had chosen to bed down in the half-empty haymow; Enid was snoring on a couple of bales laid end to end. The bale next to him was empty. I stared at it for a long five count before I realized that empty spot was where Magritte should have been. Her tether lay loose on the floor. Chill swiped through me.

"Maggie?" I moved instinctively toward the darkest part of the barn, where Goldie had gone. Surely the Source couldn't have taken her. We would have heard something, felt something.

We did hear something, my argumentative side reminded me—that big wind hitting the barn, the doors slamming wide open. And we didn't hear much else while that was going on.

"Maggie?" I called again, and behind me Colleen asked, "What's wrong?"

I was at the head of the row of stalls now. It was black on black back here, except where pale, aqua light seeped from an unseen source to ripple across the ceiling. That could be Magritte; it could just as easily be one of Goldie's light-globes.

I hesitated, suddenly afraid of interrupting something. I took another step into the gloom, drawing level with the first stall.

"What is it?"

I swung around to find Goldie watching me over the bottom half of the stall's double door. He was wearing an unmistakable aura of the palest gold.

Caught gaping like a fish, I managed to say, "I just . . . realized Magritte was gone." I met his eyes. Behind his veil of wild curls, they were dark and wary.

There was movement behind him. Light shifted as if someone approached with a lantern, and Magritte appeared over the threshold of the stall, her own aura bright, silvery, blinding.

Goldie said, "I've got her covered."

"But the tether—"

"Don't need it."

I realized, suddenly, what he meant. Each of them was the center of a radiant halo that extended to touch and mingle with the other, changing hue subtly in the process. I'd noticed it a number of times, but had always assumed that Maggie was creating the phenomenon, that she was reaching out to Goldie. Now I realized that Goldie was generating his own halo.

"A proximity effect?" I looked from one to the other.

"To all intents and purposes, Magritte disappears when she's close to me." He smiled wryly. "I'm just plain overwhelming, I guess."

Magritte snorted delicately.

"When did you realize you could do that?"

His eyes flicked away from mine, as if the subject were embarrassing. "My first day inside the Preserve. But I didn't realize what it meant until we left the Blue Mounds. I was afraid for her and I . . . just sort of reached out mentally and shut out the Storm."

Magritte looked at him with something like adoration in her eyes. "Goldie brought the power of the Mounds with him."

He returned the look, adoration mingled with something darker. "Yeah, I'm just like one of those glow-in-the-dark things."

I remembered, then, what he'd said about the Black Tower that bound our dreams together: *It's inside me.*

I couldn't imagine what that must feel like. Could I handle it any better than he did? "I'm sorry," I said.

"For what?"

"Jumping all over you earlier. It was uncalled for."

"Yeah, well, shit happens."

He surprised laughter out of me. "What are you—psychic? Doc said that."

The corner of his mouth twitched. "Doc's psychic—I'm psy-*cho*. It's important to keep that straight." He sobered, meeting my gaze. "I'm going to get through this, Cal. I have to get through this. I don't know what's in Chicago, but whatever it is, we'll deal with it."

"When I said I understood what it costs you to touch the Source," I said, "when I said I got it—I meant that. I think it . . . must feel . . . as if you're not quite yourself."

He laughed, breaking eye contact. "Not quite myself. Oh, that's a mouthful. Am I ever myself?" He shook his head. "Yeah, that's one of the feelings I get, I guess. Not myself."

"When I do . . . the maps, the contract . . . things like that . . ." I felt my way through the emotions; the words were elusive. "I wonder . . . what I'm becoming. I've always thought change comes from within. That you change yourself. You know what I'm saying?"

"Self-determination," he said. "Self-possession. Those may be chimeras now." He spoke the words as if he'd already accepted them, but they were killing words to me.

I didn't let it show. "So? For all we know, there may really *be* chimeras wandering around out there."

Magritte laughed. It was a little girl's laugh. Incongruous, slipping from between those razor-sharp teeth. I was amazed she could still make that sound after all she'd been through. "Those are the lions with the bird-legs, right?" she asked.

Goldie gave me a sly look. "Naw, those are griffins." The sly look broadened into a smile that seemed genuine. "Sweet dreams," he said, and moved back into the stall, drawing Maggie after him.

I shivered and sought the comfort of my sleeping bag.

Psychic, maybe. Prophetic, not. Having let it into my head, I dreamed of the Tower. That night there was a different twist. Tina was still trapped behind the dripping, glazed walls, but now Goldie was there with her.

Morning dawned cold and relatively clear. The blanket of clouds was higher, allowing the sun to peek beneath it at the horizon. The cloud cover wasn't quite as seamless as it had been the day before. The wind still came out of the north, but it was a tired wind.

I could relate.

The silence struck hard. I could see it in every face when at last we crept out of the barn, leading our jittery horses. It was a ghost-town silence that made our voices ooze out in whispers and our eyes dart about in search of mysterious shadows. There were none, so we imagined them. Wind stirred the tufts of dried grass that stood above the powdery snow, while tree branches nodded and creaked and ash lifted lazily from the burnt shell of the farmhouse. Then, far and away across a ruined cornfield, a crow called and another answered. Sepulcher sounds from the first living things we'd heard or seen for days.

Goldie breathed out a gust of steam. "Whoa. Where's Stephen King when you need him?"

"I used to love that sound," said Colleen. "The crows, I mean. It meant autumn: Halloween, Thanksgiving, the crunch of leaves, the smell of wood smoke, snow."

"Well, we got you some snow," Enid observed. "And I can give you crunchy leaves, if you really want 'em all that badly."

Colleen returned his grin and threw her leg over Big T's broad back. "Thanks, Enid. I was getting all morbid and mushy there for a moment."

"Any time."

We moved out. I tried to put myself next to Colleen in the hope that we might talk about certain events, but she seemed to be in one of her loner moods, keeping herself a little aloof from everyone. I tried to tell myself it didn't have anything to do with *the kiss*, but I couldn't help wondering.

It was Enid I found myself riding with at the head of the column. He was as eager as I to see what Goldie's black hole really was.

As we made our way into the sunrise and rode the last several yards to the top of the hill, I realized I was holding my breath. I'm not sure what I expected to see when at last we crested the rise. Maybe something from one of those disaster movies—a nuclear dead zone à la *Independence Day* or any one of the dozens of postapocalyptic creations imagined by science fiction authors and Hollywood script writers.

What I saw was water.

"Damn," said Enid, and Goldie sang, " 'The river is wide, I cannot get o'er. And neither have I bright wings to fly.' "

Bright wings. They'd have to be 767 wings to get five people and eight horses across that. The water stretched north to south as far as the eye could see, its flat, opaque surface rippling beneath a layer of rheumy mist, the far shore all but invisible from our vantage point atop the hill.

I knew there was a far shore only because the map—the post-Change, Griffinized map—said so. The pre-Change map only indicated that a narrow stream called the Fox River had once inhabited the landscape somewhere out there.

A current seemed to be flowing slowly and diligently south. Was this a river of epic proportions, or a migrating lake? It hardly mattered; it lay between us and our goal, effectively cutting us off.

My frustration was sabotaged by the sudden appearance in memory of a childhood icon: a large, stuffed teddy in a red shirt sat atop my horse, tapping his wadding-filled noggin and muttering, "Think. Think. Think." I felt an insane urge to laugh.

Magritte, hovering near Goldie, gestured skyward. "I'm going up," she said, "so nobody flip out, okay?"

I don't know if it did anything, but Goldie tilted back his head and began to sing, of all things, "I Can See Clearly Now."

I bit back laughter. Colleen, too, seemed amused, and Doc . . . I turned to look back over my shoulder. Doc was sitting silently amid the pack train on our rear guard, wearing an expression that made me doubt he was even in the state of Illinois with the rest of us.

I glanced up at Magritte, floating upward as if made of fluff, then reined Sooner around and circled back to Doc's side.

"You all right?"

"What?" He blinked at me like a man just awakening from a long sleep.

"You seem . . . I don't know . . . a bit lost."

"Ah, yes. That is it. I am . . . a bit lost, as you say. I . . . did not sleep well last night."

"I'm sorry about that. I'm sure I didn't help matters much with my little outburst. I apologized to Goldie."

He was regarding me solemnly, but I had the distinct impression he was only half hearing me. "And did he accept your apology?"

"Actually, he said 'shit happens.' "

"I would say that 'shit' is not all that happens. Good things also happen, even in this chaotic world." His eyes shifted into focus on my face and I was suddenly too warm, realizing he must have seen me with Colleen. "Don't let this quest we're on make you too single-minded, Calvin. Don't let it steal what small pieces of real life you are given."

His gaze shifted again and I followed it to where Colleen sat astride her roan—watching us. Her eyes flew up after Magritte as soon as mine touched them.

"Why is this so hard?" I asked, keeping my voice low. "This thing with Colleen. You know what I mean. Shouldn't it be simple?"

"I think, perhaps, it is simple, but we make it hard. With all that has changed, it seems to me that love should be the one immutable thing. I suppose that seems . . . what is the word—corny?"

"No. Not corny. True."

His eyes swung to meet mine, catching me off guard. "And do you love Colleen?"

Did I? "I don't know. She's an admirable woman—strong, resilient, smart, vital. I wouldn't have thought she was my 'type' before—whatever that is—but I . . . she . . . There's some kind of attraction there." I floundered. "Sometimes I think my soul is . . . that I'm too full of darkness to understand love. That the whole world is too full of darkness. That's what's hard—the ambiguity. I wish I could just *know* if I loved Colleen, or if it's just chemistry."

Doc carefully arranged his horse's mane so it lay all on one side of her dark neck. "For *you*, it should be simple. You are young. Unbroken. And possessed of fewer ghosts."

"We make our own ghosts," I said, "and then give them permission to haunt us."

He looked at me again, speculatively. "Your thought is your reality."

"What?"

"Abdu'l-Bahá Abbas Effendi—a nineteenth-century Persian idealist. There are infinite meanings buried in that statement. A man can spend many years pondering it, trying to apply it, yet grasp but one or two."

The words struck a chord. Goldie had grasped at least one of those meanings. He used it to manipulate light and energy. I'd grasped one of those meanings, too, the night before we left the Preserve. But I had the feeling Doc was talking about something else and perhaps speaking more to himself than to me.

"There's a land bridge!"

Magritte's excited cry interrupted my thoughts. No wonder Muhammad had favored a cave for his meditations. I urged Sooner forward. When I rejoined Goldie and Enid, Magritte was bobbing at eye level, pointing south.

"Well, it's more of a sandbar, really," she said. "But it looks like it might go all the way across . . . sorta."

Everyone turned to look at me.

"It's all we've got," I told them.

Maggie's land bridge was about three miles south as the crow flies. I considered the possibility of finding some way to turn us all into crows for the rest of the trip, but there was no time to thoroughly ponder the effect of thought on reality, so shape-shifting was not an option.

The bridge had apparently once been part of a county-maintained road. Now it was little more than a ridge of rock and dirt and pocked tarmac that had collected sand, uprooted trees, brush, pieces of human habitation, whatever had chosen to drift down against it.

It looked treacherous as hell, but it did seem to go all the way across the river (if such it was), with the exception of some visible channels where the slow-moving current had crested it. There was no way to know if those channels were passable without going out onto the ridge.

We went.

Once we left shore, the sensation of having stepped into an alien world was overpowering. The sky overhead was dull pewter, the water greenish gray. Mist rose like dry-ice vapor to carpet the river's surface and festoon the twists of wood and brush that bordered our dangerous corridor. All color seemed drained out of the world.

Even we looked gray.

We traveled single file, picking our way carefully across the debris, sometimes dismounting to lead the horses through narrow or difficult passes. I led the way, followed by Enid and the airborne Magritte, acting as lookout. Goldie trailed behind Enid, leading two of the three packhorses. Colleen came after, with the remaining "mule" sandwiched between her and Doc.

The rear horse in a train, Colleen had taught me, will always be a little skittish. For this reason, a mounted animal should always bring up the rear. The packhorses were nervous in spite of the precaution, and who could blame them? There was little visibility, the constant slap and moan of water, miserable damp and cold, uncertain footing, and a pervasive stew of smells, all of them unpleasant. Enough to give anyone the jitters—equine or human.

The channels we had seen from shore marked where the river had overwhelmed the tarmac and broken through, forming rough spillways. We hit a number of these in the first half of our crossing. The water in them was never more than about two feet deep—roughly knee high on your average saddle horse—and it was sluggish, as if rendered torpid by the cold.

If pressed to guess, I'd have to say the river was between six and eight miles across, including its flood plain. I couldn't help but wonder what was feeding it and how; none of the theories I came up with were particularly comforting.

Just past the halfway mark, we came upon a long stretch of uprooted trees and boulders filled in with coarse, treacherous sands. It took an exhausting hour and a half to navigate less than seventy-five yards. We rested after that on a high spot in the narrow ridge, ate a little, spoke less, and watched the water move by around us. It had a soporific effect. If I closed my eyes I could almost imagine myself in a rowboat, drifting down a lazy, peaceful stream, fishing, maybe. Except that I had never cared for fishing and the temperature was near freezing.

I opened my eyes to a slight disturbance out in the murky water below us. What appeared to be a large tree had caught on a submerged snag and bobbed in place about thirty yards out. A moment later it just disappeared. Sucked straight down or . . .

Adrenaline went to high tide. I got up, no longer drowsy. "Let's move out. We've still got a trek ahead of us. And the sooner we get off this strand, the better."

I didn't have to say more. Everyone was as eager to move on as I was.

"Did you see that?" I asked Goldie as we sorted ourselves back into order.

"I'm not saying," he told me, then, "What did you see?"

"A tree."

"Uh-huh. I saw a tree."

"What was *your* tree doing?"

"Exhibiting un-tree-like behavior."

"Currents," I said.

"Oh, I certainly hope so."

In what seemed like ages, we drew within tantalizing sight of the nether shore and I could make out the silhouettes of buildings in the distance. I glanced back at Enid. He was smiling. Magritte, floating at his shoulder, was also smiling. We could smell dry land.

Then hell erupted. Behind me someone shouted a warning. There was a wild thrashing of water, the thunder of hooves on rocky ground, a scream that could only have come from Colleen.

I twisted in the saddle. Past Enid, past Goldie and his two charges, I could see that another animal floundered in the water. It was Colleen's pack mare. The bank she'd been traversing was gone, undercut by the river. Where the trail had been, there was now a yawning sinkhole.

The mare's lead line, snagged around Big T's saddle horn, threatened to drag him and Colleen both into the muddy current. The big roan's hindquarters were already half in the sink, while his forelegs flailed at the slope, spraying wet sand and rock in every direction.

There was no way to turn Sooner on the narrow trail without ending up in the river myself. I dug in my heels and drove him up the ridge to the first place wide enough for to me to slide off and scramble back.

I didn't get far. Goldie's abandoned mount was charging straight at me. I had nowhere to go but into the rocks and brush that studded the side of the ridge. Cursing, I struggled back up onto the trail and turned just as Colleen's horse lost his footing and slid backward down the embankment.

Water flew. The gelding lunged upward, trying to take the bank, but the pack line snugged to his saddle horn pulled him back. He upended and hung almost upright for a moment, staggering on his hind legs. Colleen tore at the pack line. At the last possible moment she got it free and hurled it into the air, where a flash of aqua intercepted it. Magritte.

But it was too late, Big T lost his battle with the slope and pitched over on top of Colleen in a spray of dirty water.

My head felt as if it might explode. I shouted wordlessly and flung myself along the ridge, shoving past the quaking packhorses.

Magritte had pulled the pack line around the thick limb of an uprooted tree. Goldie snagged the end, using his weight to keep the line tight, playing tug-of-war with the struggling mare. He needed help, but that would have to wait. I scrambled past him, slipping and falling, tearing clothing and flesh on rock and brush.

Doc was already down in the freezing flood, grappling with Big T.

The horse struggled to right himself, his eyes showing white, his distended nostrils spouting steam. Doc had gotten hold of his headstall and somewhere found the strength to keep his head above water. With a final, roaring heave the horse twisted upright and surfaced, nearly bowling Doc over.

No Colleen.

My throat, already raw from yelling, constricted. *God, no.* I careened past Goldie on the narrow track, nearly tripping over him.

Doc was shouting Colleen's name. When I thought he would dive into the river after her, she surfaced not two feet from him, gasping for breath.

"My boot! I'm caught!"

At that moment, in one of those flukes of the cosmos that can only have been carefully choreographed, the sodden tree limb Magritte had dallied the rope around collapsed, ripping Goldie off his feet. He pitched, screaming, toward the sinkhole, the rope still twisted around his hands.

There was no decision to be made: I turned back and lunged after him, got hold of the rope, braced my feet among the rocks and threw my whole weight against it. He scrambled upright and joined me; together we brought the struggling mare closer to shore.

Only yards away there was an explosion of sound and movement. Big T flew up out of the river, steaming and shivering. Through his quaking legs I could see Doc, still up to his thighs in the current, his frantic grip all that kept Colleen from going under.

Beyond them the smooth, misty flood was cut by something that I might have taken for a large log except that logs are rarely so purposeful and never move against a current.

"Jesus-Buddha," Goldie prayed, and I knew he'd seen it, too.

So had Colleen. "Let go of my hands!" she shrieked, now fighting Doc as before she'd fought the river.

He shook his head. "No!"

"Just one! If I can reach the snag, I can lose the boot!"

"I will lose *you!*"

"No. No, you won't. Viktor, *please!*"

He shifted his grip, freeing her left hand. She disappeared beneath the water, only her right arm in Doc's grasp.

The dark disturbance in the stream slipped closer, parting water and mist. It seemed to gain bulk as it approached, ride higher in the water.

A ball of light sailed out to the water's edge and began bobbing along it, well away from Doc and Colleen. It was Magritte, trying to distract the thing.

Goldie's grip on the pack line faltered. "Oh, Maggie, be careful," he breathed.

She didn't need to be careful. Whatever was in the water, her brightness and motion made no impression on it; it had focused on Colleen's struggle.

I glanced at Goldie. "Let go."

He gave me no argument. We released the pack line in unison, letting the floundering mare slide. She staggered backward, lost her balance, and toppled into the deepest part of the sinkhole. Then she swam, not toward shore, but out into the current. We were already in motion, headed toward where Doc fought to maintain his hold on Colleen. I drew my sword, my eyes on that dark presence making its way toward shore. We were just above Doc on the bank when Colleen broke the surface, flailing and gasping for air. He locked his arms around her and wrenched her from the water.

Farther up the bar, just offshore, a horse's scream rent the heavy mists. The river boiled. I didn't have to look to know that our sacrifice had been accepted by whatever god swam the currents.

By the time Goldie and I slid down to the river's edge, Doc was carrying Colleen to shore. Coatless and bootless, she lay limp in his arms, the heaving of her chest the only evidence that she was alive. We reached down to drag them the last few feet onto relatively solid ground, supporting them up the treacherous bank to a safe place among the rocks.

"Oh-God-oh-God-oh-God." Colleen ground the words out through chattering teeth.

I held out my arms, intending to take her from Doc, but he ignored me.

"She'll become hypothermic if we don't warm her. These wet clothes . . ."

I swung around, looking for the horses. They were just up the rocky ridge where Enid and Magritte had corralled them, and now worked at calming them down. I hoped he wasn't singing to them. Goldie and I moved toward them in unison.

"We'll need dry clothes," I told him. "Doesn't matter whose. And we'll need a tent. Something to use as a windbreak."

We helped Enid tether the horses, then broke out tent, clothing, and med-kit. There was no choice location, but we managed to set the tent up among the rocks in a place that offered some natural protection from the icy wind. Magritte had rounded up a sleeping bag and wrapped it around Colleen where she huddled in the lee of a tangle of driftwood, Doc feverishly checking her pulse, her eyes, her hands.

The moment I had the tent up, Doc was there, cradling Colleen as if he feared she might break. She looked awful. Her face was white, her lips blue, her eyes huge and glazed. Her entire body quivered uncontrollably. I watched him ease her into the tent, then handed in the pile of clothing and the med-kit. Doc asked for a knife and disappeared inside.

I turned to Goldie, eager to give myself something to do. "Let's go assess our situation. I want to be ready to move as soon as they're done."

He nodded and moved, grim-faced, toward where Enid tended the horses.

The situation wasn't dire, but we had lost some supplies, including food, fresh water, and horse fodder. A tent was gone, as were some of our household utensils. I was glad Colleen had instructed us to spread the critical items out across the pack animals—for this very reason. We had less of everything than before, but we still had some of everything. I tried not to think about the horse.

I returned to the tent then, to stand guard. I kept my mind occupied with planning. Colleen's voice, rising softly through the fabric in answer to Doc's questions, was reassuring, but only served to underscore my inability to do anything for her.

"Open your eyes, Colleen." The tenor of Doc's voice suggested that the danger was far from past. It jogged me out of my fragile confidence.

"So tired," she murmured.

"You must stay awake."

"Okay. Okay . . . Oh . . . Oh, I'm cut."

"It's all right. I'll make you a patch."

"That's a big cut, isn't it?"

"Then I will make it a big patch. Can you straighten your legs?"

"Uh-uh."

"Try."

"Hurts . . . Oh, no! Not the jeans! Don't cut the jeans! I'll try!" She whimpered. "There . . . oh, sonofa*bitch*, that hurts!"

"Good work, *boi baba*."

There was a moment of relative silence, then Colleen moaned, "Oh, God, Viktor! I can't feel my skin!"

A shaft of river ice twisted itself into my gut.

"It's still there, I promise." His voice was soothing, falsely light.

I distracted myself with memories of thawing out after my dunk in the skating pond. I had survived that chilling experience. Colleen would survive this. She was tough. Tougher than I was, by a long shot. But I had done my thawing in the warmth of my home, pampered with warm blankets, hot tea, and a fire.

And I hadn't been in the water as long as she had.

Goldie slipped over the rocks and came to stand beside me. "How goes it?"

"Slow."

"Should we start a fire?"

I shook my head. "I think the best thing is just to get her out of this damned ice swamp."

"I'd be afraid to start a fire out here, anyway," Goldie told me. "Too much gasoline."

I sniffed. Among the other odors, the gasoline was almost buried, but not quite. "Good God, I'm glad you caught that. I didn't even notice."

"Well, with all the other wonderful aromas—"

"Colleen!" Doc's voice was tinged with alarm. "*Colleen!*"

I took a step toward the tent.

Goldie stopped me. "He's a doctor, Cal. What're you going to do that he can't?"

There was a stinging slap and Colleen gasped.

"Forgive me," Doc said.

"S'okay."

"Can you sit up?"

"Uh-huh."

A quiet struggle ensued.

"Breathe," he commanded her.

She breathed, audibly. "Better. I'm better. Whose socks're those?"

"Do you really care? Just a little more to go. Whose dog tags do you wear?"

"Huh? Oh, those. Those're Daddy's. Mom gave 'em to me at the funeral . . . *Men's* long johns?" She let out a choked laugh.

"Very fashionable."

"I can feel my skin a little. Your hands are warm."

"This is a relative thing, believe me."

"Sweater's *way* too big."

"It's Goldie's. Put this on, then we'll get us all onto dry land. We'll build you a fire, make you some hot chocolate . . ."

"Heaven."

I could hear her teeth chattering. Literally. I remembered that part of nearly freezing to death, too. My jaw hurt for days afterward.

"Can I sleep?" she asked.

"No!" Doc's tone was sharp. He softened it and added, "But soon. I promise."

He lifted her from the tent with great care. In the overlarge clothing, with her short damp hair sticking out from beneath a woolen cap, she looked like a little boy who'd raided his daddy's closet. And she looked vulnerable. I'd never tell her either of those things.

"How is she?" I asked, and half held out my arms again.

"She's damn cold," said Colleen, through her teeth. "An' s'not nice to talk over a person."

Doc offered me a thin smile. "I think she will be fine if we can get her out of here." He gestured with his head at the vapor rising off the river. "Sooner is better."

"Then let's pack this up and get moving." I dropped my arms and bent for the sodden clothing Doc had tossed outside the tent flap. It was already wearing a thin veneer of frost.

Goldie moved to dismantle the tent, while Magritte helped Doc reinstate Colleen in the sheltering driftwood, swaddled once more in a sleeping bag. Doc started to crouch next to her, but Colleen poked a hand out of the folds of quilting and caught his shoulder.

"Change your clothes," she told him, and I realized that Doc's jeans wore a sheath of ice from the thigh down. The hem of his anorak, likewise, was crusted with hoar, as were its sleeves where he had plunged them into the water.

"You must stay awake, Colleen."

"Fine. Magritte can keep me awake. Change your clothes. I'll be all right . . . I promise. *Spacibo*," she added, in Russian. "Thank you."

He nodded and rose stiffly.

"Viktor," she said, turning him back around. She held his gaze for a long moment, then said, so softly I almost didn't catch it, "I told you so."

He said nothing, but when he turned back to face me, his eyes were glistening and haunted. I grasped his arm as he stumbled over the uneven ground.

"What did she mean?" I asked. " 'I told you so.' What was that for?"

"We had spoken of choices." He winced, and I tightened my grip on his arm. "Of how nearly impossible it is to make the correct ones. How difficult the past makes it to put yourself where you belong in the present."

"Apparently, you belong here. If that's what 'I told you so' meant, she was right."

We had reached the horses. Doc halted at his mare's side and laid his forehead against her steaming flank. "Cal, I begin to believe she is *always* right."

We took over an hour to navigate the last stretch of the land bridge. It zigged and zagged, but presented us with no major obstacles. Colleen rode sidesaddle, still wrapped in the sleeping bag, across the pommel of Doc's saddle. He kept up a running dialogue with her the whole way, making her focus, forcing her to speak. By the end of the journey his voice was a rasp, and she was cursing him for not letting her sleep.

We made camp as soon as we climbed beyond the river's miasma, and laid a fire in the lee of a broken wall. There, Colleen and Doc went through the painful process of thawing out—stoically, silently.

Oddly enough, it made me realize how much of a kind they were. Very much, I thought, like father and daughter.

III

O Animal, Who Are You?

. . . Suleiman-bin-Daoud was not proud. He very seldom showed off, and when he did he was sorry for it. Once he tried to feed all the animals in all the world in one day, but when the food was ready an Animal came out of the deep sea and ate it up in three mouthfuls. Suleiman-bin-Daoud was very surprised and said, "O Animal, who are you?" And the Animal said, "O King, live forever! I am the smallest of thirty thousand brothers, and our home is at the bottom of the sea. We heard that you were going to feed all the animals in all the world, and my brothers sent me to ask when dinner would be ready."
. . .and now the real story part of my story begins.

"The Butterfly that Stamped,"
from *Just So Stories* by Rudyard Kipling

SEVENTEEN

COLLEEN

Life is strange. I knew that long before I pitched horse first into the new and improved Fox River; before my life was stretched out in the icy water between a submerged snag and Doc's hands. They say your life flashes before your eyes in moments like that. It's true, but where I'd kind of expected a fast-forward movie, I got a slide show of random freeze frames.

Well, probably not random. These were all moments I suspect my subconscious wanted me to know were IMPORTANT. I'm pretty sure that's what Goldman would've told me, anyway. And whereas I'd lived those moments from the inside, now I saw them from the outside, as if I were sitting in the audience, glancing at my watch and wondering how long this little documentary was going to last. At least I didn't have time to get bored.

Slide one: I am smiling up at Dad, who has just helped me turn twelve years of hoarded allowances into a real, live, kicking, breathing horse.

Slide two: I am at a graveside service cringing under a twenty-one-gun salute while Mom clutches a triangle of red-white-and-blue to her breast but does not cry.

Slide three: I am helping a crumpled lawyer lead refugees out of an office building into a Manhattan blackout that might never end.

Slide four: I am watching Rory—or what's left of him—scuttle across the street on which we live to lose himself under a manhole cover.

Slide five: I am having a quiet conversation with Doc in a moonlit wood that's slipped sideways in space. Or maybe it's a frozen plain that's slipped sideways into winter.

Slide six: I am standing in a cold, damp barn in rural Illinois, half convinced that a kiss has just caused a freak ice storm. The world seems strangely upside down.

Slide seven: I am up to my neck in a frozen river, wondering if I've come to the last slide in the show. Doc is all that's keeping my head above water, and the world has righted itself again, but not the way I expected.

Funny: in the moment that might be your last, you suddenly see everything clear as a bell.

Sometime after the slide show, I woke up late in the day from a very long sleep. I had no idea what day it was late in, but I was warm and dry. I was also bruised and stiff and my fingers and toes hurt, but all in all I felt pretty good for a person who'd almost been drowned, frozen, and eaten by a whatever.

I was alone in the tent with hazy memories of the cold and the fear and the pain, and of first Cal, then Doc, tending and watching over me. I tested fingers and toes, making sure everything still worked. Then I made a horrible mistake: I stretched. The muscles in my calves knotted, and fire raced through them, making me yelp. I doubled over and fumbled with the zipper of the sleeping bag.

The tent flap flew back and light flooded in, bringing Cal with it. He must've been hovering right outside to make that quick an entrance.

"Are you all right?"

"No, dammit! I'm not all right. My legs are cramping!"

He had no trouble with the stupid zipper. A moment later he was massaging my bunched muscles. I gritted my teeth until the knots loosened.

"Better?" he asked.

I nodded. "Thanks. How long did I sleep?"

"About eighteen hours, off and on. Mostly on."

"*Eighteen hours!* You're kidding!" Hell, that was embarrassing. "Why didn't you wake me? We don't have time—"

He put a hand on my shoulder. "Relax. You don't owe anyone an apology. How do you feel now? Ready to get back up on that horse?"

That horse. I caught a sudden chill. "Big T?"

"Is fine. Enid took very good care of him after the dunking. All your clothes are dry and relatively clean, so you don't have to wear men's unmentionables anymore. Everything smells of wood smoke, but I figured you wouldn't mind that."

He smiled and flicked a stray strand of hair off my cheek, and I relived all those moments when our eyes met and there was a fire in the hold. I relived the kiss. I'd wanted him to kiss me. What'd they call that—irony?

I realized I was just sitting there staring at him, when he glanced away, made a nervous gesture, and brushed his hands on his jeans as if touching me had given him cooties, or maybe something else.

"Well, gosh," I said, "time's a-wastin'. I'd better get moving."

"If you're ready to. There's hot water for washing up. We rigged sort of an ersatz bathroom on the other side of the wall. You're probably hungry."

I was ravenous. "How much food did we lose?" I tried not to think about the mare.

"Fortunately, not a lot. You were right about splitting up the supplies."

"Well, hell, Cal," I said, grinning and slapping his leg. "That's why you pay me the big bucks."

He gave me a weird look. "I'll have to ask Doc if euphoria is a side effect of nearly drowning. What did you have, a near-death experience or something?"

I pulled back inside myself just a little to check. "Or something," I said.

He hesitated, watching my face, and I thought for a moment he was going to kiss me again. He didn't. He just moved some more stray hair off my cheek, then slid out through the tent flap.

I took a deep breath and prepared to emerge from my cocoon.

You take certain things for granted. Like walking. After making my way to the "bathroom," I vowed I would never take that particular activity for granted again. Bathing was an adventure, too, but like they say: what doesn't kill you makes you stronger. I figured a little more cold wasn't likely to do me in, especially if I confined it to one six inch square patch of skin at a time. Still, it was a relief to finally be dry and fully dressed.

The others were carefully repacking our supplies. Except for Doc. He was sitting on a crumbling bit of masonry sipping chocolate from our hoard of dry goods when I arrived at the campfire. I sat down kitty-corner to him on a rolled-up sleeping bag and poured myself a cup of watery brown liquid. It was hot and sweet—heavenly combination.

"I guess I'm not a better man than you, after all," I told him, tearing open a packet of jerky. "You didn't sleep for eighteen hours."

He glanced at me over the rim of his cup, steam veiling one eye, a lock of thick, dark hair hiding the other. Silver ran through it. Funny, I hadn't noticed that before. Maybe it hadn't been there until yesterday.

"I was not pinned in a freezing river by a thousand-pound animal," he told me.

"No, you were just standing up to your ass in the freezing river trying to rescue the woman pinned *under* the thousand-pound animal."

He shrugged.

"What, no Russian proverb to cover the occasion?"

He tilted his head, contemplating the steam rising from his cup. "Ah, well, there's probably some saying about old oxen that would apply."

I raised a brow. "Old oxen?"

"The old ox can still plow a straight furrow. Old oxen yet may have stiff horns—that sort of thing."

I burst out laughing. "Viktor, that's *obscene!*"

He blushed violently, while across the campsite the others paused in their packing to stare at us. "I did not mean—"

"Just teasing, okay?" I reached over and touched his hand. It was warm from the steaming cup. I had a flash of vivid recall about the warmth of his hands—and about my loose lips. Embarrassed, I pulled away. "You'll have to tell me some more 'old' proverbs as we go along. They're a hoot." I drained the last of my chocolate, pocketed what was left of the jerky, stood and walked toward the picket line, wobbling only a little.

"There is no fool like an old fool," he murmured behind me.
I pretended not to have heard him.

❦

We found Cal's missing suburbia, or what was left of it. It existed as a patchwork quilt of live and dead zones. Bands of holocaust gray striped with neighborhoods that seemed almost untouched except for the abandoned cars and overgrown yards. In some places the yards had become miniature farms filled with rows of dried cornstalks and makeshift garbage bag tents that protected unseen vegetables from frost.

We saw gangs and neighborhood watch groups. There was even a little old guy out raking leaves, while a woman who was probably his wife sat watch on the front porch with a plate of cookies and a baseball bat.

There were wild plants everywhere—weird-looking shit, some of it—growing up between the cracks in the asphalt, spiraling up light posts and over mailboxes. Nothing like Enid's glass trees, though. We steered clear of it.

We steered clear of people as well. It wasn't hard. Even folks who acted as if they might be interested in us got uninterested when they saw how heavily armed we were. Then there were the ones who were flat-out scared of Magritte. At one point a couple of priests scurried across our path, waving crosses at us. They barricaded themselves in a church. Magritte laughed, but it was a harsh sound with no fun in it.

Things got more and more grim-looking as we drew closer to Chicago proper. The streets were littered with glass and useless junk, useful junk having been snapped up in a spasm of looting that must've looked a lot like the one that wracked Manhattan. A regular greed orgy. The sidewalks sparkled as if they were carpeted in diamonds—sort of a twisted El Dorado. The air was thick and almost chewy with smoke.

If there were people here, they weren't showing themselves, but every once in a while you could hear them. A child laughing, a woman crying, people yelling at the top of their lungs.

What struck me most was that there was no gunfire. Imagine that—it took an epic disaster, but the streets of Chicago were quiet.

It's damn hard to commit mass destruction without guns. Guns can be used anonymously and without fear on the part of the shooter. Knives and clubs, on the other hand, are a little more particular and a lot more intimate.

I said something of that nature to Doc as we made our way carefully south through a place called Park Ridge. He raised an eyebrow and said, "*Popalsya, kotorieh kusalsya*. The biter, bit. Intimacy breeds vulnerability."

I hate conversations that operate on more than one level at a time. I turned and gave him a long, hard look. "Message?"

He seemed startled. "None that I am aware of. Except, what you were saying—in hand-to-hand combat, one does not have the advantage of distance." He smiled again, eyes warming. "Ah, you thought I was lecturing you, yes?"

"No, I . . . Okay, yeah." Fibbing to Doc was a waste of effort.

"Do I need to lecture you about such things, *boi baba*?"

"Trust me," I said, "you don't."

His smile vanished. He nodded and turned his gaze back up to the rooftops, leaving me to wonder what the hell I'd missed.

Enid led us now, working us toward Howard Russo's offices on Polk Street. He pointed out landmarks along the way. Everything he said began with the words "That used to be." It was weird. Everything used to be; nothing was now.

As if he picked up my train of thought, Enid wondered aloud where all his musician buddies were now, and what had happened to all the blues clubs. "The New Checkerboard Lounge," he said, as if the name tasted good. "That's where I met Howard. That was my first real solo gig. My whole family's musical. Pop was a lead guitarist—a session man; Mom was a singer; big brother Carson's in New Orleans now. I gotta wonder . . ." He didn't finish the thought, but we all knew what he wondered.

"Sounds as if you were born into a ready-made band," said Cal.

"It was that. We was all into session work. Pop got me my first paying gigs. Backup, mostly, for pros. Man, I just sat there and made like a sponge, soaking up everything they did. I even got to sit in at the CBF a couple of times."

"The CBF?" Cal repeated.

"Chicago Blues Festival," said Goldie. He was dressed head-to-toe in black today, except for the paisley vest. Looked kind of like a car-toonist's idea of a Wild West gunslinger—without the gun. We were all watching him pretty closely, but if he'd gotten any news from Source Radio, he wasn't telling.

"Yeah," said Enid. "I didn't get to strut or nothin'—sidemen pretty much got to stay in the pocket—but I promised myself I'd go back someday as a headliner. That Checkerboard gig was my first step down that road. Dead-end road now. Anyway, Howie was there that first night. We hooked up and he started getting me gigs. Kinda weird, actually. When you meet Howie, you'll see what I mean. He don't come across like he'd be that jazz savvy. He's more like a—like a lawyer or something. No offense," he told Cal, grinning.

"Oh, uh—none taken."

"But I gotta admit, he knew his way around the scene." He shook his head, dreadlocks swinging. "I sure can't feature him doing this to me. Trying to control my music and all. Trying to twist it."

"People change," Cal said.

Big T chose that moment to step on a manhole cover, his hoof sending up a dull clang that made me jump in the saddle. I thought of Rory and wondered whose front door I'd just knocked on. Nervous, I checked the lengthening shadows between the buildings. Things scurried back there. Things larger than the average rat. The sky was a dull orange-red where the sun hung. I wondered if maybe the Change went all the way out to the sun, all the way to the stars, all the way to heaven.

I dragged my mind back to where and when we were. The dia-monds on the sidewalks had turned to topazes, and would soon be-come garnets. "How much further, Enid?" I asked. "Are we going to make it by sunset?"

"Well, we're on Division," he said. "If we get up on the Kennedy, we might be able to move a little faster."

We'd been avoiding the major thoroughfares up till now. I looked to Cal. "What do you think?"

He glanced around at the littered streets and the shadows that crawled across them. The hand that rested on his sword hilt looked relaxed only at first glance. "This isn't a place I'd like to be when the sun goes down. Up there we'd be pretty safe from ambush, theoreti-cally."

"Except from the air." Leave it to Goldman to remind us of how impossibly weird our situation was.

"Here there be dragons?" Cal asked, echoing his skyward squint.

"I haven't seen any," said Magritte. She'd been flying point about seven feet up, but now dropped onto Jayhawk's burnished rump. Not taking any chances.

"It's hard to see anything with this haze." Cal turned to Enid. "How do we get onto the freeway?"

We fell in behind our Bluesman again, our horses moving up Division at a brisk walk, their unshod hooves making a muted clatter on the weather-rough asphalt. Checking back along the line, I saw we had a straggler. I swung Big T around, slipped up behind Doc's mare, and smacked her on the butt with my reins. She snorted and moved out smartly.

Not a peep. Doc merely took the horse a little more in hand.

"You're awfully droopy," I told him. "What happened to the old ox?"

He glanced at me, met my eyes for all of two tenths of a second, then looked away to scan the alleys and empty cars. "I'm introspecting."

"Sounds serious. Are you sure it's good for you?"

His smile was weak. "Probably not."

"And what are we introspecting about?"

He just shook his head. A private man, our dear Dr. Lysenko.

"My daddy told me that the 'Russkies' had raised pessimism to an art form. 'Zat so?"

He shot me a startled look, then laughed. "Do not judge all 'Russkies' by this one."

"Why not? If all Russians were you, my elementary school wouldn't have come equipped with a bomb shelter."

He ignored that. "Your father seems to have had strong opinions about Russians."

"My father had strong opinions about a lot of things."

"Like father like daughter."

I grinned at him. "Thank you. Now, just so you know, my opinion about this particular 'Russkie' is that he ought to stop introspecting and . . ." I hesitated, looking for some nice safe words. ". . . and start paying attention to what's going on around him." (And if that's not the pot calling the kettle black . . .)

A smile deepened the creases at the corners of his mouth. *"Da, glavah,"* he said.

Oh, joy, another nickname. "What's that mean—*gla-vah?"*

"I said, 'Yes, Chief.' "

Oh, don't go there, I thought. "My father called me that, Viktor," I told him. "You're not my father."

He looked as if I'd slapped him.

Damn. "I'm sorry," I said. "I didn't mean that the way it—"

He raised a hand to stop me. "I understand, Colleen," he said, and kicked his horse into a trot.

"No, you don't," I murmured, then clucked at Big T and hurried to rejoin the train.

❧

The Kennedy Expressway was clotted with abandoned cars, many of which had been stripped of tires, hubcaps, even window glass and seats. Fortunately, the Change had struck before the Chicago rush hour, or the road would have been an impassable maze. As it was, we were able to move at a trot or better if we single-filed it down the center line. It was windier up here, which wasn't dangerous in and of itself, but made the horses a little crazy.

We'd been on the freeway for a while and had just swung southeast into an intricate cloverleaf when Magritte let out a cry of alarm. We all looked up at her, then followed the thrust of her arm eastward.

"Oh, God," said Goldman. "What's that?"

That was a filmy bubble of something rising over what I took to be downtown Chicago. It looked like a dome from one of those futuristic movies about the colonization of Mars, but it seemed semiliquid, like a soap bubble. A rainbow of color oozed over the scarlet-tinted surface.

"Man, that wasn't there when we left," said Enid. "Looks like it's sitting right over the Loop."

Magritte had floated upward again, bit by bit. Now she settled onto Jayhawk behind Goldie, rubbing her upper arms and shaking her head. "That don't feel right. That's bad."

Cal reined Sooner closer—intense, face all angles, eyes bright and sharp. "Goldie, talk to me. What's happening? What are you hearing?"

Goldie's face had gone as gray as the asphalt we rode in on. "A whole lot of nothing. But it . . . it feels like . . ."

Magritte finished for him: "It feels like the Preserve, but . . . but dark and sticky."

"Like the Preserve, in what way?" Cal asked.

"Like firefly stuff . . . sort of," said Magritte, nodding toward the gleaming bubble.

Every drop of color drained out of Cal's face. Watching him, I felt like I'd been plunged back into the river. If there were flares here, he'd want to believe one of them was Tina.

"No," I said. "It's not possible. How could there be flares here?"

Cal's eyes burned. "How could there be flares at the Preserve?" He nodded up the dotted white line beneath our horses' hooves. "Let's get moving. The sooner we find Howard Russo, the sooner we can get Enid free of his contract."

He left the part about finding Tina and the Source unsaid.

We hustled then, due south and parallel to the Chicago River, and submerged ourselves in the Chicago 'hoods again at Des Plaines Street. It was a better neighborhood than we'd been in earlier—or at least it used to be. That did not mean I was about to relax. I rode rear guard with both eyes on the shadowy road, my crossbow at ready, flinching every time someone poked their head out of a window or doorway.

I can't begin to describe how twitchy I was, riding down that dim corridor. The others moved ahead of me in pairs, with Magritte hovering among the packhorses. I watched their backs; there was no one to watch mine. I felt naked, the flesh between my shoulder blades crawling like ants tap-danced up and down it. I decided that if we saw a police station, I was going to go in and do some clothes shopping—something black and sexy in Kevlar.

Finally, we swung east onto Polk. Enid called back over his shoulder that it was right up ahead, in the middle of the block between Jefferson and Clinton. The buildings were low rises, neither new nor old, and it looked like the zoning was mixed business and residential. Russo's building was a four-story gray stone with that sparkly stuff in the concrete. The windows were tall, narrow, and covered with a facing of flat, vertical, fake marble columns. Very neo-something.

We drew to a stop in front of the building and Enid turned to Cal. "Now what? Do we just go in and get in his face?"

"That's my vote," said Cal.

I raised my hand. "Excuse me, gentlemen, but I would like to raise a practical issue. What do we do with these horses while we're getting in Howie's face?"

The cool thing about these older neighborhoods is the way they hid things behind their storefronts. In this case, what looked like a garage door led down an alley into a courtyard that contained a patio set with a folded-up umbrella, a woebegone Fiat, and an equally forlorn motorbike. There were also some trash cans and two bicycles sitting in a metal stand. Correction: *locked* in a metal stand.

We left the horses in the yard under the watchful eyes of Goldie, Doc, and Magritte, while Cal, Enid, and I entered the building from the rear. Cal'd drawn his sword. Enid's weapons of choice were a switchblade someone had tossed into his guitar case during one of his street corner "giggles," as he called them, and a bayonet he told us had been taken off a dead cavalryman by his great-grandfather, Soldier Heart, at Little Big Horn. In close quarters I like a good baseball bat. Especially if you don't want to damage the other guy too badly. I was glad I'd thought to bring one.

Splitting up made me nervous, since I'd noted that the locks on those bicycles were brand new. We could only hope that nothing would happen in the courtyard that would separate Magritte from Goldie by more than a few feet.

Enid took us straight up to the third floor, but started shaking his head as we came up onto the landing. "He's not here. But he's in the building somewhere—I can feel him."

Cal peered up the stairwell. "We go up or down?"

Enid's brow furrowed, then he closed his eyes. "Down."

We went down. Enid first.

I traded glances with Cal before we moved to follow. "What do we do if he's *not* here?" I asked in a whisper.

"I heard that," said Enid from below. "He's here."

Cal cracked a smile. "We search the offices. We might find something. Maybe the original contract."

I shrugged. "Which would do what for us?"

"Enid tried destroying his copy and couldn't. I had a thought that maybe we have to destroy the original first."

"Better light a lamp," Enid called. "It's dark down here."

"Could it be that simple?" I asked as Cal put a lighter to the lamp wick.

"Now that would be refreshing, wouldn't it?" He looked up, caught my eyes and smiled. In the lamplight his eyes looked more gold than hazel. Breath stopped in my throat and my face felt suddenly warm and tingly.

"You comin'?" asked Enid from the darkness.

"Yeah," Cal called down, then set the chimney firmly over the flame and started down the stairs, giving me a backward glance.

I allowed myself to breathe again and followed him.

Russo wasn't on the second floor or the first.

"Little shit's hidin' out in the basement," muttered Enid. "He probably felt me coming."

The basement was a warren of storage and utility rooms, all arranged around a central area. I could tell right away that somebody lived here. Furniture had been dragged into the corner of the main room: a table, a leather chair, a futon, a shelf loaded with books, a small but nice Persian carpet. Very tasteful. There was something wrong with the picture, though—something I couldn't quite put my finger on.

"Smells funny," said Enid.

Cal was looking over some stuff on the table. He held up a cigar butt—well chewed. A tendril of smoke curled limply from the end. "Still warm."

Enid and his great-granddaddy's bayonet stood guard in the "living room" while Cal and I made our way down the hall toward the storage areas. We got to the first door, a storage room. Cal set the lantern down in the corridor while I checked the lock. It had been jimmied.

"You open," Cal whispered. "I'll go in."

I shook my head. "*You* open."

"Colleen . . ."

"All right. I open, we both go in."

He nodded.

I mouthed a three-second countdown, then flung the door against the wall with a bang, in the hope that if Russo was in there, he'd freak and blow his cover. I mean, how used to being stalked through a dark building by armed commandos could he be?

No one leapt out of the stuff that filled the storage room. It would take a thorough search to find anyone in there. I took a step farther into the room, wielding my bat.

"Hey, Howie. Come on out and say hi."

Out in the hall a door slammed and someone pounded down the corridor. Enid shouted. Cal and I whirled in unison and vaulted out of the room and down the hall to the main chamber.

Enid was facing us, bayonet in hand, his lamp held high and a stunned expression on his face. Cowering between him and us, trying to shield its bulging, white eyes from the light, was a grunter in a brown tweed suit coat and little else.

Now I realized what was wrong with the charming domestic scene we'd stumbled into. There were no lamps.

Enid took a step forward, lowering his lantern. "Shit, Howie. Is that you?"

EIGHTEEN

GOLDIE

Moments like the one we spend in the courtyard behind Russo's place are precious. This is something I know from experience. They're photographs I can take out and look at as I please. Well, holograms, actually—like on *Star Trek*—3-D, with scents and sounds and sensations. If I could, I'd live my life in a holodeck, which is, I suppose, why the opportunity has never presented itself. I'd go in and never come out. And while I was inside, I'd be anybody but Herman Goldman.

It's quiet here, almost balmy after our sojourn on the Great Plains. And there's no gusting wind. I lie on the hood of the defunct Fiat, aware that I am stealing this moment. Magritte is curled up next to me. Her aura waxes and wanes as we talk, our eyes on the ring of buildings, watching windows.

Doc sits on the back stoop of Russo's building, watching the windows we can't see. Watching us. Given what little I know about his family, this adds a blue tint to my hologram.

The sun has just snuffed itself when lights flicker feebly behind the windows of the building that faces Russo's across the courtyard. We all tense up, clutching weapons more tightly.

My stolen moment evaporates.

Doc is on his feet, crossbow up and ready. "Perhaps we should take cover." He gives the building behind him a worried glance. "They have been in there a long time."

"Only seems like a long time," I say, pulling myself upright.

The words have barely left my mouth when the metal door behind Doc scrapes open. He's got the jitters so bad, he leaps off the stoop into the courtyard, pivoting in midair to draw down on the door. Fortunately for Cal, he doesn't have an itchy trigger finger.

"Come on in," Cal says. "We found Russo."

"The horses?" I nod at our snoozing animals.

"Russo says they'll be fine here. His neighbors, according to him, wouldn't know how to ride a horse if they *wanted* to steal one."

"Uh-huh," I say. "But I'll betcha they could probably figure out how to cook one."

"Good point. Maybe you could do something to protect them?"

I fire off my most awesome ball-o'-fire to date and leave it swaddling the horses with a dangerous-looking veil of light. The poor animals are so exhausted, they barely notice. *I* notice that I do it with much less effort than before.

I am beyond surprise when we are ushered into a basement room to meet Howard Russo. "Holy cow, Blindman," I pun, "your manager is a troll."

Enid gives me a dark look from under his dreadlocks. "Yeah, tell me about it."

The troll in question turns to look at us. His big milky eyes get even bigger and milkier when he sees Magritte, the vertical pupils squeezing shut against her glow.

"You got angelfire," he croaks.

Angelfire. That's one I haven't heard before. Given the effect Magritte has on my various synapses, it's appropriate.

"Why'd you bring her here?" Russo asks.

"She's protecting me from you," says Enid.

"From me?" He blinks myopically.

"Shit—you are no way that stupid, Howard Russo. It's my damned *contract*."

The little grunter's face goes gray. Oh, all right—it's already gray; it goes grayer. "Whaddaya mean, your contract?"

"I mean that clause about repercussions. I play my music and weird shit happens. Things get all twisted. *People* get all twisted."

Russo's eyes kind of pinball off Enid's face. Shifty little fellow. "Feedback . . . The contract . . . feeds back." The words sound chewed on. He shakes a finger at Enid. "You shouldn't play without . . . you know, without . . ."

"Permission?" offers Cal.

"Uh-huh. The contract is . . . it's—it's put together to protect the interests of the, uh, the management."

"What about *my* interests?" Enid snarls. He points at Russo's diminutive nose. "I can't believe you'd do something like this to me."

Russo blinks. "You signed. You were okay with it then."

"In the *real* world, Howard. Not in this damned Twilight Zone we're living in."

The grunter picks at a piece of lint on his tweed jacket. "So, don't play." He gives Enid a sly look out of his milky bug-eyes.

"Don't play? That's like saying 'don't breathe.' Besides, there's Maggie. I been having to make music to protect her."

Russo's eyes sort of snap to Enid's face. "To what?"

"Yeah, I know it sounds weird, but it protects her from the Storm or the Source or whatever you want to call it."

Russo looks vaguely puzzled. "You mean that big, black thing that, uh, hoovered up all the angelfire? The Dark?"

Enid nods. "Bottom line, Howard, I want out."

"Out?"

"Of the contract. I came to tell you it ain't legal no more. You're gonna tear it up."

Russo's little gray face pales and he blinks rapidly several times. I have the loopy idea that he's holding back tears. "Can't do it," he mumbles.

"You want me to tear *you* up instead?"

The grunter takes a step away from Enid and backs straight into Colleen, who snags the shoulder pads of his overlarge tweeds and holds him still. He cowers a little, but repeats, "Can't do it. Not *won't* do it—*can't.*"

Colleen literally growls. "What's that supposed to mean?"

Cal leans down into Russo's face. "It's not as if you have a choice to make, Mr. Russo. This is simple: the contract was voided by the fact that it was altered *after* Enid signed it."

Russo giggles—a strange, wheezy sound like a car that doesn't want to turn over. "You talk like a lawyer."

"I am a lawyer."

He sneezes away the giggles and sobers a little. "S'more than business," he mutters, then pulls away from Colleen and shuffles over to the table, where he picks up the cigar butt and sticks it between his sharp, nasty little teeth.

Such panache.

He's silent for a moment, chewing on his cigar butt. Then he stops and looks straight at Enid, suddenly seeming utterly human. "Look, Enid, I'm not the one you gotta deal with."

"What do you mean, you're not the one?" Enid asks.

"Primal."

"Primal," Enid repeats.

"Third party to the contract, remember? Primal got a say."

"Shit, Howard, there's no Primal Records anymore. The Storm put paid to that. There's just you and me."

The cigar butt hangs loosely in Russo's mouth for a moment while his eyes move from Cal to Enid to Magritte. "You protect her, huh?"

And I thought *my* noodle produced non sequiturs.

"I could," Enid said, "except for the fact that the damn contract makes my music feed back all over the place. I'm sick, Howard. And I've twisted the shit out of I don't know how many innocent folks."

Russo is startled. "Sick? How—sick?"

"Sick. As in dying. I play and it sucks the life out of me. I don't play and it shrivels up my soul. Rock and a hard place, Howie. And you put me there."

Russo shakes his head hard enough to make it rattle. "Not me. Not me," he mumbles. "Primal. There *is* a Primal. It—It's Primal you gotta deal with."

"Do you have the original contract?" Cal asks.

"Me? No. Primal got it. I only got a copy."

"A copy you can't get rid of?"

Russo's eyes bug out even more than they are naturally inclined to do. "What?"

"You do, don't you?" Enid presses. "You try to destroy it, but you can't. You try to lose it; it won't stay lost."

Russo's about chewed his cigar in two by now. He looks up at Enid and blinks. "Why d'you think I'm still in Chicago? Far as I can go. Right *here*." He yanks the soggy butt out of his mouth and stabs it at the floor. Then he drops it and crushes it into the concrete with a bare foot.

Enid and Cal exchange glances, then Cal says, "And you've never tried to void it?"

"How?"

"Well, gee," I say, "I'll bet you'd want to go to the Ruby City with us, Mr. Cowardly Lion, sir, and see if we can't get the Wizard to give you some ba—"

"Goldie . . ." Cal gives me a sideways glance (not completely devoid of humor) and shakes his head. "It does look as if you could benefit from a visit to Primal Records."

Russo shakes his head. His eyes crinkle at the corners and get a little milkier. "No. Not goin' into that place. Not goin' downtown."

Russo clearly has some serious angst about the Bubble. I gotta admit, it weirds me out no end, because I can't tell what's inside it. I figure maybe Howie knows, so I ask. "What's downtown, Howie? Is it . . . is the Dark downtown? Is that what makes the Bubble?"

He gapes at me. "The Dark? Here?" He's laughing, sort of, but his eyes are darting around as if the Dark might just jump right out and bite him. "What kind of crazy question is that? Nobody knows where the Dark comes from. Nobody'd want to know."

Except us. I slant a glance at Cal. *Your turn.*

Cal says, "You're stuck here. You said it yourself. If you want to get unstuck, you need to void that contract. And given how things change, we may need a guide. You help us, we help you."

"You help me?"

Cal nods.

Russo seems to consider that for a moment, then develops a profound case of Gumby shoulders. "Why get unstuck? No place to go."

Cal leans down into his face. "We know a place you can go."

"Cal's right," Enid chips in. "Maggie and I just came from there. It's called the Preserve. It was a safe place for us, Howard. Until I got so damn sick. If I can get free of this contract, it'll be safe for us again."

"Just show us where we can find Primal Records," says Cal.

"Now?" Russo squeaks.

"We're in a bit of a hurry," I say.

Russo blanches. Except for the tips of his pointy little ears, which turn a darker shade of blue. "Oh, no, no. Not now. S'after hours."

That's a chuckle. "They still keep business hours?" I ask.

"Old habits," says Russo, fidgeting.

"Sorry," says Cal. "I don't buy that. You don't know how to get in, do you?"

Russo leans toward Cal, his eyes shifting to the shadows. "I know how to get in, couns'ler. But you don't wanna go out at night around here. *Trust* me."

About as far as I could throw you, I think.

"Fine. I'd rather do this fully rested anyway." Cal lays a hand on Russo's tweedy shoulder. "But tomorrow morning you're taking us to see the Wizard."

Russo looks at the hand, then back at Cal, and giggles again. "Yeah. T'morrow. See the Wizard."

⁂

We are to spend an uneasy night in Russo's third-floor suite of rooms. There is a large, rather ostentatious office with its own minimally working bathroom, a wet bar, and what amounts to a parlor tucked into a corner beside the front doors. Through a second set of doors a small but fully furnished living room with a fireplace, and a large bedroom with a second bath, line up along the front of the building. A pocket kitchen opens up kitty-corner to the bedroom door. Only a close look at the accouterments in the living room reveal that the marble hearth and parquet floors are faux. It's been slightly "grunter-fied." Every window is covered with thick curtains, none of which seem to match. They are velvet, linen, brocade. One is a quilt.

There is no moon visible tonight, but the faerie Bubble illuminates the darkness much as Chicago's bowl of light pollution must have done once. When I pull the quilt aside from a living room window, I can see it shining dully above the rooftops about two or three blocks to the east. I try to touch it, figuratively speaking—try to lay psychic hands on it, to feel its texture. It resists me. After pulling me here, its silence is unnerving and annoying. I'm pretty sure this is what it feels like to be a cat toy.

It clearly makes Russo *ferklempt*. He doesn't go near the window; he doesn't look at the window. This strikes me as odd, because the Bubble's just not that bright. It puts out a lot less light than Magritte does, and he doesn't seem at all reluctant to look at her, even though she makes his eyes water. In fact, he can't seem to take his eyes off her, which makes *me* nervous.

"Close that," he whines at last, as if he can't stand the pale wash of ruddy light that seeps in.

I oblige, letting the quilt fall. "What's the matter, Howie? Don't like the view?"

He just grunts. Typical.

Cal has been watching Russo as closely as I have. "What can you tell me about that?" he asks, nodding toward the window.

"What?" Russo asks, then fills his mouth so full of jerky that he couldn't answer if he wanted to.

Cal's mouth quirks wryly. I'm sure he's seen similar delaying tactics in the courtroom. "The bubble of power over the Loop. What do you know about it?"

Russo chews noisily and methodically and stares at Cal for a minute without answering. Then he swallows, licks his lips, also noisily, and shakes his bald head. "Nothing."

"You don't know how it's generated? Where it came from? How it's maintained?"

A shrug.

"I think you do know," suggests Cal. "And you don't like it. Why?"

Russo's eyes glaze over a little then roll back over to Magritte, where they come into sharp focus.

I snap to immediate attention and move to stand so that Maggie and I are nearly touching. I don't know if it's her or me or both of us, but I feel as if slugs are crawling all over me. I glance at her face; she is clearly creeped out by Russo's interest.

He stops chewing and points a gnarled finger at her. "D'I know you? Sure I know you."

She shakes her head. "I don't think so. I heard Enid talk about you, is all."

"Watch'er name—Maggie, is it?"

"Magritte," says Enid. He's perched on the arm of Russo's couch, tucking into a can of hash. "Her name's Magritte. We go way back. Further than you and me. You never met that I know of."

The grunter's eyes gleam with what I take as recognition, and his wide mouth curves into a grin. "Magritte? Shit, *yeah*, we met! You're

Choir Girl, right? Worked the Rainbow Club. Had a room upstairs." He snaps his fingers and points again. "Green velvet. Green velvet and a—a crystal unicorn in the window. Little colored sparkles all over *everything*." He giggles hideously. "No surprise you don't 'member me. Didn't stand out in a crowd back then. But I remember you." He looks right at me, still grinning. "She's *good*."

Suddenly, I'm struggling to breathe and wanting to simultaneously shed tears and pound the living crap out of him. Then my hands are around his neck. And weird green flames are shooting from my fingertips. And Howard is shrieking like a banshee.

Cal, Colleen, and Enid leap in harmony to stop me from killing the little shit. They loosen my fingers, but he continues to scream like a reject from *Gremlins*.

"My eyes! My eyes! Light hurts!"

I so want to wad Howard Russo into a little blue-gray ball and shoot a three-pointer into the toilet, but the others prevail, tearing me away from him.

He scuttles into a corner, eyes wide and blinking. "What? Wha'd I do? She's a hooker, for chrissake! Doin' a job. I'm just a fuckin' customer."

Poor choice of words. I leap again, but Enid and Cal's arms are tangled around me and Enid's voice comes tight and low in my ear: "Ignore him. He's a stupid shit. He's just a stupid shit. Let it go." I'm not sure which of us he's talking to.

We are like that—an off-balance human pretzel—when Magritte screams. The sound wrenches me inside out and spins all of us around.

Her face is frozen in terror, mouth open, eyes sightless and wide. She hears the Storm's countless Voices, sees its long shadow, feels its dark hands. I know, because I feel it, too. The Storm is rising in my head—in my soul—and if I don't move fast, it will literally tear Magritte and me apart.

Freed, I cover the space between us in two strides, but she is being lifted toward the ceiling, the Storm's dark fingers tugging at her. I leap and lock my arms around her; her hands tangle in my hair.

We fall.

Enid sings, desperately, as if his life depends on it. Which it does. No less does mine. I concentrate everything I have on holding Magritte, on shielding her, dragging her so deep inside Herman

Goldman that the Source will lose her and I won't. The Voices shriek at us to let go, to give up and give in.

To come home.

Maggie shudders, her back arching, and screams again, obscuring the beat of her heart—the sound I'm focused on.

"*What is it?*" Colleen is shouting. She has a crossbow in her hands—useless against this.

Cal and Doc are frozen, watching. They know what it is. They also know they are defenseless against it. Only Enid and I are armed for this enemy.

When I think we're too late, Magritte relaxes and goes nearly limp in my arms. The darkness subsides; the predator growls and returns to its lair. *Where?* God, we could be right on top of it.

When I can breathe and think again, I'm still lying on the floor with Magritte trembling beneath me. I'm trembling, too, because I've felt that black, slimy touch before and because we now know how much a momentary lapse of concentration can cost.

I utter uncounted *I'm sorrys* to Magritte for having abandoned her in a careless moment of rage, but she blames herself. "Wasn't thinking," she murmurs over and over. "I let go. I let go."

She can't stop shaking, and nothing either Enid or I can do seems capable of erasing the terror in her eyes. It bleeds all over both of us, making us quake inside and share furtive, guilty glances.

We commandeer Russo's bedroom and install her in it on his ludicrously king-size bed. Enid vows he will sit up all night and sing to her if he has to. Sitting cross-legged on the floor by the bed—guitar in his lap, harmonica in his pocket—he's ready if she needs him to sing. I pick a deity and pray he won't have to sing—again. And that the notes he's let loose already haven't found a living target.

I lie down beside Magritte, not touching her, but close enough to feel her warmth. I'm afraid to touch her. Remembering Russo's filth is one thing, but the Source, I know, reaches beyond the body and lays hands on the soul. *But from where?*

She doesn't sleep, but she seems to drowse, even to dream, her eyes moving behind the nearly translucent lids.

Time passes. Enid mumbles to himself, trying to stay awake. His fingers brush the strings of his guitar now and again, sending up a yearning whisper of notes. I prop myself against the headboard, and get lost in memories—mine or Maggie's; they're indistinguishable. They're dark memories, gray memories, punctuated by periods of colorful, inexplicable elation and stark, bleak pain. As I sort my way through them I look down at her and find her watching me.

"Enid," she says, without looking away. "Go get some sleep."

He shifts position with the squeak of strings. "Mags, I promised."

"Enid, please. It's okay. Goldie's here."

He stands, turning to look at her—at us. She returns his gaze and something passes silently between them.

"It's what you want?" he asks.

Her eyes come back to meet mine. "It's what I need."

Enid gives me the briefest of glances before he slips from the room and closes the door behind him.

"Why?" I ask, wanting to know before reason is completely blotted out by something much stronger.

"You know why." She puts a hand up and brushes the tangle of hair away from my eyes so she can read them. "I want to be clean again. And so do you."

"Maggie, I'm . . ." I'm what—unstable? Crazy? Dangerous?

"What I need," she repeats.

Through the long night the words echo in my head, until I find myself speaking them, whispering them to her again and again. And somewhere in there, "need" transforms into "love." Transforms like a lunatic turned wizard, or a hooker turned angel. And I half believe that what we do really is stronger than the Storm.

NINETEEN

DOC

During the frantic moments in which Enid and Goldie battled the Source for Magritte, Howard Russo slunk away into his office like a cowering animal. I found him there, barricaded behind his desk in a swivel chair that dwarfed him. He was reading in the dim glow of a lamp over which he had draped a sweater. The feeble light reflected in the lenses of wire-rimmed glasses balanced precariously on a nose barely capable of holding them.

My surprise did not escape him. He held up the book. "Dostoevsky," he said. "*Crime and Punishment.* Reading helps me hold onto myself."

I came a bit farther into the room, my eyes adjusting to the darkness. "Hold onto yourself?"

His face pulled into a rueful leer. "Didn't always look like this," he said. "Feel like this."

There was a howl from the street, the sound of trash cans falling, rolling, followed by strange, guttural laughter.

Russo flinched visibly and bared his teeth. "Every night," he said. "They come out. Not always so noisy. But I know. I feel them." He chuckled, a gravelly echo of the laughter from the street. "Can Howie come out to play?"

I moved to sit on the sofa across from the desk. "And do you want to . . . go out and play?"

The street erupted with what might have been the yappings of wild animals . . . or something else.

Russo slanted a look at the window then turned his face to me. "I don't want to become that." The words were clear and deliberate. The voice almost fully human.

"So you read."

He stroked the pages of the book. "My head clears out when I read. I feel . . . like myself." He shrugged. "Probably only a matter of time, though . . . This place you guys came from—there are really people like me there?"

"Yes. And like you, they don't want to become . . . something else."

The door swung open then, and Cal stood in the doorway, light from the other room flooding in around him.

Russo blinked and shielded his eyes. "Do you mind?"

Cal hesitated, then closed the door and stepped into the office. "You have any preferences about where we sleep?"

Russo shrugged. "Anywhere's fine. Sofas are pretty comfy."

"Where were you going to sleep?"

"I sleep down below. In the daytime."

"You said you knew how to get into the Bubble," Cal said. "How?"

"There are people inside. They have to eat. Stuff has to go in. Wagons, whatever."

"So, what—we just walk in?"

To this, Russo offered a broad leer. "Only if you have something they want, counselor. Which you do."

Cal glanced at me, then shook his head. "What could we have that they'd want?"

"Angelfire."

"Magritte?"

Russo nodded.

I stood, cold to the core. "Why? Why would they want flares?"

Russo shrugged. "Don't know. But I've never seen one turned back."

Cal took a quick step toward the grunter, who flinched back as if he feared violence. "But you've seen flares go in? Angelfire. You're sure? How many? When?"

"Some," said Russo warily. "Now and again. I try not to go up that way. Messes with my head."

"Messes with your head," Cal repeated. "Meaning what, exactly?"

"Place sucks at you. Makes you itch."

I thought of the Black Tower in my dreams and understood him. "You've seen flares go in. Have you ever seen one come out?"

He shook his head.

"What happens to them in there, Howard?" Cal asked.

Russo regarded him silently for a moment, then looked down into the pages of his book, fingertips stroking the print. "I don't know."

Cal sank to the arm of the sofa. "We're going in there blind." He looked at me, the expression in his eyes cloaked by the darkness of the room. "We have no way of knowing what will happen to Magritte if we take her in there."

"If? We have no choice, Calvin. We must take her in, and hope that Goldie can keep her safe."

"Safe?" Russo's smile was feral. "Ruby City's never safe."

❦

In the hours before dawn, I lay awake on the sofa in Howard Russo's office, listening to the city, to the building, to the sounds of the others sleeping, to the beating of my heart. This bespelled place was not silent; it was merely secretive. In the walls and in the corridor beyond the locked and bolted door there was movement, sly and questing.

It was these sounds that awakened me, jolting me up out of uneasy sleep to a soft chuckle from across the room. It was Russo, perched not behind his desk, but upon it. Reading.

"Don't worry, Doc," he said now, his voice a rasp that recalled Poe's raven. His malformed head was silhouetted against the wan light that crept in through the blinds behind him. He canted it to listen, and the light caressed the wire rims of his glasses. "Just some acquaintances wondering who's company." He glanced back at me, stroking the pages of the book. "It's okay. Don't think they'll try to come in." He adjusted his glasses, looking at once familiar and alien, then poked his nose back into the book. "You sleep."

But I couldn't sleep any more than could he. The furtive sounds seemed to work on both of us alike. They beckoned to him, while he barricaded himself here, armed against them with books, clinging to what was left of Howard Russo. I, on the other hand, was afraid of something I could not name.

After a while of reading, he got up and paced the rooms, so quietly he seemed to vanish. I paced, too, but mentally. I had already, this night, worn a rut in the hardwood of the upper hall, crossing and recrossing it to the room at the back of the building where our night watch kept guard on the courtyard below.

While I was engaged in this, the office door lock clicked and the door opened, allowing a slender shadow to enter. It made its way with care past me to the living room door and in.

I heard their voices then—soft whispers exchanging information about time and activity . . . and perhaps more. Then they emerged into the office together.

"I've had plenty of rest," Cal said softly. "Don't worry, I'm not going to fall asleep at my post . . . Sarge."

"I'm more worried about you falling *down* at your post," murmured Colleen. "The windowsill's the best place to sit watch, but with the casement busted like that, you could easily take a header into the picket line."

I could almost hear Cal smile. "I'll be fine. I'm wide-awake."

He leaned into her and their forms merged briefly. She said his name beneath her breath, and they parted, he to take the final watch, she to stand immobile at the foot of the sofa where I lay, pretending sleep.

"Oh, hell," she whispered, then wheeled and disappeared into the parlor. She was back a moment later to unroll her sleeping bag on the floor between the sofa and desk and curl up within it.

I forced my eyes closed and was surprised to find sleep. I drowsed until the sun finally poured out its weak amber light to ooze around Howard Russo's shades. I woke, told myself I was not comfortable lying on my back, and rolled onto my side. My glance, disobedient, fell to the floor.

The transition between the fleeting look and the gaze was seamless. One moment I was staring into darkness, the next I was watching Colleen sleep, ruddy, predawn light flowing around her. The thoughts I was struggling not to entertain; the sensations I was fighting to ignore; the emotions I did not want to name—they, too, threatened to be illuminated in that toxic spill of light.

Dear God, but I was tired. Yes, that was it. If I could only get adequate sleep, this would pass. If. If I could only comprehend the disease, I could find a cure. If I could wipe out the memory of that moment in the barn when I discovered the impossible lurking in my soul. If I could erase the feeling of her hands slipping from mine in the numbing flood.

Time rippled, and I was transported to a rain-slick road near Kiev. There, in a brief flicker of seconds, I had a dark epiphany: the life I had lived for the past fourteen years revolved on the instant I drew Colleen from the water. I had done for her what I could not do for Yelena and Nurya.

I didn't know what it meant. I didn't *want* to know what it meant. So I struggled with the angel of revelation and called him "Deceiver." I forced his wings to fold. I begged him for mercy, for sleep. There was still time before we must rise and travel. I would simply close my eyes and no longer see Colleen.

But before I could close my eyes, she opened hers. I was unable to move, to dissemble, to hide. She held my gaze for a moment, then smiled, closed her eyes, and returned to her dreams.

The struggle was over, instantly, leaving me with nothing but a peculiar wash of relief. Her smile—that warm, sleepy, child-like smile—had said to me that she yet saw in me a friend. Regardless of what I felt or imagined I felt, I would always be that—her friend, her confidant. This, I would let nothing change.

I slept then, and for the first time in many days did not dream of Chernobyl.

The sun was fully up when we rose. The rest was regenerative. I felt, if not content, at least acquiescent. Whatever coil of melancholy had wrapped itself around my heart had released it. Colleen, for her part, reacted to me no differently than she had before. She was still easy in my presence, and I determined that I would be no different in hers.

What had changed this morning was something I might have missed were it not for Howard Russo. Almost from the moment they appeared, he tracked Goldie and Magritte with his large, milky eyes, reminding me of a cat that has caught a bemusing scent.

Goldie was not unaware of this intense regard. To say it irritated him would be understatement. He avoided Russo, turning away whenever he felt the little man's eyes on him, engaging his attention fully in our task of tucking away the supplies Enid and Cal ferried up from the courtyard against our foray into the Loop.

"Little shit's giving me the creeps," he murmured as we sorted sealed food packets into neat piles on the credenza behind Russo's living room sofa.

I glanced over my shoulder at Russo and received a sly smile. "Yes? Why does he find you of such interest, suddenly?"

He shrugged, concentrating on the Army-issue food packets he was counting out. "Only the Shadow knows."

It was, ironically, because of shadow that I saw it. Howard Russo could not abide even the weak sunlight that wedged its way into his rooms through gaps in the blinds and curtains. Goldie had undone his careful tucking of the parlor curtains the night before, and now Russo took his eyes from the objects of his attention just long enough to seal the gap with safety pins.

In that initial darkness, Goldie gleamed as if his skin had been dusted in gold and burnished. He had a noticeable aura, like Magritte's, if slightly fainter. More than that, the two of them were connected by a bright conduit of flare radiance.

My first impulse was fear. "Goldie," I said, perhaps too sharply, "Goldie, look at me."

He turned, his eyes going wide with surprise as I trapped his head between my hands to peer into them. They were comfortingly brown, with normal, round, human pupils. Had they always been that large, I asked myself, that luminous?

His brow furrowed. "Doc, what . . . ? What is it?"

I put a hand to his forehead, brushing aside the tumble of thick curls. No fever. "Close your eyes," I told him.

He did, grinning nervously. "C'mon, Doc, you're scaring me."

Cal had come into the room and caught the exchange. He dropped the packs he carried and hurried to us. "Something wrong?"

As certain as I could be that Goldie's eyelids showed no sign of increased translucence, I stepped back and shook my head, meeting Cal's worried eyes. "I had a moment of concern. The aura is so much stronger this morning." I indicated the distance between Goldie and Magritte, which she had closed since I began my examination, her own face eloquent with distress. The closer she drew, the brighter became the trail of light that connected them.

Cal followed the trail with his eyes. He turned back to me, his face going pale. "You thought he was changing."

Goldie took a startled step away from us, then caught sight of the radiant cord and blushed violently. "Oh, that. It, uh . . . I guess the longer we're together, the stronger it gets." He laughed. "I thought maybe I was breaking out in manic hives or something."

Ah, sarcasm. Dostoevsky called it the last refuge for the soul whose privacy has been invaded. At times it makes excellent camouflage. At others it simply advertises what one wishes to conceal.

Russo had turned from his task at the window and sidled up beside us, his eyes darting, his impossibly wide mouth cracked in what can only be described as a leer. A sound that was more whine than giggle emerged from between his lips. "Told you." He crooked a finger at Goldie. "*Told* you she was good."

Light exploded in my eyes, buffeting me like a scorching wind— hot, white, searing. It tore Howard Russo off his feet and slammed him backward into the curtains he had so painstakingly pinned shut. The window shattered with a sound like a rifle shot, but the thick fabric held. Russo hung against the forest green velvet for an instant, then pitched forward onto the floor.

In the stunned hush that followed, there was only the sound of our breathing and the muted rain of glass on the street below. I turned fearful eyes to Magritte, certain the spectral attack must have come from her. But she was innocent, staring at Goldie, her hands to her mouth. It was Goldie whose body pulsed with residual energy, Goldie whose eyes poured venom onto the crumpled grunter. He turned his eyes to Cal then, and whatever Cal saw there caused him to take a startled step backward. Goldie brushed past him and left the room, leaving an almost palpable charge of static in his wake. After a moment of hesitation, Magritte darted after him.

Cal and I both moved at once to kneel over Russo's crumpled body. He was still breathing, thank God, and his neck had not been broken, though by all rights it should have been. We rolled him gently onto his back and I began to check for broken bones.

He moaned and his eyes fluttered open. "Son'fabitch," he muttered, and tried to sit up.

Cal put a hand on his shoulder and held him down. "Not until Doc gives you a clean bill of health. How is he?" he asked me.

"Lucky to be alive. That was no gentle slap."

Russo grunted and Cal shook his head, his expression grim. "No, it wasn't. *Damn* Goldie. I don't know what . . ."

"Possessed him?" suggested Colleen wryly, from behind him. She reached past him to hand me my med-kit. "You know how he is about Maggie. Do you really have to ask?"

They exchanged a long look.

Cal nodded. "Yeah, I do. I'd better go talk to him."

Colleen let out a throaty chuckle. "Be careful."

She watched him leave the room, then stepped over to the window and reached up to pull the curtains back inside the casement. Outside, more glass shook free to shatter on the asphalt. "We're gonna have to board that up. I guess I'd better go see if I can score some plywood."

"Will you help me move Mr. Russo to the couch?"

She hesitated. "Do I have to?"

"Can make it myself," croaked Russo.

"Colleen," I said. "Do you not care that Goldie might have killed this man?"

She peered down at him, capturing his gaze. He looked away. "That is not a man, Doc. That is a weasel. And I'm not saying that because he's a grunter; I'm saying it because he's a weasel. That was a truly crappy thing he said to Goldie. And I'm damn sure it wasn't real pleasant for Maggie, either."

I looked up at her. "Perhaps he doesn't know any better. He is, after all, not quite himself—something of which he is painfully aware. His humanity is slipping away from him, Colleen. Can you not at least credit him for *trying* to preserve it?"

She frowned. "What do you mean? What makes you think he's trying to preserve anything?"

"The little sanctuary in the cellar where he spends his days. This carefully barricaded place where he spends his nights. The clothing he chooses to wear." I straightened a tweed lapel, then nodded at the book that lay atop the Queen Anne table beside the chair. "That."

Colleen turned to look. "Dostoevsky. One of your guys."

I did not smile. "Yes, one of my guys. *Crime and Punishment*—a book that turns upon what it is to be human. Did you perhaps wonder why he didn't try to go out during the night?"

"Uh, well, at a guess—because we wouldn't have let him?"

I shook my head. "He never does go out at night. He doesn't want to become like them." My gesture took in the streets and whatever slept below them.

She and Howard Russo shared another look, a longer look, then she turned her eyes to me. They were extraordinarily green and uncharacteristically soft. She squatted next to me on the floor, meeting me eye-to-eye across Russo's body.

"You're a piece of work, you know that? I think Goldman would probably call you a mensch. And Viktor, yesterday, when I said that about you not being my father . . ." She hesitated, her lips pressed together as if to keep words from escaping. Then she leaned across Russo, kissed my cheek, rose and went off to "score some plywood."

Russo stirred, drawing my attention to him. His eyes were trained on my face. He grunted. " 'M'not sayin' a word."

TWENTY

CAL

What can I say? When I walked out into the courtyard, when I stood face-to-face with Goldie, I realized I was afraid of him. What I'd seen in his eyes just moments before had hit me like a sucker punch to the stomach. It was a dark, red rage that, until that moment, I would have said he was incapable of.

I wanted to chalk Goldie's outburst up to battle fatigue. But that would have been naive. Of all of us, Goldie had dealt with the unknown longer and more intimately. I couldn't rule out the possibility that he was on the verge of a full-blown manic episode. I almost hoped he was. As vile as that sounds, the alternative was more disturbing.

The morning sun had turned the entire sky burnt orange, as if fires burned somewhere out of sight. The recesses of the courtyard were still in deep shadow, and Goldie, though he was standing in the one spot that caught the weak sunlight, had brought shadow with him.

Magritte hung timidly behind him, as if she, too, were afraid of him—or perhaps for him. Enid, looking puzzled and worried, stood beside her, a supply pack in his hands.

"I need to talk to Goldie," I said.

Enid glanced from me to Magritte, nodded, and went back inside.

I felt Magritte's gaze on me as I faced Goldie. His eyes were closed and he shivered as if the Great Lakes chill had sunk into his bones.

A smile pulled across his lips. "What's gotten into Goldman? That the $64,000 question?"

His eyes opened. They were unreadable. For someone who wears most of his emotions right out on the surface, Goldie can be surprisingly opaque when he wants to be. But I thought the dark fire had died.

Relief loosed the knot of tension in my throat. "I was worried," I said simply.

"Well, I don't blame you." He tilted his head back to gaze up over the rooftops. "I'd be worried, too, if I were you."

"About Russo . . ."

"Look, I'm sorry, okay?" He began rocking slightly from side to side. "I should learn to control my temper. Mom always said so. Ph.D. can't be wrong, right?" He shoved both hands into his jacket pockets. "Didn't mean to scare everybody."

"Look, Goldie, you're going to have to handle having Russo around. We don't have a choice. We don't know what's under that dome. He does."

He wrapped his arms around himself, still not looking at me. Magritte glided a little nearer, protective.

I pressed. "Can you be around Russo without trying to break his neck? I need to know, Goldie. This is too important—to all of us."

I tried to read his face for remorse or something like it, but he stolidly refused to let me in. His body language—arms straightjacketed across his chest, the rocking, the sarcasm—all told me that I was not the only one in this courtyard afraid of Herman Goldman.

"You were out of control, Goldie. We need you to *stay in control.*"

He laughed. "I wasn't out of control. I didn't *want* to be in control. I was pissed at the little rodent." He shrugged. "Look, I've cooled off, okay? I've calmed down. I'm fine."

I moved closer—less than an arm's length away. Close enough to see the glitter of tears in his eyes. "You're not fine. You're scared."

He answered the challenge with a non sequitur. "Cal, what did you dream last night?"

"What did I . . . dream?"

He smiled wryly and sang a line of lyric. " 'It's all right; we told you what to dream.' "

I recognized it: Pink Floyd's "Welcome to the Machine." A chill cut a broad swath down my spine. "I . . . I don't remember what I dreamed." A lie.

"I always remember my dreams. *Always*. Every dark, disturbing moment. That's one of the reasons I don't sleep much. It's not terribly restful. But last night, I didn't dream at all. Or, if I did, Maggie was the dream."

"What do you mean?"

"I don't know . . . Yes, I *do* know. I'm saying she . . . jams the Source. She blots it out. Silences it. Hides me from it."

"As you hide her."

He nodded. "Symbiosis."

"More than symbiosis." It was not a question.

He glanced at her, then away. "Yes."

That was possibly the straightest answer I'd ever gotten from Goldie in all the time I'd known him. I wanted to shake him, tell him to stop tearing his soul apart over something that couldn't change, that could only be gotten past. Instead I said, "Goldie, I think Magritte would be the first to tell you Russo didn't do that to her. Wouldn't you, Maggie?"

She glided over between us, her eyes on Goldie's face. He turned it away. She moved right up against him, laying fingertips to his cheek. He flinched, but she refused to let him break contact. "Listen to him, Goldie, if you won't listen to me. He's right. Russo didn't put me in that room; my uncle Nathan did that. And he didn't give me that damn name; my pimp did. A little bit ago, you told me he didn't own me. Not then, not now. That's God's own truth. No one owns me. . . . except maybe the Storm."

He looked at her then, his eyes blazing. "No."

"Then save your hate for that."

They stood like that for a moment, locked eye-to-eye, their shared aura battling the sun for brightness. I had ceased to exist. Goldie closed his eyes and leaned into Maggie's touch.

A moment later he met my gaze directly, his eyes showing emotions that once more seemed to flow within the banks of the River Goldman. "Isn't it about time we blew this Popsicle stand?"

We decided to make the trek into the Loop on foot. Russo was adamant that to take the horses in would result in them becoming food, so we were faced with the problem of how to safeguard them. Russo solved it. He hired a couple of neighborhood teens to guard them for us.

"They do stuff for me," he told us. "Y'know, get things so I don't have to go out much. I pay food, clothes, stuff from the other rooms up here. What I don't need. They'll watch."

The human talent for adaptation never ceased to amaze me. The brother and sister thought the horses were "très cool" (pronounced "tray que-well") and agreed to baby-sit them for a plaid flannel shirt, a ream of paper, and a mechanical pencil with a tube of replacement leads and seven erasers.

That settled, we spread a map of Chicago out on Russo's kitchen table and held a huddle over it, deferring to him on our travel route.

"Up Clinton to Jackson," he said, " 'cause Van Buren bridge is out. Then head in. There's a sort of checkpoint there."

"Checkpoint?" Colleen asked. "Armed sentries?"

"Not sentries . . . exactly."

"Jeez, Russo. Could you possibly be any more vague?"

"Sure. You want me to?"

Doc chuckled and Colleen opened her mouth for a tart comeback.

I cut her off. "What kind of checkpoints, Howard?"

He shook his head. "Don't have words." He pointed out the trail on a city map. Three blocks up, two over, cross the river. Easy.

I checked the map over carefully, using my "extended" senses. But the simplicity of the route wasn't what caught my eye. To my tweaked vision, the Loop district was a splash of red light so intense it obscured any other feature. It was very much like one of those Doppler radar weather maps, only the wrong color. A spot the dark red of a blood clot sat slightly off center in the larger area.

"I don't like the look of that. What is it?" Goldie pressed a fingertip to the crimson smudge.

I'd half forgotten he could see this stuff. "Howard," I asked, "what's at the corner of Randolph and Dearborn?"

Russo gave me a startled glance, then tugged at his lower lip. "Chicago Media Building."

I shrugged. "Is that significant?"

"Primal Records," said Enid. "Primal Records is in that building."

Colleen leaned over the map next to me, watching my face. She poked me in the ribs. "Care to let the rest of us in on this? What do you two see that we don't?"

"A dense concentration of some kind of power."

"Which means?"

I shook my head. "No idea. But we're going to find out. Howard, why would Primal Records give a damn about Enid's contract? Or yours, for that matter? What could they possibly get out of holding either of you to them?"

The milky eyes dodged toward me, then away. "Not sure. Have to ask them. Gotta be ready t'go." He got up and trundled away into his office.

I traded glances with the others, then went after him. He was rummaging around in a pack, putting in odds and ends that possibly made sense only to a grunter: scraps of paper, a book, a fistful of stubby pencils.

I stopped in the doorway. "Not sure—but you have an idea."

"No idea." He didn't look at me and he didn't stop his compulsive packing.

"Howard," I said, patience leaching away, "this is your chance to get free of this contract. Enid said you were his friend. If that's true, then I'd think you'd welcome the chance to free him, as well. If not for him, for the people he might harm with his music, or the ones he might help."

He hesitated, pack dangling in one hand, a book in the other. "Like your sister, Tina."

"Yeah. Like Tina."

"Doc says she was a ballerina."

Past tense. I winced. "Yes, she is. A very good one."

"Love ballet," he said heavily. "Saw Bolshoi once. *Magic Flute.*"

"That's one of Tina's favorites."

He slid the book carefully into the pack and clutched it to his narrow chest. "Music box," he said softly.

"What?"

"Choir Girl had one in her room. I remember. Had a ballerina on it. Played, uh, 'Over the Rainbow.' Huh. Funny."

I saw the jewelry box in my mind. Saw the ballerina: a delicate, blue-eyed blonde, graceful, precious.

Russo turned to look up at me, his eyes glistening. "She turned into something beautiful," he said. "And I turned into *this*. Why?"

He might have meant Magritte or Tina. "I don't know."

He was silent for a moment, then grunted. "Huh. 'N' you call yourself a lawyer." He lifted the pack to one shoulder and pushed past me into the living room.

To my surprise, he waddled straight over to Goldie and Magritte and said, "Sorry."

"Sorry?" Goldie echoed.

"Didn't mean anything by it. Didn't mean to hurt her."

Goldie's face went blank, his eyes concealing his thoughts, but Magritte floated down to the grunter's eye level and said simply, "Thanks, Howard."

Goldie gave her a sideways glance, then raked long fingers through his hair. "Shit," he murmured. "Great, you're sorry. Fine. You say anything like that again, I'll—"

"Break my fuckin' neck?" asked Russo ingenuously.

Goldie looked over his head at me, deadpan. "Roundly ignore you."

The grunter was still peering up into Goldie's face. He said, "Don't let it own you."

"What?"

"The Dark. Don't let it own you. Bad Master."

Goldie's face was ashen. "I don't know what you're talking about."

Howard pointed. "It's in your eyes."

Goldie took a step back, shouldering his pack. "Can we get moving? I'm getting the yips."

We took to the windy streets, Magritte physically tethered to Goldie with a thousand-pound-pull nylon horse lead, and Howard Russo sporting oversize sweats, the hood of the sweatshirt pulled low over his eyes. A pair of mirrored shades completed the ensemble. He looked like a mutant jawa.

I felt sorry for him. I hadn't expected to. Of course, I hadn't expected much of what had happened since the morning the world turned upside down. Since then it seemed to have turned upside down over and over again in myriad tiny ways.

We made our way up to Jackson and turned east. On either side of us buildings rose in an opaque maze. They seemed untenanted, as if we had entered some sort of no-man's-land. Ahead of us were the Chicago River and the rippling wall of light. The Jackson Street Bridge disappeared into it at about mid-span.

We stopped in unison just short of the bridge. Wind ripped at our clothes and forced stray trash to dance madly around us. It moaned through the bridge's substructure, hollow and mournful.

"Do we just . . . walk across?" asked Doc.

Russo, half crouched in front of me, looked back and nodded. "Yeah, yeah. Just walk."

"I thought it kept people out," Enid said.

"Does." Howard turned and moved forward, out onto the span.

The rest of us followed, over the gray-brown rush of water, steel and asphalt vibrating beneath our feet as if alive. When we reached the shining wall, Russo hesitated. Without even thinking, I stepped past him. I heard a startled hiss from the grunter and the translucent stuff in front of me became suddenly opaque. My hand grazed it in a sizzle of light and sound. I yelped and pulled back, scalded.

"Damn! That's like liquid fire! How are we supposed to go through that?"

Russo shook his hooded head. "Told you 'bout the checkpoint. Didn't listen." He turned to Magritte, pressed close to Goldie's side. "You gotta do it, Maggie. Take them through."

Magritte looked at him for a moment, then took Goldie's hand. She led him toward the wall. It thinned to transparency before her and she floated in, pulling Goldie along with her. The rest of us followed.

"Man," murmured Enid. "I do not like this one damn bit."

The mist tingled and was bone-chillingly cold. I'd come to associate flare magic with warmth, but this billowing, ruby fog brushed us with icy fingertips.

The reddish haze thinned and faded as we crossed the bridge. The bluff, weather-stained walls of massive buildings rose steeply before us on each side of the avenue and curved away into the gloom along the river's course. On the other side the street was deserted and littered and silent. It was nothing like the Chicago I remembered from my last visit.

When we set foot on terra firma again, we looked down an even deeper canyon than the one we'd just crossed—an avenue flanked on both sides by skyscrapers. Their upper floors were lost in the haze. Sears Tower was just down the street to our left; other giants competed with it to overwhelm us. Crimson light glittered on the windows high up, as if fires burned behind them. But there were no fires there. Those floors would be all but unreachable.

"No wind," said Goldie. "It stopped when we crossed over."

"So much for the Windy City," Enid murmured, peering around. "D'you hear that?"

Goldie nodded. "Yeah. Yeah, I hear it."

"Hear what?" Colleen demanded.

"The music," whispered Magritte.

"Blues," said Enid. "But twisted."

"I don't hear anything," Colleen said, frowning.

"Me neither," I said, trying very hard to detect anything through the gurgle of water behind us. "Can you tell where it's coming from?"

Magritte pivoted slowly in the air, head cocked, listening. The rest of us watched her, expectant.

"Goldie," she said, "go up there, to the corner. Matter of fact, go *around* the corner so I can't even see you."

Goldie stared up at her. "Maggie, *no*."

"Do it. It's all right."

"No, it's *not* all right."

"I want to taste the power, but I can't with you covering me. If this is firefly stuff, then the Storm still won't be able to hear me. If this is the Storm, we're shit out of luck, anyway."

They locked gazes for a moment, then Goldie slipped the tether from his wrist and handed the loop of nylon to Enid. Clutching his machete, he turned and made his way up to the intersection with many backward glances. With one last look at Magritte, he disappeared around the corner.

I watched her face intently. We all watched her.

She seemed puzzled, uneasy, and fearful in turns. "This is weird. It's not the Storm, but it's *like* the Storm. No, no, that's not right. It—it keeps changing. And it—" She froze, and the hunted look came to her eyes. The look I'd seen when the Source's touch was on her. The look I'd seen in Tina's eyes more than once. "I can't," she said. She shuddered and closed her eyes. "I don't want to. Please don't make me."

"Maggie?" Enid took a tighter hold on her tether, tugging her to his side.

She opened her eyes then, catching me in a hot pewter gaze. "It's trying to talk to me," she whispered. "I can't let it talk to me."

Before I could ask her what "it" was, Goldie let out a wild yell. Thrown into fight or flight mode, we ran, weapons ready, Enid dragging Maggie in his wake. Goldie was standing on the far side of the intersection, back pressed to the wall of what had been a bank. He was looking away from us, farther down Jackson Street.

"What is it?" I shouted, dread making my voice sharp. "What's wrong?"

He didn't answer.

I crossed the intersection on a wave of adrenaline, my eyes reflexively following his. At the bottom of the long city block, people strolled the sidewalks; a variety of wheeled vehicles moved through the intersection; there were street vendors. All eerily normal by any previous standard of normalcy. It was as if we'd stepped back in time to a Chicago that had not yet been through an industrial revolution.

Beside me, Goldie murmured what I took to be a quotation: " 'She is always a novelty, for she is never the Chicago you saw when you passed through the last time.' "

TWENTY-ONE

GOLDIE

Twain's words fall off my tongue into a vacuum. I don't hear myself say them, because there are wild animals in my head. They've been there since just after I went around the corner. It is as if a door has opened, letting in something that makes me doubt my already questionable sanity. In a New York minute, I'd get down on my knees and beg Cal to high tail it back across the Jackson Street Bridge, collect our horses, and get the hell out of town.

An absurd thought. I don't allow it access to my tongue. I pretend I'm utterly fascinated by the flow of people in the next cross street. Under the weird, hazy, demigloom of the Bubble, they float like varicolored motes back and forth across the intersection.

"You nuts, boy?"

I look up, wondering if I've inadvertently leaked mental chaos onto the sidewalk, to find Enid in my face. I realize I've walked about a quarter of the way down the block without any awareness of having moved. My quaking threatens to go public. If this is the beginning of a manic episode, the timing is cosmically bad.

Nuts? "That's the rumor," I mumble.

Enid plants one hand firmly in the middle of my chest. "What're you thinking? You don't even know where in hell you're going."

An interesting choice of words. An unwanted chuckle bubbles out of me. I swallow it. "Sorry . . . um, just curious, I guess."

Colleen is at my shoulder, peering into my face. "Oh, jeez, Cal, look at his eyes—he's only half here." She grasps the sleeve of my jacket, digging in her little cat claws. "We're not natives in Oz, Dorothy. Try not to wander off, okay?"

"No need to be snide," I tell her. "I get the picture."

Cal turns to Howard, who's standing a little away from us, trying to hide in the shadow of a mailbox. "Fill us in, Howard. What can we expect here?"

Howard snuffles a little and looks down the hill. "Dunno," he mumbles. "Haven't been in for a long time."

"Welcome to terra incognita," I murmur.

Cal fires a glance at me, then swings back to Howard. "What *do* you know?" Even I can tell his patience is fraying.

"Angelfire's welcome here."

Cal looks down toward the busy intersection. "We just go?"

Howard's face puckers as if the question perplexes him. "Sure."

Cal nods and turns to Magritte. "Before we go anywhere, I have to know what you sensed back there just now, Maggie. You said it was like the Storm. Is it . . . How, like the Storm? How *much* like the Storm?"

Maggie and I trade glances. She has gotten hold of herself, of her fear. She shames me and buoys me up in that look. She knows I know.

"It has the same . . . texture," I answer for her. "It . . . uh . . . *sounds* like the Source, as if it's, I don't know, speaking the same language."

They all stare at me, and Cal sweeps a hand through the luminous web that binds me to Magritte. "You were half a block away from her."

"Yeah, I know."

"Describe it."

"Confusing. Anomalous. I don't have words . . . It's like a . . . a stew of energies, sounds, voices, textures. A kaleidoscope. Dark. Sentient. Aware."

Cal's eyes are narrow cat slits. "One voice, or many?"

Maggie quivers. "One voice," she says, and I shake my head, unwilling to let the half-truth slip by.

"In front of many," I add.

" 'My name is Legion.' " Doc had probably not meant to be heard. He blinks as if our sudden regard is blinding, and shrugs. "The Gospels. Christ casts a demon out of a young boy and asks its name. That is the answer it gives: 'My name is Legion.' "

"Well, *I'm* freaked out," says Colleen, hugging her crossbow to her breast. Her tone is light, sarcastic, but she means it.

If only it were demons.

"Like Fred?" Cal asks me. "Was it like Fred Wishart? One of the Many? A shard? A piece of the Source? Or was it more?"

Fred Wishart was working on Uncle Sam's little science project when it derailed. We had met him, after a fashion, in Boone's Gap. Or at least we had met what was left of him before the Source finally tied up all its loose ends. Fred was just that, a loose end, an appendage to the Source. And he had drawn his considerable powers from it.

A piece of the Source. "I don't know. I can't tell."

"Don't know? Or don't want to know?"

I'm stopped by the look on Cal's face. I realize what he's asking and it stuns me.

He steps closer, penetrating my defenses for the second time today. Perimeter alarms go off all over the place. "You said it yourself—it costs a lot to let the Source in. I wouldn't blame you for blocking it out by any means you could."

"No, but I'd blame myself." I wipe sweaty palms on my jeans. "Okay, let's do this." I close my eyes and arm myself to sample the strange, chaos vibe. To listen to the whispers in the air. But when I let my guard down, there's nothing to listen to. There is a wall. And whatever we sensed has gone behind it. The Source has *never* closed itself off to me. *I* am the builder of the barricades; it possesses none.

And yet . . . "It's like it's hiding from me. If this is the Source, Cal, it's playing games."

Colleen turns to Cal and says, "If the Source is here, will we be ready for it?"

"We have to be," he tells her. "Enid, what do you need to do to jam Magritte from human sight? The way you did when Colleen first saw you." Mentally, he has already moved on. I try to follow him.

"I gotta sing out loud."

"Out loud?"

"Don't look at me, man. I don't make the rules, I just play by 'em. I can jam the Storm by just thinking music. I can't jam people's eyes unless they can hear me."

"Okay. If we get into real trouble, you may just have to make Maggie disappear."

Enid's dark face goes to ash. "Whatever it takes."

I snag Magritte's tether and we head down toward the intersection of Jackson and Wells and our first close encounter with local life-forms. Howard hobbles along in front while the rest of us try damned hard not to look like a troop of tourist commandos. It's difficult to appear nonchalant and harmless with a machete dangling at your hip.

Not a single soul glances our way as we approach the intersection. It's as if they can't see us. The weirdness of this makes me turn back the way we've come.

Anyone who's watched a lot of horror flicks (or lived them) knows better than to do this, but I am forgetful of these mundane details.

I catch Cal's arm and turn him around so he's facing our back trail. "Have you wondered why there are so many people down here on Wells and none up on Franklin?"

"That's . . . interesting," Cal says, because behind us Jackson Street disappears into an opaque cloud of lumpy red. Well, less like a cloud and more like dense cotton candy. My fear that we've entered a trap escalates, but Cal is not panicking. "Not real comforting," he adds.

"Maggie," I say, "look up our back trail."

She glances at me, then pivots gracefully in the air. After a moment she shrugs. "What?"

"Cal and I see a thick, red cloud. What do you see?"

"Same as before—just kinda hazy. Want me to check?" She tugs at her tether and I release it reluctantly. She's gone in a heartbeat, surprising me all over again with how swiftly she can move, how like a hummingbird or a dragonfly.

She disappears into the sticky-looking red stuff. Were we connected only by human sight, I'd be seriously freaked, but I know where she is and that she's all right. As to the wall of cotton candy, after a moment's concentration I see street, sidewalk, and asphalt arroyo—as Maggie sees it. Most comfortingly, I see the intersection of Jackson and Franklin. And I see Maggie.

She is back at my side in a flash of aqua light, shaking her head and telling me what I already know. "Like I said—same as before."

I reconnect us.

Cal affords the cotton candy wall one last, dubious look before we join the others at the corner. Intent on the street scene, they seem not to have noticed the illusory barrier. Cal sees fit not to mention it.

We turn the corner onto Wells. In one step the city goes from deserted to bustling, but I remind myself that my standards are slightly skewed. Populated by bicycles, rickshaws, pedal-cabs, the occasional horse- or dog-drawn conveyance, by any pre-Change standard it's still deserted. In and out among the larger vehicles weave people on skateboards, roller skates, scooters. It is muted traffic: no engine whine, no horn blare. Only the sound of bicycle gears, wheels against tarmac, shoe soles on asphalt, voices.

People, all looking pretty normal (to me, at any rate), move along the wide sidewalk. Many carry bags and satchels of various kinds—paper, plastic, cloth. I even see bags from major department stores—Macy's, Saks Fifth Avenue, Neiman Marcus. Some folks wheel shopping carts full of stuff.

Huh. Maybe in Chicago the bag ladies have taken over.

Someone in a particular hurry shoves past me, pinballing me into Enid. I experience a moment of claustrophobia. It's been months since I've been part of a street scene. I'd almost forgotten what it was like.

"The city that wouldn't die," I murmur.

"That's my Chicago," says Enid.

"This place is awfully well-kept for a postapocalyptic urban zone," observes Colleen.

She's right. Among the relatively untwisted wreckage of civilization, the pedal-cabs travel surprisingly garbage-free streets to deliver surprisingly well-dressed passengers to shops that seem to be open for business. A number of them have patched windows, but no glass litters the sidewalks as it does outside the Bubble. The whole place is squeaky clean by postapocalypse standards.

"No one's armed, either," Colleen notes. "At least not as far as I can see."

We've been visible since we stepped from the mists of Jackson Street, and no two people react to the sight of us in the same way. Some lower their heads, avert their eyes, shy out of our path. Others stare us down, boldly and speculatively, and make no move to give us a wider berth. I find I can predict who will react in a particular way by what they wear and how they move. Not so different than the world we left behind.

Polarities. There are those who scurry or shuffle as if apologizing to the sidewalk. Their clothing suggests they have shopped in thrift stores or Dumpsters. These are the package-carriers, the cart-pushers. Street people. I know them. I *am* them. In this city, too, they are the shy ones. Seeming to exist in a parallel universe, they see not and are not seen.

Then there are those who appear stunningly mundane, average, *untouched*. There is nothing shy about them. They own the pavement; they command it. The others weave around them, follow behind them, beg their pardon.

"I don't mean to be an alarmist, but people are definitely checking out Magritte." Colleen has forsaken her usual position at rear guard to slip between Cal and me as we make our way down the block. "A guy in a turban just slunk by whispering prayers and shielding his face, and I've seen at least three people cross themselves or clutch at something around their necks when they see her."

We stop in the middle of the block and watch ourselves being watched. Colleen is right. People are checking out Magritte. *Staring* at Magritte, and finding her noteworthy. I glance around, claustrophobic again. In the semidarkness of a doorway a man in a suit— looking both at home and out of place at once—is studying us intently. Studying *her*.

Panic rises in my throat.

Cal looks down at our grunter Sacajawea and asks, "Is there something you want to tell us, Howard?"

The little guy blinks up at Cal through his mirrored shades. "Like what?"

"Like, do these people consider Magritte a deity, or a demon, or what?"

"Let's just get the hell out of here," I whisper, tensing to run.

Colleen catches my arm in a steel grip. "Chill, Goldman."

Before I can "chill," whistles cut the air behind us, letting out bleat after persistent bleat. I have images of policemen on black and white skateboards in pursuit of us gate-crashers. Everyone else draws back from the center of the sidewalk at the first tweet, but we flock dead center like a bunch of domestic turkeys awaiting the hatchet.

Belatedly, we scatter, too. I grab Magritte and thrust her into the shelter of a wide archway before we are run down by three roller-bladers in Day-Glo spandex, knee pads, and helmets. Each wears a collection of fanny packs and a backpack, carries a baseball bat, and clutches a metal police whistle between his teeth. In a skirl of sound and a swirl of wind they are gone, flying ahead of us down the block. Our fellow travelers move back onto the sidewalk and continue their sojourns.

I take a deep breath and loosen my hold on Magritte, if only a little.

She peeks over my shoulder at the retreating couriers. "You okay?" The curve of her mouth suggests she is fighting the urge to laugh at me.

Before I can answer, another voice intrudes: "Is that your deva?"

"Day-vuh," he says, and I wonder which one of us he's mistaken for a Hindu deity. I turn, shielding Magritte with my body. It's the Suit.

"Excuse me?"

He nods through me at Maggie. "The deva, she yours?"

"Yeah, I'm his," says Magritte. "Fuck off." Her voice is harder, colder, more acidic than I've ever heard it.

The suit seems amused. "You taking her in?"

Taking her in. I'm Clueless Joe, here. "No."

"Really? That's quite a mouth she's got. Could be a real annoyance after a while. Interested in selling?"

Okay. Something less than a deity, then. "Fuck off," I say, and haul Magritte back out onto the sidewalk where the others have already collected.

"Let's get the hell off this street," I tell them. "Now."

I start down Wells again at warp speed, Magritte moving in harmony. When I finally slow down a bit, Cal catches up to me and pushes me into a defunct bus stop kiosk. The rest of the crew crowds in around us. Howard dives under the bench.

"What happened back there?" Cal asks.

I want to pace, but there's no room in the cramped quarters. I settle for shifting from one foot to the other and tapping out a rhythmic tattoo on the handle of my machete. "A suit just tried to buy Magritte off me."

"Oh, jeez," Colleen mutters, eyes on my face. "He's losing it."

Maggie leaps to my defense. "No he's not. This guy asked if Goldie was taking me in, whatever the hell that meant. Then he tried to *buy* me."

Colleen grimaces, glances at Doc, then almost meets my eyes. "Sorry, Goldie," she mumbles, and slips to one end of the kiosk to watch the traffic flow by.

"Taking her in," Cal repeats. "Maybe he was just asking if you meant to keep her, take care of her."

"No, no. That wasn't it. We'd already established that she was my flare."

"It pissed me off," says Magritte. "What, do I have a damned For Rent sign on my forehead?"

Cal glances up and down the street. "Okay, well, that gives us a little insight into the place. Apparently, some people are commodities here."

"Some things never change," says Magritte.

I ask, "Enid, do you think feedback would be a problem in here?"

He shoots me a startled glance. "Nobody's threatened Maggie. That guy's probably just doing business as usual. Maybe he's a pimp."

Maggie shakes her head. "I know pimps. He seemed more like a stockbroker."

I glance back up the street. "Yeah, well, the stockbroker is following us. Can we blow this bus stop?"

"Let's," Cal says, and prods Howie out from under the bench.

Our pace isn't brisk enough to keep the suit from overtaking us and putting himself in our path. "You didn't wait to hear my offer," he tells me, smiling. "I can be very generous."

"Really? Well, I can be very violent. Please take no for an answer." I lay a hand on my machete.

He seems not to take me seriously. "I can get all kinds of swag," he says. "Jewelry, twenty-four karat gold, precious stones. Fresh water? I can get you fresh, clean water. And fruit."

"She's not for sale," says Colleen, stepping out from behind me to face the suit. Her crossbow is aimed at his heart. "What part of this very basic concept don't you get, mister?"

Her, he takes seriously. He stiffens, eyes the weapon, and steps back a pace, but he doesn't give up. "She's useless to you. Your friend here said he wasn't planning to redeem her, so I thought perhaps . . ."

Colleen trades glances with me. "What do you mean, *redeem* her?"

An icy jolt of fear ripples through the connection between Maggie and me. I can't tell whose it is, but I think of her uncle Nathan and sermons on salvation.

"You're obviously not local," says the suit. "Devas are worth a great deal around here, but you have to know the ropes, which you clearly don't. I can act as middleman, pay you for her up front, handle the details of the redemption process myself."

"Jesus," says Colleen. "It's like she's a beer bottle or something." Her hands flex on the crossbow as if they are just dying to take this joker out.

His eyes don't miss this, but he persists. "If you don't turn her in willingly, he'll only take her away from you. You might as well derive some profit from it."

"He?" asks Cal. "He who?"

"The Boss." He pauses to glance at us askew. "You really are new here. Where are you from?"

"I'm from Chicago," says Enid. "Before any of this happened. They're from—"

"Yes, well, *this* Chicago is subject to the rule of law. That's what holds it together. Specifically and especially, the law of supply and demand. I work the supply side. And trust me, there is a definite demand for her kind."

"Why?" asks Cal. "Why her kind?"

The suit looks at Magritte, who moves farther behind me. "She's a rare commodity, for one thing."

"Look," says Enid, before I can ask about the other thing. "I don't give a shit about your laws or your demand. We're not selling."

He sidesteps the suit and moves off down the block. Cal gives the guy a last look and follows, pushing Howard a little ahead of him. The rest of us fall in behind.

When I glance back, the suit is gone. I feel no relief. My eyes brush Colleen's as I face front again. We share an unlikely moment of accord.

"We might have been able to pry some information out of that guy," Cal says.

"Yeah, maybe," counters Colleen, "but could you stand being in the same breathing space with him for that long?"

Adams is less heavily traveled; we zig right onto it and a block later zag left onto LaSalle. We hurry; our eyes miss nothing. I find myself thinking about "the Boss." My mind combines the historical with the virtual and conjures an image of a computer-generated guy in pinstripes and fedora with a tommy gun. Stupid, huh? I mean, tommy guns don't even function anymore, except maybe as door stops, and these days all reality is virtual.

I scan the skyline. An impossible task; the buildings go up into a red Forever. But once or twice I think I see something large and shadowy gliding from pillar to post many, many stories above us. I decide I'd prefer it not to be real and sanguinely chalk it up to a mixed state (the bipolar equivalent of a rinse/spin cycle). It does not occur to me to wonder, at that moment, who or what is doing the mixing. I say nothing. I find I'm less afraid of actual mania than I am of having Colleen accuse me of being manic before the world.

"Oh, man, smell that?" asks Enid as we turn onto Randolph.

Food. Cooking. I salivate, remembering that I haven't eaten since early morning. Ahead of us, people sit in a sidewalk bistro, dining. Chefs in white uniforms grill meat and veggies on barbecues under a green and white striped awning. For a moment I imagine that we really are in Oz.

"I wonder what they use for money besides gold and water?" Cal asks.

We pass by the bistro reluctantly, wistfully, hungrily, and continue east. I notice something. While the bistro's tables are peopled by the well-groomed and the bold-eyed, there are small knots of bashful bag-carriers clustered around the green wrought-iron perimeter as if waiting.

A little farther up the street curiosity gets the better of me when I spot a pair of the grab-bag people huddled near the doorway of a fragrant place labeled ROSE'S TEAROOM. He is white and twenty-something; she is Asian, a little older, worn and faded. Her skin is more sallow than golden, and there are bluish smudges beneath her dark eyes. The two stand, listless, speechless, shoulder-to-shoulder, looking at nothing, packages piled about their feet.

I plant myself right in front of them. "Excuse me," I say, when they pay me no notice whatsoever. "We're from out of town and we were, um, wondering if there might be a place nearby we could spend the night."

The woman blinks as if a patch of empty air has just spoken, while the guy says, "Huh?" His eyes lift only momentarily to my face, then glance away to my shoe tops.

I smile. "We just got here and, well, uh, all this," I gesture up and down the street, "is kind of a surprise."

The two exchange glances. Hers has an element of desperation in it that is only too familiar. I saw it all the time in Manhattan: in the underground, in the streets, in the high rises.

The guy lowers his voice. "Out of town? You came from outside?" For the first time his eyes actually make it to my face. Then they dodge to a spot over my shoulder and he says, *"Shit!"* and leaps backward, slamming against the stone railing of the tearoom's porch. The woman, following his gaze, gasps and clutches his arm, her eyes going wide.

It's Maggie, of course, hovering brightly behind me.

"Look, man," says the guy. "You just move on, okay? Just . . . just leave us alone."

The woman tugs at him. "Sammy, *no*, they're from outside. They got in; maybe they know a way out."

Sammy shakes his head, eyes trying to hold mine. "They're not really from outside, Lily." It is a statement of fact, he's that sure.

Doc and Cal have moved to flank me. Doc says, "I assure you, my friend Goldie is telling you the truth." Though he speaks to Sammy, it's Lily's face he's focused on.

"We've come from New York," says Cal. "It's taken months to get here, but we got into Chicago just today."

"Yeah?" Sammy says. "And how'd you manage that?"

"Uh, walked over the Jackson Street Bridge," I say.

Sammy's smile is completely mirthless. "Through the firewall?"

"The what?" Cal asks.

"When we came through," says Doc, puzzled, "there was only a red haze. Lily, that's your name, yes?"

She nods.

"Lily, I am a doctor. Forgive me for the observation, but you do not seem well. Are you often tired? Dehydrated?"

Now she looks at Doc as if he's just offered to raise her from the dead.

"Don't listen," Sammy says. "They're lying. He's no doctor. And they're not from outside, there's no way."

"Way," I protest. "Maybe it looks like fire to you, but it looks like cotton candy to me. It's neither. It's an illusion. You know—abracadabra, hocus-pocus, magic?"

Doc slides me a bemused look, then draws Lily a little aside.

"Yeah?" says Sammy. "Some illusion. I saw a guy get third degree burns from your hocus-pocus, bud."

I feel Cal's sudden and intense interest like a hot flash. "What did you say? Third degree . . ."

"Burns," repeats Sammy. "You heard me."

"But *outside*," murmurs Lily, still listening. "If there's really something left outside—"

"Lily, please," says Doc, his voice gentle. "Do you have pain here?" His hands are equally gentle as he draws her head back around and probes the sides of her neck just below her jaw.

"There's nothing outside," says Sammy.

"Says who?"

He looks at me as if I'm speaking in tongues. "Everybody *knows*, man. It just *is*."

It just is. Resignation? Hypnosis? Mass hysteria?

"So what do you do here?" Cal asks.

Sammy glances sideways at Lily. "Mostly wait . . . and starve. While *she's* in there. They really don't give a shit if you go hungry all day while they screw around."

"They?" Cal shakes his head.

"Them." Sammy shakes his head. "Shit, you're freebies, aren't you?"

Sigh. And me without my handy Traveler's Guide to Post-Apocalyptic Slang.

"What the hell are you doing?" The female voice is as chill and biting as Chicago's normal winter weather.

We look up and gawk like a herd of startled deer. I hear Howard snuffle and assume he has found something to hide behind.

She stands four steps above us in the open door of Rose's Tearoom, dressed impeccably in a charcoal-gray wool pantsuit, hair and makeup perfect, expression outraged. "Why are you harassing my people?"

Her people.

Cal smiles his most clean-cut, all-American litigator smile and says, "Just asking for information. We're from . . . out of town."

We watch her reaction with great interest: the widening of the eyes, the arching of the brows, the lifting of the head. Her eyes go immediately to Magritte, and the expression in them changes. Then the She-Suit checks each of us over carefully, picking at this and that, lingering on the armament, which most of us carry in plain sight.

She focuses on Doc, perhaps because he is unarmed, or perhaps because he stands so close to one of "her people." "Are these your bodyguards, sir?" she asks him.

I swivel my head toward Doc and mouth, *Say yes.*

He does, without batting an eyelash.

Her whole manner mutates, going from challenge to chagrin in the turn of a phrase. "I apologize if I was rude, but armed as they are, they tend to intimidate. Then again, I suppose that's why you have them." She offers an uneasy smile.

At this point, Doc, God bless him, sees a window of opportunity for his particular passion. "I could not help but notice," he says, "that this woman's color is not good. She is dehydrated and her glands are swollen. If she is in your employ, I would recommend that you allow her several days of rest and that she see a doctor. I don't know what the state of medicine is here, but surely something can be done for her."

The she-suit reddens and glances from Lily to Doc. "You . . . you want her to see a doctor?"

Doc smiles. "I am, myself, a physician. Unfortunately, I have nothing with me that might help."

I don't know which reaction makes me the queasiest, the She-Suit's nostril-flaring, eye-rolling expression of silent fury or Lily's abject fear.

"You want her to see a doctor," she repeats.

Doc hesitates, puzzled. "It would be for the best, yes. And her diet—if she could have leafy vegetables it would be very good, although I realize they may be hard to obtain."

Not according to the menu posted in the tearoom's front window. Spinach salad is right at the top of the leafy green list. I don't grok the price units. There are symbols in column B, but none of them are dollar signs.

Faces have appeared in the window to peer out at us, and an animated dialogue is taking place behind the glass. I catch Colleen's eye and incline my head toward the window.

She looks, steps to Doc's side and lays a hand on his arm, but he's too involved in the task of saving Lily to notice. She gives the arm a gentle shake. "Viktor, we need to go."

Doc nods and looks back to the she-suit. "My friend reminds me that we have an appointment. Please, if you are able, see that Lily gets to a doctor."

"I'll see what I can do." She glances from Doc to Magritte and adds, "sir." She watches as we move away up Randolph.

When I glance back, a man has joined her on the steps. Without a word to Sammy or Lily, they fade back into the tearoom.

Okay, that was disturbing. I find my legs are suddenly heavy and loath to move the farther we get from the tearoom and the two unfortunate people left waiting and starving there.

"Why was that woman so deferential to me?" Doc wonders as we drag our demoralized bones up the block.

"You were unarmed," suggests Cal. "She took us for bodyguards and figured you must be the VIP we were protecting. Also, of the lot of us, you're arguably the most presentable, except for Magritte."

True enough. Doc, even in his fleece-lined, buffalo plaid jacket, still looked the part of a distinguished, if shaggy, professor.

"Her people," murmurs Colleen. "God, that makes me sick."

Cal chews his lip and worries his sword hilt. "Sammy seemed completely convinced there was no way out of here."

Colleen puts a hand on his arm. "Yeah, what was all that about a firewall?"

Cal carefully describes the opaque red goo that ate Jackson Street and I repeat what Magritte said about it not being real.

Colleen echoes Sammy. "Not real? What's not real that causes third degree burns?"

"Oooh, is this a riddle?" I don't mean to sound glib, but sometimes glib just pops out of my mouth.

Colleen ignores me and Cal looks uneasy. "Magritte," he says, "when you went back up Jackson into the . . . the cloud, did you feel as if you might be in danger?"

"No. It was a mirage."

"Maybe it's only a mirage if you're a flare," says Colleen. "Maybe for normals like us, it's a one-way street."

Chilling words.

"Normals like us," repeats Cal softly.

"Maybe that's why we haven't seen any twists in here besides Howard and Magritte," I say. "They've all split . . . or been redeemed."

"It goes further than that," says Cal. "I don't recall having seen anyone in here do anything that wasn't a hundred percent pre-Change mundane."

"Which means?" asks Colleen.

I hold my breath and my tongue. TMI. Too much information. My head is swimming in it—in pieces of meaningless flotsam.

"I don't know what it means," says Cal. "But we're almost to Dearborn. Let's focus. Let's get this done, okay?"

I don't know which one of us sees it first. Irrelevant, I suppose. I only know that when we turn the corner onto Dearborn and walk into the shadow of the Chicago Media Building, a great, black, oily wave of horror breaks over me. Time, light, reality, life, all stop and I am nailed to the sidewalk by the weight of sheer terror.

This is hell, I think. *We have turned the corner into hell.*

The Tower stands fifty stories tall, slick and gleaming, beneath a canopy of dark, inescapable radiance. We've all been here in our worst nightmares. We have visited this spot in a landscape we each imagined, prayed, hoped, was entirely internal.

I'm aware of Magritte clinging to me, warmth in a suddenly frozen world. Her sobs fill up my universe for a stunned instant, then other, alien voices come screaming through my head like a gale-force wind. They tear at me—at us. They are at once sweet and sad and hungry.

And familiar.

Magritte twists in my arms. "Make them stop! Oh, God, Goldie, *make them stop!*"

But I can't. I've been ambushed—with no chance to regroup.

It's Enid who makes them stop, rolling homemade, heartfelt melody off of his tongue, weaving a field of sound. The alien voices fall silent, but only for a moment, then they are back to batter at Enid's shield.

I hide my eyes from the Tower, afraid that if I look at it, it will devour me from the inside out. I look anywhere else.

At Magritte, burrowed tight to my side.

At Colleen, who herds us back into the shadowy canyon that is Randolph Street.

Doc's face is a Siberian wasteland, and his eyes are windows into a variety of death I have never seen, for all my time on the street.

Cal, blank-faced and stoic, pulls us along the sidewalk, urging Enid to sing, to *keep singing*. And Enid sings, the tracks of tears gleaming wetly on his dark cheeks. I don't think they're for the Tower, or even for what it represents. They are for those he can't see, but who will be touched by his music in ways he never intended.

It is some time before it sinks in that Howard Russo is gone.

TWENTY-TWO

Okay, easy would've been too much to ask, I suppose. But I was surprised to find that a tiny piece of Pollyanna deep down in my soul was stunned that we hadn't been able to just march in, have our lawyer talk to their lawyers, and march out again.

The postshock aura was a bitch; tiny ice crystals jogged and reeled in my eyes and ears and blood. But that burned off fast, leaving nothing but pure mad. The fact that there was no one to aim it at only made me madder.

Anger was safe. Angry, I wasn't aware of the Tower looming behind us, playing out its miles of marionette string. Hell, I don't know which was worse, seeing it or not seeing it. I may be dense as a post, but even I could feel *something*. Something more than just surprise that the Source had thrown us another curve, another something-we'd-never-seen-before—a tweaked *building*, for godsake.

Rock, scissors, paper. Anger cuts fear. Habit breaks anger. I swung into survival mode, checking resources and escape routes, assessing damage. Doc, Goldie, and Magritte were a mess. Enid was stone cold petrified. Cal was grim, purposeful, in control. He kept us moving, parting the sidewalk traffic with a look, making a hole through which I could drive our shell-shocked herd.

Once out of sight of the Tower, I caught up with him and paced him. "Was that it? Was that the Source?"

He shook his head, kept walking hard. His face was like stone. "I don't know."

"Goldie—"

"Later. Now, we need to get out of here."

"Where to?" I asked.

"Russo's. We need to regroup."

I nodded, looked around. "Russo's gone, the feckless little shit."

"Yeah. I noticed."

I shut up and took point. I was still in the lead when we crossed the intersection of Washington and Wells, which meant I was first to confront the cotton candy wall. It looked different than Goldie described it—less like cotton candy and more like one of those computer-generated nebulas I've seen in science fiction movies.

I hesitated, glancing around to see if any natives were watching, and saw a familiar face. The Suit. And he'd brought friends. My senses came on line with a crackle of electricity; my spine felt as if it had grown rebar. They were armed—baseball bats, chains, knives. They were coming down Washington behind us, leaving very little room for friendly interpretation of their intentions. Traffic parted in front of them, people scurrying to get out of their way.

Cal had seen them, too. He'd drawn his sword and slowed up, putting himself in our rear guard.

I gauged the distance to the wall of red ick and plunged at it, hearing the others close on my heels. It was like running into a blizzard of electric red glitter. A wave of intense, stinging heat kissed my face. Surprised, I sucked in a breath of air and inhaled fire.

I twisted around and flung myself back toward the others, choking and gesturing for them to go anywhere but where I'd just been.

"This way!" Enid shouted, and darted up Wells to the right, into the pedestrian traffic.

The rest of us followed, sucking up under the eaves of the buildings. We had the advantage of a half a block of distance between our attackers and us and two guides who knew the neighborhood. We had the disadvantage of me. I felt as if I'd snorted fireworks; my lungs were still burning and my skin itched like a sonofabitch. *They say your skin itches when you change* . . . Nausea washed over me, but I plowed on, keeping pace with the others.

Enid and Magritte took point now, plowing and dodging through the people on the street, making a hole for the rest of us to slip through.

A shadow passed over us, pulling my eyes upward. Overhead, the red haze eddied as if in the wake of a large bird. I shivered and prayed it wasn't dragons. That'd be about all we needed.

Ahead of me, Cal broke stride. "Who the hell is that?"

I faced front. Someone had appeared out of an alley in front of Enid. In the next second the guy grabbed him by the shoulders and dragged him into the alley. Goldie and Magritte shot around the corner after him.

Adrenaline pumping, I hauled my crossbow out from under my jacket and bolted for the alley. When I cleared the corner with Doc and Cal hard on my heels, our guys were nowhere in sight. The stranger was crouched at mid-alley next to a large Dumpster. He was wearing a hooded sweatshirt and shades, and for a moment I thought it was Howard, until I realized that this was a full-scale model. He seemed to be unarmed.

He stood and waved us on. "C'mon, boys 'n' girls!" His voice echoed strangely off the walls and rattled the fire escapes. "We don't got time for proper intros."

Good point. It was either him or a bunch of guys with baseball bats and chains. I lowered my crossbow and pounded down the alley, trying not to notice that my legs felt like licorice whips.

When I reached him, Mystery Man snagged me by the shoulder, wheeled me around the edge of the Dumpster, and shoved me down into a window well. Before I could catch my balance, someone grabbed me from below and pulled me into a cold, dark, musty hole. I opened my mouth to squawk, but a cool blue light flared practically in my face. It was balanced in Goldie's palm. He lifted a finger to his lips. A second later Doc and Cal poured themselves down through the window well, followed by the Mystery Man. The window casement slammed shut behind them.

"This way." Our guide crossed the basement in a few strides. We followed without question.

We climbed down farther into a subbasement, crawled (or floated)

through a manufactured hole between the foundations of two buildings, then went up a flight of rickety metal stairs and out another window well. We crossed an alley, trespassed into the creepy backstage
area of a defunct movie theater, and moved from there to lose ourselves in the sublevel of an abandoned office building.

There were times I was sure there were people along our route, but
I couldn't see anyone. Magritte and Goldie supplied our only light.

Once in the office building, our guide slowed to a stop. He'd long
ago pulled off his shades, but only now did he turn to face us, tugging
his hood back as he did. By Magritte's light I could see he was young,
maybe a little older than Enid. Skin the color of coffee with cream,
eyes so dark brown they were almost purple.

Enid let out a sudden crack of laughter and threw his arms around
the guy, squeezing him so hard I thought he'd break him in two.
They went way back apparently, and there was much backslapping
and bear-hugging to prove it. When that was done, Enid turned to
the rest of us and introduced our rescuer as "Tone, one hell of a session man."

I stood aside and watched as the guys shook hands all around, thanking him for the neat rescue, and Enid asked, "How'd you find us?"

"Funny about that," Tone said. "We got this old guy in the 'hood
that sort of passes for an oracle. He just seems to know all sorts of stuff
that goes on downtown."

"How?" asked Cal. "How would he know about us? How would he
know you'd care?"

"Well, when devas come into this place, just about everybody
knows—it sort of changes the vibe in the Red Zone."

Goldie's eyes rolled toward the layers of concrete over our heads.
"There's a disturbance in the Force, Luke."

Tone gave him a glance. "Yeah, sorta like that. Anyway, when stuff
like that happens, the old guy always seems to have the story. We ask
him how he does it, he just smiles and says, 'I got friends in high
places.' He told us about you guys when you first come in. Says
you've got a deva and that you didn't turn her over to the first scum
bucket that comes along. That's a remarkable thing, around here.
Had to check it out. Seeing Enid again, man, that's a pure surprise."

"We need a place to sit down and do some serious thinking," Cal
said.

"Sure thing. You all ready to commence onward? Your lady there don't look so good."

Everyone turned to look at me. I was leaning against the handrail of a staircase that went up into nowhere. The sudden attention made me want to straighten up. Somehow the message got lost between my brain and my legs. I reeled.

Next thing I knew, Cal was standing in front of me, holding me upright. "You all right? Jesus, Doc, she looks like she's been scalded."

Doc was there in a breath, concern pinching his face. He took my hands from Cal, held them up to the weak light from above.

"I can't see. Goldie . . . ?"

Goldman pushed past Cal, bringing a neat little glow ball for Doc to see by. Doc murmured something in Russian and pressed a finger gently to the back of my hand. "Does that hurt?"

"Just a little. Look, I'm fine. Really. Just kind of winded. And I think Goldman's cotton candy singed me a little. But I'm okay." I flashed a weak, nervous smile.

Doc raised a hand to my face, brushing my upper lip. It came away smeared with blood. He looked to Cal.

"What is it?" asked Enid from behind Cal.

"Colleen's hurt," said Cal.

"I am not hurt," I said. "I've got a bloody nose. Hasn't anybody ever seen a bloody nose before?"

Tone was peering at me over Doc's shoulder. "Man, you musta run into the firewall, huh? That's gonna sting for a bit. We got stuff that'll take care of it, though. And I suggest we move on now, if you can, miss, 'cause I can't guarantee how safe it is down here."

"The toughs?" Cal jerked his head back up toward where we'd left the Suit and company.

"Hell, no. That surface scum don't come down here. Other things, though."

Other things. I didn't want to find out what kind of other things. "Can we go?" I asked.

Cal brushed hair off my forehead, his eyes searching my face, and something shivered in the air between us, making me wriggle inside. "Are you sure she'll be all right?"

"Well, not a hundred percent sure," said Tone. "But I've never seen anybody die from it."

Cal nodded and put us back in motion, at my side every step of the way.

Tone and Enid used their travel time for catching up. You know: "Remember old Fly-by-Night Jones? Well, he got turned into a fruit bat."

Okay, I'm kidding, but close. Tone let loose with a rush of what happened to the old crowd and who'd been turned into what and who'd just plain disappeared. It wasn't pleasant. Enid was hearing bad news with practically every other word. This friend or that had gone missing, this family or that was scattered to the four winds, most of the places he called home had been blasted to rubble or looted or both. Weird-looking things were growing or roaming or had taken up residence in parts of their once mundane neighborhood. Made street gangs sound downright cordial.

We finally emerged out of the musty cellars into the cheery red light of day and took a look around. The street was filthy, covered with debris, garbage, and little dunes of blown dust that glittered with glass—normal, comforting urban decay.

"Where are we?" I asked Enid.

He smiled. "Near South Side. Home."

There wasn't much left of home. But there was something. The farther we went into the Near South Side, the more people we saw. Some of them recognized Enid and stuck to him, so that by the time we got to where we were going, we'd collected quite a handful of interested parties, musicians mostly.

Tone led us to a night club/restaurant on Wabash. Buddy Guy's Legends. To Enid, this was something of a religious shrine. To Cal and me, it was the perfect bolt-hole—dark, warm, and inhabited by the first friendly faces we'd seen since we left the Preserve. In the restaurant, I fell into a chair at one of the tables, hoping I didn't look as bad as I felt. My hopes were in vain. In a matter of minutes Doc had commandeered rags and water and some sort of curative liniment and was all over me with the stuff. I drank some sort of special tea that tasted like licorice and went down like slippery maple syrup.

Meanwhile, Tone told the story of our rescue with only the least bit of exaggeration. His audience didn't seem either afraid or in awe of Magritte, and they applauded the fact that she hadn't been lost to the Tough Guys.

Weird. It was almost like being back in the previously real world.

Candlelight and lamplight reflected off polished tabletops, making the place feel real cozy. Of course, there's nothing unusual about muted lamplight in a bar. There was a constant throb of rhythm in the air, too, as if a jukebox played somewhere out of sight.

Behind the long, curving bar was a chubby old fellow named Jelly and a stunningly beautiful young woman he introduced as Venus. I wondered if anyone around here kept the names they were born with. Tone, it turned out, was not short for Anthony, but a reference to the fact that Tone was a guitarist obsessed with the sound of his "axe." The death of electricity had put a nasty crimp in his universe. He'd taken up the acoustic guitar, he told us, and was learning to play the saxophone from the neighborhood oracle.

Tone and his friends wrangled food and drink for us and for the restaurant's other patrons. I didn't see money or barter change hands, so I suspected it was less a restaurant than a neighborhood mission.

Not to look a gift-horse in the mouth, but I did wonder where the food came from. Asking, I was told simply, "Grant Park."

I drank the broth off some stew and carefully chewed up and swallowed some potatoes. My throat was sore, like it had been scoured with steel wool.

Cal didn't eat. He asked questions. Foremost of which was what anybody knew about the Source or Storm or Dark or whatever they called it here. They said it was powerful, they said it was dangerous and terrifying and that they didn't need to know any more about it than that. They did not say that it lived in a gleaming, glass tower at the corner of Randolph and Dearborn.

Naturally, they wanted to know things in return—like why were we so absurdly interested in something that really ought to be avoided at all costs—and Cal told them about what had happened in New York, and Boone's Gap, and everywhere else along our trail. And he told them about Tina, about the fact that the world as we knew it was being invaded by a sort of metaphysical kudzu and that we were determined to find a way to stop it.

"Whoa, son, whoa!" Jelly interrupted Cal in mid-sentence, grasping the rim of the bar with both of his beefy hands as if it was trying to fly away. "You tellin' us you're trying to find the Storm *itself*?"

Cal nodded. "Yes. I don't pretend to understand how, but it's at the heart of this. At the center of the Change."

"Shit," said Tone, and Jelly added, "That's crazy."

Cal's face didn't change expression. If being accused of insanity undermined his self-confidence, it sure didn't show.

Jelly said earnestly: "The Storm is bigger than we are, son. I don't think any of us realizes just how much bigger."

"Well, we're not as small as we look," Cal told him, and there was a sharp edge to his smile.

"Oh, yeah?" said Tone. "So when you find it, what're you gonna do, stick that fancy sword in it? Shit, you can't fight a damned tornado with that."

"It's not really a storm," said Goldie quietly. He sat hunched over the bar, his hands around a steaming cup of chicory, Magritte hovering protectively at his side. "It's . . . more than that. And it's less than that. It has a core, a heart. That's what we hope to stick a sword in. Figuratively speaking."

"And you think it's *here?*" Tone asked Enid, eyes narrowed. "Where? In the lake? In the underground? Riding the damned El? That's fuckin' crazy."

Cal looked at Goldie, who dived back into his chicory.

Enid said: "I don't know if it's here. I do know that Primal Records is here and I come to get out of my contract with them."

"Your contract?" repeated Tone, sitting back in his chair. "What d'you mean?"

Enid explained it all: the effect of the Change on his contract, how the contract bound him, the way the music could charm, could shield . . . could twist. "Cal's gonna cut my music free and I'm gonna help him find his sister and cut her free. Maybe cut us all free."

Tone laughed, raucous. "I don't know which is more crazy, thinkin' you can get someone back from the Storm, or thinkin' you can get 'em back from Primal."

Whatever Tone saw in Cal's eyes cut his laughter off at the pass. "It sounds as if Enid isn't the only musician with a . . . contractual problem."

Tone lowered his eyes. "There've been others."

"I'm not surprised," said Cal. "Strange as it seems, the legal bindings in Enid's contract are still in effect, they just work on a different level. In theory, if we confront the Primal executives, we can void the contract. Which is where we might need your help. Is there a safe way to get into the Chicago Media Arts Building?"

"You're screwin' with me, right? You ain't goin' in there. Man, that thing'll eat her alive." He jerked his head in Magritte's direction. "The rest of you it'll just chew up and spit out."

Cal shifted from one foot to the other like he'd borrowed some of Goldie's bees. Made me wish he'd sit down. "What thing?" he asked.

Tone looked at him as if he'd dropped in from another planet. "Primal, what else?"

Cal held up his hands. "Wait a minute. Primal is a record company."

"Primal is a monster." Venus was perched on a stool at the end of Jelly's bar, watching us. She shrugged. "Or a savior, or both—depending on how you look at it. I suppose if it weren't for Primal, this city would've imploded on itself in the first week after. But it didn't, because of whatever it is that Primal does."

Cal turned slowly to look at her. "*Primal* generates the firewall?"

She nodded. "Somehow it keeps the Storm from reaching in here."

"So Primal isn't . . . the Storm. Isn't related to the Storm."

Our new acquaintances exchanged a series of glances that spoke volumes about the uncertainty of present-day life. Then Venus said, "I don't see how that could be. Like I said, Primal keeps the Storm out."

"Or at least it seems that way," added Jelly. "Hell, I don't think a one of us can pretend to know jack-diddly about anything these days. All we know is, when Primal's Red Zone went up, the Storm went away."

"But *you* think it's a monster," said Cal. "You hide from it—why?"

"Back in the beginning, we had some like her," Venus said. She canted her head toward Magritte, who drifted closer to Goldie. "The Storm got some of them, then Primal put up that bloody canopy and it didn't get any more. Right about the time we were thanking God for that, they started disappearing again. This time it was Primal doing the taking."

Cal paled. "Why?"

"We don't know," said Jelly. "It just takes them whenever it gets the chance. It can't suck them up like the Storm does, though, so it lures them or sends its goons after them."

"The Tough Guys?" guessed Cal.

Tone curled his lip. "Surface scum."

"But why would this Primal create the Red Zone?" asked Doc rocking forward in his chair. "What would it have to gain from putting this place under a bubble?"

"Maybe it's hiding out, too," said Magritte softly.

Tone was nodding. "A king in its castle."

Or a spider in its web.

"But where's it getting the power to do that?" I asked, rubbing my eyes. Damn, I was having trouble tracking suddenly—craving sleep. "If it's all that powerful, why didn't it take Magritte when it had the chance? We were right there. Standing out in the street like a bunch of gawking tourists. Hell, even I could feel . . ." I hesitated, not wanting to remember what I'd felt.

"I was jamming," murmured Enid, his eyes on Cal's face. He tugged at one of his dreadlocks, shaking the little course of bells at the end, pulsing out a rhythm. "I was jamming harder than I ever jammed in my life. Maybe it couldn't reach past the music."

"I think you were a surprise," said Goldie. He was still sitting at the bar, aimlessly sloshing chicory around in his cup. "You'd been silent up till then. And we were being drawn in, right to them."

That sent a jolt of slimy electricity up my spine. Damn that troll, Russo. If I ever saw him again, I was going to skin him, tan his hide, and wear it for a rain slicker.

Cal was shaking his head. "*It, them* . . . what are we talking about here? I'll ask again: What *is* Primal?"

"One Voice in front of many," mumbled Goldie. His own voice was flat, gray, all the normal colors leached out of it. From what I could see of his face, it matched.

I caught Doc's eye and canted my head toward Goldie. *He all right?* I mouthed.

Doc's expression did not ease my mind one bit. He got up and moved over to the bar. I watched for a moment as he put his head close to Goldie's, their foreheads nearly touching. Viktor Lysenko, Guardian Angel. My lips smiled without me telling them to.

"What are we up against here?" Cal asked. "You say we're facing a monster—do you mean that literally? We'd gotten the impression that Primal Records was still run by a group of *people.*"

Tone opened his eyes so wide, I could see the whites gleam in the dim light. "Who told you that?"

"Howard Russo, not in so many words."

"Russo? Shit, he's nobody you'd want to be givin' head space too. That rodent sold out I don't know how many devas before we got on to him."

"I knew it," I said. "I friggin' knew it. He delivered us right to the front door. Like Chinese takeout." I remembered five lousy words of Shakespeare. They twisted in my head: *All the world's a puppet theater.*

Enid's face had lost most of its color. "Why, Tone? *Why* would he?"

"T'save his own ass, I s'pose. He's under contract, too, isn't he?"

Cal sank into Doc's chair and leaned across the table, eyes on Tone's face. "*What is Primal?*"

"We don't know." Venus slid off her bar stool and moved to our table, her arms wrapped around herself as if keeping out a chill. "Says it was the first thing the Storm birthed."

"Then you've seen it."

"I came close one time," she said. "Too damn close."

"I seen it."

The voice came from the darkest corner of the room, where a hallway fed back into the private quarters. I didn't see anyone at first, then there was a shuffling sound and a dark figure moved unsteadily into the light of the room.

It was an old man. A tall, lean old man, a little stooped, hair grizzled white, clothes the same tones and colors as his skin—a walking, talking gingerbread man. Lamplight fell across his face. His eyes were completely white with cataracts. It'd been a long time since he'd seen anything.

"Now, Papa . . ." said Venus.

"I seen it," the old man insisted quietly.

"Who . . . ?" Cal looked to Tone and gestured at the old guy.

"They call me Papa Sky," the old man said. "You must be our travelers. Welcome to Legends."

TWENTY-THREE

DOC

Goldie was not all right. And it took no medical degree to know it. Like a man whose fever had just broken, he quivered in icy perspiration. He sat hunched over the bar, clinging to his mug as if it possessed powers of salvation, while Magritte hovered in suspended animation by his side.

I slid onto the bar stool next to him and leaned in, keeping my voice low. "What's wrong, Goldie?"

He raised his eyes to my face, giving me a fleeting glimpse of a place even my deepest grief had never taken me.

I caught his shoulder in a hard grip. "Goldie, I have some valproate . . . enough to start you on a course—"

Lips pressed tightly together, he shook his head. "That's not what this is, Doc. Valproate won't help."

"What, then?"

He looked me fully in the eye, and might have told me, when the old man came into the bar. Goldie's revelation was lost in the moment, for here was Tone's oracle—a living, breathing man. A blind man, appropriately.

We made introductions and he seated himself in a pool of lamplight between Tone and Enid, turning his face to Cal. "Bet you're full of questions. Young people are, as I recall. They think old folks like me are full of answers. Or just plain full of it."

Cal said, "What can you tell me about Primal?"

"No patience, either. Want all their answers this minute." He shook his head. "Primal. Well, I can tell you it's not what it seems."

Beside me, Goldie stirred, a strange mixture of pain and fascination in his face. He slid from his stool and moved toward the old man with the languid motion of a sleepwalker.

"You said you'd seen it," Cal persisted.

"Papa Sky is real big on metaphors," said Jelly. "He means to say he saw it in a vision."

"Now, don't you ever scoff at a blind man's visions, Mr. Jelly," said Papa Sky. "I see things a whole lot clearer sometimes than folks with two good eyes."

"What did you see?" asked Cal.

"Chaos. With a kernel of will. A tiny, tiny kernel of will. The first shall be last and the last first," he added cryptically. "The least shall be greatest and the greatest least."

Cal traded a glance with Enid, disappointment written on his face. He erased it with a sigh.

"Papa Sky's big on riddles, too," said Tone. He turned to the old man. "If you could answer these folks straight up, Papa, it'd be best."

"Sometimes a straight answer ain't the best answer," Papa Sky observed.

"Our friend Calvin is on a quest. His sister's been taken by the Storm and he means to get her back." Tone grimaced. "And save the world while he's at it. But first he's gotta pry Enid free of Primal."

Papa Sky's head swiveled toward Cal. "Imagine that. That's a pretty tall order, boy."

Cal twitched. "So everybody keeps telling me. But that's it. That's the quest. Crazy or not. We have to try."

Papa Sky nodded as if in time to the music that drifted down on us from upstairs. "Oh my, yes. We have to try. Lord, if I'd've gave up every time I was so inclined, I'd've never made it all the way out here from New York."

"New York?" echoed Enid. "That's where they're from." He made a sweeping gesture that took us all in.

"Are they, now? Ain't that a fluke?"

"What the hell possessed you to come to Chicago?" Enid asked.

"I come with a friend. He needed me. Turned out, I needed him, too. Never would've made it but for him. Would've died right there in Manhattan. He got me here an' I got him here. So, I know what loyalty is and I can see that you do, too." He leaned forward toward Cal. "Your sister's name's Tina, ain't it?"

Cal was visibly stunned. I suspect he wondered, as did I, whether our new friend was a sage or a madman. "How . . . how did you know?"

Papa Sky laughed. "Well, maybe I overheard you talking about her. Or maybe that kind of knowing is what God give me to make up for these bunged-up old eyes. Or maybe—" He broke off and smiled. "What's your plan, Mr. Cal?"

Cal told him, then added, "Before we can do anything about Tina, or the Storm, or anything else, we have to get into the Black Tower— the Chicago Media Building—and deal with Primal."

Papa Sky scratched his bearded jaw. "Well, I have to say, that ain't gonna be as easy as you make it sound. But, now the thing is, I might just know somebody who can help you out. I can't promise, but I can ask."

"Somebody . . . this friend you mentioned?" Cal asked. "The one who brought you here?"

Papa Sky nodded, then pulled himself to his feet. "Don't you folks go runnin' off and doin' anything crazy now. You wait for Papa Sky to check things out."

Cal glanced from Enid to Colleen to me, seeking accord. "I . . . I suppose we could wait a little," he said, "but—"

The old man pointed an arthritic finger at Cal's nose. "Don't you do nothing crazy, Mr. Cal. Let's see what my friend has to say."

Colleen cleared her throat. "About what, exactly?" she asked. Her voice was frayed, her head propped on her hand.

I considered ordering her to rest, then discarded the idea as fruitless.

"Well, my friend is a queer sort of fellow. He got a lofty point of view, you might say. Gives him insights."

"Could you bring him here so we can meet him—talk to him?" Cal asked.

Papa Sky smiled crookedly. "Oh my, no. He don't go out. Well, not where folks'll see him, anyway."

"Shy guy?" asked Colleen, rubbing her eyes.

"A tormented soul," answered Papa Sky thoughtfully. "A massively tormented soul." He held out his hand. "Toney-boy, can you help me get where I'm going? You can come back to your new friends after, if you like. But I need a guide dog."

Tone looked at Enid, hesitating. Clearly, it was leaving his *old* friend that gave him pause.

Papa coaxed, "I'll let you play my axe."

Tone's eyes lit up with obvious pleasure. "Serious?"

"Serious as can be." He held out his arm and Tone took it.

Before they could move, Goldie stepped in front of them. "You said it's not what it seems. What does it seem like to you?"

Papa Sky paused and cocked his head to one side. "And you are?"

"Goldie. My name is Goldie. Which is neither here nor there. What does Primal seem like that it's not?"

"It seems to be one thing when it's another."

Goldie rolled his head around on his shoulders as if every muscle in his neck had spasmed at once. "No, no, no. No games, please. Not now."

Cal came to his feet and moved to lay a hand on Goldie's arm.

Goldie shrugged the hand away. "Tell me, old man, tell me what you hear when it speaks to you."

Cal flushed. "I'm sorry, Papa—"

"Oh, it never speaks to *me*. Not directly, anyway. But I hear it. Sometimes it sounds sweet and mild and wistful-like. And sometimes it blows like a storm." A slow smile spread across Papa Sky's face. "A man of many voices, is our Primal."

"It's not a man," murmured Goldie, and Calvin shot him a troubled glance.

Papa, still smiling, shook his head. Then he and Tone moved around Goldie to disappear the way he had come in. A long silence eddied in his wake.

"Maybe we should follow him," said Colleen.

Cal shook his head. "His friend could be imaginary, for all we know. I'd rather concentrate on the problem at hand: how we're going to get into that building, find Primal, and confront it . . . whatever it is."

"Them," whispered Goldie.

Cal grabbed Goldie by both arms and turned him around so that they stood face-to-face. "Jesus Christ, Goldie, what is it?"

Goldie looked like a man with a message he did not wish to deliver. "When Primal reached for me and Magritte, when it called to us . . ." He hesitated.

"You said it was one voice in front of many," prompted Cal.

"The many . . ." He shook his head. "Shit. They're *flares*, Cal. A flare . . . collective. *Resistance is futile*. Oh, God." He raked unsteady fingers through his long hair. "I don't mean to sound flippant. But when it speaks, I hear *flare* voices."

Cal's face went completely still. "What do you mean you hear flare voices? How can you tell that's what they are?"

"I can. I didn't want to believe that I could, but I can, maybe because Magritte can."

Cal glanced at the flare, reading confirmation in her eyes. "Why didn't you say something before?" he asked Goldie.

"I didn't know how," Goldie said. "And I wanted to be wrong. And I was confused. One second I was sure this was the Source; the next second I was just as sure it wasn't. Whatever it is—they are—there's power here, and lots of it."

Cal let go of Goldie and stood motionless. "Are you saying . . . are you saying *flares* are enslaving other flares? Flares are binding Enid in this contract from hell? Turning his music into a—a weapon?"

"I don't know. I just know what I hear. What *we* hear." Goldie looked to Magritte for support. "I don't know what it means."

"But now you're sure it's not the Source." Was that disappointment or relief in his voice?

"I told you before—I'm not sure of anything. I'm still not. But if it's the Source, it's learned some new tricks."

Magritte was watching him, eyes like dark moons. "The music in here—it's like twisted blues . . ."

Colleen sat back in her chair, making it creak mournfully. "Now that'd make sense, wouldn't it?" she asked. "The flares need protection from the Source; tweaked music protects them from the Source; if they can draw in tweaked musicians, they've got the real-world equivalent of a force field." Unexpectedly, she giggled. "Real-world. Did I really say that?"

"Wait a minute." Venus, who had been watching in silence, broke in. "Are you saying that Primal is a bunch of *devas*?"

Cal was staring at Colleen, brow furrowed, but when he spoke, it was to Jelly and Venus. "Do you know any other musicians who had contracts with Primal Records before the Change?"

Jelly looked at Venus and said: "One or two."

Venus looked away across the bar.

"Are they still around?"

Jelly shook his head. "We . . . we just thought they found some way out. Except for Charlie Gwinn."

Venus had wandered to the front window, to be silhouetted by the seep of light through the blinds. "Charlie . . ." she said, her face obscured by the slices of brilliance, "Charlie hung himself. Smashed his horn to pieces and hung himself. We buried him in the park."

"Jesus, Lord," said Jelly. "Do you think it was the same with him as with Enid?"

"Maybe that was *his* way out," said Venus. "Maybe it's the only way out."

"No," Jelly whispered.

"No, there's another way, and we're going to find it." Cal looked to Jelly behind his bar. "How well do you know Papa Sky?"

"He's a mysterious old dude," said Jelly. "Keeps to himself mostly. Like he said, he came from New York a while back. Just showed up on our doorstep like a stray cat. Comes back every day to eat." Jelly shook his head and smiled. "Man, but he plays a mean sax. Some sweet horn, too. A 1922 Selmar. You heard him bribe Tone just now. That old guy is the riff king. He's teaching Tone to blow some serious chops."

Venus snorted. "He could have the Angel Gabriel's chops, Jelly. That doesn't mean he's right in the head."

"What about this friend of his?" asked Cal.

Jelly shook his head. "He's a bigger mystery than the old man. Papa talks about him once in a while, but that's about it. The way he tells it, this guy practically carried him all the way from New York."

"So, what's next, Cal?" Colleen asked him. "Are we going to wait for our new friend to come back, or do you want to just try to bust into that place on our own? Blind."

Cal did not answer directly. "It'll be dark soon." He took a deep breath and released it. "I assume bad things come out at night around here."

Venus turned back toward us, shaking her head. "Not in the Red

Zone. Primal pretty much takes care of things there." Her mouth curved into a sardonic smile. "It doesn't let the creepy crawlies get to its people. One of the perks of being a normal in Primal Land."

"Perks?" Colleen laughed without humor. "You can't friggin' get out. I know—I tried."

Venus shrugged. "A trade-off, I guess. We can't get out, but other things can't get in. If we behave ourselves, we do just fine."

Colleen shook her head. "That's still a prison, any way you cut it."

"Yeah," said Venus. "It is."

"And we could be trapped here," said Colleen, looking to Cal to refute it.

In the lamplight, the dark circles under her eyes were more pronounced. Colleen put on a brave show, always, but she had not recovered from her brush with Primal's arcane fences.

"If this is a trap," I said, catching Cal's eye, "then I'm sure we will find a way to spring it. In the morning." I canted my head subtly toward Colleen.

Cal glanced at her, then asked Jelly, "You have someplace we can crash?"

Jelly smiled. "That's about the first sensible idea you've had since you got here. If you're going to go out questing, you at least ought to do it on a good night's sleep."

I cannot speak to how good the night's sleep was, but it was sleep, and welcome. We spent the night in what had been Jelly's private residence. He now shared it with others who called this place home. Thanks to the cleverness of our hosts, we were blessed even with showers. They were hot, if brief.

By unspoken consensus, we granted Goldie and Magritte the right of a room to themselves. The rest of us slept in a pleasant bedroom made up with a large canopy bed and several cots. Colleen first opted for one of these, but after some argument, Cal convinced her the bed offered the best chance of comfort. She agreed, but only on the condition that one of us share it with her. It was not an unreasonable request; we had shared tents, plots of earth, and straw bales for months.

Calvin, eyes spilling worry, took me aside to ask, "Is Colleen all right, really?"

"You know Colleen. It is impossible to tell how much discomfort she is hiding."

Cal glanced over to where Colleen sat cross-legged before a pot-bellied stove, drying her hair, wearing nightclothes composed of long, gray thermal underwear and a man's red and black plaid woolen shirt. Shapeless, androgynous. "You take the bed. In case she needs you."

I closed my eyes and thanked God my friend could not possibly see the precipice my thoughts teetered above. "*Da*," I answered, not trusting myself to say more.

"So, who's my bunkmate tonight?" Colleen had gotten up from the stove and moved toward us, combing her hair. It had grown in the past weeks and curled disobediently around her ears, framing her face.

Cal nudged my shoulder. "Here's your man," he said. "He looks like he could use a soft feather mattress and a down comforter, doesn't he? Besides, I'm not really ready to turn in yet. Enid and I are going to do some sleuthing. See if we can find out a little more about Papa Sky and his mysterious buddy. Maybe unearth some more tales of disappearing musicians."

"Good luck." She yawned. "Jeez, I'm tired."

He leaned over and kissed her forehead. "Sleep tight," he said, touched my shoulder again, lightly, and left us alone.

Neither Colleen nor I spoke again until we lay side by side under the canopy, veiled slightly from each other by the semidarkness of the room. Firelight wove itself through the bed curtains and played across the ceiling, having crept from the slotted door of the wood stove, which Colleen had carefully banked down for the night. There was moonlight, too, equally clandestine, slipping between sash and sill. It was a luminous violet.

We lay in silence for a time, then she reached up and knocked on the headboard. "God, this thing reminds me of my childhood. I ever tell you about the bedroom set from hell?"

"No, I don't believe you did." I glanced sideways in time to catch her grimace.

"I was about, oh, thirteen, I guess. We'd just moved . . . again, and Mom wanted to make up for it by buying me new bedroom furniture. Well, I'll tell you, what I really wanted was Mom and Dad's bed. Big, old, heavy, mahogany four-poster. I came home from school one day and here was this wretched gold and white French Provincial thing with dust ruffles and pink roses all over the quilt. *Pink*, for God's sake. She'd bought me *her* dream furniture, not mine. I wanted a pirate's bedroom, not a princess's."

Pirate Colleen. I could almost picture her at the helm of a ship flying the Jolly Roger. I smiled in the soft darkness. "Did you tell her?" I asked.

"Yeah. Eventually. She really did feel bad about it. About six months later she bought her and Dad a new bed and gave me theirs." She reached out a hand and tugged at the brocade draperies. "Okay, so this isn't exactly a pirate's bedroom, either. More like a lord and lady's. But it's closer. I asked her why she got me that trashy white stuff, and you know what she said? She said she thought I was just pretending to be a tomboy. So Dad would treat me like the son he never had. She was afraid I thought Dad had wanted a boy and that was why he'd taught me to play baseball and shoot and ride a horse."

"But you weren't pretending."

"Hell, no. And neither was he." She rolled over on her side to look at me. "Pretending sucks, Viktor. Promise me you won't pretend with me."

Were I not a doctor, I would have sworn my heart had stopped beating in my chest. "What do you mean? What pretense would I make with you?"

"The 'old bull' shit. You're not old, Viktor. But you've let yourself feel old. You don't have to explain why. I know why. But it's a lie you've made up about yourself and I don't buy it. Neither should you. Promise me: no more old bull shit."

"Yes, *boi baba*. No old bullshit."

"Okay. And you can also stop pretending to be a father figure."

"Colleen . . ."

She raised herself up on one elbow and looked down into my face. "Viktor, *you are not my father*."

I looked up at her for what seemed an eternity, her face illuminated by the warm, red amber of firelight on one side and cool moonlight on the other. Fire and ice.

I wanted to kiss her. I wanted to take her in my arms and hold her, and sleep, and awaken in the Preserve where there was no quest and no danger and no dreams of blood and death. I wanted more than that, and it terrified me. *She* terrified me. I tried desperately to call Yelena to mind, but she would not come. She left me alone with Colleen.

"No," I whispered. "I am not your father."

She gave me a smile that was at once smug and shy, then put her head down on my chest, wrapped her arms around me, sighed deeply, and slept.

I lay awake as long as I could, savoring her nearness, while my heartbeat slowed and desire ebbed.

By morning I had convinced myself I had suffered some sort of mental confusion. I was glad, desperately glad, that I had not acted out of misbegotten passion. Colleen could not possibly have meant what I had taken her to mean through my veil of exhaustion. I had seen her with Cal. I had seen the way he looked at her, spoke to her, touched her. I had seen them kiss.

Certainly, my dear friend Colleen had only meant to keep me from becoming old before my time.

I might have asked her, but she had risen and was gone; only Enid still snored peacefully in a nearby cot. That was good. It saved me further confusion, further possibility of betraying myself. Daylight grounded me, ordered my thoughts. I was well-rested, sober. And I recalled clearly that I had not let slip anything revealing. I recalled, with equal clarity, that I had promised to forswear pretense. Honor would have me go to Colleen and confess . . . what?

Say it, you old fool. What possible good is to be gained from lying to yourself?

Old bullshit, indeed. Here I was late in my forties, pretending to myself that life was over. I had told myself life was over when I took up that damned hot dog cart. And since then, since I had given up on myself, look where I had been and what I had done. And I had not taken a single step of the journey without repeating that old chestnut: *Your life is over, Viktor Lysenko. You are an old, dead, hollowed-out man.*

I sat up in the empty canopy bed, hand over my heart, and felt it beating. I was not old, she had said. Most assuredly, I was not dead . . .

yet. And at this moment, I did not feel hollow. Truthfully, I had not been hollow since Cal brought me to his apartment to examine his sister. Since the four of us had set foot on the road together. With that first step outside myself, the cavity within had begun to fill, until this moment when I was forced to recognize that it was half full. Perhaps more than half.

Downstairs in the restaurant, breakfast was on. It was simple but substantial fare, and it seemed the whole neighborhood, such as it was, had shown up to partake. I took bread and porridge to a table near a window, where Colleen sat drinking hot tea.

She smiled at me as I sat down across from her. "I'd kill for some coffee," she said, "but Jelly says they exhausted the supply about three weeks ago. He thinks he can arrange to get some more from 'a certain warehouse on the waterfront.' We'll probably be out of here by the time he gets the deal set up." She cocked her head to one side and checked me over thoroughly. "You look better this morning. Still like to see you get rid of those dark circles under your eyes, though."

"I feel much better this morning. But I'm afraid the dark circles are a permanent fixture. You didn't give me a chance to check your burns this morning."

"You mean that little rash?" She leaned forward into the wan sunlight. Her softly tanned face was completely unblemished. "All gone. And I slept better than I have since we left the Preserve. Thanks. You make a nice pillow."

Her green eyes were warm and open down to her soul, but she did not speak of last night, nor did I. There was nothing I could say, no question I could ask, that would not lead somewhere I was uncertain she wanted to go. I would die before I shattered these comfortable bonds.

Cal came in before long, trailing Goldie and Magritte. The three of them generated sufficient nervous energy to power Jelly's cook stove. When I thought Cal would be unable to resist a blind thrust into Primal's domain, Papa Sky reappeared on Tone's arm. He accepted his breakfast with sincere gratitude and sat at table with us. Calvin showed admirable restraint, holding his questions until the old man had done with his meal.

When Papa had finished, he put aside his porridge bowl, picked up his mug of chicory and sat back with a sigh of contentment, his face warmed by the crimson stained sunlight that poured through the street-level windows. "So, you still want to go charging off into the heart of darkness, do you, Mr. Cal?"

"We don't have a choice."

"Surely you do. You could stay here. Here, you don't have to search and Enid don't have to play."

"Staying here doesn't get my sister back," said Cal. "Staying here is giving up—not just on Tina, but on everything. I can't do that. I couldn't live with knowing I'd done that."

Papa gazed at Cal in such a way that I almost believed he could see him. "Well, you got this far. I didn't figure you for a quitter. You're a lot like my friend in that, Mr. Cal. He understands your desire to persevere."

"Does that mean he'll help us?"

"He can't do miracles. But he did tell me some things. About that Tower? He says you oughta find the seventh floor real interesting."

"Why?" Cal glanced at Goldie, who sat at one corner of the table with his back pressed against the wall. "What's on the seventh floor? The legal records? Primal? What?"

"He didn't enlighten me on that point, son. He just said to tell you that you'd find the seventh floor of interest. His words. He also suggested you leave Enid and the pretty flying lady outside the building. Said it'd be bad for both them in there. And he said you should go in through the car park underneath. There's a delivery exit on the northeast corner, and a fire stair that goes up from the sublevel. Now, I'll tell you something I know. You go in there, you gotta be ready. Up here." He tapped his temple. "I told you before, that thing ain't what it seems. You gotta watch yourselves and keep your heads in what you're doing."

"You've said that before—that it's not what it seems. But you won't say what that means. Primal is powerful—we understand that."

Papa Sky sat forward in his chair, blind eyes on Cal. "Primal is a trickster."

"Puppet-master," murmured Colleen.

Papa Sky cocked his head toward her. "Smart girl. Don't forget that."

"You seem to know an awful lot about Primal," Cal pressed.

The old man shook his head. "I only know what I hear and see and feel. I know what my friend tells me. He's a very observant soul, my friend." He finished his drink, then rose and held out his hand. "Toney-boy, it's time for me to go. Could you take me to my place?"

Tone got up from the table and came to Papa's side.

"Oh, yeah, one other thing." He felt in his coat pocket and drew out what looked like a small triangle of shell-hard leather. He held it out to Colleen. "I'm supposed to give you this."

Colleen took the bit of hide and turned it on her palm. "Weird. What is it?"

Enid leaned across the table. "Looks kinda like a guitar pick. Too thick, though."

"You feel anything from it, do you?" Papa Sky asked Colleen.

She stared at it, then enclosed it in her fingers. I found my muscles knotting, as if I believed this harmless old blind man might put something in her hand that would injure her. Yet, had he not himself observed that some things were not what they seemed?

I shook myself. Whatever else this changed world did to me, I could not let it turn me to knee-jerk distrust.

Colleen looked up at Papa Sky and shook her head, then apparently remembered he couldn't see her. "No. No, I don't feel a thing. Am I supposed to?"

"You ain't been touched by the Storm, girl. You're as pure as you were before the change was made. Backwards as it seems, that means you can see stuff that can't be seen by them that's been touched. But that stuff can hurt you like it can't hurt them. My friend says you carry that on you all the time, you'll get through. Wear it next to your skin," he added, and shuffled off on Tone's arm.

I looked at the thing in Colleen's hand. It was dark, gray-green, and oddly textured. Hesitantly, I put a finger on it. It sent a strange, uneasy tingle through my fingertips.

Cal reached over and took the thing out of her hand, then dropped it as if it had burnt him. It fell to the table with a click, firing a faint blue spark. "Damn," he murmured. "I don't like the feel of that, Colleen. It's . . ." He shook his head, wiping his palm on his jeans. "I'm not sure you ought to carry it."

Colleen retrieved the strange chip and slipped it into her pocket. "After colliding with Primal's little force field, I think I'd just rather be safe than sorry."

"Yeah," murmured Goldie, "but which is which?"

Cal swung into high gear then, formulating plans. He, Colleen, and Goldie would try to gain entrance to the Black Tower; Enid, Magritte, and I would remain outside, on watch. We would rely on Magritte's connection with Goldie for instant awareness if anything should go awry inside.

We prepared as if for battle, taking only emergency food and water, concealing small weapons. Except for Goldie. Goldie's arsenal consisted of such things as his rattle, a wooden flute Kevin Elk Sings had given him, tiny bells laced upon a string about his wrist. Only when Colleen pressed him did he consent to slip a knife into his boot.

As preparation went forward, I was consumed with a sense of dread. But as closely as I watched Colleen, I saw in her nothing but a bulldog's determination. When I would look up to catch her watching me, I would wonder if she feared, as I did, that she might walk into the Black Tower and never come out again. I could not help but remember that in my nightmares the Tower was associated with loss.

For me, the tension was unbearable. While they pored over Cal's map, settling on a route that would take us into hell, I slipped into the scullery off the bar and made myself busy finding odds and ends that might have medicinal value. I am not a man who paces the floor. Action must at least *seem* to have meaning.

Deeply engaged in some inconsequential task, I didn't realize I was not alone until I heard the door click shut behind me.

"I think you've got enough stuff there for a field hospital, Doc."

I turned.

She was dressed from head to toe in black leather: leather pants, a jacket that hung to mid-thigh. She was a biker Valkyrie. She grinned at me. "Venus's stuff. Pretty tough, huh? At least, it makes me *feel* tough. Leather's good protection." She patted her thigh, then took another step into the room. "Time to go."

I was mute.

She gave me a long, level look, then dropped her eyes to the floor. "Look, Viktor. I'm pretty dense a lot of the time, but I don't have to be hit over the head more than two or three whacks to know . . . What I'm trying to say is that I think there's something we need to, um . . . to work out here." She paused, raising her eyes to my face. "Isn't there?"

No pretense. I had promised her that, and I knew it would be impossible for me to break a promise to Colleen. "Last night," I said, "you accused me of playing the father figure for you. I suppose I have done that, at first unintentionally, and then . . . with purpose. It was a safe role. But you are right when you say that I am not your father." I halted, the impossible words frozen on my tongue. "Dear God, how can I say this to you?"

She took another step in, her eyes searing my face. "Just say it."

"Colleen, the feelings I have for you are not a father's."

She hesitated, as if waiting for me to say more, then shrugged. "And this is a problem?"

"Is it not a problem? I am old enough —"

"To know better. So am I, come to it, but self-knowledge hasn't been a real high priority for me until just recently. Look, Viktor, here's the flip side. I'm not your daughter. I don't want you to think of me as a daughter, or treat me like a daughter. I want . . ."

She struggled for a moment, her eyes locked with mine, then muttered, "Dammit, Viktor." She took a final step, put her hands to my face and kissed me.

I ceased to analyze and agonize and simply allowed myself to live inside the moment, allowed the cascade of emotion to flow over and into that hollow space. The kiss began with tender discovery and ended with a passion that stunned me to the marrow.

So, this was rebirth.

Finally, Colleen drew back in my arms, releasing a long sigh. "Glory hallelujah," she said. "You know, I came in here thinking that I was going to tell you how I felt because, well, who knows if we'll have another chance, right?" She looked up into my eyes, stunning me anew. "But I promise you, Viktor, we're going to come out of this alive."

"If you say it, I have no doubt," I said.

In the hallway outside, someone called our names. Cal. I felt a sudden, swift stab of guilt.

"Damn," said Colleen, and moved to answer his call.

Like a sleepwalker, I followed.

He was standing in the hallway behind the bar, and saw us the moment we emerged from the scullery. "I was wondering where you two went. We're ready to move out." He scanned our faces, then asked, "Something wrong?"

Colleen smiled. "Not a thing. Just wanted to make sure Doc wasn't assembling an entire MASH unit."

Cal nodded, but as I passed him on the way into the bar, he laid a hand on my arm. "She's all right, isn't she?"

I could barely look him in the eye. Stupid, yes? Perhaps it was only in my mind that Colleen and Cal belonged together, but I suspected the connection existed in his mind as well.

"Don't let her take unnecessary risks. I shall ask her to do the same for you."

Cal grinned and pressed my arm. "Thanks."

There was about him the exhilaration I have seen on those who are about to go into battle. In Afghanistan, where I was stationed at a field hospital, I saw it every day on young, ardent faces. At the time, I was horrified by how eager they were to die. I have come to understand that it was not death they yearned for, but action. Action of any kind. Anything but the waiting.

In the bar, we prepared to move out, grimly purposeful. I looked at the leather-clad Valkyrie and wondered if this hard-bitten warrior was really the same woman who had just come to me quaking with uncertainty. Already, my arms felt the ache of returning emptiness.

"This is it," Cal told me, patting the sword at his thigh. He looked over at Tone and Jelly, who hovered uncertainly behind us. "Wish us luck."

Tone shook his head and held out one hand. "You're a crazy shit, Calvin. Hope you're a lucky shit, too."

Cal took the hand and shook it.

We headed up the stairs to the street then, Goldie trailing the double tether that joined him to Magritte — nylon and light. My connection to Colleen was, blessedly, invisible. Before Cal could lay a hand on the door, it opened, admitting a shaft of amber light. The soft radiance framed a short, misshapen figure.

"Boy howdy," said Goldie. "If it ain't the prodigal troll."

Enid swore, Colleen threatened, and Howard Russo shuffled from one foot to the other, glancing at each of us in turn. He looked down at the floor, nudging a knothole with his toe as if he might cover it up or erase it.

He finally looked up and met Cal's eyes. "I feel like shit," he said.

"I'm not a bad man. Just a scared man. Just wanted to go home. Couldn't get out." His eyes darted about, making him look like a trapped thing. "It wouldn't let me out."

"So you came crawling to us," said Colleen. "How noble."

Russo nearly snarled at her. "Didn't have to. Could've gone to Primal. Maybe if I gave him something he wanted, he'd cut me loose."

Colleen snorted. "You would've cut a deal for Enid? Fed him to the contract so you could get out of it?"

Russo's eyes snapped to her face. "*Would've*. Didn't. I didn't. See?"

Colleen ran a hand through her hair, leaving it in wild disarray. "So that's it? You've come back to apologize for dumping our asses on Primal's doorstep?"

"No. To help." Russo turned to Enid. "Feel like crap. I like you, Enid. Always have. Didn't want to hurt you. Just got cold feet." He curled his bare, gray toes as if to illustrate. "Came back 'cause I can help you get in. I can set you up to talk to Primal."

"Set us up," repeated Colleen. "Good choice of words, Howie."

The color of Russo's face altered subtly. "Wouldn't do that. I mean it."

Cal was focused tightly on Russo's face. "All right. Let's assume for a moment that we take you up on your offer. How do you intend to get us in?"

The big milky eyes were suddenly very direct. "I only look useless. Primal's got my contract, too. He wants something from me."

"What?"

"I'm a manager. Manage talent. S'posed to help him hang on to what he's got." He turned his milky gaze up into Enid's face. "I let you get away. Let a couple others get away, too. S'pose he figures I owe him something for that."

Enid took a step back, steadying himself against a table. "You *let* me get away?"

Russo nodded. "He was pissed as hell. That's why he took over the contract."

Cal dropped his gaze to the floor. "All right, Howard. You come. But for your sake, be straight with us."

"Straight," said Russo, making a vague gesture over his heart.

We walked out into the amber daylight then. At the top of the steps, Colleen paused to adjust the crossbow that hung beneath the skirt of her jacket.

I put a hand on her shoulder. "You have the talisman Papa Sky gave you?"

She smiled and fetched the thing out of the front of her shirt. She had cut a hole into it and hung it on the chain that bore her father's dog tags. She laid the charm and tags in my hand. They still carried the warmth of her body. I felt a soft tingle of something more from the strange chip of leather.

"I'm taking all my good luck into that place." Her smile became lopsided, eyeing me. "Well, almost all."

Around my own neck, I wore a silver cross. Nurya had made up the fable that reformed vampires haunted the blood bank at the hospital and that the cross would protect me if one of them should "fall off the wagon," as the Americans say. I pulled the chain off over my head and draped it around Colleen's neck, then returned the charms to their place.

Her smile was gone. She grasped my hand and held it over her heart for an instant before we turned and went after the others.

IV

In the House of Suddhoo

A stone's throw out on either hand
From that well-ordered road we tread,
And all the world is wild and strange:
Churel and ghoul and Djinn and sprite
Shall bear us company to-night,
For we have reached the Oldest Land
Wherein the Powers of Darkness range.

—In the House of Suddhoo
by Rudyard Kipling

TWENTY-FOUR

CAL

Howard didn't lead us back through the business district. He swung east toward the lake and up through the rail yards to Grant Park. It was nothing like I remembered it. The defunct trains had become a neighborhood on useless wheels. Boxcars, passenger cars, cabooses, even engines had been converted for human use. It had to beat trying to maintain a household in a twenty-five-story walk-up.

The park's lawns, which once seemed to go on forever and had been dotted with picnickers, volleyball games, and joggers, were now divided into farm plots, tent towns, and graveyards littered with sad little markers. There were no flowers, but some of the graves seemed to have collected piles of offerings: bows, feathers, ribbons, other odds and ends.

It was easier going here, oddly enough, because the people seemed not to care about us. Neither Magritte nor Howard, shambling along smothered in his sweatsuit, aroused any particular interest. Maybe it was because an armed group of normals with two twists in tow merely looked like a successful hunting party. Whatever the reason, they looked at us; they looked away, they went about their business. And, I noticed distractedly, there seemed to be a lot of business going on in some quarters.

"Balbo Market," said Howard, apparently catching my curiosity about the busy clumps of tents, stalls, and makeshift wagons. "People gotta eat, and they gotta have stuff, y'know, so . . ." He waved an arm at the small but bustling throng.

I slowed my pace a little to watch the patrons of Balbo Market interact. I saw haggling, items changing hands, hands being shaken in accord. Adaptation passing for normalcy.

"Life finds a way," murmured Goldie.

I focused my attention on the cluttered path ahead. I couldn't yet see the Black Tower through the combination of fey red haze and smoke, but the closer we got to it, the tighter my nerves twisted.

I distracted them with a study of Howard Russo. Who was this guy, really? Was he the victim of circumstance who bravely allowed Enid and others to escape Primal's grasp, or was he the weasel who sold out flares and a handful of musicians to save his own hide? Was he both? Was there any way to find out before we walked into Primal's fortress? Was there any way to find out what Primal was?

"Howard, the devas that Primal keeps—are they his allies or his slaves?"

Howard glanced up at me from inside his hood, his mirror lenses nearly blinding me. "I didn't sell those people."

"Chill, Howie," said Colleen. "Cal's just trying to get at the truth."

"Is Primal a group of flares?" I asked bluntly.

The lenses flashed at me again. "Primal is Primal. But it *likes* the devas."

"Why? What does 'it' want with them?"

"Not sure," Howard said.

"Maybe the question is backward," suggested Colleen. "Maybe the question is: What do the flares want with Primal?"

I shook my head. "We've never known flares to be devious or dangerous."

"But they could be, couldn't they? I mean, look at the pull the Source has on them. Alice, Faun."

The memory of losing Faun raised an ache in my heart. It carried its own freight of agony, on top of reminding me of what I'd gone through with Tina. "Faun and Alice weren't . . ." I hesitated.

"I think *evil* is the word you're searching for," Goldie said baldly.

"They weren't evil. They were tortured, pulled between opposing forces. Look, this conversation is pointless."

"Is it?" Colleen asked. "If we knew how the flares figured in this, we'd have a lot better idea what to expect once we're inside. What d'you think they're gonna do, Cal? Give us a hero's welcome?"

I guess I had expected that—or at least that we'd be viewed as a rescue party.

"Colleen may be right," said Doc. "What if this is the way these flares protect themselves from the Source? Might they not take us as a threat?"

I turned my attention back to Howard. "Is Primal protecting the flares, Howard?"

He considered it, his mouth puckering. "They're safe there. Safer than they'd be anywhere else."

"And what does Primal get out of it?"

"Shit." Colleen gripped my arm so tightly I knew I'd bruise. "We're forgetting something. *Primal's a tweak.* Maybe even a flare. He'd have to have some way of protecting himself from the Source."

One Voice in front of many. A mutual protection society, very much like Enid and Magritte's. We wouldn't be heroes; we'd be invaders.

"Tweak?" echoed Howard.

"Like you," said Goldie, "or Magritte."

"Primal's not like any of us," Howard said, and my blood congealed in my veins.

"Shit," Colleen said again. "This sucks."

We approached the Chicago Media Building with dread, but forewarned really was forearmed, in this case. Magritte could hear the flare voices, but only faintly. And she could drive them almost completely from her head if she kept one of Enid's songs in mind. Enid, wrapped in Magritte's flare shielding, heard nothing. He sweated the situation anyway.

"This doesn't seem right—me hangin' while you get into this up to your armpits. If I went in with you—"

Cal was adamant. "You can't. If you went in, you might never come out." He glanced at Magritte. "Either of you. We don't know what might happen if you went in there before your contract is voided. I'd rather not find out."

Enid took a deep breath and stared up at the Tower. In the strange gleam of Chicago daylight, its darkened windows and steel frame spat iridescence back at the sun. "Yeah," he said. "Me neither."

The front doors of the Chicago Media Group were massive, glass-and-brass revolving mechanisms set in two ranks with a ten-foot windbreak between. We watched them for several minutes from the half-shattered lobby of a building across the street. No one came in or out.

"We go?" Howard asked from beside me.

"No time like the present." I patted the copy of Enid's contract I carried in an inside pocket of my jacket and turned to Doc. "You're our backup contingency plan. If this is a trap, or if something goes wrong, you may be our only way out."

Doc nodded grimly and worried the hilt of a knife that had never been used for anything but cutting bandages.

Colleen put her hand over his, stopping the nervous clenching of his fingers. "Don't cut yourself on that thing, Viktor. It'd be pretty embarrassing if I had to patch *you* up."

He smiled faintly. "I will try not to cut myself. Good luck."

Colleen smiled and squeezed her odd collection of charms. I noticed there was a silver cross among them now. Funny. I hadn't thought she was particularly religious. "I'll see you later," she answered, and started for the street, leaping nimbly over a fall of broken glass and mortar.

Howard and I followed, leaving Goldie behind to make his good-byes. We'd reached the great doors by the time he came loping up behind us. They weren't guarded, and in my eagerness to get in, I simply put my hand out to give one of them a push.

"No! No!" Howard howled, and Colleen threw a body block, bowling me over. When she hauled me upright, she and Howard and Goldie were all talking at once.

"What the hell was that for?" I asked.

"Didn't you see it?" Colleen flung an arm at the doors.

"See what?" asked Goldie, glancing from me to Colleen.

"Can't just walk in," Howard lectured. "There's protocols." He swung away and shuffled over behind a pillar.

"See what?" Goldie asked again.

Colleen squinted at the doors. "The . . . the force field."

I grabbed her arm and physically moved her out of my way, trying to keep an eye on what Howard was doing. He was peering at a mail slot centered in a brass plate. He poked the end of one finger into the slot, then jumped as if he'd been shocked and stuck the finger in his mouth to suck on it.

Strange. "I don't see anything," I said.

Goldie shook his head. "Me neither."

"Whoa. Well, neither do I now, but a second ago there was this . . . Well, it looked kind of like a curtain of static electricity. Yellow and green and all . . ." She made a circular motion with her hand.

"Wax on, wax off?"

She threw Goldie a dirty look. "Staticky."

Howard had shuffled back to us. "Okay. *Now* we go in." He led the way, turning the doors as if they were made of balsa wood instead of thick, tempered glass. I will forever be amazed at how much strength is contained in a grunter's body.

We crossed the windbreak and went through the second door into the foyer. It was a huge, vaulted chamber, harshly lit by sun filtered through the ruby veil. Banks of elevators lay in the semidarkness beyond, useless now; twin escalators, reduced to toothy staircases, led to the second floor.

I looked up as we entered the hall, our footsteps tapping out echoes on the gray marble underfoot. The upper floor was dimly lit by globes of light much like the ones Goldie produced. These were the color of dying embers and filled the upper reaches of the building with a dull, red gleam that made me think of volcanoes, lava lamps, and hell.

In the center of the floor the artfully combined letters CMG — apparently the Chicago Media Group logo — were inlaid in solid brass. Howard squatted in the middle of the logo with an expression of resignation on his face. "We wait."

"You're kidding," said Colleen. "Wait for what?"

"For me."

We glanced up in unison toward the farther of the two escalators. A man was descending. He was dressed in a long, silk Chinese robe, his hands hidden among the billows of fabric in that archetypal pose that probably had little reality outside of Saturday morning cartoons and old Charlie Chan movies. On his head was an extravagantly tall hat of the same fabric and pattern. His face was heavily made up, more like a kabuki dancer than a Chinese noble. He even sported a Fu Manchu mustache. In spite of that, he did not look the least bit Asian.

"Trick or treat," Howard singsonged. He looked back over his shoulder at me, his mouth wriggling with what I would have said was derision on a fully human face.

The faux Chinaman set foot on the marble and glided to meet us, his feet moving invisibly under the robe. It dragged the floor in a soft whisper. He stopped in front of us. "I am Clay," he announced, then cocked an eye at Howard. "You've brought . . . friends?"

Howard nodded and pointed at me. "Cal here wants to talk to Primal. Cal's a lawyer."

Clay's eyes wobbled up to meet mine. They were strange eyes. One of them seemed to focus in a different place than its mate. They held an expression of perpetual surprise, probably because of the curved eyebrows penciled in arcs above them. "A lawyer? Why does a lawyer want to see Primal?"

"He wants to . . . er . . . serve notice," Howard informed him.

"Notice? What sort of notice? I need more specifics, Cal . . . ?" His brows rose with the inflection of this voice.

"Griffin. Cal Griffin."

"Ah, Cal Griffin, attorney at law. Do you have a business card?"

I glanced at Howard, who looked the other way. Primal had interesting taste in toadies. "Sorry, I seem to have left them in my other pants. Primal has a musician under contract named Enid Blindman."

Clay's eyes fluttered and his lips formed a wordless O.

"You've heard of him."

"Oh, my, yes. Everyone here has heard of Enid. Primal's been waiting for him to come home. He thought he might be in the neighborhood. Have you brought Enid home, Mr. Griffin?"

"That's an issue I need to raise with Primal."

We locked eyes for a moment, then Clay's lips curved into a smile. "By all means, come up. I'll announce you."

We followed him up the escalator into a broad second-floor gallery, then turned the corner, mounted a second escalator and climbed to the third floor. He turned left down a wide, marbled hallway, Howard moving just behind him, the rest of us walking three abreast like a trio of gunslingers.

"Freaky," mumbled Colleen. "I feel like I'm in a production of the *Wizard of Oz*."

The words were no sooner out of her mouth than Goldie began intoning the chant of the Witch's Guard, "All we owe, we owe her," under his breath.

"Wrong scene, Goldman," Colleen murmured.

He switched to a mumbled rendition of "Follow the Yellow Brick Road." I glanced at him sharply. His eyes glittered and a grin was tugging at the corners of his mouth, giving me vertigo.

The end of the corridor disappeared into red twilight. Up ahead I could see people moving back and forth across intersecting halls. We traveled all the way to the end of the north-south corridor and turned left toward the front of the building, which gave us every opportunity to see the denizens of Primal's domain up close.

"Normals," murmured Goldie.

They seemed to be. Among the dozen or so people we saw roaming the corridor, not one was a tweak. At least, not as far as we could tell. Just like the rest of the Loop. At the same time, Howard's presence didn't seem to cause them any pause at all. He had pushed off his hood, fully displaying his distinctive features, but no one had given him any but the most cursory notice.

We reached a point in the east-west corridor where a huge set of wooden doors, decorated with the CMG logo, halted our progress. Clay did an about-face and looked from me to Colleen to Goldie. "Do you need to bring your people with you or shall they stay outside?"

"They're not my 'people,'" I said. "They're my friends. We stay together."

His eyes repeated the journey from Colleen's face to Goldie's. "I see. In that case, they may enter."

I steeled myself for my first sight of the monster that might be Primal, and followed Clay into the room. Somewhere in the back of my mind I think I actually expected to enter a boardroom—the sort of regal wood, chrome, and glass chamber that Ely Stern had favored, decorated to intimidate or impress. But this was a grotto, a cavern, dimly lit, seemingly boundless, a place the dragon-Stern would comfortably hang out in now, if he still lived. The walls and ceiling were invisible, obscured by gloom and glistening streamers of what looked like wet silk. Woven among those were strands of something like silver Christmas garland. Some of the banners hung so low I had to duck to avoid them. Eerie light in shades of blue and green oozed from unseen sources overhead.

There were people here, collected in small groups and draped in long, strangely kinetic shadows. Their voices made soft, pink noise like the murmur of moving water. I thought of the Indian Caves at Olentangy and was surprised at the depth of my longing for the place. As we passed through the chamber, a wave of silence followed in our wake.

"It's like an underwater cocktail party . . . or a disco," murmured Colleen. "All it needs is the damn glitter ball."

I barely heard her over the trip-hammering of my own heart. Looking up, I had found the source of the spectral light. Floating high up amid the trailing banners were several flares, gleaming emerald and aquamarine. They watched us, lazy-eyed, and drifted aimlessly, as if their only purpose here was to light Primal's world. I found myself trying to make out the features, coloring, and clothing hidden beneath Saint Elmo's fire. Hoping to surprise something familiar and beloved.

"Wraiths," whispered Goldie. "They're like lost souls."

Colleen peered up at them. "Really? They look downright comfy to me. Well, as comfy as you can be on a leash."

I didn't have time to ask what she meant. Our progress through the long, cavernous room had stopped. I looked up to where Clay stood waiting for us. There was nothing there at first, only an inky, sticky blackness that filled the northeast corner of the room. But the blackness eddied and, as if on cue, light sprung up around it, revealing a dais, a throne, and the undisputed Emperor of the Red Zone.

Suddenly I was Alice. Having just eaten the wrong side of the mushroom, I was too small. I would have to flood the room with giant tears to get face-to-face with Primal. He was immense—seated, he was at least ten feet tall—and gave the impression of great mass. He was human in form, but his naked, coiled body gleamed blue-black, as if it were carved out of solid obsidian. It reflected the tendrils of light in the room and gave up a kinetic radiance of its own. Beneath the skin—or whatever passed for skin—delicate traceries of red pulsed, like neon tattoos, like veins full of luminous blood. His face had the smooth, perfect features of a pharaoh's death mask, frozen but for the eyes. Those were the size of baseballs and bright as burnished brass. He was horrible and he was beautiful, and I was confused and disturbed by the paradox.

And the eyes were on me. On us.

Beside me, Colleen had come up short, her stance changing subtly, as if she meant to spring or run. She drew in a hissing breath and exhaled, "Holy shit."

I don't know if Primal heard her, but Clay did, and raised a hand to his mouth to hide a grin.

Primal spoke. In a voice like rocks being crushed, he asked, "What amuses you, monkey?" The aurora brilliance increased, spiking with reds. I didn't see the lips move or the eyes blink.

Clay's entire demeanor changed. His face went flat and colorless, as if made of wax, and he groveled—literally, groveled—rubbing his hands together in their obscuring sleeves, twisting his head sideways like a beaten dog. "I'm not amused, Primal. I'm *pleased*. Pleased that you have such . . . presence. You really wow 'em. It, eh, it tickles me a bit."

"*Tickles* you?" Primal repeated. Without preamble, he swung one huge arm in a sweeping arc. A flash of bloodred light rolled down the length of the arm, caught Clay under the chin, and tossed him a good six feet through the air.

Colleen shouted, flipped open her jacket and reached for the crossbow strapped to her hip. I grabbed her arm hard, stopping her.

Amid derisive laughter, Clay unfolded slowly upright, like a paper doll. He shook off hurt and derision alike, straightened his robe, and turned toward us, a smile on his lips. His hat was gone and blood from his nose had run over lips and chin to stain the silk.

"You've ruined your outfit," purred Primal. "Why don't you go change into something else?"

Clay merely nodded and bobbled away, stopping only to pick up his hat. The rest of the people in the room ignored him. Their attention was on us again.

"Howard Russo."

The grunter, who'd turned to watch Clay disappear, swung around and squinted up at the being on the throne. "Yessir."

"You've come to honor your contract, have you?"

"Nosir."

"No?" The voice was like smooth, musing thunder. "Then why have you come?"

"Brought friends to see you."

"You don't have friends, you wizened little toad. According to my information, these are the friends of Enid Blindman."

"Oh. Yessir."

"And where is Mr. Blindman?"

Howard's eyes squinted to wrinkled slits. "Don' know. Around. Haven't seen him since—"

"Yesterday," said Primal.

Howard blinked. "Yessir. Yesterday."

He'd actually seen him about fifteen minutes ago. That was encouraging. It meant there were holes in Primal's information.

The brass eyes swung to me. "You're a lawyer."

"That's correct. I represent Enid Blindman and Howard Russo," I said, and heard Howard mew in surprise.

"*Represent*, Mr. Griffin?"

"You are the holder of a contract of which they are cosignatories. Recent events have caused revisions to that contract which neither of my clients have approved. Those alterations have resulted in severe penalties."

Primal's eyes seemed to glow brighter momentarily. "The Source Project," he said.

"Oh, God," Goldie murmured, and Colleen took a quick step closer to me.

"I'm . . . surprised you've heard of it." I lied. Surprise didn't begin to cover it. "How did you come by your intelligence?"

Primal laughed—boulders rolling down a hill. "My intelligence," he repeated. "Let's just say that . . . there was a leak."

My throat had gone bone hard and dry. "What do you know about the Source?"

He put a massive hand over the perfect, unmoving mouth. "Mum's the word, Mr. Griffin. Why do you care?"

"I believe the Source Project is responsible for . . . the changes in the environment."

"You mean the hocus-pocus." He waved an arm over his head. Neon pulsed wildly in the pattern of veins, and the hand extruded a smear of ruddiness that was nothing like light. It was viscous, gelatinous, and it hung in the darkness over his head, gleaming dully, before drifting downward.

The room around us gave up an audible sigh. I could feel people pressing forward, straining toward the oily gleam. The flares, high up in their tinsel forest, were drawn to it, too. The tide of desire was palpable; they wanted to lap it up, to bathe in it.

My gaze was drawn unwillingly upward to where the aqua glow of flares met Primal's crimson and altered hue, becoming muddy, opaque, the color of clotting blood. I pulled my eyes away.

"I realize all this, of course," Primal said, forcing my attention back to him. "My more superstitious people call it the Dark, or the Storm, or any one of a hundred other folksy and inaccurate things. It's not dark. It's blindingly bright."

"And is that why you hide from it?" asked Goldie. He pushed himself up next to me, and I glanced at his face. He was sweating, pale—like an alcoholic fighting DTs.

Primal sat up just a little straighter. "And who, exactly, are you?"

"I'm irrelevant. You're hiding from the Source, aren't you? Pretty much the way the rest of us are."

"Ridiculous." Clay's voice came from behind us.

We turned in unison to see him working his way through the cavernous room. He had, indeed, changed into something else. He had changed into a mime, replete with whiteface, Alice Cooper eyes, beret, white gloves, and leotard.

"Oh, jeez," muttered Colleen.

"Primal is afraid of no one." Clay came to a gliding stop in the same place Primal had bowled him over, as if it were policy to place himself in harm's way. There was a smile painted on his face. I doubted it was echoed beneath the paint.

"Thank you, monkey," Primal told him. "Your new attire suits you."

Clay struck a dramatic pose, pointing a finger at Colleen. "The bitch doesn't like it."

"The bitch has a name," said Colleen tartly. "Colleen. That's Queen Colleen to you, monkey boy."

"You dislike mimes, Colleen?" Primal inquired.

"Doesn't everybody?" Colleen asked. "The only thing I hate more than mimes is clowns. They give me the creeps."

Clay postured exaggeratedly, making a sad mime face, and for a moment, in the slow eddy of light and dark, the weirdly watery luminance of the flares, the strangeness of the room and conversation, I was sure I'd been tossed head first into a Fellini film.

"She's scrappy, isn't she?" Primal observed. "You could learn something from this young woman, Clay. She seems to have found the balls you misplaced."

Clay was silent, his mime face smiling sadly into the insult.

Primal watched him for a moment more, then turned back to me. "So, you represent Misters Russo and Blindman, and you want to strike a compromise on their contract with us."

"Actually, I'm here to effect their release from it."

"Release. I see. And why would I consider releasing either of them?"

"Quite simply because you have no choice. The contract is no longer binding. I'm here simply to inform you of that fact."

All sound in the room stopped as if everyone in it had suddenly held their breath. Primal sat back in his throne and underwent a metamorphosis. His obsidian skin flushed with color until it seemed his entire body was cut from garnet.

"What do you mean, no longer binding? They signed the contract, Mr. Griffin. We signed the contract."

"No. No one signed *this* contract," I said, drawing the papers out of my jacket. I held them up before Primal's bright gaze, which followed them as if they were a mesmerist's charm. "This document and the stipulations in it have changed since the original was signed. Drastically. Those changes invalidate the agreement. In addition, I seriously doubt that you personally signed the original contract. If I'm not mistaken, you didn't exist before the Change. At least not as you are now."

I glanced down at the signatures on the page. "This contract was signed by Daniel Freemont, Glenford Blaker, and Shirley Cross. Are you one or more of those individuals?"

Primal changed aspect again, seeming to grow and inflate, his body blazing golden and glorious. "I AM PRIMAL."

The voice was immense, room-shaking. Primal's shadowy courtiers drew back in fear and Howard Russo cringed and quivered against my legs. I was struck with the absurd image of Dorothy and her three stalwarts quaking before the Wizard of Oz. Life imitates art. Except that I wasn't going to rattle, cower, or shed my straw innards on Primal's throne room floor.

"Irrelevant," I said. "The legal fact remains: this contract is invalid. It is no longer binding on either Enid Blindman or Howard Russo." I nudged Howard out from behind me and held the contract out to him. "Howard Russo, are you prepared to void this contract on behalf of yourself and your client?"

Howard blinked up at me and lifted an uncertain hand.

Primal said, "DON'T," with a voice in which wind howled and trees collapsed.

Howard squinted at the contract so hard his eyes watered. For a moment I thought he might run and hide. Instead he snatched the pages from my hand.

"DON'T."

Howard stepped out of my shadow, faced the gleaming giant, held up the contract, and ripped it in two. It gave up a flash of sickly green light that lingered like the after-image of fireworks before weeping to the floor. This time the damn thing stayed torn. Howard grasped it with new vigor and ripped it again and again into tiny pieces. He flung them to the floor and danced on them. Then he pointed a finger up at Primal and said, "*Done* with you! I am *done* with you!"

I steeled myself for an explosion from Primal—the tirade of a thwarted tyrant. Instead he sat back in his throne with a sound like the roll of low thunder. His eyes, half lidded, looked like twin suns. He guttered toward garnet. "So . . ." was all he said, and raised an arm the size of a tree trunk. Red mist cascaded down it. Howard flinched back a step, but there was no menace in Primal's movement. "Not so hasty. This contract is voided, but might we not strike a new deal?"

Howard glanced at me, then back to Primal. "What deal?"

"I still want Enid Blindman. I still want . . . devas." He might have been announcing that he craved chocolate.

"Why?" I asked.

"I like having my very own pantheon of little gods and goddesses. I like the way they gleam through the darkness. They soothe my troubled breast." He folded a ruby hand to where a heart might have beat were he human. "They . . . light up my life."

"Wow," said Goldie. "I'm impressed. Half-assed literary allusions, bad song title puns. We could be twins. I think you and the flares protect each other."

"You again. You're annoying. You realize that, don't you?"

"Protection. Isn't that why you've enslaved the flares . . . and the musicians?" Goldie pressed.

"There are no slaves here. The flares, as you call them, are my guests. The musicians . . . are in protective custody."

"Why?" I asked.

"Their music is dangerous—to themselves and to others. Surely you've realized that. You've seen what Enid's music does. It not only depletes him, it bends things. Reshapes them. Makes them hideous. I don't like hideous things." He rolled a glance toward Howard, who bared his teeth. "I bring the musicians here and I channel their abilities. So they can't hurt themselves or anyone else. A noble cause, don't you think?"

"You use them to imprison the flares," Goldie accused.

I put a hand on his arm and squeezed, my eyes on Primal. "The music only feeds back because of the contract."

Primal's perfect head moved slowly back and forth. "Because of the Source."

"No. The Source gave the music power; the contract made it dangerous."

For the first time, Primal's lips moved, showing teeth that might have been made of diamonds. "Are you sure? Are you absolutely sure?"

I ignored the question. "No one's going to cut a deal with you."

"Oh, Howard will. Howard's always ready to make a deal. And Howard wants what's best for his client . . . and for himself. He'll convince Enid to stay under contract."

"Fuck you," said Howard, then turned and shuffled toward the door.

"You haven't heard what I'm offering you in return."

Howard wheeled, beating at his chest with balled fists. "Can you take this back? Make me human? You can't do that. *Nobody* can do that." He flipped Primal a pointed gesture and trundled away.

"I think we got what we came for," I said. "Let's go."

Goldie shook himself as if we were waking from sleep. "What we came for," he murmured. "No, no, we don't have that." He stepped in front of me and looked up into the full blast of Primal's gaze. "The seventh floor."

Primal seemed to freeze, and Clay said, "There's nothing on the seventh floor."

"Yes, there is," Goldie insisted. "There *is.*"

I tried to pull him back. "Goldie, come on. We're done here." I ignored the wraiths hovering around us. Ignored what leaving them here in this state might mean. We had to go on. If we could break the Source, this trap, too, might be sprung.

Goldie shook me off. "There's something on the seventh floor, Cal. Something he doesn't want us to see."

Primal opened his mouth and an earthquake rolled out. "GET OUT!"

Goldie's aura was suddenly bright enough to make me blink. There was an even more dazzling concentration of light building up in his hands. I lunged at him, grabbing his forearms, desperate to keep him from doing something deadly. He turned his head to look at me. The moment our eyes touched, I was struck with the stark, horrific image of Tina, floating like a Lorelei in an aquarium, listless, almost lifeless, her eyes empty, her fine, pale hair fanned out on the ether. One prisoner among many.

The seventh floor.

I let go of Goldie. His lightning went off like a fragment of Armageddon, filling the room with stark white flash-fire. I was blinded. He shoved me toward the door.

I heard Colleen shouting behind us, heard Primal roaring, Clay shrieking. Then we were in the hall and the doors closed, shutting the cacophony out. Through the sparks that danced in front of my eyes I expected to see guards, armed and ready to bring us down. What I saw was a guard's boot just visible around the corner to the main corridor.

Howard, standing at the corner, looked down and nudged it out of sight with one foot, then straightened his sweats. "Not dead," he told me pointedly. "Just . . . inconvenienced."

Goldie shoved past me, heading for the fire escape. "We don't have time," he said. "We've got to go."

I snagged his jacket. "Not that way."

He swung around to face me, eyes desperate. "*Tina.*"

"Not now." I redoubled my grip on his arm and started moving him toward the intersecting corridor where Howard waited impatiently.

He struggled in my grasp. "Cal, for God's sake! He's got Tina!"

"How, Goldie?" I kept him moving. "How'd he get her? The Source has Tina. This isn't the Source. "

"You don't know that! None of us knows that!"

"This is not the Source," I repeated, and told myself I believed it, though I found I didn't want to.

I'd just marched him around the corner when Howard looked up and said, "Where's the girl?"

I spun around. Colleen was nowhere in sight. We'd left her behind.

Goldie picked that moment to bolt. He caught me completely by surprise, bowling Howard and me both over and onto the floor. From the darkness of the hallway I watched him disappear around the corner. A second later there was a wash of red light and the fire door slammed.

I scrambled to my feet, pulling Howard up after me. I took a step toward the cross corridor, then realized I didn't know which direction I should go. Colleen was still in Primal's lair. Goldie . . . and maybe Tina . . .

Goldie's vision washed back over me, making my legs quake.

Howard tugged on my jacket. "I'll get the girl," he said, jerking a thumb toward the throne room. "You go for the crazy guy."

Hesitation gone, I flew around the corner after Goldie, through the fire door, and out onto the escape. I felt the cadence of Goldie's frantic steps as a dull vibration in the concrete and steel. I looked up. The stairs seemed to zigzag into infinity; I only needed to go as far as the seventh floor. I sprinted, taking two steps at a time.

On the seventh-floor landing the fire door hung open. I didn't stop to think. I dove into the gloom and dodged swiftly down the hall to the left, guided only by the tentative light from the open fire exit. Within seconds that had dwindled to nothing. I slowed, put my back to the inner wall, and listened.

Nothing.

I moved cautiously along, keeping my back to the wall. When I'd sidled about ten feet I paused again to listen. Still nothing.

"Goldie?"

Behind me the fire door slammed shut, leaving me in total darkness. Someone was behind me in the hallway. My heart rate spiked. I turned back the way I'd come, slipping my sword from its sheath.

"Goldie?"

The building around me seemed to moan softly. Hair rose up on the back of my neck and I was overwhelmed by the sudden conviction that something very unlike Goldie faced me down the hallway. The darkness stirred and shifted. I pivoted and ran, keeping one hand on the inner wall.

Three doors slipped by beneath my trailing fingers. Then the wall fell suddenly away. I turned right. Remembering the escalator core, I shifted to the opposite side of the hall. Four more doors slid by before the wall fell away again. I turned left and stopped.

Ahead of me the corridor glowed a strange, dim green, like light through many layers of thick glass. The walls themselves were black and seemed to be dripping with some kind of viscous fluid that flowed in every direction, unconstrained by gravity. Just beneath the surface, gleaming green runnels of light wriggled as if sentient. Like the veins beneath Primal's skin.

Behind the walls, or maybe trapped within the walls, amorphous shapes moved languorously and gave up a light of their own. Flares, caught like butterflies in a giant's display case. There seemed to be dozens of them.

I stood immobile in the middle of my own nightmare—a dreamscape I'd walked right into, in spite of the steps I had taken (or thought I had taken) to avoid it. Colleen was four floors down in God knew what kind of predicament. Goldie was somewhere ahead of me in this maze. My thoughts eddied there, floating with the disembodied shapes behind the thick, translucent walls.

A great sigh breathed over me. I looked ahead, my eyes filling to the brim with the glow of fey light. Without meaning to, I moved forward, feeling a horrible, palpable sense of déja vu.

My worst nightmare.

I moved deeper into the labyrinth, reached another juncture, turned another corner. I heard my name called again, only this time it sounded in my head.

"Cal . . ."

"Tina?" My lips formed the name against will or reason.

A gleaming shape wavered behind the wall just ahead of me. It seemed to draw nearer to the barrier, taking on more and more definition. The shape was human, but every limb gleamed with spectral light, and the hair, so white it was almost blue, floated in a bright banner from the head. It moved with the grace of a swan, closer and closer to the barrier.

I moved closer, too, until I had nowhere to go. I pressed my hands against the icy wall and looked into a delicate face with huge, azure eyes, the features blurred by the glass but still recognizable.

"Oh, God," I sighed, and wept.

TWENTY-FIVE

One thing I'll say for Goldman—he doesn't do things by halves. He'd let loose the fireball to end all fireballs and then skeedaddled. In the flash of white light, I saw everyone around me frozen in the act of shielding their eyes. All except Primal. He was just frozen, staring into the blast as if it were no brighter than a candle.

In the speckled darkness after, I did a full 180 and headed for the doors. But there were people in the way, milling, shoving. I pinballed off of them, trying to stay upright and moving toward the doors. I shouted for Cal, for Goldie, even for Russo, but I was drowned out.

I was somewhere near the doors (I thought) when a pair of hands took hold of my shoulder and spun me around.

"Cal?"

"Sorry," said a voice in my ear. "But your friends seem to have left you behind."

Clay. I turned my head, trying to see him through the purple and green blotches in front of my eyes. In the flare light, his whiteface gleamed moonlike. The eyes were black craters.

"They'll come back for me," I said.

Painted lips curved upward into an exaggerated smile. "Of course they will. And when they do . . ." He cocked his head back toward the far corner of the room, toward Primal.

Primal was still sitting godlike in his throne, while his toadies milled around him and his flares floated above him on their neon tethers. His head was turning from side to side, the wolf-yellow eyes raking the walls of the place as if he could see through them.

God. Maybe he could.

Clay leaned in, bringing his face close to mine. He was sweating, little beads of perspiration standing out all over his face, making him look like he was wearing a veneer of gleaming bubble bath. "You want to save your friends, don't you?"

"Duh."

"I could help you persuade Primal to let them go—at least your lawyer friend and the little gnome. That Goldman fellow's behavior was just plain insulting. Primal will have to deal with him. He can't afford to appear soft or weak, after all."

"What can *I* do? I'm not a deva or a tweaked musician. I don't have anything Primal would want."

"No, but Primal's not the only one here with . . . wants."

I glanced at him sharply. His eyes, still trained on me, had a glassy, intent look that suddenly and uncomfortably reminded me of the look Rory used to get when we . . .

I shit-canned the thought. "Oh, really? And exactly what would you get me? You're just a bootlicker—and a fashion disaster, I might add."

His hand bit into my upper arm, right through the leather. "I lick no one's boots. There are other centers of power in this place. One of them is right down the hall . . . in my rooms." He gestured with his head.

Following his eyes, I realized we were literally on top of the exit. If I could get out into the hall . . .

"Yeah, right. Look, you're a grunt." I flicked my gaze toward the far corner of the room. "Primal's the power in this place. If I want to save anybody's ass, I'll kiss his, not yours."

I brought my eyes back to his face and got the shock of my life. The whiteface was running. Little rivers meandered down his cheeks, leaving trails of naked flesh that were green-white and glowing.

He realized I was staring at him and raised a hand to his cheek.

His white gloves came back smudged with paint. Beneath the translucent gleam of his cheek, I could see the fine tracery of blue-green veins.

Clay was a flare.

But he didn't fly, I argued with myself, and his eyes were wrong. He seemed more like an *attempted* flare, as if the Change had lost interest before it was done with him.

"You glow in the dark," I observed, and licked my lips. I wasn't trying to be sexy. They were just suddenly parched.

Clay smiled, no *smirked*, and pulled off one of his gloves. The hand gleamed like moonlit snow. The next second, he shocked the hell out of me by putting the shining hand over my left breast.

Flesh crawling, I knocked it away.

Rage contorted the mime face before he slammed the door open and dragged me out into the hall. The guards were gone. I imagined they were in pursuit of Goldie and Cal. Clay didn't seem to notice their absence. I coiled to run, but he yanked me off balance and shoved me against the wall, his face only inches from mine. The crossbow bit into my hip.

"Here's the deal: Primal's a little touchy about . . . the seventh floor. If he catches your boys—and he will—they're toast. Literally. Unless I intercede for them. Now, why don't you slip down to my rooms with me for a while? I'm sure we can negotiate something."

I thought of Viktor and suddenly wanted out of this madhouse so badly I could taste it. At that moment I would've cut off a finger or an ear or gotten a tattoo to be back in the Preserve. Anything to send us all back.

"What'll it be . . . Colleen?" he murmured, and my skin crept at the sound of my name.

Damn me, I considered it, but I knew better than to believe the creep had any real influence with Primal. He was a pet. "What'll it be? Well, it won't be you, glow-boy."

Anger, sudden, dark, and real, twisted the whitewashed face. There was surprise under the rage, as if he hadn't expected me to reject him. He grabbed at my breast again, but I twisted sideways and his fingers clawed the thick denim of my shirt, wringing it. His fingernails dug painfully into my skin.

"You stupid bitch." His voice was soft, velvety, the whole outrage of rejection boiled down to a sticky syrup. "You just threw away your only bargaining chip, you know that? You want out of here, *I'm* the one you have to go through, not Primal. He doesn't give a shit about your kind." He gave me a fierce, feral grin and shook me so hard my head thumped the wall. "*I do.*"

His face was too close, his eyes too hot. I brought my hand up in a defensive chop, twisting sideways. He released me for a split second, then grabbed again, catching skin, fabric, and a fistful of lucky charms. Blue and green static shot up in front of my eyes, nearly blinding me. Clay was suddenly crawling with eerie blue-green static—a fishnet made of Northern Lights. He shrieked and flung himself away from me.

Something quick and low to the ground slipped behind him and he toppled over the sudden obstacle, dragging me after him. Dad's old chain broke. The charms scattered, dog tags and weird guitar pick thing flying away into the gloom of the hall. Clay ended up in an awkward heap on the floor.

Howard straightened from a crouch and grinned at me. "Thud," he said.

I didn't laugh. I couldn't pull my eyes away from Clay. Strange static still crept over him. And in the whiteface, leotard, and tights he looked like a marionette with its strings cut. If we couldn't find Cal and Goldie and get out of here, Primal might just have a whole troop of marionette mimes. A dream come true.

I put a hand to my throat. Viktor's cross on its silver chain was still there. I thanked God for that and looked around for the other stuff. In the dim light of the hallway it wasn't going to be easy to find, but I wasn't about to leave it behind. I'd worn Dad's tags since the day he was buried, and I suspected Papa Sky's lucky chip had just saved my bacon.

Something tugged at my jacket. I spun, going for my knife.

It was only Howard. He held out my missing charms. "Yours."

Dad's Air Force–issue links were totaled. I slid the tags and the leather chip onto the chain with the cross. Then I tugged my shirt back into place and glanced down at myself. I had lost a couple of buttons and some skin; beads of blood stood up in a row of angry-looking welts across my chest. This wasn't going to play well in Kiev. Ripping my knife out of its belt sheath, I headed for the fire exit.

Howard shadowed me so close I almost tripped over him. "What'd you do to him?" he asked.

"Just a little something I picked up." I kicked the fire door open.

"But you're a normal!"

I threw myself out onto the fire escape and came face-to-face with Viktor. I stared at him stupidly for a moment. "What're you doing here? You shouldn't be here." I grabbed him and tried to force him down the stairs; he swung me around and headed up instead. I had no choice but to follow.

"The contract is broken," he told me over his shoulder. "We came in through the garage as Papa Sky's friend suggested. But then . . . something happened. Magritte flew off up there and Enid went after her." He nodded at the layers of building above us.

"Yeah, yeah, yeah. Goldie and Cal are up there, too. There's something about the seventh floor." I snatched at him again, trying to slow him down. "Look, I'll go. You take Howard and get—"

He shrugged me off, taking the stairs two at a time. I leapt after him, using every foul word I could think of.

Climbing four floors takes time. In this case, it took enough time for me to do the math. We were no surprise to Primal. How could we have been after weeks of wretched dreams, hours spent burrowing our way into the Loop, minutes ticking by under his hot eyes? I suspected he'd connected with us through Enid, found out what made us tick, and used it to pull us here like moths to a flame. If that was true, could Goldie's taking off to the mysterious seventh floor be unexpected? For all we knew, Papa Sky might've been a mole.

And there was this: Why would a building that was all castle keep, with a moat at the front door and a dragon guarding the treasure, have unlocked doorways that let little old us waltz in and out? The answer was obvious: we'd been shuffled, cut, and dealt like a pack of playing cards. And the only question worth asking at this point—the $64,000 question, as Goldman would say—was: Why? What did Primal want? Really.

At the seventh-floor landing, we paused to survey the fire exit. The *open* fire exit.

Oh, this was just too damn convenient.

Doc caught my arm and turned me around to face him. He raised a hand to the torn front of my shirt, fingering the stained denim. "Is this blood?"

"It's nothing, really."

He pushed the fabric aside to bare the welts Clay had left. "These are claw marks. What in the name of God is in that place?"

"Nothing a can of mace wouldn't cure. It's fine, really. I just had a disagreement with somebody over my . . . charms." Yeah, and I said it with a straight face, too.

Behind me Howard made a snuffling noise that sounded an awful lot like laughter.

I turned on him. "You got a problem?"

He shook his head.

"Good. Weapons?"

He just grinned at me, baring a mouthful of incredibly sharp teeth. Would've done a T-Rex proud.

"How about you?" I asked Doc.

In answer, he reached up under his jacket and pulled out his knife. It was about six inches long—a very effective weapon in the right hands.

"That'll do," I told him. "But only if you're prepared to use it."

The look he gave me was grim. "I am prepared."

Yeah, but for what? I could've shared my certainty that we were stepping into a trap, that there were too many open doors in this place. I didn't. What good would it have done? Instead I said, "Back at the Preserve . . . I wish I'd realized . . . I just wish there were more time."

He smiled. "There is always time," he said, then turned and walked into the darkness of the seventh floor.

God, let him be right, I thought, and stepped through after him.

TWENTY-SIX

We were smothered in cold, clammy darkness the moment we entered the building, and made our way along a corridor that seemed to go forever up its north side. When at last we turned into the transverse hallway and the carpet ended, our footsteps made scrapes and whispers on the marble sheathing. Amplified and echoed by the escalator galleries, it seemed as if an army trod the halls. This was not such a bad thing, I reasoned. At least we should be able to hear as well as we were heard.

We turned from the escalators into a broad hallway that glowed with eerie green light and whose walls seemed to run wet with liquid. Colleen slid her crossbow out of its harness and set a bolt. I put a hand out to stay her.

"Don't worry," she said, her eyes probing the shadows between the tiny rivers of green light. "I'll make damn sure what I'm shooting at before I empty this thing." She turned her head toward me, green luminance washing across her face and into her eyes. "It looks like a haunted house. You ever been in a haunted house, Doc? Besides the Wishart place, I mean."

"No. Never. I have been in field hospitals, though, in Afghanistan. When there was bombing, they would extinguish all the lights, and it would be this dark and this silent between explosions. It smelled like this. Like decay."

"Cheery thought. We're gonna have to work on that attitude, Viktor."

I should not want to smile. Not here. "Thank you," I said.

"*De nada.*"

"I been in haunted houses," Howard said. "Holy Family put on a good one at Halloween. Used to like 'em."

Colleen let out a crack of laughter that echoed off the living walls. "The Holy Family put on a haunted house?"

Howard blinked at her, eyes like pale marbles in the wash of sickly light. "The *church*—over on Roosevelt."

I found I could not tear my eyes from the strange green capillaries. They reminded me of blood vessels. A network of veins beneath the skin of . . .

Colleen was right. I needed to work on my attitude.

We went down the broad, bleeding hallway, Colleen at point, me slightly behind, Howard watching our backs. I could not say I was entirely comfortable with him there.

We had not gone far when we began to see vague patches of radiance moving behind the walls. As we worked our way down the hall, turning this way and that, they began to take recognizable form, as if each turn peeled away an obscuring layer of film. Flares—dozens of them—floated somehow behind these glazed walls like bright fish in an aquarium.

"What is this?" Colleen's voice oozed out in a whisper. "Some kind of giant stasis chamber? Cryogen— Cryo— Oh, hell, you know what I mean."

"Cryonics," I said. "And no, if it were something like that, it would no longer be working. This is not science, Colleen. This is something else."

She moved to stand next to one of the glistening walls, staring up at the bright, blurred figures. "It's like an aquarium."

Like. Like an aquarium, *like* a stasis chamber, *like* a haunted house. It was like nothing we'd ever seen or even imagined, but still we tried to tell ourselves that it was. In this way we fooled ourselves into thinking we could grasp it, could deal with it. To do otherwise would have been a form of surrender.

We turned as the walls willed, and I came to think that perhaps they moved with us, changing shape to guide us deeper into the labyrinth. I was hopelessly turned about by the time we heard other voices somewhere in the maze. We couldn't make out what they said, but they were raised in high emotion and punctuated by the ring of metal against stone.

"That's Cal," Colleen said, and picked up her pace.

Without warning we emerged into a square chamber twice the size of Cal's entire Manhattan apartment. Cal and Goldie were there, faced off against each other like boxers. Cal had drawn his sword; Goldie gestured emphatically at the wall. Enid and Magritte were nowhere in sight.

"You're wasting time, Cal," Goldie was saying. "This is a dead end."

"No. This *is* the way, dammit! There was a doorway here—I saw it. It closed up. We're being intentionally blocked. They've given us one way out—back the way we came. *I* intend to go *this* way!"

He wielded the sword, and for an instant I thought he meant to use it on Goldie. But instead he swung it at the wall, connecting with a sound like the ringing of a bell. Sparks flew, the room seemed to shudder, thunder rolled around us.

I froze, struck with the impossible idea that the building was a living thing and that Cal had wounded it. Colleen shouted and vaulted across the chamber, Howard and I strung out behind.

Relief flooded Cal's face at the sight of her. "Colleen—thank God—"

"What're you *doing*?" she asked, gaze darting into the dark corners of the chamber. "Where're Magritte and Enid?"

Cal stared at her, seemingly stunned. "I'm trying to get to Tina." He pointed up at the wall, his eyes bright and sharp, his face gaunt in the play of light and shadow. A flare drifted there behind the dark, translucent surface—hair and clothing wafting as if in a breeze.

Colleen and I both stared up at her. Her long hair was the color of moon on wheat; large azure smudges marked her eyes; her skin had the sheen of sunlight through milk glass. She was a watercolor, no feature distinct enough to recognize.

Colleen grasped Cal's arm. "*Where are Magritte and Enid?*" she repeated. "They were with Doc. They got up here before we did. They should be here."

"Magritte is fine," said Goldie absently. "She's nearby. I can feel her."

His lack of concern raised a chill in my breast. "Goldie, are you sure?" I asked. "Do you trust what you feel in this place?"

The look he gave me I have seen often in the eyes of men who wake to find themselves paralyzed. "I think maybe I'm a little fucked up right now. Hard to tell."

"But why aren't they *here*?" asked Colleen.

Howard made a funny noise somewhere between a whimper and a growl. "Place has a mind of its own. Does what it wants."

Yes, and it had wanted us to come here.

Goldie murmured something under his breath and wandered off, gazing at the walls, trailing his fingertips across them. I shuddered. I had set my hands to the most horrible wounds imaginable, but the thought of touching the green blood of the Tower made me reel.

Cal was staring at Howard as if the import of his words had finally struck him. After a moment he uttered a growl of frustration and stabbed his sword point first into the floor. It gouged out chips of stone and sent them dancing across the polished surface. He dropped to his haunches behind it, pressing his forehead to the hilt, his lips moving.

Did he pray? I strained to hear him, catching the whispered words.

"Come on, Griffin, use the Force. Think, think, *think*."

As if on cue, flute music trilled—a high, mournful melody from the near corner of the room. Goldie, wooden flute at his lips, meandered back and forth, playing. The building rumbled as if in response, vibration passing through the floor beneath our feet.

Cal glanced up at him. "Damn," he murmured, then turned his eyes to the dully gleaming flare behind the wall. "Is that Tina? I look at her and I see Tina. Goldie sees Tina. Tell me what you see, Doc."

"I must be honest with you, Calvin. I see a flare who may or may not be your sister. Her features aren't clear enough for certainty."

"Colleen?"

She made an impatient gesture. "Yeah. I'd have to agree with Doc. I can't tell who she is. Look, can we get out of here?"

"Sha-*zam*!"

Goldie's shout brought us all about, pulses pounding. We turned in time to see him disappear into the wall, grinning.

"Oh, shit," said Colleen. "Not again."

But Goldie reappeared immediately, beckoning to us with the flute. "Don't lollygag, folks. Let's go."

We moved in unison to the place where he stood, and found a doorway where before there had been none.

"What did you do?" Cal asked.

"You heard Howie: the place has a mind of its own. If it has a mind, the mind can be tricked. Right?" There was an exultant gleam in his dark eyes. He bowed, flourishing the flute. "After you."

We went through the new doorway into another corridor. When it dead-ended in a few yards, Goldie played another doorway and another. We drew nearer to the flare, spiraling toward her. She grew brighter, clearer, until any of us who had known Tina might recognize her . . . if we could trust the testimony of our own eyes in this place. Still, looking at her I could believe this was the wraith-child I had treated in Manhattan. Or perhaps I only *wanted* to believe it.

At the final barrier we stood, listening to muted thunder rolling around us, while Goldie played Kevin Elk Sings's flute. In the space beyond, the flare that might be Tina held out her arms to us.

Then the barrier was gone and we were through into a long, narrow room from which the ceiling seemed to have been blown away. Wires and cables had been ripped free and in some places hung nearly to the floor. There were a number of flares here, most of them hovering high above us amid the tangle of wiring and mangled ceiling tiles. They seemed not even to mark our passing.

Tina, or what we hoped was Tina, floated against the wall in a near corner. She pivoted to look at us, and Cal rushed toward her, arms outstretched. She didn't come down to meet him, but merely hung there, just beyond his reach, looking down, her face devoid of expression.

"Tina? It's me. It's Cal." His voice shattered on the words; his arms reached up to her.

"It's Cal," she repeated, her voice seeping out in a hushed monotone.

"Tina, I've found a place. A place you'll be safe from the Source. A home."

"Home?" she echoed.

"Come down, please. There's nothing to be afraid of."

"Afraid," she echoed, and turned her head toward the far end of the room.

Cal mirrored the movement, sickly green light licking across his face. Out of the gloom an oily bloodied spray arced outward to wrap itself around the bright flare. Cal cried out and leapt back, wrenching his sword from its scabbard, wielding it in both hands. There was nothing he could do. The crimson stain invaded the flare aura and altered it, polluted it. And the poor child, writhing in agony, moaned Cal's name.

He shrieked rage and launched himself toward the source of the red power, Goldie in his wake.

Something rose up out of the darkness there. Something huge and bright—the titanic golden statue of Nebuchadnezzar's dream. I knew this must be Primal, and I suspected I already knew the penalty for failing to offer veneration. It raised gleaming arms and the building rocked. I kept my feet with difficulty, but Cal and Goldie, in frantic motion, tumbled to the floor.

It spoke then, twisting thunder into words. "What an amusing novelty you normals are. Except for you, Mr. Goldman, you're not quite normal, are you? You have . . . a delicious strangeness about you. You also have a most receptive mind. I wouldn't have been able to spring this trap without your help."

With a wordless cry, Goldie flung out his arms and unleashed an explosion of gold-white light in Primal's face. It met a wall of crimson but was not repelled. Instead, the scarlet ooze seemed to filter Goldie's power, to stain it, as it had stained the flare's aura. Then it spat the stuff out again in a vivid pulse aimed directly at Cal. It caught him in a breaking wave, flinging him backward into the room. He rebounded off the wall and crumpled into a heap nearly beneath the flare.

I scrambled to his side, whispering scraps of prayer. Chaos had entered the chamber, voices shouted, thunder rolled, the very walls seemed to shake. I ignored all. By flare light, I could see that Cal lived. His pulse was strong. Before I could check beneath his eyelids, they fluttered and his eyes opened. They focused, not on me, but behind and above me. They filled with the aqua radiance, grew wide and troubled.

"No," he said.

I twisted to follow his gaze. Above me, the girl hung, her glow strong but tarnished with red. Her body moved as if in a current, and I thought for a moment that it was her pain that Cal was responding to. But when I gazed into her face, I knew the lie of that. Beneath the fathomless eyes her mouth was curved in an unholy smile.

TWENTY-SEVEN

CAL

I hurt all over and tingled as if I'd connected with an electric fence. But for the first time in what seemed an eternity my mind was clear. Every perception, every sensation, cut like a shard of glass.

I looked up into that face, a face that should have been Tina's, and saw something fundamentally and inexpressibly alien. This was not Tina, had never been Tina.

"You all right?" Colleen leaned over me, cutting off my view of the flare, her own face barely recognizable in the ripples of light and dark. Howard peered over her shoulder.

The wave of futile bitterness passed. I took up my sword in one hand, grabbed Colleen's arm with the other, and hauled myself upright, turning toward the front of the room. Primal stood there in a blaze of his own light, flinging out bright spheres. The flares in the room had congregated above him.

It was as if a veil had been lifted from my eyes. I could now see what Colleen had commented on before—that the flares were tethered to him by a visible web of power. He was drawing on them, sucking up their life to fuel his own.

Goldie was the target of Primal's volleys. He was huddled in the middle of the room, tucked into himself, rocking back and forth. The fireballs detonated with a fizzing sound, exploding like trick snakes and writhing about him. His golden halo, so bright in the semidarkness, was tinted crimson.

"He'll kill him," I said. "He'll kill Goldie if we don't get him out of here."

"What do we do?" Colleen asked.

"Split up. Try to distract Primal. Confuse him. I'll get Goldie."

I sheathed my sword and crab-crawled toward him on my hands and knees, using dangling hanks of cable for cover, flattening myself to the floor when slivers of Primal's light flew too near. I wasn't sure what I'd do when I reached him. I'd have to trust my instincts—pray there was some way to separate Primal from his power supply.

Your thought is your reality, Doc had said. Colleen had complained that life's rules had been suspended, and Mary that they had changed so much she no longer knew them. They were right. There were new rules, new laws of nature; perhaps even nature itself was fundamentally changed. Before, if you wanted to set off an explosion, you had to take the indirect route offered by science. You had to manipulate matter. Now, the connective tissue between thought and reality was exposed. And that exposure presented us with a whole new set of tools, a whole new realm of arts and sciences.

New rules, new ways to set off explosions.

I heard a shout from the shadows somewhere near the front of the room. Colleen. A moment later mundane fire flared and rocketed toward Primal on a crossbow bolt. I didn't see it connect, but Primal let out a roar that sounded like a train wreck and flashed white-hot. The red missiles stopped falling.

I scrambled to Goldie's side, grabbed him with both hands and shook him as hard as I dared. "Goldie, come on! Get clear. *Now*."

He shook his head, cringing as Primal roared again, firing lightning in every direction. "No good. He's turned me into a boomerang. I could've killed you."

"You didn't. Goldie, come on. I need you. *Clear your head.*"

He raised his hands, tangling his fingers in his rampant hair. "*He's* in my head, dammit! I'm a fucking puppet!"

I shook him again, cringing as Howard let out a wild howl somewhere in the dark. "Let it go. I have an idea. Take my hand." I held it out to him.

He raised his eyes to my face. He looked less like a man and more like a wild thing—a satyr surprised in a forest glade. But he obeyed, lacing his fingers into mine. I could feel the power in him, hot and raw and reckless. Darkness and light colliding; converging and separating. I'd had no idea how strong he'd become.

Looking down into his eyes, I drew my sword. "Feed me power," I told him. "He may have your number, but he doesn't have mine. Not yet."

He gripped my hand tighter. "Be sure of this, Cal. Be fucking sure of it."

"I'm sure." I stood, hauling him to his feet, and aimed the point of my sword approximately at Primal's head. "Fire."

I can't even begin to describe it. A wild tide of power leapt the physical connection, welded the two of us together, and roared through me like hot lava, scalding every nerve. The sword erupted with it, spewing gold glory at the target I held in sharp focus. We were a cosmic flamethrower—Agni, Lord of Fire. Rage and exultation, pain and ecstasy, tumbled through me. I think I screamed. Maybe we both did.

Primal couldn't absorb the attack. All he could do was throw up a shield, and he was too late to save himself completely. The blaze of power caught him, spun him around and flung him against the deeply tinted window behind him. A thousand tiny traceries of brilliance raced out from the point of impact, letting in a ruddy glow from outside. The wash of light caught Colleen in a far corner of the room, frozen in the act of reloading her crossbow.

I lowered my sword. It still burned white-hot and vibrated in my hand as if an electrical current crackled through it. Beside me Goldie hummed under his breath, quaking. Chills rolled between us through our entwined fingers.

"Anything left?" I murmured, my eyes still on Colleen.

"Nothing," he panted. "Nothing left."

That was bad news. Primal was staggering upright. In a moment he might be raging and sending bloody missiles at us again. We had to move fast. I grabbed Goldie and forced him into a shambling walk. To our left, in the shadows along the walls, I could see Doc and Howard. They were also moving toward the head of the room.

Fire flared again to Primal's right as Colleen unloaded a blazing crossbow bolt right at his head. The thing's reflexes were good. He wrenched his head aside and the bolt caught his shoulder instead, carrying away a volleyball-size chunk of it. There was no blood, only a spew of blood-colored light.

We were maybe twenty-five feet from him when Primal reared back and unleashed a fresh storm of power. It rolled over us in a crushing wave, smearing itself on Goldie's aura, darkening it. Goldie groaned and went to his knees; nausea hit me like a gut punch. Doubled over, I saw Doc and Howard buckle, saw Colleen duck and roll.

The flares above Primal pulled close, pulsing radiance, giving up their energy to him along the bright umbilicals—energy he was going to destroy us with. And I noticed for the first time that luminous cords also connected them to the walls—to the pulsing arteries in the walls.

A tether? A conduit? If so, which way did the power run?

I didn't have time for conjecture. Primal raised his hands above his head, a ball of fire raging between them. The deadly star grew swiftly—it was the size of his head, then three times the size.

"Now," he roared. "Now, you die." He loosed the thing.

The sword, still gleaming with the residue of Goldie's power, was the only defense I had. I stepped in front of Goldie and raised it, hoping it might deflect the deadly ball and recalling that an angel with a burning sword had driven Adam and Eve from Paradise.

A brilliant streak of aqua sizzled over our heads, slashing between Primal and us. It met his blast head on, engulfing it in a billow of pale fire. In the center of the billow Magritte blazed into being, electricity in every line of her body. She flung her hands defensively toward the enemy, and what rolled out of her grasp was a roaring piece of the sun. It hurled Primal's missile right back in his face.

He recoiled, throwing up a shield of the clotted magic, then fought back through it, aiming all his powers at Magritte. She weakened swiftly—she was alone; Primal had a dozen flares in his rear guard.

Beside me Goldie let out a shriek of useless rage, trying to gather his resources. Amber light flashed around him, but it wasn't enough to help Magritte.

Sword in hand, I rolled away from him, out from under Magritte's protective cover. As I came upright, melody surged over me, cutting through the chaos in the room like a sonic knife. Around Goldie and

Magritte, Primal's furious onslaught melted, the murky colors of carnage muting to pastels.

I turned. Enid stood in the dark opening at the rear of the room, harmonica to his lips, blue notes—piercing and bittersweet—cascading from it. Over Primal's head the flares pivoted toward the musician in eerie unison and began to drift toward him as if Primal had ceased to exist. The giant's glory dimmed, blushing ruby.

I started toward the head of the room again, sword ready. Once the flares were gone, Primal would be at a disadvantage. I intended to be in a position to do something about it.

But I'd reckoned without Primal's will to live. In a movement that belied his size, he reached out and literally snatched Magritte out of the air.

Straightening, he held her out before him and thundered, "Enid Blindman! I swear to you I'll break this creature in two if you don't *stop now.*"

Enid faltered, and the flares—who had almost reached him—hesitated, bobbing in place.

"No!" Magritte cried. Primal's bright hand, wrapped around her neck, squeezed off any further protest.

"Stop," Primal repeated.

Behind me Goldie made a choking sound.

Enid held the flares before him for a second more, then sagged against the door frame in defeat. They turned and began their journey back toward Primal. Magritte's eyes, desperate, locked on them.

"No. This can't happen." Goldie pulled himself to his full height and staggered toward Primal, flames leaping from his hands. They spread wildly up his arms, over his head. He was turning himself into an incendiary device. In a matter of seconds his entire body was cloaked in arcane fire.

Magritte's eyes were filled with it. Then she, too, seemed to burn brighter in Primal's hands, her aura swelling into a blazing sphere. In seconds her nova was so intense I had to turn my head away and screw my eyes shut.

There was a flash of unbearable brilliance, a whoosh of sound, a burst of heat, and the room was plunged into chilly gloom.

I opened my eyes. Primal had faded from ruby to bronze and stood frozen, his empty hands extended before him. Magritte had crumpled to the floor in front of him, her halo dimmed nearly to nonexistence. Goldie was beside her in an instant, pulling her into his arms. She sagged against him, strength gone.

That was the opening I needed. I leapt into motion, sword swinging, while from the darkness to my right came a flash of real fire. Colleen's third shot buried itself in Primal's neck in the same moment I lashed out with my sword. The blade sang through the air in a radiant arc, catching Primal thigh high. Sparks exploded. The blow was bone jarring, as if I'd hacked into one of the oozing walls rather than a living thing. Bits of something hard flew in all directions. But the blade sliced through the leg, severing it. There was no blood.

Primal toppled, clutching at Colleen's bolt. He fell backward in slow motion, into the spiderweb of light from the cracked window. The thick glass sagged, gaps widening, lengthening, and then the whole thing gave way, sending the monster and several hundred pounds of glass shard down seven floors onto the sidewalk. Ruddy sunlight poured through the yawning hole.

The world around us took a deep breath.

Then we converged on Goldie and Magritte, Enid hovering protectively, Doc immediately falling into the medic's drill: check eyes, check pulse, check respiration. She was spent but conscious.

"Damn!" Colleen stopped in front of me, shaking her head. "I thought that thing would never die. That was my last shot."

"Tough cookie," muttered Howard.

I looked down at Magritte. She glowed a bit brighter now, seemed to rest more lightly in Goldie's arms. "Can we move her?"

Doc flashed me a glance, nodded.

"Oh, shit. That can't be good." Colleen said the words so softly I barely heard them. She was staring at a spot behind me and over my head.

I followed her gaze. The flares hung in limbo in the middle of the room, still bound to each other and to their prison with blazing manacles. There was still power here. The building around us pulsed with it. I felt its oily static on my skin.

"They're still trapped," I said. "But by what?"

Magritte's eyes widened. "Didn't get all of it," she said. "Still something . . ." She shook her head. "Weird. Flare. A flare, but . . . but *not.*"

"Oh, son of a bitch," said Colleen. "It's Clay." She flung her useless crossbow aside to clatter and skid across the floor. She paced after it, swearing.

I followed her. "What's Clay? Colleen, *what's* Clay?"

"Our puppet master, that's what. The power behind the fucking throne. Why didn't I *see* it?"

I shook my head in confusion. "She said *a flare.*"

"But *not*. Shit, I didn't even think to tell anybody—if you wipe off his dazzle paint, Clay glows like a damned lightning bug."

"But he doesn't fly; his eyes aren't—"

"Yeah, yeah. That's the *not* part. Oh, damn, why didn't I *see* it?" She grabbed my arm so hard I gasped. "We've got to find him, Cal. Find him before he can—"

She was cut off by the sound of applause from a single pair of hands. We both turned toward the middle of the room.

Clay stood there in the wash of muted sunlight, having appeared seemingly out of nowhere, clapping slowly, rhythmically. He was wearing what looked like an orange hazmat suit, and the flesh of his face and hands gleamed greenish white. His hair, uncovered, was long and curling and had a similar tint. And although he didn't fly, I caught, not for the first time, the strangeness of his gait. Gliding, as if he merely skimmed the ground he walked.

As he moved toward us he drew the flares down from their dark aerie. They bobbed about him, tethered, as they had been tethered to Primal. He stopped applauding and clasped his hands together over his heart. "Oh, Colleen, you are such a clever girl. I had no idea. None of my normals are nearly as clever as you and your friends. You've been quite an amusement. I'm sorry this has to end."

"That makes one of us," Colleen returned acidly. She fidgeted, in her own unique way, rolling the haft of her knife over and over in her hand. "We're nothing to you. Why don't you just let us go?"

"You're not going anywhere. None of you. Oh, well, maybe Howard. He's pretty much outlived his usefulness. But the rest of you are going to stay to populate the king's court with life, laughter . . . and love," he added, affording Colleen a wry leer.

"Like hell," Colleen assured him.

"You really don't get it, do you?" Clay asked. "I'm not the loser here. You are. You destroyed a figurehead, an effigy. You killed a machine." His eyes swept the walls around us, lips curving in a smile. "No—you killed *part* of a machine. And the master of the machine is very much alive. You still have to deal with *me*." He slapped a palm to his narrow chest, pulled out a bright green ball of energy, and balanced it on the palm of his hand. "Which one of you gets this?" he asked, then swung gracefully toward me, puckering up to blow the thing in my direction.

"You are so fucking predictable," Colleen said.

Clay pivoted. The blazing orb caught her in the chest and flung her across the floor. She skidded almost to the gaping window and rolled into a fetal position.

Adrenaline sang in my veins. I took a wild slash at Clay with my sword, but he was too quick. He dodged lightly out of reach, laughing. I kept after him, parrying, thrusting, keeping his attention on me. From the corner of my eye I saw Enid hovering uncertainly behind Doc, harmonica still in his hand.

"Enid!" I shouted, keeping my eyes on Clay. "Enid, the flares!"

Familiar melody rose around me. Enid's refugee song. He broke away from the group gathered around Magritte and moved toward the flares, harmonica wailing out the very depths of his soul. It was a siren song; the flares melted to it, turning their bright eyes away from their master. Their auras changed subtly, shedding reds, shading toward aqua. Playing, Enid headed for the doorway, the harmonica's haunting voice echoing through the hollow room. The flares moved with him, the cords or conduits that connected them to the building dissolving. Behind the walls the bright veins of light dimmed.

The building shuddered, and panic flashed in Clay's eyes. He shot a sphere of light at Enid. It hit the barrier of Enid's music and melted harmlessly away. He lobbed a second salvo at me. I met it with my sword. It fizzled in a shower of golden sparks.

I went straight at him. He released a barrage of arcane grapeshot. I caught the brilliant pebbles with the blade, swept them aside, and advanced, careless of where they landed. Enid and the flares receded into the darkness; the Tower sighed and moaned. Clay laughed and danced away from me. But he sweated now, his eyes wild.

I will probably never shake the feeling that I caused what happened next. I know I could have prevented it.

Four feet from where Doc and Goldie shielded Magritte, Clay stopped and extended a hand toward the nearest wall. The fey arteries blazed, their pulse quickening. I could almost hear the drumming of a great mechanical heart. A second later a green streamer of light leapt from the wall to Clay's outstretched hand. It enveloped him, fed him.

I lunged, hoping to land a blow while he was distracted, but before I could touch him, he turned and pointed at Maggie. A bolt of energy shot from his fingertip straight to her heart. She spasmed, aqua radiance backwashing along the connection. There was a flash of light, a sizzle of sound, and the emerald trail sucked itself back up, wreathing Clay in a rainbow. He broke his connection with the Tower.

Magritte went limp in Goldie's arms, light extinguished.

He screamed—one long, piercing note of anguish that I will hear until the day I die. Longer, if there's any life after this one. Doc bent to revive her, but I knew she was gone. Because Goldie knew.

The building shook as if the ground beneath it shivered. The walls pulsed with lurid Light.

In the moment of vertigo, Howard flung himself at Clay, snapping with animal fury, claw-hands reaching, ready to rend and tear. But Clay, exultant, danced out of the way. He was suddenly able to leave the ground and, if not to fly, at least to levitate. He grinned at me, vibrating with new power, ablaze with it, his hair tossing in the breeze from the blown out window.

"Christ, what a rush! I had no idea . . . Here I'd been keeping those creatures alive, taking only what I needed—what I *thought* I needed. I had no idea it could be this . . . powerful an experience." He smiled beatifically and rubbed a hand over his heart as if petting the new power that infused it. "Do you know how many devas are in this place? Dozens. Scores." He giggled. "So much for saving something for a rainy day."

Dear God, I'd taken a garden-variety monster and driven it to become a flare killer. Somehow, we had to bring him down before he could reach any of the other flares. But how? He was no longer a man. He wasn't even a flare. He was an unknown, connected to this damn Tower in ways I didn't understand. I shook myself. Understanding was irrelevant. We had to stop him.

Out of the corner of my eye I saw Colleen raise her head from the floor. She fumbled her necklace off over her head, made a beckoning gesture with her fingers, then dropped her head and lay still. Clay didn't seem to notice her, though she was only about five feet from him.

I took a long, gliding step to my left.

"Maybe," Clay mused, "my diet doesn't need to be limited to devas. You can read changed texts, can't you? Maybe I'll sample you next. Lord knows what I could do with your little talent."

I stepped left again, raising the sword.

He glided right, laughing at me. "You don't actually think you're going to get near me with that thing, do you?"

In answer I raised it over my head and came right at him.

At that exact moment Colleen wrapped a hand around his ankle, then sliced through the leg of his coverall with her knife. His skin gleamed through the tear for an instant before she reached in and grasped his leg.

He shrieked, convulsing as if caught in a powerful electrical current. A swarm of shimmering sparks raced up his leg to engulf him, devouring his bright new aura.

No hesitation. Not now. I knew what this thing was—what I had to do. I redoubled my grip on the sword, took two strides and ran Clay through. I felt the power in him kicking back through the blade, still battling me. The sword bucked in my grasp as if alive, but I held on—*willed* myself to *hold on.*

In a spray of light and blood he pitched backward, sliding off the blade toward the shattered window, dragging Colleen with him.

I flung the sword aside and threw myself down practically on top of her in the debris, wrapping my arms around her as tightly as I could. She let go of his ankle as he went over, stopping our slide just short of the jagged border. We watched as the spot of orange receded into the twilight.

A sigh seemed to issue from every corner of the room, from the building itself. Then the entire place shuddered. There was a loud, long wrenching sound and bits of ceiling tile rained down into the room.

"Shit, the whole place is coming apart," said Colleen.

I rolled to my feet, drawing her up after me. "Let's go!"

The Tower shook again, then settled into a rhythmic quaking. Ceiling tiles continued to fall, exploding dully against the floor.

We scrambled from the room, half dragging Goldie, who still clutched Magritte's frail body to himself. The building no longer toyed with us. It was dying, groaning, pelting us with debris as it disintegrated around us. We escaped through its death throes to the escalator core and descended, sometimes conveyed by tides of other refugees.

Out in the street we put as much distance between us and the Tower as possible. We'd barely gotten across Dearborn when it seemed to sag, settling toward the parking garage at the rear. We took cover in doorways and under ledges, and while we watched, every window in the place blew out, showering debris everywhere. Then flares poured from the building into the sky, which even now was clearing, losing its ruddy gleam. There were dozens of them.

Primal's ruby dome was evaporating.

For the space of several minutes the sky was amber-washed cerulean. A cold wind whipped the streets and flayed the clouds overhead. But then, in the west, a swift unnatural darkness gathered, blotting out the sunset. The sky went yellow-gray, the way it does before a tornado.

From where I hunkered inside the blasted foyer of the building across Dearborn from the Tower, I saw Enid move out of cover into the middle of the street, his knot of rescued flares hovering close behind him. They were enclosed with him within a shimmering nebula. The light was pure, blue—a weave of flare magic and music.

Enid raised his eyes to the twisted, static-filled clouds, to the fingers of lightning. He'd seen this before. We all had. He put his harmonica to his lips again and played, the sharp, sad wail of sound reaching up into the sky to grasp at the escaping flares, to do battle for them with the Source.

In the end fifteen more flares made it into the safety of Enid's protective pocket of sound; the others were lost—sucked up into the whorl of unnatural wind. When it had taken them, the Storm raged above us, opening and closing its maw, roaring, spewing bright rage, while Enid led the rescued away toward the Near South Side. I had to pray they'd be safe there.

The Storm lingered for a time, reaching after the lost flares, then retreated into the sunset, taking its lightning and thunder with it.

The broken skeleton of the Chicago Media Building pointed up into a clear, dusky sky. Wind scraped walls and windows, whistling around corners. Normal sounds. Natural sounds.

I sagged back against the facade of the building, weakness flooding my limbs. Nearly at my feet, Goldie sat cross-legged on the sidewalk, Magritte's body limp across his lap. Howard hunkered next to him, sucked into himself.

"I'm fine," said Colleen in answer to a murmured question I only half heard.

"Let me look at you." Doc's voice was gentle, as always, but had an undercurrent of alarm.

I turned, fearing what I'd see. Doc had Colleen's head between his hands; Colleen was trying to push them away.

"*Ni smyesta!*" said Doc sharply. "Don't *move*."

"Viktor, stop!"

"You're bleeding—"

Colleen grimaced. "It's not my blood. It's *his*." She glanced across the street to where the puppet master and his puppet lay in a mound of debris. "Look. See? Just little cuts. Nothing major. Stop fussing." She imprisoned his hands with hers and looked up into his face. "Stop, Viktor. *Parestanya.*"

He kissed her. With a passion she obviously shared. And all I could think was, *Now, why didn't I see that coming?*

I pushed myself away from the wall and walked across Dearborn toward the ruined building. I tried to think as I walked. What to do next? We'd have to find some way to protect the flares. With Primal/Clay gone, we might be able to find other musicians like Enid who were now "released" from their contracts. Maybe they'd help us against the Source, too, or maybe they could help get the flares back to the Preserve.

Maybe, maybe, maybe.

I paused to look back across the street at Goldie, slumped over Magritte in the lengthening shadows with Howard still huddled beside him. That was a mistake. Just seeing them like that made me feel hollow inside. The way I'd felt as I watched Tina change. The way I'd felt in the days after she was gone.

I took a deep breath and moved to where the bodies lay, Primal's and Clay's, in a sea of fallen glass and tile. Primal's remains weren't so much a corpse as they were a heap of rubble.

Behind me, I heard the crunch of boots on debris.

"This was Primal?" Doc asked, stepping carefully over the littered ground. Colleen was at his side.

I nodded and knelt to pick up a clod of the detritus.

"This was never flesh and blood," he said. "This was—"

"Clay," said Colleen. "Primal was *clay.*" She glanced over to where the onetime puppet master lay on the ground, gray as burnt ash.

"A golem," I murmured.

"A golem?" Colleen repeated. "What the hell's that?"

Doc answered. "An effigy. A lifeless figure made of earth and powered by wizardry."

Colleen shivered and pulled the front of her shirt together. "He did like word games."

"What did you do to him?" I asked her. "At the end, when you grabbed his leg. It paralyzed him. What was that?"

She reached into her pocket and held up the wedge of leather Papa Sky had given her. Mr. Mystery's talisman.

"Before I realized what he was, he tried to . . ." She glanced sideways at Doc. "He made a grab at me and got a handful of this instead. Derailed him. I thought, hell, why not? Nothing to lose, right?" She shrugged, returned the thing to her pocket, then moved to kick at the wreckage.

A moment later she called out, "Hey, look at this."

She picked her way out of the debris and laid something on the ground at my feet. It was a metal tool kit about the size of a shoe box.

"Where'd you find that?"

"There was a little cavity of some sort in the torso." She nodded back toward the broken golem. "It split wide open when it hit the ground, but I figure it was right about here." She gestured at her own midsection.

I knelt to inspect it. It wasn't locked; in place of a lock, what looked like a piece of bone was shoved through the hasp, holding the box closed. I knocked the bone out with a chunk of rubble and opened the lid.

Inside, sitting in the half-empty metal tool tray, was a sheaf of papers, binder-clipped and held together with a fat rubber band. More specifically, it was a sheaf of contracts. Enid's, other musicians whose names I didn't recognize, one I did—Charlie Gwinn, who had chosen death over slavery. He and a Vanessa Gwinn had signed on with Primal as a duo.

I turned them over in my hands. "Huh. What do we do with these now?"

"Burn them." The voice was Goldie's. He was standing behind me in the wan light of the setting sun, looking wasted, pale, all the luster gone from his eyes. "So we can move on."

He wandered off around the field of debris. I followed him with my eyes, wondering why tears wouldn't come when I so felt like weeping.

"Cal, what do you make of this?"

Colleen had come around to hunker down next to me. She'd moved the tool tray to reveal a collection of pitifully mundane objects. There was a wallet, a badge, a small velvet bag, and an envelope.

I picked up the wallet and flipped it open. There was a photograph in it. In the waning light of a natural sunset, I made out a man, a woman, and two children. Smiling. A normal, happy family. The only other contents were three dollars and a driver's license issued to one Clayton Devine of Rapid City, South Dakota.

The velvet bag contained a wedding ring.

The badge was DOD issue. A security badge, also in the name of Clayton Devine: MAINTENANCE CREW CHIEF. The face of the man on the badge was round with delicate features, eyes that had a vague, unfocused look, mouth cocked in a slightly loopy grin.

"Level seven access," Colleen read over my shoulder. "If that's anything like the Air Force security ratings, this guy had a pretty high clearance somewhere."

"Yeah, but where?"

"Somewhere near Rapid City, looks like," she said.

I flashed momentarily to Mary's office, to Goldie twirling the little Lakota prayer drum in his hands. *Badlands*, he'd said. I remembered something Clay's golem had said, too, when I asked how he'd known about the Source.

There was a leak.

I picked up the envelope. *May*, it said. A month? A name? Inside was a single piece of notebook paper with writing on one side. In a barely legible scrawl someone had written, *Baby, I know you won't understand this, but I've gotta get out of here. It's not you or the kids. I love you. Always love you. But something's happening to me I don't understand but it's happening and I've got to go away. They know why it's happening and I wish I could make them tell me what this is and what it means and if it's good or bad. One minute I know it's good and the next I know it's bad just as hard. It's power, May. But I don't think I'm supposed to have it. If they find out I have it I don't know what they'll do so I've got to go away. I don't even know if I should be telling you this.*

The letter just ended. Was it an aborted first draft, or had he never sent it? I looked at the date scrawled across the top of the letter. A full three months before the Change.

A leak.

I put the stuff into my pocket. "Let's get back to Legends. Without Primal protecting this place, who knows what's going to be out tonight? We can get back to this in the morning."

❦

Her name was Gwen, not Tina. She was sixteen, not twelve. A child of abusive parents. They were grunters now, and gone. She didn't even really look like Tina in the light of day.

I wasn't devastated. Just resigned.

The city was different now. With Clay's bubble removed, things roamed at night. Chicago would finally face the full effects of the Change.

There wasn't much sleep for anyone that first night. Most of it we spent realizing our losses and gains, sorting things out and trying to make coherent plans. Papa Sky showed up at Legends about eight o'clock, according to my wind-up Timex. We owed him a tremendous debt, him and his secret friend. Colleen and I cornered him and asked if we couldn't meet Mr. Enigma now, to thank him personally for his help.

Papa Sky just laughed. "No sir, Mr. Cal, I don't think he'd've let you near him on any account. Not yet, anyhow."

"What do you mean, not yet?" asked Colleen.

"Well, the way he put it to me, he's got some thinking to do before that happens."

I was puzzled and didn't bother to hide it. "Why should he have to do any thinking about meeting us?"

Papa Sky shrugged.

Colleen chuffed in frustration. "Well, if he won't see us, will you at least tell him thanks? For all of us." She waved an arm at the strange rabble in the room.

"I don't think thanks means diddly to him. I don't think he helped because he was lookin' for thanks."

"What then?" I asked, hoping maybe the answer would shed some light on our mysterious benefactor.

"I asked him that myself, son. He said you and him had something in common. And before you ask—no, he didn't say what. And before you ask—I *can't* ask him, 'cause he's gone."

Colleen and I exchanged glances. "Gone? Gone where?"

"Moved on. I think he's looking for something, too. Maybe that's what you have in common. Hope he finds it, whatever it is. Hope both of you find it."

So much for tidy conclusions. Only on TV does the masked man come out of the shadows and reveal himself to be your long-lost cousin, or the twin brother you never knew you had, or Batman. TV was dead, maybe forever. I was disappointed, but not surprised that its conventions didn't operate in the real world, if they ever had.

I also wasn't surprised when Enid pulled me into the dim little hallway behind Jelly's bar to tell me he wanted to take the flares back to the Preserve. The pain of losing Magritte was etched on his face. His mouth, for which laughing had seemed the most normal state, drew downward at the corners. I was amazed he was still on his feet, still jamming the Source.

"I'm sorry, Cal," he told me. "It's just something I feel I gotta do. For Maggie. For the other ones like her. And . . . for the folks I screwed up back there. Maybe there's something I can do for them, too, now that I'm clear. I know that don't make sense, but seems like I ought to try."

I understood. In fact, it seemed like the most logical, practical, humane thing to do. "It makes sense," I said. "And I know it'll make Mary happy."

"You all could come back with us."

I shook my head. "I can't. But, hey, you ask the others. Maybe they'll want to go."

He gave me a weird look. "You crazy? You don't believe that. They'd never leave you. Not in a million years."

I knew that. Maybe it was the only thing I knew with any certainty, when it came right down to it.

"Something else I gotta tell you before I crash and burn." He rubbed a hand over his eyes. Even in the feeble light that filtered through from the bar, I could see they were bloodshot and red-rimmed from tears and exhaustion. "That guy Clay, the guy on that badge you showed me? I met him before. Just didn't recognize him. He was one of the maintenance guys at Primal. I seen him working around there when I done some late session work. Funny about all that, 'cause I'd swear the guy wore makeup, even back then."

Clayton Devine had twisted *before* the Change. And come here. From Rapid City, South Dakota. Which meant, what? That the Change had happened there first? By how long? And why? I tried to wrap my mind around that and failed. It made me recognize how close to crashing and burning *I* was.

"Enid, you're going to have to sleep sometime. Who's going to shield the flares when you do?"

"I am." Venus appeared in the hallway behind Enid and moved into our puddle of light.

I swear all I could do was stare at her. "You're a musician?" I meant "a tweaked musician" but didn't want to say it.

"I was. Vocals, keyboards. My . . . Charlie played horn. We'd just signed with Primal Records when everything changed. We got stuck here on the inside. When Charlie . . . when I saw what happened to Charlie, the music in me just dried up. Just stopped. I haven't written or sung a note since the Change."

Enid shook his head. "God Almighty, I only been holding it in since Wisconsin. I can't even imagine."

"You're Vanessa Gwinn," I guessed.

She nodded.

"She's going back to the Preserve with us," Enid told me, then hesitated. "Look, Cal. I owe you . . ."

I shook my head.

"Yes," he said, "I *do*. I'm free because of you guys. After I get them all home safe, I'll come find you. Catch up."

I started to answer him, realized I didn't know what to say. I wanted him to find us, but how likely was that, really? I nodded, mute.

He put a hand to my shoulder. "Take your own advice. Man's gotta sleep sometime. That includes you."

Man's gotta sleep. I was terrified of sleep. How badly I needed it, I only realized when I sat down to consider *where* I would sleep. Most certainly *not* in the room I'd slept in last night, nor in that company. The thought of sharing a room with Doc and Colleen made me feel like a teen who's terrified of what he might catch his parents doing. What did they call that?

A "primal" moment?

I started to laugh. Sitting alone in a corner of the restaurant with the murmur of other people's lives going on around me, I laughed. I caught Jelly gaping at me from behind his bar. But that only made the laughter more fierce.

Then, when I thought I would never stop, the tears finally came.

TWENTY-EIGHT

GOLDIE

They say the ritual of burying or burning the dead gives a sense of closure. I've never known that to be true. Not when I sat shiva for my grandfather. Not for all the deaths since. Most especially not now.

I'm familiar with the phases you supposedly go through. Denial, anger, grief, acceptance, whatever. I don't know what phase I'm in as we stand out in Grant Park under a clear dawn sky with dew scattering jewels across grass and lake and watch Magritte burn. The packet of twisted contracts burns with her.

God, that sounds wrong. It isn't Magritte we burn. It's a shell Magritte lived in for twenty-two years and then abandoned.

That's Denial talking. Anger is the next scheduled speaker. I think I feel it coming on as I murmur kaddish, a prayer that I am now sure is more for the living than for the dead.

So, we are standing here and Enid and Venus are crying out the blues—he for Magritte, she for her lost Charlie. All the words have been said and Maggie's embers rise on a slight breeze—bright little birds freeing themselves from gravity for the last time. And I am a black hole. I suck light in, but no light comes out.

The air is chill and tastes like snow and ash on the tongue. Already the clouds have banked to the north, hesitant, as if unable to believe Chicago is once again open for their trade.

Away to the west I can hear the Voices again, dark and insistent, clear as this day, no longer muddled by Clay's Black Tower. But I still have the nightmare, because my Black Tower doesn't stand at the corner of Dearborn and Randolph. My Black Tower, like the Kingdom of God, is within.

And as I stand at Magritte's pyre with the music draining away and my friends standing close beside me and watching me with apprehension, I think perhaps her death here and now is a good thing. She will never look at me the way Cal is looking at me, the way Doc and Colleen are looking at me. She won't have to watch me become whatever it is I am becoming.

People are wandering away from the park now. Even Enid and Venus are taking their leave—along with the inscrutable Howard, who will also return to the Preserve, and who, I'm forced to admit, grows on you like fungus.

This morning, as we laid wood on the pyre, he came to Cal and said, "Enid says once we get angelfire to the Preserve, we'll catch up to you." He moved in close and fixed Cal with those bulgy, marble eyes and added, "We *will*. Sometimes miracles happen." He held up his hand, turning it back and forth in the sunlight, and it seemed to me it looked more human.

"Yeah," Cal said. "Sometimes they do." They were words of hope, but I saw little of that in his face. And he wasn't looking at Howard when he said them; he was looking at Doc and Colleen, who seem reluctant to stray more than three feet from each other today. I recognized what I saw in his face then—loneliness.

I look up from the delicate act of constructing a facade and catch their eyes on me. Caught out, Colleen glances at her feet, Doc gazes out over Lake Michigan, and Cal looks straight up into the sky, shivers in the chill wind and says, "It looks like Chicago's the Windy City again. It's got to be at least twenty degrees colder than it was the day we got here. I wonder what else Primal was holding at bay. I don't envy these people what they're going to go through this winter."

"How long will it go on?" Colleen asks. "Is this like a—a chain reaction? Will the world just mutate until . . ."

"Until it comes full circle?" Doc finishes. He continues to gaze out over the lake. "They say a fisherman's children look to the sea. I wonder what our children will have to look to."

Colleen sways toward him, the thick fabric of their jackets just brushing. A subtle movement. I wonder if they realize how bright are the cords that bind them together.

Cal glances at them and away. He shifts uncomfortably from one foot to the other and says, "We need to get the horses saddled and packed. If you'd like to stay out here for a while longer, Goldie—"

I shake my head. "No. There's nothing out here. And you're right: we need to get going."

"Where?" asks Colleen. "Have you settled on a route yet?"

Cal rakes a hand through his hair. "Settled, no. But I have an idea. I want to take another look at the map. See what it tells me."

He says more, but I don't hear him. The sparks are turning to ashes. The breeze lifts them out over the water, where eventually they will settle and melt away. I think, for a moment, of joining them in the great, sparkling lake. Beneath the great, sparkling lake. But I still have work to do.

The lake and the dying fire and the sky blur, looking like a glittering watercolor. I turn my back on the pyre and walk away. There are Voices calling me and I must listen.